**He fitted his hands to her waist and leaned toward her.**

She met him in the kiss, her mouth parting, her hands sliding around to the back of his neck, combing through his silky hair. Dear Lord, she'd forgotten how good a kiss could be. She nibbled at his lip, only pausing when his tongue thrust between her teeth, invading, exploring, rousing a long-unsatisfied need deep inside. Moving intuitively, her hands glided over soft cotton that covered the lean muscles along his spine. When they reached the rougher texture of jeans and leather belt, the tips tingled, like the briefest touch of a live wire, singeing and searing and sparking pleasure through her body.

It had been so very long...would be so very easy... back up one step, don't let go, take him to the bedroom or, better, the couch, strip off their clothes...

# Acclaim for the Tallgrass Novels

## A Promise of Forever

"Heartbreaking and heartwarming...Pappano blends a realistic vision of returning soldiers with a tender love story."
—***Publishers Weekly***

"A good military romance with strong characters that will truly touch your heart."
—**HarlequinJunkie.com**

"A heartfelt read...With beautifully honest storytelling, Pappano expresses the vulnerable hearts of Ben and Avi."
—***RT Book Reviews***

## A Love to Call Her Own

"Deeply satisfying...Pappano's characters are achingly real and flawed, and readers will commiserate with and root for the couple...This deeply moving tale will remind everyone who reads it of the great sacrifices made by those who serve and the families they leave behind."
—***Publishers Weekly*** (**starred review**)

"A solid, tender plot, well-developed, vulnerable characters and smart, modern banter are the highlights of this heartwarming story."
—***RT Book Reviews***

"A wonderful romance with real-life, real-time issues... [Pappano] writes with substance and does an excellent job of bringing the characters to life."
**—HarlequinJunkie.com**

"Poignant and engaging... Authentic details of army life and battle experience will glue readers to the page."
*—Library Journal*

# A Summer
# to Remember

# A Summer to Remember

Marilyn Pappano

FOREVER

NEW YORK  BOSTON

Copyright © 2016 by Marilyn Pappano
Excerpt from *A Hero to Come Home To* © 2013 by Marilyn Pappano
Cover illustration by Judy York
Cover design by Elizabeth Turner
Cover copyright © 2016 by Hachette Book Group, Inc.

Forever
Hachette Book Group
1290 Avenue of the Americas
New York, NY 10104
forever-romance.com
twitter.com/foreverromance

First Edition: June 2016

Forever is an imprint of Grand Central Publishing.
The Forever name and logo are trademarks of Hachette Book Group, Inc.

The publisher is not responsible for websites (or their content) that are not owned by the publisher.

The Hachette Speakers Bureau provides a wide range of authors for speaking events. To find out more, go to www.hachettespeakersbureau.com or call (866) 376-6591.

ISBNs: 978-1-4555-8817-6 (mass market), 978-1-4555-8818-3 (ebook)

Printed in the United States of America

OPM

10 9 8 7 6 5 4 3 2 1

# Acknowledgments

To the military personnel who have served our country well in peace and in war, with honor and courage, and the families who stood by them. We owe you such a debt.

To the people who made these books possible: my incredible agent, Melissa Jeglinski, and my two wonderful editors, Selina McLemore and Michele Bidelspach. Your input and advice and tweaking have been a huge gift.

To Chance and Shadow, my fur babies, and their bubbas who have gone on to dog heaven: Olivia, Beau, Lucky, Jack, Jasper, Spencer, and Duc. These guys have been the basis for all the pets in my books (yep, even the cats) and have brought me more joy than I could have imagined. If you don't have a pet, adopt a dog (or even a cat) and gain unconditional love. You'll never regret it.

And as always, to my husband, Robert. It's a wonderful life.

The truth of the matter is that you always know the right thing to do. The hard part is doing it.

—Norman Schwarzkopf

Valor is stability, not of legs and arms, but of courage and the soul.

—Michel de Montaigne

# A Summer
# to Remember

# Chapter 1

His neck aching from hours behind the wheel, Elliot Ross gave in to just a bit of relief when lights became visible a few miles ahead. He'd been driving a long time, most of it through spring storms, wind buffeting the truck, rain falling so hard that the windshield wipers couldn't keep up. Every muscle in his body was knotted and sore. If he had the money, this would be a good night to check into a motel, to take a shower as long and as hot as he wanted, to sleep in a real bed with real privacy.

He didn't need to pull out his wallet to know that he didn't have the money. He wasn't broke, but his funds were reaching the level that always made him itch. With any luck, he'd be able to find work in Tallgrass, short-term if nothing else. He could build up his safety net, maybe run into some old friends, maybe even find a place to settle. Eight years in the Army had left him with buddies all over the world, and though he was alone by choice, he always appreciated meeting up again with friends.

Rustling from the passenger seat reminded him that he wasn't exactly alone. His companion, fifteen pounds of lazy, shedding tan hair, and giant puppy-dog eyes, uncurled and sat up, tail thumping against the console, then raised her gaze to him. He hadn't known her long enough to read all her cues, but he was pretty sure that look was universal in the canine world for *I need to take a leak*.

"Hang on, Mouse. According to Matilda, we'll be in Tallgrass in a couple minutes." Elliot had given the name to the truck's GPS the first time he'd ever used it and found the previous owner had set it to a woman's voice with an Australian accent. He'd traveled to Perth while he was still on active duty, and all it took was one simple *turn left* in that accent to remind him of good times with Aussie girls soft enough, sweet enough, and sexy enough to almost make him think about renouncing his U.S. citizenship and spending the rest of his life becoming a sandgroper.

Almost.

Mouse stared at him a moment before blinking and looking away. Elliot had found her in eastern Tennessee two days ago. A group of kids had been messing with her in a McDonald's parking lot, offering the starving pup a scrap of burger, then kicking her away before she could get it.

Worthless punk cowards. Elliot flexed his still-tender right hand. He'd made sure they understood they'd picked on the wrong dog before he'd loaded the scrawny pit into his truck and headed for the nearest vet.

*Always a white knight*, his sister used to tease, but it wasn't anything so noble. He just didn't like seeing anyone mistreated, and luckily he was tough enough and strong enough to put a stop to it most times.

The lights grew brighter despite the heavy cloud cover, and within minutes he was passing the main gate to Fort Murphy. It seemed strange to drive past with no plans to turn into the entrance. He'd spent most of his adult life going to work on similar posts, places so familiar that they felt more like home than anywhere else.

Another mile or so, and a shopping center appeared on the right. With a glance at Mouse, he slowed, then turned into the lot. The only businesses open this late on a Friday night were a Mexican restaurant at the front and a pharmacy at the back. A strip of grass separated the pharmacy from the parking lot, only a few feet wide and maybe twenty feet long, but that was more than enough for Mouse to do her business.

He parked near the median and shut off the engine, then contemplated the rain for a moment. "I don't suppose I could just open the door and you'd jump out and do your thing, then come back?"

Mouse held his gaze with a steadiness he found unsettling. He'd known his share of animals that had been mistreated, but he'd never seen one less skittish than this one. She showed him no fear. She'd trembled and whimpered with the punks, and with the vet and his assistants, but she was steady as a rock with Elliot.

*She trusts you, idiot*, his sister Emily's voice commented. *Females always trust you.*

The truth of her statement made him grin.

Tugging his jean jacket collar a little closer, he slid out of the truck, jogged to the other side, opened the door, and hooked Mouse's leash on before lifting her to the ground. She didn't dart off the ten feet to the grass like he'd hoped but instead hunkered underneath the truck, still giving him that long, steady look. "Come on, Mouse, I'm getting soaked here."

She didn't move.

"Come on, you're a pit bull. Big, fierce dog." He growled softly at her. "You can't tell me you'd rather hold it than piss in the rain."

No response.

With water dripping from his hair and trickling down his neck, Elliot gave the leash a tug. When she didn't move, he sighed and reached under the passenger seat. The umbrella he brought out had been in the truck when he bought it. He hadn't used one in...well, ever—he was a tough guy, right?—but he'd never bothered to throw it away, figuring someday he might find himself with a pretty female who cared about things like staying dry. Mouse was a good-looking dog, or would be once she'd put on some weight, but she wasn't exactly the kind of female he'd had in mind.

He popped the umbrella, tilting it at an angle that would provide protection for the pup, and Mouse instantly came out from under the truck, walking alongside him to the grass.

"Grown man holding an umbrella for a prissy little dog so she doesn't get wet," he grumbled as the dampness spread over him from the outside in. His jeans were sticking to his legs, and even inside work boots, his feet were getting wet and cold. His hair was soaked, his jacket sodden, and his shirt—

"I think I'd worry more about talking to myself than pampering the baby."

The voice came from behind him, soft and amused, its accent muddled, and very definitely female. Abashed at being caught off guard, he turned to face a slight woman an inch or two shorter than him. A neon green slicker covered her clothes, showing bare legs and feet shoved into disreputable sneakers, and its hood kept most of her face in shadow. Not the smile, though. Her smile was wide and happy and made a guy want to smile back—at least, a guy who wasn't turning red to the tips of his ears.

"She, uh, doesn't like the rain." He gestured toward the dog, who'd turned her back to them before squatting carefully over the wet grass. "I've never done this before. Held an umbrella for a dog, I mean. Hell, I've never held an umbrella for a person, either, except for the time I tried to hit my sister with one, if that counts." Jeez, he was rambling. He hadn't rambled with a pretty girl in his life. His mama called him a natural-born charmer, but his best hope for charm now was his smile.

"Did you succeed?" At his blank look, she pointed to the umbrella. "You said you tried to hit your sister. Did you succeed?"

"No, she outran me. Emily was six feet tall by seventh grade, and I hadn't hit my growth spurt yet." He grinned at the obvious fact that his growth spurt had never come. He reached five feet nine only by standing on his toes, but he'd compensated for lack of height by building strength.

At his feet, Mouse barked, the first sound he'd heard from her that wasn't pain-filled. When he looked down at her, she stared back, her way, he guessed, of saying she'd had enough of the rain.

The woman apparently thought the same thing. "She probably needs her feet dried. I assume you carry a towel for that purpose?" Adjusting the slicker hood, she took a few steps away, then turned back. "I think it's sweet, you holding the umbrella for her."

He grinned again. "That's me. Sweeter than honey."

Once again she smiled, and anticipation crackled around them, like lightning about to strike. He even took a quick look at the sky to make sure they weren't about to get fried, then reconnected gazes with her. If he didn't say something, she was going to make another move to go, and he'd be left standing in the rain, watching her drive away, full of things to say, just too late. He hated being too late.

"Could Mouse and I interest you in a drink?"

She stood there a long time, as still and steady as Mouse, probably considering the wisdom of going to a bar with a total stranger. She could be married, for all he knew—could be a nun, for all he knew—but he wouldn't recall the invitation if he could. She was pretty and nice and seemed to like his dog, and her voice could make a man weak, and her smile...

"Sorry. I don't drink," she said at last. "But how about a burger? There's a Sonic just down the street, so Mouse wouldn't have to stay alone in the truck."

A drive-in on a rainy night, cool air drifting through the windows, fog steaming the glass, privacy without risk. "Burgers sound great. You want to leave your car here?"

She hesitated again before beeping the door locks of the only car parked nearby. "You can follow me."

He watched until she'd reached the car before giving Mouse a tug and heading back to his truck. After lifting the dog inside and tossing the umbrella into the rear floorboard, he climbed in and started the engine.

"Yes, ma'am," he murmured. "We'll be happy to follow you, won't we, Mouse?"

\*   \*   \*

"What are you doing?" Fia Thomas asked aloud as she peered through the rain on her way through the lot to Main Street. "You should be home in your pajamas. You shouldn't be out in the rain. You certainly shouldn't be driving in the rain, and having a hamburger with a stranger... You don't even know his name! That's so far off the top of the scale of shouldn'ts that it doesn't even register."

Shoving her hood back with one hand, she checked her appearance in the rearview mirror and grimaced. "No makeup, you didn't even comb your hair, and... Oh, my God, when did you start talking to yourself like this?!"

A paper bag crinkled in her slicker pocket, the pills she'd picked up at the pharmacy. It was one of the multiple medications her doctor had her on to treat the symptoms of the illness they hadn't yet identified. She could have waited for it until tomorrow morning. She could have called any one of her best friends, and they would have picked it up and brought it to her. Wind and flood wouldn't keep them away when she needed them. That knowledge warmed her heart almost unbearably.

But she'd had a good day. No vision problems, no muscle spasms, no stumbling or headaches or nausea. For the first time in a long time, she was feeling like herself, and she'd grabbed the first excuse to come to mind for rushing out into the rain and driving a car for the first time in months. She'd relished the feel of sitting behind the wheel, hands clasping it firmly, the radio tuned to the loudest and most favorite of her country stations. She'd felt strong. Empowered. Independent.

After more than a year of fearing she would never be any of those things again.

The white pickup followed her through a green light and into the center turn lane, then into Sonic's driveway. Overhangs protected the cars on both sides from the downpour, and bright lights made it feel like midday.

With a glance in the rearview mirror, she drove to the last spot on the row and shut off the engine. The wipers stopped in mid-swipe with a squeaky-smudgy sound, replaced almost immediately by the powerful engine parking beside her. She pulled the pills from her pocket and tossed them on the passenger seat, combed her fingers through her hair again, patted her other pocket to make sure her tiny purse was there, then reached for the door. Her hand stilled on the handle.

Was she really going to do this? Get in a stranger's truck, eat a hamburger, make small talk, maybe even flirt with him? All because he was sweet to his dog and had a great smile and gorgeous eyes and radiated *nice, sexy guy* with every breath he took, and because she'd had a good day and those times came so rarely that it seemed wrong not to celebrate? And maybe partly because she hadn't sat with a man, sharing a meal or a drink or a laugh, since Scott, and twenty-four was way too young to be so alone?

Her fingers tightened as the defiant voice in her head answered, *Yeah, we're gonna do this. Scott's dead. He's not coming back, little girl, and he'd never want you to live alone like this.*

The words hurt her heart, a tug so powerful that nausea

stirred deep in her gut, but she pushed it back. Scott *was* dead, and she hated that fact with all her soul, but she couldn't change it. And he *would* be pissed if she'd given up without him. Warrior girl, he'd called her, the strongest, the toughest, the baddest-ass woman he knew. The one who could do any damn thing, could survive any damn thing. Hell, yeah, she was gonna do this.

With a deep breath, she opened the car door and slid out. The rubber soles of her sneakers made a sound similar to the wipers as she pivoted through the narrow space to the pickup's passenger door. Mouse's owner leaned across the truck and opened the door a few inches while Mouse sat halfway between the front and the rear seats, still and sniffing the air. Was it Fia's unfamiliar scent that had caught her attention or the burgers-grease-fries aroma that announced, *Good food found here*?

Obvious answer. The dog's nose was twitching, and drool was starting to form at the corners of her mouth.

But it was Fia who held the man's interest. A shiver ran deep inside her. Oh, man, it had been so long since she'd felt the tingle brought on by a man's interest—so long since she'd let herself feel it, since she'd wanted to feel it. The sad truth was, she didn't have much to offer a man besides worry and frustration and a whole lot of hassle. But for one night she could pretend that the medical issues didn't exist, that she was a perfectly normal, healthy woman who'd been asked out by a perfectly gorgeous man.

She climbed in the truck, settled in the worn seat, and closed the door before looking his way. *Perfectly gorgeous* was an understatement. He was incredible. His hair was dark brown, falling over his eyes and past his shoulders, sleek and shiny. His features were sharply defined: blue eyes with ridiculously long lashes, strong nose, stubborn jaw, and a mouth that sensuously softened the angles. He wasn't tall, as he'd pointed out, but he was compact, with broad shoulders, rock-hard muscles, strength tempered by gentleness. There was an air about him of peace, decency, Zen, but also a sense of limits. He was a man who couldn't be pushed too far.

*That's a lot to read into one look*, she mocked herself. Honestly, he was damn good-looking. The rest was fantasy.

*Nothing wrong with a little fantasy*, Scott whispered.

"So…" The guy's husky voice broke the silence, along with the sound of his window sliding down. "You know what you want?"

An innocent question to conjure so many answers in her head. She stuck with the pertinent one. "A number one combo, no onions, and a cherry limeade."

He pressed the order button, waited for the tinny response, and ordered two of the same. She breathed in the cool air that filled the cab, catching a faint scent of dog and a fainter scent of man. Men had the best smells. All it took was the slightest whiff of the cologne or shampoo Scott had used, a cup of coffee brewed strong the way he had, and in a flash, she would be in happier times. Definitely better ones.

He swiped his fingers through his hair, then took a band dangling from the gear shift and pulled it back into a ponytail. She'd never been a fan of long hair on men, but it worked for this one. After drying his hands the best he could on his wet shirt, he extended the right one. "I'm Elliot Ross."

The introduction reminded her how out of character this was for her. Meeting a man for dinner, even if it was at

Sonic, without learning his name first was something the before-Scott Fia would have done, certainly not something widowed, struggling Fia should do. *But now you know his name, and it's a nice one.* Not too common, not too unusual, masculine without sounding too macho.

"And you are?" His brows rose, and so did the corners of his mouth. She liked a good-natured man. Angst was nice to read about in a novel, and it worked fine for some of her besties and the men in their lives, but Fia was happy with balance, good humor, and optimism. She tried to be that way herself. It made life easier.

"Fia Thomas," she said, and after an instant, she took his hand. Shaking hands was such a common, ordinary thing. She'd done it a thousand times, and nine-hundred-ninety-five of them had been brief, impersonal, barely worth classifying as contact. But on a few rare occasions, there had been more: a charge, a spark, the recognition of the potential that this person could actually rock her world, good or bad.

Elliot's palm was warm, the skin toughened from years of work. It was twice the size of hers, and it gave her that spark, that warning, that he could shake things up. Trouble was, things were already shaky. Any more shaking, and she could end up like the woman in the old commercial, knocked on her ass and unable to get up.

Though he showed no sign of letting go, when she tugged, he released her hand. She clasped both hands in her lap with an internal sigh of relief, feeling...safer that way.

What had happened to the days when being safe was the last thing on her mind?

"You don't have the typical Oklahoma accent," he remarked.

"I'm from Florida."

"What brought you to Tallgrass?"

"My husband, Scott, was in the Army." The air between them changed, a flutter of discomfort, or maybe disappointment, accompanied by his quick glance at her bare left hand. Good. She appreciated a man who cared whether the object of his flirtation was married. "I was here when he deployed to Afghanistan, and I stayed here when he died."

Elliot's expression turned solemn, his eyes going darker, his mouth flattening. "I'm sorry."

She'd heard those words a thousand times—said them ten thousand—with little real meaning. *I'm sorry I was late, I'm sorry I missed dinner, I'm sorry to bother you.* But there was genuine emotion in his voice—not just sympathy but empathy, too. It wasn't something he automatically parroted but something he actually felt.

She couldn't bring herself to offer the other bland, automatic response—*Thank you*—so she forced a small smile instead. "What about you? You don't sound like a native, either."

"I'm from West Texas."

Instantly an image of him in Wranglers, cowboy boots, and a Stetson, with no shirt but a lot of smooth brown skin begging for a caress, formed in her mind. It warmed her enough inside to require the unzipping of her slicker. "And what brings you to Tallgrass?"

"The highway and my trusty steed." He patted the dashboard with a grin before shrugging. "I'm just looking for a place that feels like home."

"West Texas doesn't anymore?"

A distant look came into his eyes, resisting the casual smile he offered. "Nah. I went off to join the Army, and while I was gone, the town where I grew up pretty much shriveled up and blew away. My folks moved to Arizona, my sister to New Mexico, and me... like I said, I'm looking."

"I get that. I was looking for a while, too." For most of her life, she'd been on her own, except for those too-short years with Scott. Absent father, disinterested mother, no family to help her... It had made her strong, but damn, that strength had come at a price. There was a part of her that would give it all up in exchange for a normal life, good health, and a man who would protect and keep her safe. She knew what it was like to be fierce and independent. Sometimes, just for a change, she wanted to be pampered and coddled.

Elliot's gaze fixed on her, searching, before he asked, "You find what you needed here?"

There was such intensity in his eyes that it seemed almost physical, warming her face, sliding along her skin, tying a knot in her gut. She had to shrug out of the slicker to slow the heat burning through her, had to clear her throat before she could answer, and when she did, the words came out husky. "Yeah. I did." What she needed, what she wanted, and the hope for maybe, someday, what she only dreamed about.

Movement blurred on the sidewalk, a carhop on skates rolling their way. Elliot's gaze didn't waver, though, not until it softened, not until he quietly, with some satisfaction, said, "Good. That's good."

* * *

Elliot liked women. All women. He didn't have a type, no preference in hair color, physical characteristics, sometimes not even personality: He had great memories of a few women who would have driven him crazy if they'd stayed together one minute longer. Women were the best idea God had ever had, soft and funny and smart and difficult and beautiful and sexy and aggravating and intriguing and frustrating and so incredibly sweet.

Fia Thomas—he wondered if that was short for Sofia— was making a great start on being all those things. He wouldn't be surprised if he drove away from her tonight with one of what Emily called his serious casual crushes. He always fell a little bit in love with the women he dated. It never lasted long, and he was okay with that, since he wasn't eager to get his heart broken. He'd volunteered for a lot of dangerous things in his life, but heartache wasn't one of them.

He paid for their dinner, brushing away the five bucks Fia produced from one of her slicker pockets. Handing her a paper bag and a drink, he grinned. "You can buy next time." Since he would be in Tallgrass awhile, might as well make sure she had a reason to see him again.

"That sounds fair." She unpacked her bag: fries on the dash, hamburger staying warm in foil, ketchup squirted from plastic packets onto an edge of French fry packaging. "It can even be home-cooked as long as it doesn't have to be my cooking."

"Hey, you provide the kitchen, I can do the cooking. I like to cook."

She studied him a moment before licking a dab of ketchup from her fingertip. "I like a man who knows his way around a kitchen," she said at last.

If she would lick her finger like that again, all innocent and tempting and unself-conscious, he'd gladly do the shopping, the prep, the cooking, the serving, and the cleanup for the best meal she'd ever had—and breakfast to follow.

Mouse climbed into Elliot's seat as he unwrapped his burger, breaking the tension that surrounded him, making it easier for him to draw a breath. When he tore off a bite, she took it delicately from his fingers, chewed it carefully, then set her butt on the console, and waited, quivering, for the next.

"How long have you had her?" Fia asked around a mouthful of her own burger.

He gave the dog an affectionate nudge with his elbow. "Two days."

"Is she a rescue?"

He didn't need to study Mouse to see what Fia saw: scrawny body, ribs showing through her skin, old injuries to her legs and torso. "Yeah. Some kids were playing soccer with her. She was the ball." He flexed his hand again, taking satisfaction in the aches there—and greater satisfaction that the teenagers were in a lot more pain than either him or Mouse.

"Poor baby. Lucky you and your trusty steed rode to her rescue. I hope you gave them something to remember you by." She smiled, softening the lines and the thinness of her face. Mouse wasn't the only one who needed a few pounds to fill her out. In her loose-fitting T-shirt and shorts, Fia looked as if she hadn't found much interest in food lately. Grieving a husband who'd died so young could do that to a woman.

He thought briefly of Scott Thomas, wishing him peace,

respecting his sacrifice. Not every service member saw combat, but everyone who signed up during wartime knew it was a serious possibility, and they were willing to accept that. Elliot had been lucky enough to come home, as tough and determined as when he'd left, thanks to his parents, Emily, and his own hardheadedness.

He'd lost a lot of people he'd loved, though, and a lot he'd hardly known. He was glad to be out of it, to be home in the United States, but if the Army needed him to go back, he would. *Live for something rather than die for nothing*, General George S. Patton Jr. had said, a fine sentiment, but Elliot preferred to switch it around: *Die for something rather than live for nothing*.

There had always been passions in his life, so he'd never had to settle for nothing. He never would.

"What kept you in Tallgrass after your husband passed?" He softened the words, the way he would soften any personal question, maybe a little bit more given the subject.

She pinched off a piece of her hamburger, including a generous hunk of meat, and offered it to Mouse. The dog hesitated, glanced at Elliot, and he nudged her to let her know it was okay. She took it in her mouth, then retreated to the backseat to eat it.

"There was nothing in Florida to go back to. And Oklahoma has the best people. All my friends are here." Fia paused long enough to dip a French fry in ketchup, then studied it a moment before adding, "Though all of them are transplants except Bennie and Patricia. They're all Army wives. Army widows. They're my family."

He understood the value of family, both the one a person was born into and the one they picked for themselves.

He stayed in close contact with his parents and Emily; he talked with his nieces and nephew every week; he'd attended the last two family reunions and felt like a better person for it.

Holding what was left of her burger in one hand, Fia gestured toward Mouse. "Can she have..."

"Sure. I don't want her to get used to people food, but right now, I figure she needs all the calories she can get. She's been hungry too long."

Finishing off his own sandwich, Elliot watched her feed Mouse one bite at a time. When she was done, she crumpled the wrapper, then swiped one hand through her hair. It was brown like his, just a few shades darker, and shorter by inches. Even with the dampness in the air, it lay smooth, framing her delicate face and, at first glance, making her look dangerously young. At second glance, though, it was clear she'd passed legal age a few years back. He would guess she was in her mid-twenties, maybe a year older, maybe a year younger.

At first glance, second, and third, she was beautiful in a fragile, innocent way, though he knew appearances could be deceiving. She might rouse his protective instincts— most women did—but she was physically strong, evidenced by impressive biceps and triceps and long solid muscles in her thighs and calves. Emotionally, she was probably pretty strong, too. Being an Army wife wasn't for the faint of heart.

Even though she'd lost her husband, her smile came quick and easy and found its way from her mouth into her dark eyes. It was something to behold, that smile. "I've never met a pit bull before. She's sweet."

"The breed's gotten a bad rap. Worst damage I ever

suffered from a dog was from a miniature poodle with pink bows on her ears. I've still got the scars on my ankle." He moved as if to pull up his jeans leg to show her, earning a laugh from her that was so damn appealing, it made him laugh, too.

Just think, if Mouse hadn't needed to take a leak, he wouldn't have been standing in that parking lot in the pouring rain, he wouldn't have been holding an umbrella for the pup, and he wouldn't have met Fia.

Damned if he didn't owe the dog a T-bone.

\*  \*  \*

Marti Levin had been through the worst life could throw at her: her parents' divorce while she was in college; her father's sudden death from a stroke at the age of fifty-one; her husband Joshua's death in Iraq at the age of twenty-six; her best friend Lucy's heart attack; her mother Eugenie once coming to stay with her for a month that, thank God, had lasted only a week. Those things had been horrible—okay, Eugenie's moving in had been more scary than horrible—but none of them had prepared her for what she was facing on this rainy Friday night.

Another relative moving in.

Her fourteen-year-old niece.

Marti paced the baggage claim area at Tulsa International Airport, checking her cell every time she pivoted in front of the large plate glass windows. Cadence's flight had arrived on time according to the arrival-departure board. Getting off the plane, stopping at the bathroom, and making the short walk from the terminal to baggage never took long this time of night in Tulsa, but twenty-five minutes had passed, and there was still no sign of her. Twenty-five minutes that Marti had used to rethink her brother's plan.

No, not his plan. Marti's insane agreement to it. Frank had always been all about his career, so she hadn't been surprised when he'd e-mailed her about the job transfer he'd accepted to Dubai. She hadn't been surprised that her sister-in-law was going with him; Belinda was a good corporate wife—would have made a great military wife, always willing to follow Frank wherever he chose to go, to take on whatever responsibilities he required. She hadn't even been surprised that they'd chosen not to take their only daughter with them. The Middle East, in this political climate, was no place for a shy, quiet Western girl.

But asking Marti to take Cadence for a year—that had been a surprise.

Her agreeing had been an even bigger one.

It wasn't that she didn't love Cadence. She did. She was sweet and studious and practically the role model for The Good Girl. How could anyone not love her?

But Marti wasn't a real warm and fuzzy person. Joshua was the only one she'd ever wanted to live with, share her home with, looked forward to seeing every hour of every day. She loved and even liked her family, but she did it best from a distance. Phone calls, texts, e-mails, Facebook...that was plenty of contact for her. Actually opening her home, trading long-distance and occasional for up close and personal...

She'd agreed a month ago and still didn't know why. Had still wanted to call Frank every day and say, *Sorry, I changed my mind.* Still dreaded what constant companionship—and of a kid, no less—would do to her peaceful, contented, solitary life.

A glance at her phone showed that nearly thirty minutes had passed. Only a few lone bags spun on the luggage carousel; stragglers talked on phones or waited impatiently for rides.

Surely Cadence hadn't gotten lost between Connecticut and Oklahoma. Her mother had put her on the plane in New Haven, and there'd been only one stop, without changing planes, in Chicago. She couldn't have gone past without Marti seeing her, wouldn't have been forcefully taken without screaming her head off. She'd had personal safety drummed into her head since she was an infant. She would ask for help if she needed it, would make a scene if she had to.

Marti started toward the long corridor that connected the baggage claim to the terminal. Usually someone sat at the desk there to answer questions and block passage into the hallway from this end. If that was the case tonight, they could call someone for assistance; if not, Marti would risk a scolding to go find her niece herself.

Ten feet from the desk—manned by a sour-looking gentleman reading the newspaper—Marti saw a slender figure entering the far end of the corridor. Her black hair was pulled back in a ponytail that bounced with every step, and she wore an expensive yellow leather backpack slung over one shoulder, Marti's gift the Christmas before. Though she was too far away to make eye contact, when the girl saw Marti, she picked up the pace until, at the last fifty feet, she was jogging.

"Aunt Martine!" Cadence threw herself into Marti's arms, the enthusiastic hug putting their usual sedate embraces to shame. "I'm sorry I'm late. I had to go to the bathroom. I'm so glad I'm finally here."

"You've grown." The words were out before Marti's brain engaged, and she gave herself a mental slap. However true it was, it should have at least waited until she'd said, *Hi, good to see you, I was starting to worry.*

Cadence took a step back and smiled sheepishly. "I'm fourteen. That's what I do."

"I'm glad to see you. Good flight?"

"As good as commercial's ever gonna be."

They both laughed at the reference to their last family vacation, when Eugenie's then-current boyfriend had taken them to Bermuda on his company's private jet. They'd all agreed that going back to coach or business travel was going to be a letdown, and it had been.

As they walked the few yards to the luggage carousel, Marti took a closer look at Cadence. She had grown about five inches since the last time they'd been together, and though she was still willowy, she had curves now, too. Her face was paler than usual, her gray eyes seeming darker in comparison. The contrast made the redness and puffiness around them starker as well.

Marti's gut tightened as she realized the long bathroom stop had included a good cry, and guilt flushed through her. All this past month, she'd worried about the changes *she* was facing, the hardships *she* would be taking on. She hadn't given any thought to how tough moving for a year would be for Cadence. Leaving the only home she'd ever known, her friends, her parents, everything familiar and dear. It was a lot to ask of a grown-up. How much harder would it be for a barely-a-teenager?

"Those are mine." Cadence gestured toward two suitcases, pink polka dots and stripes, circling at the far end, then made a face. "Duh. They're the only ones left."

They watched the bags approach for a moment before it occurred to them that they could meet them halfway, then continue out the door. Sharing an awkward laugh, they did just that, stepping out into the dreary cool night. Lights glistened on the wet pavement as they hustled across the street in the rain, then entered the short-term parking lot, where Marti's SUV waited. Cadence tilted her head as the lights flashed, giving Marti a knowing look. "Dad said you'd have something cute and pricey. I won that bet."

An image of her brother's garage came to mind: immaculate, obsessively organized, three expensive vehicles sharing the space. Frank didn't do cute, but he did love his luxury. "I traded the Beamer last winter after the fourth storm hit before Christmas. This baby's got all-wheel drive and handles ice like a gold medal skater." Though the problem driving in Oklahoma winters wasn't so much the road conditions as the other drivers. "Did your mom leave today, too?"

They hefted the suitcases into the cargo area, then slid into the front seats at the same time, reaching for their belts at the same time, too. "Yeah, her flight left two hours after mine," Cadence replied. "She's spending a few days in Paris before she meets Dad in Dubai."

A few days in Paris sounded like heaven...The queen of yearning inside Marti darn near salivated over the mere idea. Shopping, eating fabulous food, sipping café au lait at a sidewalk café, just soaking in the atmosphere of *Paris*. The queen of reality smacked yearning down with the reminder that she didn't have to travel halfway around the world to find good shopping, food, and coffee. And one of the reasons Belinda was free to visit

Paris now was because Marti had taken on her greatest responsibility. Maybe, when this year was over and Cadence had gone back home to her parents, Marti would treat herself to a trip to the City of Lights. Exactly the way she preferred it.

Alone.

# Chapter 2

The rain still pounded on the corrugated metal overhead, and the traffic circling through the driveway had picked up. Tallgrass had a number of restaurants, bars, and coffee shops where teenagers could hang out, and Sonic was the one of choice for the guys too young to get into the cowboy bars and the girls who crushed on them.

Fia caught the reflection of her smile in the window glass. Scott hadn't been a cowboy, but he'd done a pretty good impression when they'd met. She'd thought he was one of those good ol' boys who signed up to do their service to their country but couldn't leave behind the well-worn jeans, the flashy belt buckles, and the Resistols and Stetsons that had molded to fit them perfectly after years of wear. Turned out, it was a look he affected because everyone knew women liked cowboys.

Elliot was a real cowboy. He'd grown up on a ranch in the rugged West Texas landscape, starting chores when he was four, caring for his own horse from the time he was five, doctoring animals and driving heavy equipment and even doing a bit of rodeoing all before he was old enough to shave. He'd even shown her his Stetson, sitting upside down in the back where Mouse couldn't reach it.

She smiled again. Satisfaction was a big, complicated thing, but it could be created by the simplest little things. Listening to the rain drumming against the carport. Watching headlights flash across the wet world. Scratching an underweight, overcautious Mouse's belly. Listening to Elliot's deep gravelly voice with its Texas twang. Feeling like a woman with no cares in the world beyond enjoying this evening.

Her gaze slid across the clock in the dash, and her brows arched high. "Oh, my God, is it really almost midnight?"

Lazily he checked his watch. "Yep. Do you turn into a pumpkin when the clock strikes twelve?"

Her surprise gone, she arched one brow again. "Cinderella's coach turned into a pumpkin. She just went back to being herself." The plain girl with nothing to offer and no one to notice her. The obvious similarities gave her a mental *ouch*.

He leaned past her to look at her car. "It doesn't seem to be transforming."

She found herself gazing at his dark hair, dried now in a smooth curl that dipped underneath the band holding it, at the warm tan of his skin, the fine lines at the corners of his eye, and a small scar at the edge of his mouth. Had he gotten it in combat? In a bar fight? From some recalcitrant animal that liked its testicles exactly the way they were, thanks very much?

Probably his sister Emily had taken that umbrella from him and beaten him with it.

Bittersweet longing spread through Fia. What would she have given for a sibling who loved her enough to squabble with her? But then his gaze met hers, and the longing morphed, just like that. Forget siblings and squabbling; what would she give for a hunky, sweet hero like this in her life? To be the sort of woman who wouldn't burden a man like him?

Swallowing hard, she tried to remember what they'd been talking about, even though every hormone in her body wanted to shut down all thought and just feel instead. Inhale his scent. Touch his muscular arm. Grip his strong hand. Lean into him, just a few inches, just close enough so his mouth could brush hers.

"If I have a say in its transformation, I'm voting for a Challenger." Her voice was muddled, breathy, sounding like the kind of idiot who'd never talked to a gorgeous man, and the words didn't even register with her until they were out. It was self-preservation speaking, she realized, because if they'd stayed like that much longer, wrapped in a warm, muggy cocoon of desire and longing looks and parted lips, who knew what would have happened next?

She did. Elliot did, too, judging by the disappointment that flashed across his face.

He blinked, and the dazed look disappeared. "Man, my uncle Vance had a Challenger in high school. He promised he would hold on to it until I was ready to take it off his hands."

"Did he?"

"I don't know. I'll have to ask him."

"You should. Your steed is nice, but a vintage Challenger...damn. I'd even help you restore it."

"You can restore cars?"

"I'll have you know, I'm the best tool handler west of

the Mississippi. Just don't expect me to know their names or measurements."

He laughed, and the last bit of tension seeped from her body. Once it was gone, she became aware of a niggling behind her eyes. A headache was trying to dig its way out from the recesses of her brain to take over her world, the kind that required medicine, a dark room, a cool cloth. It reminded her once more of the things she couldn't even fantasize about with Elliot, of the things she couldn't offer him or anyone else, and that made her suddenly, unbearably weary.

"I appreciate the meal and the company," she said, avoiding looking at him, "but it's past my bedtime." She didn't reach for the door automatically, but lingered, waiting, wondering, hoping he would say or do...something.

He did, flipping open the center console, his fingers brushing her arm, sparking tiny tremors. From inside he pulled out an ink pen and an old receipt, and he scrawled his cell phone number before offering both paper and pen to her. She hesitated, told herself not to be greedy. All she'd asked for was one evening of normal, and she'd gotten it. But instead of pushing the pen away, she gripped it awkwardly in her left hand, her hold less sure than it should have been, and wrote her own number. She laid the pen in his hand, tore the paper in two, and handed him half while tucking the other half in her pocket.

"Can I call you about that home-cooked meal?" he asked. His voice was quiet, his expression serious, but there was optimism, hope, in his tone.

She couldn't think of anything smart or lighthearted or snarky to say, so she opened the door, slid to the ground, then turned back to face him. "I would like that."

With the smile crinkling his eyes, the long silky hair, the bit of stubble on his jaw, and the cream-colored Stetson in back, oh, yeah, he was definitely a damn good-looking fantasy.

And Scott was right: There was nothing wrong with a little fantasy.

Her answer erased any hint of disappointment from Elliot's face, replacing it with triumph instead. He was a man who savored small victories, something else they had in common. She'd learned the hard way that big problems were resolved one step at a time, sometimes with a few fallbacks along the way. She would have liked a kiss from her handsome stranger, would probably fantasize tonight about that and a lot more, but she was going to see him again. He was going to cook a meal for her, and she was going to melt into a puddle of emotional goo...if she didn't have to turn him down instead. A sharp pain behind her left eye reminded her that was possible.

She closed the door, and he rolled down the window. "You okay getting home by yourself?"

"I would have made it fine if I hadn't run into you in the parking lot."

"My lucky day." He flashed a grin that would have done any ladies' man proud and said, "I'll call you."

She acknowledged him with a nod, then slid into her own car. It hadn't turned into a pumpkin, but it wasn't a Challenger, either. Just the same bland car it had always been. She backed out of the parking space, navigated around the back of the building while still watching Elliot in the rearview mirror, then sighed loudly. Happy, contented, disappointed, blue—she couldn't tell exactly what that sigh held. She might never see him again—how many millions of times had people used *I'll call you* as a brush-off? She might see him again but things might not work out, or he might decide right off the bat that Tallgrass didn't feel like home. He might love Tallgrass and want to stay, might even like her and want to pursue something serious, but her health might not let it happen.

*Day by day*, her margarita girls advised. When times were tough, all you had to do was get through the next day, the next hour, the next ten minutes. That gave you a tiny bit more strength to get through the next ten minutes, the next hour, the next day. If all you could do in that very moment was breathe, then breathe and be damn grateful for it, and then breathe again.

If one evening with a sexy cowboy was all Fia could have, she would be grateful for it. Small victories. It might not be fair, but she'd built an entire life for herself out of them. She'd been happy then, and she could be happy again.

It took less than six minutes to reach her house, a squat, rectangular building of cinder blocks painted white. There was a small square stoop at each end, one for each of the two apartments housed inside, and neat windows with flower boxes mounted beneath them ran the length between the doors. When Fia's increasing bad days had made it too risky to climb the stairs to her second-story apartment, she'd been forced to move. Instead of a handicapped-accessible place, she'd chosen this duplex because it reminded her of her first home with Scott. There were still steps but only three. She desperately wanted to believe that she would always have the strength to climb three small steps.

Her headache intensified as she let herself in, and she automatically locked the door behind her. The only light on was in the short hallway that led to the bathroom and bedroom.

She didn't switch on any other lamps—didn't need to. Her illness had pushed her into a minimalist decorating style: no excess furniture to move while cleaning, no clutter to deal with, no sharp instruments to lose control of during a spasm, no cat to trip over. It was better for her, but she dreamed of cozy, not bare. Of health, not weakness.

Fingers brushing furniture, counters, wall, she made her way to the bathroom, located the medicine she needed, and swallowed it at the sink. Her hand trembled when she wadded the paper cup, and when she tossed it at the trash can, it bounced and landed on the floor instead.

"Later," she sighed, pulling off her shirt, kicking off her shoes, retrieving her cell phone from her pocket, and shucking her shorts. The bedroom to her left was her haven: cool, quiet, dark. The hall light didn't penetrate as far as the bed. The window blinds were always closed, the black-out drapes always drawn tightly. When these episodes came on, light was not her friend.

She pulled back the covers, slid onto soft, clean sheets, lay back, and groaned. Her skin tingled peculiarly as the full force of the migraine hit her. Her stomach churned. Her hair roots hurt. Even her eyebrows quivered individually. Breathing shallowly, throbbing, and missing Scott almost more than she could bear, she curled onto her side, eyes closed, her breathing sounding like jet engines in her ears.

The ring of the cell phone startled her, fingers clenching the hard plastic case as her heart rate increased. It was past midnight. No one called that late unless it was an emergency. She *hated* emergencies. Besides, she didn't know the number, wasn't familiar with the area code. It was probably just someone who'd misdialed, pumping up her heartbeat for no reason.

Or it could be...

She lifted the phone to her ear. "Hello?"

"Hello." The husky voice sent shivers through her that had nothing to do with the crap going on in her head. "It's Elliot."

Carefully she relaxed onto her back, bending her knees to ease the pressure on her spine. "Yeah, I recognized your voice." Recognized it and, for an instant, felt carefree again. It was sweet that he was keeping his word. The first time Scott had said, *I'll call you,* she'd been so sure she wanted to see him again that she'd replied, *Screw that. I'll call you.* She'd waited barely twelve hours. Elliot had waited less than one.

"I was thinking about that meal I'm going to cook for you. Mouse and I are pretty easy to please, but I figured I should find out what you do and don't like."

*I'm damn easy to please.* He could bring a packet of Twinkies and a bottle of water, and she would be happy, because it wasn't the food she was interested in. Too bold?

Not for the old Fia. Sadly, yes for the new, unimproved model. "No Italian," she said.

"Aw, and here I just dug out my grandma's recipe for lasagna."

"You travel with your grandma's recipes?"

"You're not gonna laugh, are you? Because, yeah, I keep her old cookbook with me."

That touched her. She had only vague memories of her maternal grandmother, who'd died when Fia was four or five, and she'd never met her father's mother. His family had written him off long before he'd met her mother.

She settled more comfortably on the bed, her fingers loosening their grip on the phone, a little of the stress easing from her body. The healing magic of Elliot's voice, she would like to think. The medicine taking effect, she knew. "I won't laugh. And I'll eat practically anything— even Italian with the right incentive."

"I'm good at providing incentive," he teased, and she knew he was telling the truth. "When and where?"

She gave him her address, and they agreed on six o'clock Saturday night. "I'll be there," he said, "ready to impress."

After saying good-bye, she slid the phone aside and smiled in the dark. *Ready to impress.* He'd done nothing but from the moment she'd seen him, and Lord, she needed impressing.

\* \* \*

In the last eight years, Dillon Smith had lived in West Texas, Nebraska, North Dakota, Wyoming, and Utah. The years before, he hadn't lived anywhere at all: traveling the rodeo circuit, working little, playing hard, and living harder. For a while, it had been fun, and then it had been okay. After that . . .

He'd been back in Tallgrass a year come June. It was the best place for him and the worst, the easiest and the toughest. His parents had forgiven him for his absence— and silence—and his kid brother, Noah, more or less had. His other brother, Dalton, still treated him with distrust and wariness. He expected more of Dillon than the others just because they'd shared a womb for the first forty weeks of their lives. Nothing Dillon did was good enough in Dalton's eyes.

Never had been.

It was Saturday afternoon, and Dillon had driven to one of a hundred small towns where he'd spent time. This one was in South Dakota, a dusty little place that kept itself running on hope and sheer will. In the four years he'd been gone, the high school had shut down; so had three of its five restaurants, all but one of the doctors' offices, and the tiny hospital. The motel on the edge of the town was the only one in the entire county, and it was about as beat-up and run-down as Dillon.

The day was still, the sky faded, nothing on the move besides him and a few birds circling overhead. Swiping at the sweat on his forehead, Dillon figured the only thing that could make the scene any more perfect for him was if the birds were vultures instead of common swallows.

His boots thudded on the sidewalk as he passed a Baptist church, then a mom-and-pop diner that made pancakes as fluffy and buttery as his grandmother's had been. Across fifteen feet of empty lot was the next building, two stories built of stone and weathered by wind and rain. The big windows were painted black, forming a backdrop for the childish red scrawl that read *BB's Bar*. There was no place in this town for fancy or trendy; BB's was a solid building with tables, chairs, a scarred floor, a long bar scavenged from barn wood, beer on tap, and cheap strong liquor.

He stepped inside, gave his vision a moment to adjust to the dim lighting, then headed for the bar at the back. To the right was a flight of stairs that led to the apartment on the second floor, stairs he'd climbed a thousand times when his shift behind the bar was done. It had been a part-time job, paid with free rent. His living money had come from his work at the grain elevator just north of town.

The place looked empty, but he knew he'd find BB

kicked back in a shabby recliner behind the bar. Times were rare when the old man could afford help, so he made himself comfortable with the chair, a TV, and a microwave where he could heat frozen meals for himself. He'd never been married, he used to say, but he'd consider giving up bachelorhood for a woman who could cook. Apparently, no one had ever taken his offer seriously.

When Dillon stopped at the end of the bar, BB looked up, a slice of pizza halfway to his mouth. No surprise crossed his face, nothing but recognition. "Dillon Smith." His voice was raspy and loud. The worse his hearing got, Tina had teased, the louder he talked.

An ache stirred deep inside, but Dillon had gotten pretty good over the years at ignoring it. Never a day went by that he didn't think about Tina, but if he let himself hurt every time, he'd have no reason to keep on living. And he did have a reason.

"In the flesh," he replied, and his own voice sounded pretty damn raspy.

"You looking for work?"

"Not right now. I hired on with my brother down in Oklahoma."

"Didn't know you had a brother."

"Got two." It was one of the things he'd liked about living away from his hometown. No one ever had to look at him twice before making a stab at what name to call him. He'd been mistaken for Dalton his whole life in Tallgrass, by their parents, their friends, even their girlfriends. Hell, Noah had been so young when Dillon left home that he never had known which was which. But in those hundred small towns, no one had known Dalton Smith existed. No one had held him up as an example of what Dillon should be.

The old man gestured to the cooler, a silent invite for Dillon to help himself to a cold one, before asking, "What brings you back to Dullsville?"

Dillon circled the bar and opened the cooler, feeling the chill radiating from the bottles. He pulled out a long-neck, popped the top, then went to sit on a lawn chair next to the TV. It was older than he was, made of aluminum, the seat formed by strips of nylon webbing. It sagged and shifted under his weight, but today wasn't its day to collapse. "I'm looking for someone."

BB finished off the pizza slice, licked his fingers, and wiped them on a paper towel, all the while studying Dillon intently. He swallowed a gulp of Pepsi—he'd run the bar his whole life and never had so much as a taste of the product he sold—then belched. "You know Tina's gone."

Gone and buried. Dillon had gotten that news just before the start of his trial, when the district attorney had upgraded the charges against him to manslaughter. But for all practical purposes, she'd been gone the moment her head had cracked against the windshield. Brain-dead, and it had been his fault. He supposed the end had been a mercy for her family—no more vigils, no more prayers, no more hopes. It would have been damn easier for him if she'd continued to live, even in that state. Less guilt and sorrow and blame and hatred. But it hadn't been about him, had it?

He forced his voice through tight vocal cords. "Her family used to live over in Granite. They moved a year or two back. Either no one knows where they went…"

"Or they're just not telling you."

Dillon took his first chug of beer, savoring the sharp flavor, the iciness sliding down his throat. "You ever hear where they went?"

BB took a long breath, then blew it out through his nose. "Heard it was to North Dakota. Some little town in the middle of nowhere." His laugh scraped like sandpaper. "Also heard they went to stay with family in Wyoming. Nobody's said nothing about them in a long time. I might could ask around for you. You got a phone number down there in Oklahoma where I could get in touch with you?"

Dillon heaved himself out of the chair and got a note pad and an ink pen, right in the same place they'd always been, and scrawled his name and number on the top sheet. He'd bet not a single thing in the entire bar had been re-arranged since he'd left. If he wanted to tend bar tonight, he wouldn't need even a glance to familiarize himself. Memory would guide him.

"You gonna spend the night?" BB asked.

He'd thought he would. He'd brought a couple changes of clothes, a toothbrush, the charger for his cell phone. He'd thought he might drive to a couple other towns in the area and ask around—the Hunter family had been pretty well known throughout the county—but now that he was here, he didn't see the point. He'd figured out without BB's help that people didn't want to talk to him about Tina's family. Even the ones who didn't remember him hadn't been willing to share information about one of their own with a stranger.

BB was a different story. He'd known Tina, her mother and father, her sister—hell, her aunts, uncles, and grand-parents. No one would question his curiosity; no one would think twice about giving him answers. Unless they con-nected him with Dillon.

And South Dakota, with all its memories, was no damn place for him.

"Nah, I don't think so. It's a long drive." He'd left hours before dawn, hit the interstate, and driven through Kansas, Nebraska, and half of South Dakota. It would be an even longer drive back because he was tired and just being here had stirred feelings he didn't often let get stirred.

BB nodded. "Anybody that don't come in tonight will be at church tomorrow. I'll let you know if I find out anything."

"Thanks." Dillon handed him the paper with his phone number, hesitated, then extended his hand. When the old man took it, the tension in Dillon's gut uncoiled a little bit. "Thanks a lot, BB."

\* \* \*

Elliot couldn't recall the last time it had taken him so long to buy groceries, and for one meal, no less. He'd wandered the aisles and wished for the days at home when he could walk into the garden out back to pick whatever produce he needed, open up the extra freezer in the pantry and take out whatever recently butchered meat he wanted, and make the rest from scratch. That was ten long years ago in a life that hadn't turned out quite the way he'd envisioned.

But that was okay. Sure, he'd like to have more money; extra cash was always nice. He was more than ready for a steady job, to prove his worth to himself if no one else, but that would come someday, when the time and the place were right. He loved his nieces and nephew and envied Emily the whole family experience, but he had a lot of years left. Maybe. If there was one thing war had taught him, it was that life was fragile. Scott Thomas was proof of that.

He arrived at Fia's house a few minutes before six,

wearing jeans, boots, and a white button-down. He'd shaved before coming, and his hair was pulled back with an elastic band. For good measure, he was wearing the straw Stetson he kept handy in the backseat of the truck with a nicer dark brown felt one, and a championship bull-riding buckle he'd won when he was in high school. Hey, if ladies loved a cowboy, he was more than happy to take advantage of it.

Juggling shopping bags, he climbed the steps and rang the doorbell with his elbow. At his feet, Mouse tilted her head back to sniff the bag containing the meat. She licked her lips with anticipation.

Elliot could have done the same when Fia opened the door if his mama hadn't taught him better. She stood there in cutoffs that might have started at a modest length but now reached high on her long, lean thighs and nestled an inch or two beneath her belly button. Her shirt was like his if he only looked at them in broad strokes: both white, both long-sleeved, both buttoned. But where his was utilitarian and provided full coverage, hers was thin and light and shifted when she did, following the natural curves of her waist, her breasts, her biceps and triceps. She wore a little makeup, no shoes, and the only fragrance he smelled was bath soap or shampoo, and damn, it was enough to make his gut tie itself into knots.

"I like a man on time."

"I like a barefoot woman." He stepped inside and turned toward the kitchen before stopping. "I forgot to ask if Mouse could come. I didn't want to leave her alone in a strange place." Not that he had any place besides the truck to leave her. Like the last four or five nights, he'd slept in the truck, parked in the dark corner of a quiet parking lot. It had actually been pretty peaceful, with Mouse curled in the front seat snoring and the rain hitting the roof most of the night. This morning he'd driven to a truck stop on the west side of town for breakfast and a shower. He'd had worse accommodations, even before he'd joined the Army.

Fia slid the leash off his wrist, then bent to unhook it. "Of course she's welcome. I don't have any pets who might say otherwise." She scratched Mouse's ears and under her chin, and Elliot watched. Well, more accurately, he watched the way the faded denim stretched over her butt and how the muscles in the backs of her thighs and calves flexed. He'd said it before, and he would say it again: Lord, he loved women.

When she cleared her throat, he started, his face warming at being caught staring. He grinned big for her, then carried the bags to the kitchen counter. As he began unpacking them, she pulled a stool to the bar and slid onto it, her fingers moving to the stem of a half-filled wineglass. "Would you like something to drink? I have tea"—she raised the glass, clinking the ice cubes in it—"and there's milk and a couple cans of pop in there somewhere." Her thin shoulders shrugged. "Sorry, no booze."

She started to rise, and he waved her back. "I'll get it in a minute." That was the second time she'd apologized about alcohol. He appreciated a cold beer in the right setting and, of course, a good wine paired with the right food, but he'd never seen the point in criticizing anyone for their beverage choices unless they were overdoing it. Fia not drinking beer was no more important, and no more his business, than him not eating cauliflower.

"I decided to start out simple with hamburgers," he said before wadding the second plastic bag inside the other and pushing them aside. "Even though we had them last night, I like to think mine are better than the average fast-food place. If you don't have a grill, I can pan-fry them."

"I do have one. It's been so long since I've used it, though, that we might have to clean out small rodents and such."

He grinned again. "Hey, rodents don't scare me. I'm tough." He did his best Hulk impression, shoulders hunched, fists clenched, drawing a laugh from her, then washed his hands before turning his attention to the kitchen. "Glass?"

She gestured toward the cabinet nearest the sink, where he found coffee mugs, tall insulated cups, and on the top shelf, a wineglass that matched the one she held. They were fine-quality crystal, edged with gold, the sort of glasses a couple might get as a wedding gift, maybe even drink their first toast from.

Feeling suddenly clumsy, he picked up an insulated cup decorated with sunglasses instead. "This okay?"

"Whatever you want."

After filling his glass from a jug of sweet tea in the refrigerator, he found a large bowl and dumped the ground beef into it, added salt and pepper, then pulled out a cutting board.

"You appear to know my kitchen better than I do," Fia remarked.

"Nah, we just think alike. Everything's in its logical location. Do you cook much?"

"It depends. My friends are incredible cooks who keep my freezer well stocked. And sometimes a peanut butter sandwich is the only thing I need."

He wondered if that was because cooking for one was a lot more effort than seemed logical. No matter how hard he tried, it just wasn't possible to make a bunch of his favorite recipes without having leftovers. "Peanut butter is one of my major food groups. I like it best with sliced banana and a drizzle of syrup or caramel sauce."

"Oh, no. Just plain smooth Jif. On a slice of white bread. Folded in half." She made a *yum* noise, then smiled. "Pure comfort in a sandwich."

She looked like she'd needed that comfort more in recent months than anyone should. He respected the sacrifices Scott had made, but Fia had had to make them, too. That was the reason Elliot had never looked for a serious relationship in the Army, not when he'd spent all his time in Afghanistan, getting ready to go there, or just coming back. He'd chosen that life for himself. It wouldn't have been right to choose it for someone else.

At least, that was one of the reasons. Mostly he'd been unattached because he hadn't met the right woman. For her, he would have given up a lot. Just as Fia had given up a lot for Scott.

"You like onion?" Elliot tossed a sweet yellow onion into the air, catching it easily. "I noticed last night you didn't want it."

"Close quarters and onion breath?" She shuddered. "Besides, I knew I'd be sharing with Mouse if you didn't mind, and my friend Jessy says dogs shouldn't eat onions. But tonight, Mouse will have to look elsewhere."

He laid the onion on the cutting board, and then reached for the knife roll he'd carried in with the groceries. Fia's gaze sharpened, then widened. "Oh my gosh, you travel with your own knives? I buy mine at Walmart, and then throw them away after I've sharpened them down to a nub. You *are* a serious cook, aren't you?"

He removed a six-inch utility knife, and sliced the ends from the onion. "I considered going to culinary school when I got out of the Army. Seriously. I thought it would be nice to be in a field where the only danger is an occasional cut or burn or a fallen soufflé."

"Okay, I am officially impressed. I can't remember the last time a man cooked for me"—the flash of emotion in her dark eyes suggested that, to the contrary, she knew to the day the last time Scott had cooked for her—"and I've never known a man who had his own knives. I mean, cooking knives. Every guy I've known has pocket knives or switch blades or hunting knives."

"It's hard to chop an onion with any of those." He let his gaze shift for a moment around the living room. The furnishings were a little sparse for his tastes, but the clean lines and lack of clutter worked. The colors and patterns were subdued, with only the textures varying, except when it came to the wall that held the television. The bright-colored, energetic photos there were the only personal touch in the room: portraits and snapshots of Scott, in and out of uniform, smiling, somber, weary. Almost all of the pictures of him in the desert were taken with the sun setting in the background. It was the same in the one photo that included Fia—their wedding portrait, gazing at each other with the sun sinking behind them.

She was beautiful. Scott was sharp in his dress uniform. They were both incredibly happy.

*Life isn't fair.* But Elliot knew it never had been and never would be. Horrible people lived and prospered; good people failed and died. Man's cruelty to others had reached historic highs, with the weaker, the younger, and the innocent bearing the brunt of it. People believed they were special and everyone else was expendable. Soldiers died, and brides became widows.

But that was the big picture. There were good, kind people who did the best they could, who protected what they could, who loved and laughed and honored those in their lives. His own parents were a fine example. His sister and brother-in-law, aunts and uncles, grandparents. Most of the people he'd known growing up and in the Army.

He'd met bad people. He'd met truly evil people. They had their power, but in numbers, they were a vastly smaller group than the good guys. And he was proud to be a good guy.

Movement across the counter brought his gaze around. Fia had slid off the stool to pick up Mouse, and now they were sliding back on, Mouse sitting like a lady in Fia's lap. Rubbing the pup's shoulders, keeping her gaze down, Fia said, "We were married four years ago. I never expected anyone to really want me because my mom and my dad sure didn't. I was kind of wild back then, but then I met Scott, and it was so strange. He adored me right from the start." Her gaze darted up, barely making contact, then away again. "Crazy, huh."

While listening, Elliot had diced a pile of onion into little more than mush without noticing it. "I don't think so," he said as he scraped them to one side, then carefully cut the rest of the onion into the proper-size dice for the burgers. "I thought you were pretty damn adorable, too, right from the start. And while I may be many things, take my word: Crazy ain't one of them."

*  *  *

While the fat hamburger patties stuffed with balls of moz-zarella cheese and onions came to room temperature on the counter, Fia took her guests on a guided tour, pointing out the bathroom, the door that led from the laundry room to the back patio, and down the steps to the small square of concrete. Elliot reattached Mouse's leash, then looped it over the doorknob to keep her from wandering too far.

The propane grill at the far edge of the patio had been her gift to Scott for the last birthday they'd spent together. No matter how cold, they'd huddled together on the tiny balcony of their apartment through that whole winter, grilling burgers and brats, chicken and steaks, ribs and zuc-chini and bread. Come spring, he'd deployed, and she had never seen him alive again.

Her heart squeezed, and her hands shook, making her wonder if one of her episodes was coming on. *Please, God, not right now,* she prayed, and in a moment she realized it was just the usual heartache. All day she'd worried whether she would be able to keep this date with Elliot. All day she'd rested and prayed and thought happy thoughts, and it was working so far. She was strong and confident she would stay that way at least until the evening was over.

Looking, acting, and feeling normal had never been as important to her as it was tonight. Hope was pretty damn important tonight, too.

Elliot carefully removed the vinyl cover from the grill, shook it out to dislodge spiders, then lifted the lid of the grill. "Aw, no rodents, no birds, not even a nest. Darn."

"What would you have done if there had been? Make friends and persuade them to let you move their nest? Take them in the way you did Mouse? Maybe whistle and get the mama mouse and all her babies to follow you?"

"My whistle is pathetic, but I have other charms to soothe the savage beast." He checked the gas line connections, turned on the propane, then pressed the igniter. With a whoosh, gas came on beneath both burners, glowing yellow through the slits, heat immediately drifting into the air. "We'll let it warm up, then I'll scrub it." He brought out a wire brush that had hung next to the tank.

"You want to sit?" There weren't any chairs to use. Those were in storage in the tiny shed across the yard. But the concrete steps were sturdy and narrow, barely room for the two of them, which made them just about perfect.

At his nod, she sat on the top step, still warm from an afternoon in the sun, and Elliot took the spot beside her. His hip bumped hers, and her shoulder brushed his as she settled her feet flat on the lowest step. His boots, with their worn heels and scuffed leather, made her feet look small and delicate and—and womanly. She hadn't felt that in a long time.

"Nice night." His voice was quiet, only a few inches from her ear. He smelled fresh and fruity and intoxicating, and his brown skin appeared even darker against the contrast of his white shirt. His lashes were long, his blue gaze directed across the yard, and a sense of contentment radiated from him that was at once distantly familiar and curiously alien to her.

When his gaze shifted minimally and the corner of his mouth tilted, she knew he knew she was studying him. Leaning forward to rest her elbows on her knees, she ducked her head so that what he saw was mostly hair and asked, "How old are you?"

"Twenty-eight."

"Ever been married?"

"Nope. I intend to do it only once, so I'm waiting for the right woman."

It was his turn now to study her. She could feel his gaze as surely as she felt the evening air against her skin, warm and sweet and with the promise of cooling breezes. As he'd done, she stared out across the grass. The duplexes were part of the apartment complex where she and Scott had lived in their tiny two-bedroom apartment. There were eight small houses with small yards, carports, and sheds. They looked like a lot of base housing she'd seen over the years, not fancy but clean and well maintained and sturdy. The duplex's eight hundred square feet suited her just fine.

"Finding the right woman shouldn't be hard," she murmured, twisting to see him.

"Sometimes it's not. You found Scott before you were twenty. My mom knew she was going to marry my dad when she was fourteen. But sometimes it takes a while. Uncle Vance was coming up on fifty when he met his wife."

"And you hope it's only once." She and Scott had amused themselves planning their retirement: where they would live, where they would travel, what adventures they'd take with their grandchildren and great-grands. It had never occurred to either of them that they could possibly have less than three years together. Even if the thought had crossed their minds, they wouldn't have believed it. They'd been too young, too much in love, too invincible.

And even if they'd believed it, they still would have gone through with it: gotten married, started a life, planned a future, because they'd been young, in love, invincible, and incredibly hopeful.

That lovely, smoky residue of food cooked on the grill

drifted on the air, adding its perfume to the white-flowered bush blooming one house over. Fia's stomach growled, making Elliot chuckle, a good sign to her. She ate because life required nourishment, but she couldn't remember the last time she'd actually been hungry. Food smelled good. It tasted good. In the last year or so, it just hadn't seemed worth the effort.

Elliot gently elbowed her. "I hope you have a good appetite. I'd hate to go through all this effort just to end up sharing it with Mouse."

"No, you wouldn't," she disagreed. "You like the prepping part. And you like Mouse." She shifted so she could see him better. Unfortunately, that meant putting a few inches of space between them. Her left hip, rib cage, and arm cooled after losing contact with his body. "Where have you lived since you got out of the Army?"

"Nowhere. Everywhere." He shrugged. "I spent a few weeks with my folks at their new place in Arizona. They ranched in West Texas, which is never a very easy proposition. After a few years of drought and unstable market prices and skyrocketing expenses, they decided to head someplace friendlier. Dad works for another rancher now—gets to do the things he likes with the livestock and the cowboys and doesn't have to worry about the stuff he doesn't like, like paying bills and making a profit."

Tired of checking out her new location, Mouse climbed the steps, looked at Fia for a moment, then slid between Elliot's knees so he could scratch her head. Like the well-trained creature he was, he immediately accommodated her.

"It was kind of hard when they told me their plans. That ranch had been in my dad's family since the 1880s. It had always been tough, but the Rosses always made a go of it, and I was afraid it would take a toll on them, losing it after all those years." He smiled. "Turned out, he and Mom couldn't wait to shake the dust of West Texas off their boots. They live outside Phoenix, a short drive to everything they could possibly need, and they have a lot of friends who've never set foot on a ranch or branded a cow or castrated a steer. They love it."

For a brief moment, Fia wondered what her parents were doing with their lives. In the time she'd known them, neither one had ever held a job for any length of time. They had never accepted responsibility for that, either, or for anything else. They'd brought her into the world with no intention of taking care of her. When she was little, she'd wondered why. What was so wrong with her that even her mother and father couldn't love her? What had she done to deserve their neglect?

It wasn't her, Scott had insisted. The failings were her parents'; they'd been selfish, lazy, too focused on themselves. It was the first time anyone had told her she wasn't to blame, and he'd been so sincere that she'd believed him. She had given up trying to love her mom and dad, had quit trying to maintain some semblance of a relationship with them.

But Lord, there was still a place way deep down inside her that wanted to know how a mother's and father's love felt. There was still a part of her that regretted she would never know.

Beside her, Elliot exhaled. "So I decided Arizona wasn't for me, and I didn't want to cramp Mom and Dad's life by trying to fit in where I didn't. Next I went to New Mexico and stayed a few weeks with Emily and her family." He reached into his pocket and pulled out his phone, then began swiping one finger across the screen, scrolling through pictures fast enough to create a blur of color and activity. "You'd like Emily. She's a tyrant but in a good way. Her kids are well behaved and respectful, and they say stuff like 'please' and 'thank you' and volunteer to do chores. They live in a little town about an hour out of Albuquerque where everyone knows not to cross Emily. Everyone gathers at her and Bill's house—all the school kids, the neighbors, the folks from church—and everyone is happy."

She leaned close to see the photo when he held out the phone. The woman was a few years older than him, tall, lean, and really pretty in a wholesome-girl way. In the shot, she hugged her husband and kids close. *Everyone is happy.* They really looked it.

"But you didn't stay there because...you'd already spent enough years under her thumb but in a good way?"

"Nah." He gazed at the photo a moment with pure affection before looking back at Fia. "She and Bill have lived there six years. She loves it, and it works for her. It's *her* place. But not mine."

"How will you know your place when you find it?"

Even though his attention turned serious, there was still a hint of amusement in his eyes. Fia wondered if it ever totally went away. "I made a list once. Maybe sometime I'll show it to you. In the meantime, let's get this dinner on the grill."

He stood, then offered his hand. She laid hers in it, liking the feel of his warm callused skin and the way his fingers folded around hers. With little effort, he pulled her to her feet. With just a little more, he could have pulled her into his arms. She would have been startled—or just plain happy—and he would have smiled and his blue eyes would have lit up. Her breathing would have gotten fast and shallow, and his slow and raspy, and then slowly he would have pulled her even closer, until nothing more substantial than a breath could come between them, and by then she would have been shivery and hot, and he would have—

"Aw, come on, don't pee on the patio. That's just not dignified."

Fia blinked, and the shivers and fever disappeared. Instead of moving closer, Elliot had taken a step back and was chastising the dog near his feet, who looked back at him from the other side of a puddle, her expression as unrepentant as any rebellious teenager's.

His scowl good-natured, he shook his head. "I'll clean that, then start cooking. Want me to get you a chair?"

Fia was still in a daze, still thinking about contact and intimacy and other girly desires. She shook her head to clear it. "No, I'm fine. You go on and get the food, and I'll get the hose."

He protested but went inside when she insisted. As the door closed solidly behind him, she gave Mouse a measuring look. The dog gave back the same expression.

"Consider yourself lucky if I don't turn it on you and me both."

# Chapter 3

Elliot quickly prepped the last few vegetables and loaded them onto a baking tray—zucchini sliced in thick planks, seasoned and drizzled with olive oil, and portobello caps—and swiped oil across the surface of the buns before carrying the tray outside. He found the patio rinsed clean and Fia sitting on the grass near the grill, Mouse curled up a short distance away.

That dog and her bladder... First, she'd dragged him out into the rain so he could meet Fia, and then she'd pulled him totally out of the moment when he'd thought he was going to kiss Fia. She'd looked so sweet and soft and willing—Fia, not the dog—and he'd felt the tiny tremors in her hand, and he'd wanted more than anything to lean forward and wrap his arms around her and slide his tongue inside her mouth and—

*And.* Who knew how far it would have gone, but he did know one thing for sure: It would have been a hell of a good time. The best he'd had in months. Maybe ever.

He set the tray on the side shelf of the grill and lifted the lid, fierce heat escaping into the evening. The zucchini and the mushrooms hissed when he put them on the grate, smoke rising into the air, hanging there before drifting away. After closing the lid again, he faced Fia. "What kind of workouts do you do?"

"What makes you think I'm not lazier than Mouse?"

"Because you don't get muscles like that being lazy."

She considered her long, lean legs for a moment. "It used to be the most strenuous thing I'd do all day was dancing in the clubs all night. Then I met Scott, and his idea of a perfect date was a long walk or jogging three miles to breakfast. I kind of got hooked on the activity, so I went back to school and got licensed as a personal trainer. After a while, I decided running was more stress than I wanted to put on my joints since I intended to chase after my grandkids when I was old, so I began mostly swimming, weight training, walking, yoga."

"Did you work as a trainer?"

"Yeah. I still work at the gym, but I gave up my clients after…" A pensive look on her face, she shrugged one thin shoulder, and he finished the sentence himself: *after Scott died.* "I see them around while I do other stuff at the gym."

Loss was a bitch, Elliot thought as he used tongs to flip the zucchini slices. His grandmother had been widowed fairly young: She was thirty-nine when his grandfather's horse had thrown him and broken his neck. She'd had family living right there on the ranch, though—Elliot's dad and mom, him and Emily, Uncle Vance and Uncle Marvin and his wife, Amy. Grandma had sucked it up and gone on with the business and with life, but she'd never stopped missing Grandpa until the day she died.

Just like Fia would never stop missing Scott, and her friends would never stop missing their husbands. It could prove a bit of tough competition for some people, but Elliot was nothing if not tough. And competitive.

Facing the grill again, he loosened the foil covering the two fat burgers, then slid each one onto the grate with a smoky sizzle. "The perfect sound: beef over heat."

"Pretty near the perfect aroma, too." Fia pushed to her feet, nudged Mouse with her toes, then laughed before joining him. "I've never been much of a burger griller."

"Aw, it's easy. First you start with your own grass-fed beef, tomatoes off your vines, and onions so fresh that there's still clumps of dirt clinging to them."

"You didn't grow any of this," she pointed out.

"Nope, you're right. But back in the day, that's how we did it. Grandma made the buns, and Aunt Amy made the cheese with milk from her own cows, no kidding. The only thing they ever bought was the mustard and the mayonnaise. Even the pickles were homegrown and canned."

"Let's see, hamburgers in my family back in the day meant unwrapping the paper and biting into a piece of mystery meat, a squirt of mustard and one of ketchup, and a single slice of pickle. If you wanted cheese, they slapped on a cold slice just before they wrapped it and handed it to you."

Elliot gave her a phony pitying look. "That's just damn sad. You should have grown up in West Texas, where people know how to eat right." And live right. And, especially, treat their kids right. He hated the casual, straightforward way she'd thrown out comments about her family: *There was nothing in Florida to go back to. I never really expected anyone to want me because my mom and my dad sure didn't.* As if they were simple facts of life, deserving no more importance than any other detail.

Tamping back that annoyance, he continued with the same phony tone. "I take it your mother didn't like to cook."

"She preferred a liquid diet most of the time. Food was just one more thing she didn't bother with, along with housekeeping and working."

*And child-rearing.* What a shame.

To shake off the gloom that line of thought brought, he pointed to the burgers with the pancake turner. "Rare, medium, shoe leather, or in between?"

"Medium well. I'm not a fan of any pink food except strawberries mashed with vanilla ice cream."

"Home-churned ice cream and served with a thick slice of fresh-baked angel food cake."

She gave him a look. "Or those little round sponge cakes that come four to a package and are usually piled next to the berries in the produce section."

"Man, you're killing me here. Your life has been so deprived."

To his surprise, she shifted until her shoulder bumped his. It was similar to a thousand nudges Emily had given him growing up, but it felt like a whole different universe. "Yeah, but I also didn't have to get up at oh-dark-thirty to feed cows and horses and chickens."

"Can't-see," he murmured. When she glanced at him, brows lifted, he shrugged. "That's what Grandma called it. You work on a ranch from can't-see to can't-see. Dawn to dusk." For a moment, he concentrated on the food, removing the zucchini and portobellos from the grill, testing the doneness of the burgers with the press of the pancake turner, sliding the buns over the heat. He'd learned the perfect timing of burgers and buns years ago, always finishing one just as the other was ready for it. It was his singular talent, Emily claimed. That, and being every female's knight in shining armor.

Hey, some men had a lot less to offer than perfectly timed food and a stand-up guy complex.

Within five minutes, they were back in the house, Fia helping him gather condiments, napkins, and plates. Once everything was on the small dining table that separated the living room from the kitchen, he presented her with one medium-well-done portobello-mozzarella-onion burger on a perfectly grilled bun.

"This smells incredible. Why didn't you go to culinary school?" she asked as she spread mustard and mayo, added lettuce and pickle, then took her first bite. She made the same kind of pleasure-filled moan that Mouse had made at her first-ever taste of hamburger. It was so much sexier coming from Fia.

"I don't know. Time. Money. Differences of opinion. I have my way of doing things that I don't want to change." He took a bite of his own burger while considering it further. "I'm not interested in exotic ingredients or impressive plating or mastering overly complex techniques. I'd never make it as a chef in a five-star restaurant. I'd want to have my own place, cooking the sort of food I grew up with, serving it to the sort of people I grew up with, and for that, thousands of hours in the kitchen with Grandma count for a hell of a lot more than a culinary certificate."

"So is that the kind of job you're looking for here?"

Elliot shrugged with an easiness he didn't feel inside. There weren't many topics in his life that made him uncomfortable, but his lack of employment did. With all the skills that the Army had taught him, added to what he'd already known, finding a job should be easy. Instead, he'd found too many people who said, *Oh, you were in the Army. Thank you for your service, but we don't have anything for you.* That was hard to accept for a guy who'd worked practically his whole life.

"I'm not picky. Cowboying, tending bar, construction, chief bottle washer...Something that will pay the rent." Obviously, he'd been getting by the past two years, and more comfortably than a lot of veterans. He might sleep in his truck as often as not, but it was better than the ground. His only luxuries were the pickup and the cell phone, but he needed one to find the right place to live—and to get to any job he did get—and the other to keep in touch with his family.

"Hmm. My friend Jessy's husband owns a ranch north of town. His brother works with him, but they hire seasonal help, or maybe he knows someone else who's looking for someone. I'll ask her." Fia sliced into a piece of zucchini, her fork cutting through the charred marks, then tasted it. "This is really good."

"Thank you, ma'am."

"What was your MOS in the Army?"

Deliberately he took a large bite of his hamburger, more than his mouth should hold, because his specialty in the Army was one of the other topics that could make him uncomfortable sometimes. He had no regrets. He'd done his job and done it well, killing his share of the enemy, saving his share of his buddies.

Some people, though, didn't care about the training, the discipline, or the people he'd saved. All they'd wanted to hear about was the ones he'd killed. Their questions were pushy and rude: *Did you know the guy in that movie? Could you shoot as well as him? Could you see their heads blow apart in the scope? What was it like? How did it feel to know you did that from a mile away?*

"I was a sniper," he said at last.

Fia wasn't some people. Her eyes didn't widen; her thoughts didn't race to thrills and deadly skills or media hype. She nodded once and quietly said, "Tough job." She didn't pry. She didn't look at him like he was some big bad killing machine. She just made her comment and continued eating.

Every time he learned something about her that he really liked, it gave him a warm feeling in his gut. It took a strong man to be a warrior, and an even stronger woman to be a warrior's wife. Scott Thomas had met his match in Fia. That always-falling-in-love part of Elliot was wondering whether he might turn out to be as lucky.

\* \* \*

Marti's neat spacious house was quiet as usual Sunday morning. She'd gotten up at eight—it was the one day she allowed herself to sleep in—and made herself a cup of coffee, along with a bagel slathered with cream cheese. Her friends teased her about merely tasting foods rather than actually eating. Her rule was to eat as much as she wanted of most foods, which wasn't a lot, but there were exceptions: a carton of salted caramel ice cream; a bag of vanilla cookies; a bagel almost as big as the dinner plate on which it sat. *As much as she wanted* then became an embarrassing amount of food. Like enough to sustain a family of three for a day.

With the local newspaper tucked under one arm, the plate in one hand, and the coffee in the other, she was on her way to the back door to enjoy the cool morning and the patio furniture delivered just last week when a sound down the hall stopped her. It came from the bathroom, and it wasn't pretty. Cadence was puking. Again.

Marti hesitated. Should she knock on the door and ask if her niece was all right? Should she write it off as nerves, Cadence's explanation when it had happened after lunch yesterday? Maybe she should pretend she hadn't heard anything, go outside, and enjoy her breakfast while her coffee and bagel were hot, and let Cadence tell her whatever she wanted.

"Man, you suck at this," she muttered, but before she could take two steps toward the hall, the toilet flushed, the sink ran, then the door opened.

Cadence stepped out, still drying her face on paper towels, and stopped suddenly as she saw Marti. Her face was pale, her smile an automatic gesture that looked more pitiful than pleased. "Oh. Hi. I didn't know if you were up yet."

"You okay?"

A flush filled in the unnatural paleness of Cadence's cheeks. "Yeah. Just nervous. About meeting people. Being different." She shrugged her thin shoulders. "Fitting in."

Marti studied her a moment, wondering if she'd ever worried about stuff like fitting in when she was a teenager. She couldn't recall it if she had, but then, she'd been a pushy kid, the one making the decisions about who fit in and who didn't. She hoped none of her friends twenty years ago had fretted this much about it.

"I'm taking my breakfast outside," she remarked, turning toward the back door. "If you want to, grab something and join me."

The furniture she had bought for the patio was vintage stuff, dating back to the 1920s, solid wood and curves and soft lines, once painted white, now showing mostly flecks of white paint. It needed a fresh coat of something if for no other reason than to protect her clothing and skin from its worn wood, so for nearly a week, she'd studied it in the morning sun, at midday when she was able, and in the setting sun, but she still hadn't found a clue what to do with it.

Careful of her pajamas—one of Joshua's old gray and black PT shirts with a pair of her own shorts—she pulled a chair out from the table and sat down. It had thick curved arms and turned legs and made her feel like a small child in a chair that wrapped around her. She took the first creamy, chewy, delicious bite of her bagel as the door behind her opened. A moment later Cadence settled across from her with a bowl of dry cereal and a small bottle of orange juice.

"Mom says drinking all that fresh-squeezed orange juice when we visited Grandmommy ruined her for OJ," Cadence remarked as she twisted the top, "but I still like the bottled stuff, as long as I remember that fresh juice and bottled juice are two totally different things."

Marti smiled faintly. The only time she had conversation with breakfast was on the rare occasions when the margarita girls took an overnight trip. She didn't even like the television on first thing in the morning, when her brain was still waking up, still debating how or even whether to face the day.

"So we're having dinner with these friends of yours after their church gets out." Cadence grinned. "I owe Daddy five bucks. He bet you hadn't set foot in a church since Uncle Joshua's funeral. I figured you to be on better terms with God."

Mention of Josh brought Marti a bittersweet smile. "You don't owe him the entire five bucks. I've been to a wedding or two." And a few funerals too many.

"How well do you know Abby?"

Abby Matheson's stepmother, Therese Matheson-Logan, was one of the original margarita girls, left with the additional burden of raising stepchildren from her husband's first marriage. There had been times when all the margarita girls had wondered which was the more tragic for her: Paul's death or getting stuck raising his children. Sad but true.

"About as well as you know your mom's childless friends." Abby was the only fourteen-year-old girl Marti knew in town—the only teenage girl, period. Since her family lived a few blocks away and Abby went to the middle school Cadence would start tomorrow and Therese had offered introductions in the lower-stress environment of a backyard barbecue, Marti had jumped at the chance.

Cadence lifted a few fingerfuls of cereal to her mouth, crunched loudly, then washed them down with juice. "Does she make good grades? What kind of activities does she do? Does she like horses, music, cheerleading, computers?" Translation: *Will she like me?*

Marti took another bite of bagel to avoid answering right away. Though she'd met Abby numerous times, the things she knew about the girl weren't the sort she would share. Grieving her father's death and her mother's abandonment of her and her brother, Abby had gone through one hell of a rebellious phase. Princess of Whine, Queen of I-Hate-You, Girl in Need of Smacking—she'd earned plenty of nicknames, none of them flattering.

But things had changed last year, when Keegan and his daughter, Mariah, came into the Mathesons' lives. His respect and little Mariah's unquestioning love had gone a long way toward making Therese, Abby, and Jacob a real family, not just three people sharing a house.

Aware that Cadence was patiently waiting, Marti shrugged. "She's bright, like you. She likes clothes and boys and school, and she's pretty good at computers. She's something of an artist, too. She's short, blond-haired, brown-eyed, and she has a deformity to her left hand, this rectangular growth that beeps, buzzes, and interrupts normal life a million times a day."

At mention of the word *deformity*, Cadence's eyes had widened. Now she gave Marti a chastening look as she nudged her cell phone into the shadow of her cereal bowl. "You sometimes suffer from the same condition. What is it called? Cell-itis?"

They both laughed, then Marti fixed her gaze on her niece and turned solemn. "You're going to fit in perfectly here. You and Abby may not be best buds, but you and someone will. A lot of the kids you're going to meet in Tallgrass, they're Army kids, so they know what it's like to leave behind everything familiar and start over in a new place. They adapt to new situations and new people all the time, and you're just so darn adorable that they're all going to love you."

Reaching across the table, Cadence patted Marti's hand. "It's been a long time since you were fourteen, hasn't it?"

"Ugh, that was kind of cheesy, wasn't it? Just...be yourself. And remember that it's only for a year." She thought briefly of life with Josh, and life without him, and squeezed Cadence's fingers tightly. "You can endure anything for a year."

\* \* \*

Fia's head was pounding when she awoke, and the numbers on the digital clock were too blurry to read. Heaving a sigh, she rolled onto her back and stuffed the extra pillow beneath her head, keeping her eyes closed. She'd had a wonderful day Friday, a wonderful day Saturday, and now she was going to pay for it. Two steps forward, one step back, though her bad days sometimes outnumbered the good by a whole lot.

The only thing on her schedule for the day was a cookout at Therese's house. All of the margarita girls would be there, significant others in tow for the ones who had them, and three of them had offered to pick her up on the way. She'd told them all the same thing: *I'll have to let you know that day.* Lord, how she hated those words!

If she could go, she could invite Elliot, the woman inside her whispered, and heat filtered through her veins. She hadn't enjoyed an evening so much since...too long. The food, the conversation, the serious interest in his eyes, and that whole calm-peace-satisfaction thing he had going. The entire evening she'd felt alive and tingly and aware of possibilities she thought she'd said good-bye to.

This morning, reality and its limitations fizzled the heat and left her feeling weary and hopeless. Damn, she hated feeling hopeless!

Slowly sitting up, she threw back the covers and swung her feet to the floor. Warrior girl didn't lie in bed moping around, especially when her bladder was full, and blurred vision or not, it was way past time to start the day. Nausea tumbled in her stomach when she stood, but after a moment it passed, and she headed to the closet, grabbing a dress from its hanger, snatched up underwear from a drawer, then made her way to the bathroom.

After washing down her morning medications and brushing her teeth, she climbed into the shower. While she was luxuriating in the sensation of hot water pounding her body, her left hand began to curl, the fingers bending, pulling into a fist of their own accord. She watched, the image still fuzzy, regret sour in her stomach, and wondered how bad it would get this time. Would her right hand follow suit? Would the muscles in her arms and shoulders tighten until her wrists were drawn inward against her chest, her arms basically useless until the spasm or whatever the hell it was passed? Would her feet start to turn in, too, forcing her to walk on the outside of her ankles, her calf muscles knot, her speech turn slurry like she'd been on a three-day drunk?

*Please, God, no.* She wanted to go to the cookout. To see her friends. To see Elliot. To be normal just one more day.

But even as she prayed, the cramps started in her right hand and her fingers began to bend as if pulled by invisible cords attached to the tips. Cautiously she slid one foot forward, then the other, until she was directly under the flow of water and let every bit of lather wash away before nudging the faucet to Off. She climbed out carefully, wrapped a bath sheet around her, then sank to the floor, pretending that she wanted to sit there, pretending that the moisture on her cheeks was dripping from her wet hair.

Fia didn't know how long she might have sat there—the whole day?—if the cell phone hadn't rung. Her gaze went automatically to the counter before she remembered it was on the nightstand. All the crap she'd gone through the past year, and she still couldn't remember to keep the damn phone with her. Getting up took time, pushing herself first to sit on the edge of the tub, then on the commode, finally making it to her feet. Nausea rushed through her again and, thankfully, passed just as quickly, and with her fisted hand, she scooped up a towel to blot her hair as she shuffled to the bedroom.

"Warrior girl, my ass," she snorted as she squinted at the cell screen, trying to decipher the jumbled letters showing on caller ID. "Only twenty-four, and you need one of those phones for old people with a super-big display and numbers."

Giving up on ID'ing the caller, she stabbed uncooperative fingers to call up the voice mail. It was worth every wince and mistake.

"Hey, Fia. It's Elliot." A bark sounded in the background, and he chuckled, adding, "And Mouse. I wanted to thank you for a nice evening." His voice turned teasing. "You're making me feel at home here, you know that? Are you sure you want that?"

*Oh, hell, yes, I want it.* Of course, it was just infatuation at this point, but the idea of Elliot settling in Tallgrass, of running into him from time to time, maybe going out with him from time to time...Just knowing he was there would soothe something in her soul. Not a romantic something, just a lifelong need to know there were good people around. Like Scott and the margarita girls, Elliot was good people. She would be better for knowing him than not knowing him.

"Anyway, Mouse and I found a pretty spot at Tall Grass Lake. Water's still cold for skinny-dipping, but the sun's shining, the wildflowers are blooming, and there's lots of peace and quiet. I thought maybe we could share it with you if it's not too late to ask. Just give me a call." A moment of fumbling came through the phone, then he spoke again, his voice huskier, more Texan. "By the way, if you were thinking of kissing me good night last night, you should have gone ahead and done it, because I was sure thinking about doing it to you. And I know you were. You get this look... You had it in the truck Friday and on your porch last night. Come have fun with us today, and I'll show you the look I get *after* I've been kissed." He followed with another *Call me*, then the automated voice asked her to save or delete the message.

She saved it.

Fia's mouth curled in a crooked victorious smile. They'd stood on the porch just before Elliot had left last night, the air heavy and damp and close, the night sounds muffled, the heat simmering off both of them. Only two feet had separated them. Two feet was no obstruction, not even when her feet were pointing every which way but right. Hell, she could trip and fall that far.

But she hadn't. She'd wanted to almost as much as she'd wanted her next breath, but ugly words kept echoing in her head: *Bad days. Sick. Getting worse. Not a stroke, not MS, not MG. Needy. Exhausted. Burden. Burden. Burden.*

All her life, until Scott, she'd been a burden—to her parents, grandparents, schools, the system. Scott was the first person who'd ever looked at her and seen a woman worth having. He'd made her want to be a better person, to want to deserve him. Thank God, he'd never had to know what happened to her after his death. It would have broken his heart.

*I'd still be here. For better or worse, remember?*

She smiled. She wasn't the only margarita girl who talked to her husband. They found comfort or reassurance, sought hope and the enduring love they'd shared, vented their frustration, or did it out of habit.

"But you took vows," she said as she rubbed the second towel over her hair. "You knew what you were getting into the first time you asked me to dance. You knew I was crazy and wild."

*Crazy's just an opinion, and wild can be tamed—but no more than a little bit. I loved a healthy dose of wild.*

Feeling a little steadier, she returned to the bathroom to dry off, then dress. "I'm not the girl you met, Scott. I was young and energetic and full of hope and defiance. And kinda cute, too. You would have those memories to hold on to. But Elliot's never known the real me. He'd be getting some pasty version of what I used to be, and all it would be for him is work. Disappointment. Medical bills." She paused before bitterly adding, "A burden."

After shimmying her dress over her hips, she sank down on the commode. "No guy in his right mind is looking for a burden. No guy would listen to my story, watch me on a bad day, then ever show his face again."

Her voice came out on a self-pitying exhale.

"I really want to see his face again."

\* \* \*

Elliot had been totally honest when he told Fia's voice mail that he'd found a pretty spot at the lake, though he may have left the impression that it was a more recent discovery. When he'd left her house last night, he'd been too wired to sleep so he'd taken an aimless tour of the town, saw a sign for the lake, and followed it, and he'd been rewarded with exactly the kind of place he liked to spend the night.

The lake was a few miles out of town, and the spot he'd chosen was a ways off the road. The first spring mowing hadn't taken place yet, so the weeds were high, but the wildflowers blooming among them were a dozen shades of yellow and purple and white. He'd parked at the edge of a clearing, trees nearby for shade from the morning sun, and for a while he and Mouse had lain in the back, watching for shooting stars and far-off planes. The only noises he'd heard all night were the birds in the trees, fish breaking the water's surface, and distant coyotes. It would have been a perfect night except that Fia wasn't with them. She wouldn't even have had to kiss him, or let him kiss her. Just sharing the peace and the beauty of nature with her would have been enough.

For now.

So far this morning, he'd driven to the campgrounds down the road to shower and change, then returned to the clearing, where he fed Mouse and ate his own breakfast of peanut butter and crackers. He and Mouse had worked on her training for a while, and he'd waited for a call back from Fia. He never sweated calls back. Women liked him. They always called him back. It was as sure as the sun rising in the east.

Though he'd checked the phone approximately every thirty minutes to make sure it hadn't lost its signal.

Okay, he liked women. So he liked *this* woman a lot.

He was on the shore, contemplating bringing out his fishing rod to see how big those puddle jumpers were, when the cell rang. For an instant, his pulse accelerated, then calmed again immediately. That ring tone belonged to Emily.

"Hey, older sister." He put emphasis on *older*, since she'd been determined as a kid never to let him forget it. He figured he owed her a reminder now.

"Hey, little brother." She'd also been determined never to let him forget he was shorter. "Where are you?"

"Tallgrass, Oklahoma."

"Are you stopped for gas, lunch, or sticking around?"

"I'm gonna stay a..." *A few days* was his standard answer, then he would reevaluate, stay on or move on. But so far there wasn't much standard about this stop. "Awhile."

"Hm. Job or woman?"

"You think that's all I'm interested in?"

"A job makes living possible. A woman makes it worthwhile." The teasing faded from her voice, caution replacing it. "Can I send you some money?"

"Nope." Every couple months, she and their parents offered him money, and he always gave them the same answer. He didn't have a regular job. A lot of people didn't. He picked up day jobs when he could, worked part-time gigs when necessary, and when he did have a job, he budgeted his money carefully. No splurges, except for Mouse's vet bill, and that hadn't been an option.

"Bill and I can afford it, El. Consider it an early birthday present."

"No, thanks. I'm fine, Em." He really was. The day he had to choose between food for Mouse and gas for the truck, he'd point the pickup west and spend some time with his family. He wasn't too proud to accept help. He just wouldn't do it until he needed it.

"Tell me about the town."

He gave her the rundown and noticed the change in tone of her *hm*s as he talked. He didn't have to wait long for her to explain them.

"You spent five months in Jackson, Tennessee, and never sounded like this about it. And four months in Tampa. And three months in Austin. And yet after only a few days in Tallgrass, you're sounding..."

"Like I'm home?"

"Yeah." She sighed wistfully. "I wish home could have stayed home for all of us."

He did, too. But when a town just up and died, one business after another closing down, and everyone who depended on those businesses having to move away, it had made keeping the ranch going that much harder. He was glad he hadn't been there, like Emily, when their parents had been forced into the decision to give up. His family spread across different states wasn't what he had expected for the wife and kids he planned to have someday.

"Now tell me about the woman." Emily's tone was cheerful again, and he could tell even with nearly seven hundred miles between them that she was grinning from ear to ear. "Come on, bubba, don't deny it. There's always a woman."

Mouse brought him a stick, dropped it on his boot, and waited impassively. Bending to pick it up, Elliot threw it across the clearing, expecting the dog to chase after it. Instead, she crawled into the shade of the truck and curled up. Nudging her gently with his boot, he shook his head.

"Her name is Fia. I met her about two minutes after I got to town. She's..."

When he didn't go on, Emily laughed. "Man, when you're at a loss for words, things get interesting. What does she do?"

"She used to be a personal trainer. Now..." A knot formed in his throat, part sympathy, part dread about what he was up against. "She's a widow. Her husband died in Afghanistan."

"Oh." The word came out on a soft rush of sympathy. "That sucks. You won't break her heart, will you?"

"I don't break hearts, Em." At least, he didn't like to think so. Most of the women attracted to him just seemed to understand the temporary nature of their relationships. They had fun and good times and sometimes considered more, but it usually ended on a pretty even keel for both of them.

"No, you're right. You either stay friends with 'em or piss 'em off eternally. Remember that girl you dated when you were home on leave? The one who took a tire iron to the windows of that old pickup truck you borrowed from Aunt Amy?"

Oh, he remembered. Beautiful and sweet as an angel until things didn't go her way. Then she turned flat scary. "She tried to take that tire iron to me, too," he reminded her with a wince, recalling how the wooden fence post blocking him had shuddered from the blow.

"Lucky for you, I was there before she did any significant damage, little brother."

"I was." Not just that time, when she'd snatched the tire iron away from the crazy woman, gripped it like a baseball bat, and warned, *He won't hit you because that's the way he was raised, but if you don't get in your car and drive away,* I'm *gonna beat the crap out of you.* He was lucky for *all* the times Emily had been there, usually at his side, behind him when he needed it, in front of him when he needed that. Looking out for him, she'd claimed, had been practice for when she had kids of her own.

"Listen, El, I've got to get the kids together for the late service at church. If I talk to Mom and Dad before you do, I'll tell them where you are. Good luck with the whole job-home-Fia stuff." Deviltry returning to her voice, she offered their childhood good-bye. "I hate you."

"Hate you more." He ended the call, his grin slowly fading. He was with her a hundred percent in her wish that home could have stayed home for the family. He'd never imagined anything other than the Army that could pull him away and had never imagined *any*thing that could drag Mom and Dad away. They'd lived their whole lives within twenty-five miles of where they were born. West Texas ranching had been in the blood pumping through their veins and the oxygen keeping them alive.

Until it wasn't.

The whole experience had taught him the truth of the wooden plaque that had hung over Grandma's front door: *Home is where the heart is.* He'd learned for a fact that it wasn't a place, roots dug deep in the soil, but a feeling. A satisfaction. A spiritual connection.

And thank God his cell phone rang again before he got any farther down that sappy road.

A glance at caller ID made his grin return, and he settled comfortably on his back in the truck bed, hat tilted over his eyes, as he answered. "You've reached Elliot."

Fia laughed. "And his lovely dog, Mouse?"

"Lazy is more like it. We're surrounded by birds to bark

at and fields to run through and water to swim in, and she's asleep under the truck."

"Sometimes lazy is the best way to be."

Lazy and comfortable and feeling everything was right in his world. Exactly the way *he* was feeling. "Aw, I bet you've never been lazy a day in your life. I bet you run and go biking and hiking and even ride a motorcycle from time to time."

"How'd you guess that?"

He considered teasing her a moment longer, then admitted, "When I got the trash bag out of the laundry room last night, I saw running shoes, hiking boots, and helmets."

"You get points for being observant."

"How many points? And what can I redeem them for?" he asked, but he was thinking that he *was* observant, and something was off in her voice. It wasn't distress or regret or about-to-give-the-brush-off, just a little something: unsteadiness, weariness.

"However many points you want."

"Can I redeem them for any*thing* I want?"

She laughed again. Did she know how incredibly sexy she was when she laughed? And when she smiled. When she was serious. "We'll have to talk about that."

"Oh, honey, talking is not *at all* what I'm after." From beneath the truck, Mouse rose and stretched, then with one graceful leap, landed on Elliot's stomach, making him grunt. "I swear, that pup is doubling her weight every day. Next time she jumps on me, it'll probably crush me."

"Big man complaining about such a delicate baby."

He switched the phone to his other hand so he could rub Mouse's belly, finding the spot that made her leg twitch. "Any chance you're going to join us out here at the lake?"

Fia's sigh was soft and wistful and echoed deep inside him. "Not today, I'm afraid. I've got this thing…"

*What thing?* he wanted to ask, but it was none of his business. He'd known her less than forty-eight hours. Her Sunday plans could have been made weeks ago. He should consider himself lucky that she'd spared time for him Friday and Saturday evenings, and he did. But disappointment still twinged in his gut.

"Not a problem," he said, adding extra cheeriness to cover the letdown. "Maybe tomorrow night? We could make a real picnic of it. You bring a blanket, and I'll bring fried chicken, potato salad, and brownies."

The silence on the line grew heavier as it stretched out. Finally it was broken by another sigh. "I really can't say for sure. Could I call you tomorrow afternoon and let you know?"

*You won't break her heart, will you?* Emily had asked.

His disappointment was childish in its proportions, and his smile was phony to keep it from creeping into his voice. "Yeah, that would be great."

His sister should worry about Fia breaking *his* heart. It had never happened before, but one lesson he'd learned damn well…

There was a first time for everything.

*   *   *

It had been a long time since Dillon had felt comfortable around people. Being in prison, never alone twenty-four hours a day for five hundred sixty-seven days, had a way of making a man value his privacy. But when Jessy Smith said, *You're going*, a wise man shut his mouth and went. So here he was, in the backyard of a nice middle-class house surrounded by nice middle-class people, a cold bottle of water in hand, smoke from a couple of grills perfuming the air, and a niggling feeling working up his spine that he couldn't shake. Though he'd met everyone there, he felt alone in a bunch of strangers.

Damn, he'd always been the center of attention at any party, not the odd one out. Now he was so odd, he didn't want to even be there.

"Are you new here, too?"

The question came from his right, from a girl who'd sidled into the shade of the patio, standing very still as if doing so would keep anyone from noticing her. He wasn't good at guessing kids' ages, and once they hit about twelve, all bets were off, but she seemed very young. Very alone.

"Not exactly. I came with my brother and his wife. They're over there." He gestured in Dalton and Jessy's general direction, and the girl looked at them, then back at him. Her mouth quirked a little, but she didn't state the obvious: *Oh, you're twins.* Like he and Dalton hadn't known that their whole lives.

"I'm with my aunt Marti. She's the dark-haired one in the white dress."

She pointed, too, and he looked, though he didn't need to. He knew Marti Levin by sight—tall, cool, always in control. Too pretty, too elegant, too sophisticated for a man like him, if he was looking.

He wasn't sure he would ever look again.

"I'm Cadence. I'm staying with Aunt Marti for a year while my dad's working in Dubai. I just got here Friday." The girl extended her hand, as composed and elegant as her aunt.

"Dillon Smith." He tried to remember the last time he'd shaken hands with a kid. It wasn't coming to mind. Her hand was delicate in his, her palm damp, her handshake less than steady. Underneath all that composure, she was feeling out of place much like him. Poor kid was at a bad age for being uprooted and sent off to live with strangers, though he wasn't sure what was a good age for that. At least leaving Tallgrass and his family had been his own choice.

"These the first people you've met here?"

She nodded. "They're Aunt Marti's best friends. Jacob"—she pointed out their hosts' son—"is nice. Into sports and all. Abby, his sister, is my age. She went inside to recharge her cell. She's nice, too. We'll have classes together at school." Her smile quavered. "Tomorrow's my first day."

Dillon thought of all the things a responsible adult would say: *You'll be fine. The kids will like you. It'll be fun.* He shrugged instead, and said, "That sucks, doesn't it?"

Apparently, she'd heard enough bland reassurances that she'd expected another from him, so his response earned a choked laugh. "Well, it's better—by *this* much—than being the new kid at boarding school at the end of the school year. That was Mom and Dad's option if Aunt Marti said no."

He wondered why Mom didn't stay home with her daughter rather than ship her off to an aunt or to school. If Dad was old enough to take a job in Dubai, he was old enough to go by himself. But it wasn't really Dillon's business, was it? "How old are you?"

"Fourteen." She shrugged thin shoulders. "I'm an only child. I've spent my entire life in private schools or with grown-ups. Are you a cowboy?"

He glanced at his clothes—faded jeans, blue button-down, scuffed boots, and leather belt. "What gave it away?"

"I'm from Connecticut. I don't see many cowboys there. Where's your Stetson?"

"In the truck. And it's an O'Farrell."

She smiled, and the faint scared look disappeared. "What kind of horse do you have?"

"My brother raises palominos." He added, "I work for him." *For* him. If he hadn't run off when he was a kid, he'd be part owner of the ranch now. He'd been raised to do that. Hell, he'd been *named* to do it. The Double D Ranch had always been run by Smiths whose first names started with D. "Do you ride?"

"Since I was seven. I rode dressage for a while, but it was more work than fun. Is riding a horse on the ranch fun?"

"Yeah, it is." Even when it seemed like his butt had gone stone-cold numb from too many hours in the saddle, he'd never been on a horse, even the ones that had tried to kill him, that he hadn't found peace somewhere deep inside.

Cadence started to speak, then stopped herself. After a moment, knowing what he would want if he were fourteen and in her situation, he asked, "If your aunt says it's okay, you want to come out and ride sometime?".

Her expression brightened, then dimmed again just as quickly. "I'd love to see the horses, if that's okay."

Before he could respond, the door behind them opened, and a pretty little blonde burst out, followed by a pint-size version. "Sorry it took so long. I got a text from Monroe. He's, like, the cutest boy in the whole school. You'll meet him tomorrow. Come on." She grabbed Cadence's left arm, and the little girl took her right. "I've got pictures to show you."

As they pulled her away, Cadence glanced back over her shoulder. "It was nice meeting you, Mr. Smith. I'll ask Aunt Marti about the horses."

He responded with a nod as he watched them go. The older blonde chattered, the little one bobbed her head enthusiastically, and Cadence smiled through a very thin veil of anxiety.

As they disappeared into the shade of a broad oak, he shifted his gaze across the yard until it reached Marti Levin. She was laughing with some of her friends, her posture as erect as any ballerina's without being rigid. Her white dress was modest enough for church—sleeveless, curve-hugging, barely brushing the tops of her knees—and it made a pretty good contrast to the olive tone of her skin and her black hair.

The resemblance between her and her niece was faint but there: Both were cool, controlled, pretty, and elegant. From their few interactions in the past, he'd never figured Marti the sort to do the kid thing, but Cadence was a teenager, and the situation was temporary, only for a year.

But a year could fly by in the blink of an eye, leaving good memories and contentment, or it could crawl one damn hour at a time, taking a man's strength, his courage, his self-respect, his dignity.

Dillon knew that from experience.

# Chapter 4

Elliot had job hunting down to an art. He started with the ads in the Sunday paper and found they were typically sparse for the kinds of jobs he was qualified for. He had better luck finding *Help Wanted* signs taped to store windows or asking everywhere he went who was hiring. It was, in general, a demoralizing process that he'd been through a few times too many. He'd occasionally considered using his Veterans Administration benefits to get a college degree, but the idea of sitting behind a desk, working more with computers and phones than with people, and wearing a coat and tie just didn't set well with him.

After making sure the shirt he'd taken from the clean pile in the backseat really was clean, he tugged it on and tucked it into a fresh pair of jeans. He fastened his belt, pulled his damp hair into a ponytail, and turned toward Mouse, watching from the passenger seat. "How do I look?"

The pup yawned, unimpressed. Elliot rubbed her ears anyway.

It had taken a long time for Sunday to pass after Fia had turned down his invitation. He and Mouse had walked, played, snoozed, caught enough fish for dinner over an open fire, and slept well. Now it was Monday; he'd showered and shaved at the campground's facilities, and after breakfast somewhere, he was starting his job hunt.

Job hunt. Sounded so easy. Employers needed employees. The problem was, just being available and willing to work hard didn't always count for much. Some people looked at his list of jobs, scattered all over the country, and lost interest. Some saw his service in the Army and lost interest even quicker. The facts that he was single and had no ties to the town were a negative, too, since it made it awful easy to pick up and move on. And damn it, he hadn't yet found a classified ad that said, *Wanted: Sniper.*

He'd had enough of that job anyway.

So he would look at the *Help Wanted* ads in the local paper over breakfast, then drive around town for the third time, make note of signs taped to the windows of businesses. He would be charming and pleasant and politely persistent and flexible—any job, any hours, pretty much any pay.

On his other trips through town, he'd noticed a little bakery on North First named Prairie Harts that reminded him of a place back home—the only place to eat out back home: a squat cinder block building, large windows, a crowded parking lot on Saturday. Usually, nothing indicated good food like a full parking lot.

He drove into town, bought a newspaper at QuikTrip, then traveled a few more blocks to Prairie Harts. There were only a handful of cars this morning, but given that the workday had started more than two hours ago for most folks, that was pretty good.

He rolled down all four windows a few inches, then gave Mouse a pat. "I won't be long. You behave, and I'll bring you a treat."

Her nose quivered—he'd bet she smelled every good scent on the air—and though she remained sitting, her tail wagged double-time.

The aromas when he stepped inside the bakery just about stopped him in his tracks. Whoever ran Prairie Harts definitely knew his or her business. There were savory smells, too, but he focused on the sweet: sugar, cinnamon, vanilla, almond. Add strong rich coffee, and what more could a man ask for?

*A beautiful woman to share it with.*

And a *Help Wanted* sign in the window.

Hallelujah, God had chosen to smile on him.

The bakery had a happy, homey feel to it, if home happened to be somewhere near a beach. The tables and chairs would be a great place to settle and listen to the waves; the pastels and pops of hot pink and turquoise brightened the dining room and made it look bigger; and the iron flowers clustered around the room were cool. There was even a flamingo in the corner, complete with sunglasses, Hawaiian shirt, and flip-flops.

None of which would matter if the food in the display cases wasn't worthy. He didn't even need a taste to know it was. There was no way something that smelled and looked that good could possibly not taste good.

A half-dozen customers sat around the room, each at their own table, each immersed in their laptop or cell phone. Remembering the hundreds of times he and Emily had met their friends at Rosey's without a single electronic device in sight made him shake his head as he walked to the counter.

"Welcome to Prairie Harts," the woman behind it greeted him. "What can I do for you?"

Breakfast or application first? The rumbling of his stomach made that decision easy. After scanning the rows of fresh-baked muffins, biscuits, cookies, turnovers, and more, he chose a cinnamon roll the size of a dinner plate, drizzled with cream cheese frosting, and a cup of coffee.

"Is this your first time here?" the woman asked as she scooped the roll onto a plate. As soon as she set it on the display case in front of him, he drew a deep breath, causing his stomach to rumble again.

"Yes, ma'am, it is. I just got into town on Friday."

Her gaze skimmed over him, stopping for a moment on his ponytail. "I'm guessing it wasn't the Army that brought you here." There was a gleam in her eyes when she put a flip-flop-decorated porcelain mug of steaming coffee next to the plate.

"No, ma'am. I'm looking to settle down." He offered her a ten-dollar bill, and she counted the change into his palm.

"Well, I hope we see you again. By the way, I'm Patricia."

"Elliot." He returned her smile and would have tipped his Stetson if he was wearing it just for the added charm factor, but instead he picked up his breakfast and carried it to a table near the front windows, where he could keep an eye on Mouse.

His first bite of roll was enough to make him moan if he hadn't been in public. His first impression was sweet and walnutty and chewy, thanks to the raisins in the filling, followed by a moment of pure sensory pleasure, then the explosion of the cinnamon: heat and spice and bite. Incredible.

A customer left, and Patricia came out from behind the counter to retrieve the dishes and wipe the table. "How's that roll?" she asked.

He gave her a thumbs-up before wiping his mouth. "Ceylon cinnamon or Vietnamese cassia?"

"You're the first customer who's ever asked that. Vietnamese cassia." She rested one hand on the back of the chair opposite him. "Are you a baker?"

"I learned to make biscuits when I still needed a footstool to reach the counter. Cakes came after that, but piecrusts had to wait until I started fifth grade." If Emily were there, she'd point out that he hadn't grown much since then, but Patricia was too polite to comment on his lack of height.

"Aw, my kids would help me in the kitchen sometimes, but none of them grew up to like cooking. Luckily for me, they still like to eat."

He sipped the coffee, hot enough to scald his tongue, and nodded appreciatively. "Excellent coffee."

"It's kind of an Oklahoma product. We try to source locally as much as we can. The coffee is shipped straight from the estates in El Salvador to a roastery in Tulsa. Lucy, my partner"—she gestured toward the kitchen—"drives to Tulsa every Saturday to pick up the beans, and we grind them as we need them."

"The only way," he said with a grin, though if he was in bad enough need of caffeine, he would chew the beans and be happy.

She shifted position, folding her arms across her middle. "Are you married, Elliot?"

"No, ma'am."

"From southern Oklahoma?"

"Texas."

Her grin was sly. "That's what I said." She winked, then pulled out the other chair and sat. "Do you have a job here?"

"No, ma'am, I'm looking." His gut tightened. He'd never worked in a bakery a day in his life, but instinct said he would like this place, just as he'd known right off he was going to like Fia. He couldn't think of much he'd rather do job-wise than spend his shift working with food: making it, serving it, cleaning up after it. If he could get a job here, if it might pay a living wage, it would be the best damn luck he'd ever had, other than surviving his tours in combat.

It, and meeting Fia, would be like coming home.

He nodded at the *Help Wanted* sign. "I was figuring on putting in an application when I finished here."

Patricia's smile widened, and she went to the counter, where she could see her partner through the pass-through. "Lucy, do we have application forms?"

A younger woman, face framed by dark hair, appeared at the window, looking perplexed. "Um, no. I didn't think...It was on my list..." After a moment's search, she called, "Let me see what I can find online."

Elliot hid his grin behind the coffee mug. He liked the informality of their approach. If he had his own place, he would get sound advice for financial matters and depend on gut instinct for everything else. He'd spent a lot of years honing his instincts. Why not use them?

"We just put the sign up this morning," Patricia confided

as she sat down again. "We opened in February and didn't plan on hiring anyone at least until summer, but things have been pretty busy. Lucy's trying to plan her wedding in June, and I can't run the place alone while she's honeymooning, so we decided we'd better get moving. So, Elliot, do you cook, or is baking your talent?"

"Bread is my talent, but yes, ma'am, I'm a pretty good cook, too."

Delight spread across her face as Lucy hurried out from the kitchen. "His specialty is bread, Lucy. How cool is that?"

"Great! I make a killer no-rise bread, but I can't do a decent loaf of anything else to save my life." Lucy extended her hand. "Lucy Hart."

"Elliot Ross." He shook hands with her, then she thrust out a sheet of paper ripped from a spiral notebook. "My printer doesn't want to print today. We really just need the basics anyway." As she was walking away, she said, "Can't stay. I'm making crepes."

He took the sheet, and the ink pen Patricia offered, and scanned the page. Lucy hadn't been kidding. In a column down the left she'd scrawled *Name*, *Address*, *Phone*, *Date of Birth*, *Social Security Number*, and *Hours Available*. There were no blocks for the twenty or so jobs he'd held in the previous couple years, no block for his Army service, so it took him only a couple minutes to fill out, even with his hesitation over the address line.

"Like I said, I just got into town Friday, so I don't have a permanent address yet, but the cell phone's always on." He slid the paper and pen across to Patricia. "Anything you want to add?"

She skimmed it and returned it. "An emergency contact, please."

"Yes, ma'am." He wrote Emily's name, cell phone, and identified her as his sister.

"I'm impressed that you know her number from memory. My kids are lost without their smart phones. When I tell my grandkids of family reunions where we ate and played baseball and hide-and-seek, they say, 'Oh, Grandma, what about the Internet?'" She snorted. "I think our youngest generation is losing its ability to communicate face to face."

"I agree, ma'am. But on the good side, my sister lives in New Mexico, and I've spent time in Iraq and Afghanistan, but I still get to see my nieces and nephew grow up, read to them, sing to them." It was the only way he could be a regular part of their lives without moving to New Mexico, whether it suited him or not.

She squeezed his hand. "I know. I've gotten to do the same with my grandbabies. Oh, and forget the *ma'am*, Elliot. I spent twenty years as an Army wife, and I have been *ma'am*'ed enough for a lifetime."

Lucy called Patricia from the kitchen, and she stood. "Though I have to admit, *ma'am* from a handsome Texas cowboy has a whole other appeal than when it comes from an eighteen-year-old private."

He'd been one of those eighteen-year-old privates, too, so he'd gotten a double whammy of respect drilled into him. He wasn't sure it was even possible for him to call a woman his mother's age by her first name.

While Patricia took care of business in back, Elliot scooped what was left of his roll onto a napkin, picked out the raisins, and ate those himself. With the uncanny sense she had, Mouse's head popped up above the dash, and her tail and everything else began quivering. Good dog, though: She didn't bark. She knew she would get the treat, sooner rather than later, and would wait patiently for it. In the meantime…

"She's gonna drool all over my truck," he murmured.

"I hope you're talking about your dog and not your girl-friend," Patricia teased as she returned.

"My girlfriends don't drool."

She gave him a long look head to toe, then murmured, "I may be from a whole different generation, but I know that's not true. I've got a few single friends who would very much appreciate looking at you, seeing that grin, and hear-ing that voice. But don't worry. We'll give you a chance to meet someone on your own before we start matchmak-ing." She patted his upper arm the way Emily often did, but without the force of a full-fledged punch behind it, the way Emily's often had. "We're about to get busy here, so you go give that pretty little puppy a treat and come back around two thirty. Lucy will have time to sit down and talk with you then. Does that sound good?"

"You bet, ma—Patricia." He stood and reached for his dishes, but she brushed him away. Picking up the napkin-wrapped roll, he thanked her, then went to the truck. By the time he got the door open, Mouse was standing in her seat and, yep, there was drool trailing from there to the console to the dashboard.

"Man, you're lucky I'm such a sucker for cute," he said as he handed her a chunk of roll, then reached in back for baby wipes and paper towels. She inhaled it, then sat—barely—for the next. He was pretty sure she would have eaten the napkins and licked the seats if he hadn't been faster, scooping her into one arm while he cleaned her mess.

That done, he had about four hours to blow. He could go

back to the lake or check out the bakery's competition. He could look for other *Help Wanted* signs to cover his bases if he struck out with Lucy. Instead, he reached for his phone. After two rings, a sweet voice picked up.

"Hey, Fia. It's Elliot. Is there any chance I can buy you lunch today?"

\* \* \*

Fia had plenty of those times when her brain told her mouth to stay shut and her mouth ignored it, so it was no surprise when it happened again. Brain ordered her to say no to Elliot's invitation; she was still a little shaky, her vision still a little blurred.

But Mouth went ahead and said, "I'd like that," and Fia was siding with Mouth.

She'd stayed home all day yesterday, either in bed or curled up on the couch, and missed Elliot and Mouse and all her friends at Therese's welcome barbecue for Marti's niece. Patricia had brought her a plate of food on her way home with grilled chicken, a garden salad, roasted baby red potatoes, and a bowl filled with Lucy's special angel food cake with fresh strawberry sauce. Fia was grateful the choices hadn't included any barbecue sauce, salsa, onions, garlic, or tangy dressings, and she'd managed to eat most of it, despite the queasy state of her stomach.

She'd appreciated Patricia's thoughtfulness more than she could say. Her own mother had never done anything nice for her, so it was still a surprise every time someone else's mother did.

But she'd still missed being at the party, seeing her friends, meeting Cadence. She'd felt left out, and she hated it. That so wasn't the strong, independent person she used to be.

"Are you at work?" Elliot made no effort to hide his pleasure that she'd agreed, and that warmed her all the way through. Scott had been that way, too, unabashed about the things that made him happy. He'd never tried to play cool or hard to get. He saw something he wanted, and he went for it.

"I'm working at home today." Since her body had begun its relentless betrayal, she'd switched jobs at the gym from trainer to general problem solver and paper handler. She didn't love the desk job but was happy her boss had done his best to keep her on staff when he so easily could have booted her to the curb.

"Do you want to go out or should I bring something?"

Staying in was probably safer in physical terms for her. Though she'd showered, shaved her legs without so much as a nick, and gotten through all the payroll forms for April—it was amazing what an eighteen-point computer font did for blurry vision—she still wasn't a hundred percent.

No doubt, though, *out* was safer in emotional terms. When it was just the two of them in a small, private space, it was impossible to avoid the intimacy that came naturally. And there was a heck of a lot of intimacy in the wings just waiting its chance. Who knew which spark would set it off?

Still, Mouth wasn't listening to Brain. "Do you mind coming here?"

He laughed. "One thing you'll learn about me, Fia: If I offer to do something, I won't mind doing it. I'm pretty easygoing, but I can dig in my heels like the most stubborn critter in the world when I need to. What would you like?"

He reeled off choices—Mexican, Italian, Chinese, Greek, barbecue, fish—and she reeled off answers: too spicy, not her favorite, too heavy, too unfamiliar, too toma- toey, not her favorite.

"Okay, you tell me what you want, and I'll bring it."

After a moment's thought, she replied, "I think I need comfort food. Soup, chicken and noodles, macaroni and cheese."

"I can make chicken and noodles as good as my grandma's. I'll stop at the store, then be there in ten."

After hanging up, she closed the lid of the laptop and set it on the coffee table, then stood, stretching out the kinks from the morning's work. She was steady on her feet and felt good enough to care how she looked, so that was progress. She changed from T-shirt and shorts into a dress, finger-combed her short hair, and even dabbed on a bit of foundation, blush, and mascara before her doorbell rang.

Her stomach took a tumble, and for the first time in twenty-four hours, it wasn't due to nausea. She gave her- self a quick once-over in the mirror hanging on the back of the bathroom door—hair looked good, mascara wasn't smeared, dress covered everything it was supposed to— then she walked more quickly than she normally would have to the front door.

For an instant, she stood there, mentally repeating warn- ings to herself: This couldn't go anywhere; she wasn't the woman she used to be; Elliot wanted a woman for a lovely fling or a lifetime; either way, she wasn't looking to be- come anyone else's burden.

But none of that stopped her from grinning ear to ear when she opened the door. He held Mouse's leash in one hand, a grocery bag in the other, and wore jeans, a buttoned-up shirt, and boots, and took her breath away with nothing more than his presence on her stoop. Lord, was there anything better than the giddiness when a woman first began falling for a man?

The satisfaction of living happily ever after with him, a solemn voice whispered in her head. Of not having to dress up or be on her best behavior and knowing he still loved her. Of facing him with morning breath and bed head and knowing he still thought she was beautiful. Of losing her temper and wishing mightily that she'd never met him but still loving every awful thing about him.

Falling in love with Scott had been incredible, but being in love with him, living day to day, through good and bad and nothing special, had been the real reward.

*Why are you thinking about me when Elliot's standing right in front of you?*

Bittersweetly, she pushed back the memories and crouched to scratch Mouse's chin. "Hey, sweetie, I'm glad you came over and brought your person with you. Come on in."

Elliot switched the groceries to his other hand, then gave her a hand up. Oh, she loved the warm touch and easy strength of a helping hand. The old Fia had never needed one, but she'd sure been happy to take it. In her growing-up world, men had rarely raised a hand unless it was to smack whoever had annoyed them. Her father had never opened a door for her mother, carried a load for her, or helped her around the house. He'd been the king, commanding others to do everything for him, unable to even pronounce the word *chivalry*, much less practice it.

When she was on her feet again, a smile spread slowly

across Elliot's face. "Hey, you," he said in a low, intimate voice.

Shivers danced down her spine, and her stomach looped crazily. Trembling, she stepped back, the move sadly pulling her arm free of his hand, and she offered another smile that wasn't quite as steady as the first. "Hey."

"I'm glad you agreed to see me."

She could protect herself, play it cool, brush it off, but she didn't. So she was tempting herself with something she couldn't have, not long-term. That was okay. Feeling this way was definitely worth any pain that might come later. "So am I."

He followed her inside, disconnected Mouse's leash, and carried the groceries into the kitchen, where he unpacked a large carton of chicken stock, a package of chicken, and a bag of frozen noodles.

Sitting on a bar stool, Fia leaned across to pick up the noodles. "Your grandma's chicken and noodles, huh? So your grandma is Mrs. Reames?"

He stuck his tongue out at her. If they were a little bit closer, she could bite it. Or kiss the mouth it came from. "Actually—well, no, she wasn't, but she used Reames noodles. Remember, she had a ranch to run and a family to keep in line. Now, me, normally I'd buy a whole chicken and simmer it slowly all afternoon with carrots and celery and onions, and I'd make the noodles by hand, and after I stripped the tender chicken from the bones, I'd cook it all in the steaming fragrant broth until the noodles were just perfectly tender, and then..."

He was looking at her, but his hands were making quick work of tearing open the chicken package, setting two breasts, two wings, and two thighs on a paper towel. He

knew she couldn't bring herself to look away from him—
she could see it in the amusement in his eyes—and he
knew, too, that talking about his attention to detail in cooking was inexplicably making her warm from the inside out.

"And then," he repeated before mimicking setting a big
bowl in front of her, waving away imaginary steam with
one hand, and adding, "you would be transported away
by the best chicken and noodles in the whole universe.
But since I have a job interview at two thirty, Grandma's
chicken and noodles will have to do."

He turned to rinse the chicken pieces then, and she
waved away some imaginary heat of her own, wondering
if she could turn the air conditioner low enough to get
her internal temperature back to normal. "Cool about the
interview," she said, really meaning it. No matter what happened, or didn't, between them, Tallgrass with Elliot was a
better place than Tallgrass without him. Besides, he needed
that home. That place to belong. "Where is it?"

"A little bakery where I had breakfast this morning. The
best cinnamon roll I've eaten since the last time I made my
own. Name's Prairie Harts and—"

*"Ohhh!"* Almost immediately, Fia clapped her hands
over her mouth as he whirled around. "Sorry about that.
I don't usually interrupt. I don't usually squeal, either,
at least not since I was twelve. But I *know* them—Lucy
and Patricia. They're two of my margarita girls." When
no comprehension appeared in his eyes, she added, "My
Army widow friends. My family. They're the reason I'm
here." And she meant that in every way possible.

Remembrance sparked in his expression. "They seem
like nice people, and they can damn well bake."

"Yes to both. Man, leave it to you on your first weekday

in town to meet two of the margarita girls. I bet Patricia's first question was, *Are you available?* because she's determined to marry off her single friends and Brianne, her younger daughter. And Lucy was there in body but probably about a hundred miles away in her mind."

"Standing in front of a pastor with her fiancé, grinning big, and saying, 'You bet I do,'" Elliot said with a laugh. He dropped the chicken into her biggest stockpot, poured in the whole container of broth, and set it on high heat on the stove. After that, he washed his hands, fixed two glasses of tea, and came to sit on the stool beside her. "I'm guessing her feet haven't touched the ground since they got engaged."

"They have not." Sliding off the stool, Fia went into her bedroom, then returned with a large framed picture. Again, Elliot gave her a hand to help her up, and again, she went all soft and hot inside. *I love chivalry.* "This is about sixteen months ago. That's Carly and Therese—they started the margarita club—and the little blonde is Ilena. She was pregnant there and gave birth to a beautiful little boy last June. Jessy's the redhead, there's Bennie, and that's Marti, Lucy—"

"And you." He leaned close enough that his shoulder bumped hers, and he laid his hand over hers on the frame to steady its sudden shaking. One breath capturing all the man-cowboy-Elliot scents of him, and she could totally forget what she was saying, what they were doing. She could just sort of slide against him, rest her head on his shoulder, raise her mouth to his, and forget all about lunch. No food was as comforting as a make-out session with a really sexy, really gorgeous, really nice guy.

"Lucy looks different."

Fia smiled at his polite way of saying, *She's lost a whole lot of weight.* Losing Mike had turned Lucy to food for comfort. Finding Joe had turned her back.

"I don't see Patricia."

"She didn't join us until the colonel died the end of last May."

His long finger traced Fia's image. "When did you join?"

A kinder way of asking when Scott died. "It started with Carly and Therese. The next week, Marti and Lucy were there, and I heard about it from a teacher at the post school, so I showed up the week after. Scott had been dead seven months at the time."

He got up to check the chicken, turn down the heat, and top off their tea. When he came back, he continued to study the photo. "A buddy of mine died in Iraq. I'd known him and his wife for a couple years, so I called her, visited her when I got back to the States, still keep in touch with her from time to time, but not once has she ever mentioned his name or let me mention it. We talk about everything in the world except him. That's the way she wants it. It just makes me sad."

"Before I met the girls, I wondered if I was doing things wrong because I wanted to talk about Scott, but it made people uncomfortable. I'd never lost anyone I'd loved before"—sad truth was, she'd never loved anyone before—"but the first time I had dinner with the margarita club, our husbands were all we talked about. They understood. They saved me."

"And you saved them." He looked at her picture again. "You look different."

Also a polite way of saying, *You've gone to hell since then.* She'd lost ten or fifteen pounds she hadn't needed to lose when she was already operating on a low body mass indicator. Her hair had turned dull, and her complexion looked healthier in the picture.

"It's been a tough time," she murmured.

Elliot didn't say a word, but he set the frame down, wrapped his arms around her, and hugged her tight for a long, soothing moment. She knew too well that she couldn't always rely on others; she had to be strong enough to do everything for herself. But in those forty or sixty seconds, she recalled the confidence Patricia and Jessy and the others always displayed for her. *You're gonna be all right. We're gonna kick some ass and get some answers, and the doctors are going to give your life back to you.*

For that moment, she didn't know if she shared their positivity or if she just wanted it badly enough that it felt like she did.

Without letting the embrace turn sexual, Elliot released her, then went into the kitchen. She missed his warmth instantly but appreciated his judgment tremendously. "I didn't pick up anything to go with lunch, since comfort foods don't generally need go-alongs. Well, other than what's implied by the name. Macaroni needs cheese. Chicken needs noodles. Spaghetti needs meatballs."

She sneaked a swab at her eyes before smiling. "And cheese."

"I thought you didn't eat Italian."

"Put enough cheese on it, and I'll eat dirt."

"I'll remember that," he said with a flash of a grin. "But I did notice Saturday night that your candy dish was running low, so I brought these." From the bottom of the shopping bag, he took out a small package of Hershey's Kisses with almonds and tossed them to her.

Fia's laugh was choked as she caught the bag and tore it open, emptying it into the small crystal heart on the counter in front of her. "I keep my dish for Kisses small. Otherwise, my butt wouldn't fit through the door anymore, but it makes for some great disappointment when it runs empty."

"I'll make sure that doesn't happen."

Something fluttered in her chest and stirred a knot in her throat. "Remember what you said on the phone. If you offer to do something, you do it. Always. It wouldn't be nice to disappoint a chocolate kiss-aholic."

"You have my word." He raised one hand in the air, holding the other palm down as if swearing on a stack of Bibles.

When Scott made a promise, he'd raised two fingers up. *Scout's honor,* he'd always said, and she'd always thrown back at him, *You were never a Scout.* He would give her that lazy grin and correct himself. *Scott's honor.*

Smiling at Elliot, she wondered: Was there anything in the world sexier than a man with honor?

\* \* \*

Two o'clock arrived much more quickly than Elliot had expected. He put up the last of the dishes, dried his hands, and hung the towel neatly on the bar, then faced Fia. "Should I change clothes for the interview?"

She took her time checking out his appearance, and he didn't mind. Her gaze scanned side to side, reminding him of a mapping device producing a one-dimensional image. And the whole time she looked, she continued to smile, in fact smiling even a little bigger by the time she finished. "Nah. If you showed up in dress clothes, Lucy would probably feel obligated to run home and dress up, too. She thrives on making people comfortable."

"That's a good quality for someone in the restaurant business. So many servers treat their customers like annoyances these days."

"So many people treat other people that way these days. I had clients who came thirty minutes late to every session, expected me to put my other clients on hold so I could give them an extra thirty minutes at the end, and assumed that I was happy to clean up their sweat and spit when we were done."

"That's just gross."

"Yeah. I learned after a while to say, 'Well, I've done all I can for you. It's time to move on to a more experienced trainer.' Everyone loves to believe they've outstripped your abilities, especially in such a short time."

Elliot gave her a lingering look. "I can't imagine many clients, not male, at least, who were willing to move on so quickly from you. If I'd wandered into the gym seeking a trainer and got you, I would have forgotten everything I'd ever learned about exercise just to prolong our time."

She laughed as she slid off the bar stool and walked to the couch to scoop up Mouse. "A few guys tried that, but it's not hard to tell when their muscles have muscles upon muscles. Besides, I was married. I never thought once about a client after I walked out the door each evening." She nuzzled the soft patch between Mouse's ears, then asked, "Can she stay with me while you do your interview?"

"You wouldn't mind?"

She shook one finger at him. "One thing you need to learn, Elliot. If I offer to do something, then I do it. I never offer just to be nice while hoping to get turned down. I think I'm perfectly capable of watching Mouse while she snoozes."

On cue, the dog opened her mouth wide in a yawn and snuggled closer to the warmth of Fia's body. Elliot envied the pup for that. "I appreciate it. I left her in the truck this morning with the windows rolled down, but soon it'll be too warm for that."

"She'll be fine here. She's already comfortable, and she already likes to pee on the patio." Fia shrugged as if that settled it, then hesitated a moment before speaking. "I could call Lucy and tell her we're friends."

He straightened the leash he'd dropped on the couch when he arrived, folded it neatly, and laid it on the cushion back. He'd never had anyone put in a good word for him, other than in the Army at promotion time, when a yea or nay was part of the evaluation. In all his jobs since then, he hadn't known anyone who could pull strings, but he hadn't minded. "I appreciate the offer. Thank you. But no." He shrugged sheepishly. "I'd rather have a job because I'm good enough to have it than because someone else smoothed the way."

A bit of ease spread through Fia's eyes. He was guessing that she hadn't been totally comfortable making the offer, but she'd been willing to do it for him. That meant a lot.

"You think my friends would hire you just because I asked them to?" she asked, head tilted to the side.

He brushed his hand lightly over a strand of hair that rested against her cheek, combing it back into place behind her ear. "I think your friends would do just about anything for you." And he was including himself in that group. She was a good person who'd had some really crappy luck. She deserved all the help she needed to come back from that.

She glanced at her watch, then moved to the door, easing him that way. "Well, don't worry about the interview. You'll love Lucy and Patricia. And don't worry about Mouse. I'll take very good care of her."

The dog, still nestled in her arms, obviously had no argument with that. Elliot stepped outside, holding the storm door, then hooked his finger in the thin braided belt around Fia's waist and pulled her a few steps. He kissed her left cheek, then right, then grinned. "Soon I'm gonna do that for real."

Instead of blushing or being coy, Fia gave him a steady look. "I'm counting on it. Go before you're late. Charm the girls. Get hired."

He laughed as he took the steps to the driveway. His cell phone showed two fifteen. He was pretty sure there was nowhere in Tallgrass he couldn't reach in fifteen minutes, unless it involved entering or exiting the fort during morning and evening rush. The radio was on, the windows down, and he was singing along with a classic George Strait song when he pulled into the Prairie Harts lot.

Though the sign was turned to *Closed*, the door was unlocked. He stepped inside, the bell overhead dinging, and called, "Patricia? Lucy?"

"In the kitchen," Lucy replied.

When he walked through the wide door, he found her standing next to a counter filled with trays of tiny cupcakes. He didn't exaggerate with *filled*, either. There was barely space on her side for a bowl of green butter cream frosting and a pastry bag.

"Wow. How many cupcakes are here?"

Her forehead wrinkled. "Please don't make me do the math again. Enough, I hope. All of them in the black and white liners"—she gestured to the ones on the right half of the table—"are for a soccer tournament. They're getting grass frosting, and each one will have a candy soccer ball on top. The rest of them are for a reception tonight, and we're doing different shades and flavors of butter cream. Do you mind helping?"

"I'd be happy to." He washed his hands, then fitted a 233 tip to a pastry bag, filled it with frosting, and took up a position across from her. The tip was cylindrical, with multiple openings that forced the frosting out in thin lines. With the streaky color of the frosting, it made for pretty realistic grass.

"Patricia's running some errands. She'll be back soon. But you already know she was pretty impressed with you."

He grinned. "My sister, Emily, says women like me. I tell her it's because I like them, too. You have a great place here."

She raised her head for a moment to glance around with deep satisfaction before she returned to piping the frosting. "We're expanding a lot faster than I'd expected. Initially I thought if we stayed in business for a year, then we'd add sandwiches, salads, and a few specials like chicken pot pies or beef stew for lunch. Well, the shop did great, and there was an interest in lunch right away, so we started that last month. Patricia and I were amazed. Of course, it might help that my fiancé"—she broke off, gazed at her engagement ring, then repeated the word as if it were still new to her—"my fiancé is the head football coach at the high school, and football is a very big deal to a small town."

"It might help." Elliot finished the twelfth cupcake on the

tray, slid it aside, and reached for another tray. "But not as much as the fact that your cinnamon rolls are incredible."

"Thank you." Her cheeks flushed. "Have you ever worked in a bakery or a restaurant before?"

"I've waited tables a few times, but I've never been in the back of the house. I haven't had any sort of classes, either, but I grew up helping the women in my family bake, cook, serve, and clean up every day. I like food. I like planning menus, prepping it, making it taste good and look good. When I was in the Army, I did holiday meals for all my buddies who didn't have family nearby or couldn't go home, usually between forty and sixty people at a time. I'm used to hard work—I grew up on a ranch—and I know my way around a kitchen, and I make a damn good loaf of bread."

"Artisanal breads," she said with a sigh. "We've had requests for those. What are your favorites?"

"Ciabatta. Focaccia with caramelized red onions and black olives. Sweet yeast rolls. Brioche. Sourdough in loaves, sticky buns, or with herbs and spices. I had to learn soda bread to satisfy my aunt Amy, who's Irish."

Lucy sighed again, this time with a hint of longing. "I love sourdough bread. Neither Patricia nor I have a starter, but I know where we can get one, unless you have your own."

He shook his head regretfully. "My mom and my aunt weren't into bread, so my grandma's starter died with her." Emily had tried to keep it going for him, discarding half of the flour-water-lactobacillus mixture, then feeding it every week, but it wasn't habit for her, and life had gotten in the way. When she'd finally admitted it had turned to nothing more than a crusty, stinky mess, it had been a second loss.

If he'd had less self-confidence, such sentimentality might have embarrassed him.

When all the tiny cupcake cases in front of him held frosted cakes, he asked for the soccer ball candy, and Lucy directed him to a shelf behind her. Dozens of candy balls filled a huge stainless bowl. He set the bowl on the stool on his side of the counter, put on gloves, and started adding one ball per cake. He took care of the four dozen he'd frosted and the six dozen Lucy had finished, snapped on the lids bearing the Prairie Harts logo, and moved the trays to the cake refrigerator.

"What was your MOS?"

Elliot moved the candy bowl to the shelf and slid on the stool to start frosting more cakes. "I was a sniper." The same tension that had clenched in his gut when he'd given that answer to Fia, to really pretty much everyone, was there again, but not quite so sharp. After all, like Fia, Lucy was an Army wife.

She stopped to refill her pastry bag with more frosting. "My husband, Mike, used to say a lot of people can do a lot of jobs, but it takes a special person to do certain ones, and sniper was one of them. He said he couldn't do it, but God love the ones who do." She met his gaze. "*We* love the ones who do, too."

Now it was his turn to flush. "Thank you."

They worked in silence a few moments before she returned to business. "We're open Monday through Saturday from six thirty to two. It usually takes a while to get the last few people out and clean up, and then we have our catering clients to take care of. That's what got us into the business, so we stay loyal to them.

"What we would like to do to start is have you make

bread for our lunch specials. We've been buying a white sandwich bread from another bakery, but I'm convinced our walnut-celery-chicken salad sandwich would be so much better on brioche. We're also getting ready to add gourmet grilled cheese sandwiches, so your breads would be a great help there. Then, of course, if you have time, we'd appreciate help with the baking and cooking and decorating. We pretty much do each other's jobs, except for the bread. That would be your province."

"Sounds good." Elliott candied, lidded, and refrigerated another dozen boxes.

"We offer two weeks' vacation, and we're flexible about that, but please, not during the weeks of my wedding and honeymoon. We don't have health or dental insurance yet, and we don't offer a retirement plan. But we want to. We want to be that small business that pays better than anyone else in town and keeps their staff so happy, they won't go looking anywhere else." She wrinkled her nose. "Patricia and I and our friends—we've all had those jobs where you're lucky to make minimum wage, and getting sick is a fireable offense, and to top it all off, your boss is a jerk. We promised we'd be as much the opposite as profits allow us to be. So what do you think?"

What Elliot thought was, *God isn't just smiling on me. He's grinning ear to ear.* "If I can have access to the kitchen tonight or early tomorrow morning, I can bake you a sample of my breads, then you and Patricia can decide if I'm worth it."

Lucy snorted. "I can tell you what Patricia has decided; she told me so before she left. 'Tell Elliot we'll have our first company dinner at my house, Wednesday night at six.'" She slid off her stool and stretched the kinks from her back before returning to the cakes. "She's already put in her vote for yes. She likes you. I like you. Can you start tomorrow?"

"Sure. And I thought this was a test." He indicated the entire workspace in front of him.

"Nope, this was me needing help." Then she relented. "Though it's good to know that you can handle pastry bags and pick a 233 tip out of that messy cabinet filled with tips without asking which one you needed."

He had the job. Because they liked him and thought he could handle whatever they asked him to do. Strong satisfaction swept through him. He always felt better with a job, even if it was one a blindfolded monkey could do, and this one felt like...more. For the first time in a lot of years, it felt like all the lights had turned green at once.

He couldn't wait to tell Fia.

"I understand you have a dog," Lucy remarked. "Do you have a place to leave her where she'll be safe?"

"I don't yet." He intended to get an apartment first thing, definitely one that allowed pets. Until he found such a place and moved in, maybe Fia would be willing to extend her dogsitting a few days more.

"My office is a tiny corner in the back of the storeroom," Lucy went on. "If you need to bring her in, she should be fine there, and I think we're covered as long as she doesn't come in the kitchen or dining room."

"Thanks." The way his luck was running, he should drive to the nearest casino and bet every dime he had. But his parents hadn't raised a fool. A job was a great first step. An apartment would be a great second step. Having money in the bank, though...that was the goal. Fitting in, in a town that seemed to have chosen him as much he'd chosen it. Living a normal life like a normal guy, with all the responsibilities and payoffs of that.

And Fia. She was an important part of the town, the normal life, the payoff.

Maybe the biggest part of all.

# Chapter 5

Marti did something Monday afternoon that she rarely ever did: She took off work early. Not by a lot, only ninety minutes, so she could be at the house when Cadence got there. Cadence would have been fine alone, or she could have stayed with Abby until Marti got home at her normal time. Marti just felt the need to...be there.

Her niece was as unobtrusive as a teenager could be. Given that Abby had put Therese through several years of hell, Marti's expectations, she had to admit, had been pretty low. But Cadence was quiet, respectful, helpful. She was trying to fit into a situation that no one thought was ideal, least of all her. *Ideal* would have been her mom staying home in Connecticut and not disrupting her daughter's life while Frank tended to his career. But so far, this was working out well.

Even though Cadence wasn't home yet, the house felt different when Marti walked in. The energy, the vibe, had changed, as if the place itself knew it was no longer just

Marti's space. It was a strange sensation, and Marti couldn't say she loved it, but she loved her niece, and that was what counted.

After changing into a sleeveless dress and her favorite ballet flats, she got a bottle of water from the fridge and went outside, leaving the kitchen door open for a little fresh air. She was standing there, studying the patio furniture, when Cadence called her name from inside.

"Out here," Marti replied.

Cadence came to stand beside her, considering the furniture, too. After a couple of moments, she asked, "What are we looking at?"

"I'm still trying to decide what color to paint the furniture." Marti glanced at her: hair in an elaborate braid, her uniform—burgundy plaid skirt, white shirt, and burgundy sweater—looking as fresh as when she'd left this morning. "When I was in middle school and high school, I had to wear a uniform almost identical to that. The skirts were never short enough, the shirts were never fitted enough, and there was zero opportunity for individuality."

"And that suited you just fine, didn't it?"

Marti's brows rose. "No, of course not. I wanted to wear colors—"

"Subdued ones."

"And patterns—"

"Subtle ones."

"And different styles—"

"As long as they all quietly whispered 'class.'"

Cadence was trying to contain her grin, and Marti found herself wanting to smile with her. She feigned huffiness instead. "Are you saying I'm a uniform sort of person?"

"Well...I've been in your closet, Aunt Marti. Everything you own is timeless. There's a few bright colors, but everything else is white, black, navy, or gray. It's all tailored and elegant, the lines are uncluttered, it's all balanced."

Marti looked for a point to argue with but couldn't find one, so she exaggerated a sigh. "You've spent far too much time shopping with your mother."

"Tell me about it." Cadence rolled her eyes before looking at the table again, her head tilted to one side. "Why not just leave it the way it is? It's old. Let it look old. If that doesn't work, then restore it to its original state. But not everything needs to be shiny and new and perfect."

That wasn't a sentiment she'd learned from her parents, Marti knew. It was a good thing Frank made excellent money, because Belinda insisted on only the best for her family. They liked *everything* perfect. Including their daughter.

How did Cadence feel about that? Eugenie had had certain standards, and Marti had met most of them, but not out of some desire to please her mom. They were just rules that made sense to her when she was a kid. It seemed Cadence had done a lot of things to please Belinda: Ballet (*It doesn't change the fact that I'm clumsy,* she'd confided to Joshua); gymnastics (*When I tumble by accident, it's clumsy; when I do it on purpose, there's a point to it?*); piano (*Whyyy, when I can listen to much better stuff on my iPhone?*); and dressage (*All I wanted was a western saddle, jeans, and boots and to ride the trails in the woods*).

Eugenie, for all her flaws, had never signed up Marti for one single activity that Marti hadn't begged for first.

She turned her attention back to the patio furniture. "You make a good point. I'll find out what it needs to be protected from the weather, and then we'll do as little as possible to it. Okay?" She went to sit in one of the over-sized chairs and nodded to Cadence to join her.

"Let me get something to eat first. I'm starving." She went back inside, then returned with bottled water, an apple, and a granola bar.

"How was school?" God, how long had it been since Marti had imagined asking that of a child? Since the last time Joshua had brought up the subject of babies. At least eight, maybe nine years ago. She'd known before she married him that he wanted kids, but she hadn't been so sure herself. She'd wanted him, though, and had been convinced that her feelings would change. That Joshua's baby would be more special than any other baby. That sheer love would turn her into good mother material.

Since his death...She'd experienced a lot of yearnings, but the need for a child wasn't one of them. The need to replace Joshua wasn't, either. She wouldn't be like her mother after their parents' divorce. Eugenie had been married four times and engaged another four times that Marti knew about. Her mother found comfort in men—temporarily—before realizing that they were crazy-making and fleeing for her own sanity.

Everyone else in the family agreed that Eugenie was the crazy-maker.

Cadence drew her feet into her chair, tucking her skirt snugly, and crunched into the apple. Politely, she waited to swallow before answering. "It was okay, I guess. Abby introduced me to all her friends, and I met kids in my classes. It'll be okay."

"Such a ringing endorsement."

Cadence's smile was small, disappearing as she bit into

the apple again. When she could speak again, she asked, "Aunt Marti, do you know Dillon Smith?"

Marti blinked, an image of Jessy's brother-in-law popping into her mind. The whole identical-twin thing had been a little disconcerting to start, especially when Dalton was more than a tad formidable, and frankly, Dillon came close. Jessy had coerced him into showing up for parties and dinners, but he didn't seem to fit in. He stood on the outside, figuratively as well as literally on occasion, and made no effort to make friends.

But he was damn fine to look at. He was a leaner, tougher version of Dalton, and he did an outstanding job of filling out a pair of faded jeans, and he loved Jessy the way family should. That made him good in Marti's mind.

"I've met him. I didn't know you had."

"Yesterday. While Abby was inside." Cadence wrapped the apple core in a napkin, then tore open the granola bar wrapper. "He lives on a ranch. He's a cowboy. His brother is married to your friend, Jessy. He seems nice."

When had her niece lost the ability to form compound sentences, and why? Had Dillon said something inappropriate to her? Had he been too friendly—a situation Marti simply couldn't imagine—or otherwise set off Cadence's warning alarms?

Marti's stomach was starting to knot when Cadence drew a deep breath and said in a rush, "They raise palominos and he said I could come out and ride if it was okay with you and I don't want to start riding again yet, but..." She breathed again. "I'd like to see the horses."

Everything around Marti relaxed. Horses. Of course. Cadence had been crazy about them from the time she was in diapers until about a year into dressage. It had taken her another four years to let her mother know she wanted to quit.

"So you want to go out to the ranch and see the horses? Maybe, if that old excitement is still there, ask Dillon to let you ride?"

"I didn't bring riding clothes or my saddle," Cadence said, her nose wrinkled. "I just...I haven't even petted a horse since I quit dressage. Mom's kind of all or nothing, you know. I didn't want to do dressage, but quitting that meant quitting horses completely." She shrugged. "I miss them."

Marti understood being taken away from something—someone—she loved, and she remembered proud notes from Cadence's parents relating every compliment her trainer gave her. *A natural horsewoman. Has an affinity with all the animals. Firm hand, excellent instincts.*

"You go change, and I'll call Jessy and see if this is a good time."

"Thank you, Aunt Marti." Cadence didn't squeal the way Abby would have, or jump to her feet and run inside, texting all the way. She picked up the trash from her snack, took her bottle, and walked sedately to the back door. Fourteen going on middle age.

Shaking her head, Marti pulled out her cell phone and found Jessy's fiery red hair in the contact photos. "Hey, Jess, it's Marti. Your brother-in-law invited my niece out to see the horses. Do you think today would be okay?"

*　*　*

Mouse was the best office mate. She didn't ask distracting questions. She didn't interrupt when Fia was double-checking her math. She didn't get in Fia's way, asking, "What's that? What's it for? Why did the boss ask you to do it?" No, Mouse slept in the armchair until she tired of its comfyness, then she slept on the floor, then she disappeared down the hall. Fia assumed she was drinking out of the toilet bowl instead of the one filled with bottled water in the kitchen or sleeping in the middle of the bed like the princess she clearly thought she was.

All of Fia's work for the day was done, so she changed into workout capri pants and the smallest T-shirt she owned, still a size too big, and spread out a mat on the floor in front of the TV. When her muscles cramped, there wasn't much she could do, but she took advantage of the good times to stretch and strengthen every muscle that cooperated.

It was after five, and she'd been tempted every half hour since three thirty to call Elliot. She couldn't imagine Lucy and Patricia not hiring him. Truthfully, when she thought about her friends making hiring decisions, she saw them taking on every person who filled out an application. They were so softhearted. Lucy had never made a bad decision in her life, and Patricia had made some awful ones that she'd learned serious lessons from.

She started her yoga routine with easy, gentle stretches, savoring the pull in her muscles, slowing and deepening her breathing. Tensions eased a bit at a time from her forehead, her jaw, her neck, down her shoulders and along her spine. She moved through the sun salutation, then while in a tree pose—standing erect, right foot flat against the inside of her left thigh, hands clasped together above her head—the sensation of being watched drew her gaze to the door.

Elliot stood on the other side, one shoulder resting against the door frame. The Prairie Harts bag in his other hand swayed, and a smile of victory and of pure primal man-likes-what-he-sees sent a shiver through her. It was funny. His face was the same as it had been the day before and the day before, but there were such contrasts between the feelings seeing him inspired in her. At times he struck her as the sweetest, kindest guy in the world. Other times, he was so sexy that a single touch from him might spark a fire that would leave behind nothing but ashes and some serious satisfaction. Still other times, he was such a care-giver that she couldn't remember ever feeling safer.

And always, he displayed balance, a good nature, an un-willingness to let minor annoyances disturb his peace.

Slowly she lowered her foot to the floor, wobbling only once before her legs realized their job was to hold her in place even if they had gone weak. She half wished she'd changed into her regular yoga clothes—snug tank top, even snugger capris—but based on his expression, her successful-dieter-in-baggy-clothes look was fine with him.

Twisting the lock, she pushed the storm door open and pressed back against the wooden door to let him come in. Fairytale flavors perfumed the air around him as he moved past: sugar and chocolate and butter and vanilla. Four of her favorite scents in the world. "Well?" she asked when the storm door swung shut behind him.

"I went. I charmed. I got the job." He dangled the bag between them. "I also brought treats."

She folded her arms over her middle. "I knew you would."

"Get the job or bring treats?"

"Both. Do you love Lucy and Patricia?" Before he could

answer, she went on. "Of course you do. Everyone does. And I won't even ask if they loved you. Of course they did. Everyone does."

He set the bag on the back of the couch, and it rattled. An instant later, four paws hit the floor in the bedroom, then Mouse trotted in, sniffing the air. "I wondered where she had gone," Fia said as the puppy circled Elliot. "I guess all that snoozing out here made her tired so she needed a real nap."

"Yeah, getting to sleep on a real bed again is pretty high on my list, too. You want to go out with us tonight? Just drive around, show me which cheap apartments are okay and which ones are rumored to have roaches bigger than Mouse?"

Fia did a quick systems test. No headache. Her muscles were tingling in a good way—no, wait, that was her nerves, but still good. Her stomach wasn't churning; her sight had improved from double vision to single with an extraneous bit of fuzz. She was having a good-enough-to-go-work moment, so she certainly felt good enough to ride around town with Elliot and Mouse. "I'd be happy to. Just let me change clothes."

"Aw, do you have to?" He hooked on Mouse's leash. "I'm going to take her for a quick walk. Come on out when you're ready."

Since giving up her trainer job, Fia had discovered she could live days at a time in the same outfit—stained, worn, sweaty—and on those same days, she could forget to comb her hair even once. She hadn't let herself sink so low that she'd stopped brushing her teeth twice a day, but for a while, when everything seemed so hopeless, she'd figured that was inevitable. She would have been carted off to some facility where she would live with people in equally dark places until the margarita girls rescued her.

Or maybe this time Elliot could be her white knight.

*No, no, no,* she chastened herself. The only rescue she needed was from the medical establishment. There would be no putting her troubles off on someone else. Not until she was strong again and able to bear them all by herself again.

By the time she walked out the door in a short white skirt and a sleeveless chambray shirt with tiny ruffles down the placket, Elliot and Mouse were waiting next to the truck. He gave her an admiring look as she descended the steps to her usual silent mantra: *Don't fall, don't fall.*

"You look good enough to take a turn around the dance floor at Bubba's." He met her at the foot of the steps, rested his hand on her elbow, and walked around the truck with her.

"You've already heard of Bubba's?"

"The rowdiest cowboy bar in five counties. Good burgers, good music, and good entertainment."

"I know what passes for entertainment there. Dance contests, drinking contests, wet T-shirt contests, and of course, at least one ass-kicking a night."

"Ah, my kind of place. Actually, Lucy suggested a lot of places to take a woman before Bubba's. She's not a cowboy bar sort. She's familiarizing me with the town because Patricia says if I don't find a woman for myself, she's gonna find one."

Jealousy twinged in Fia's heart. Would Patricia even put her on such a list, or would she think Fia was too big a mess?

Elliot opened the passenger door, and Mouse jumped inside and into the rear. Next he helped Fia in, his fingers warm and solid on her arm. Even her worst muscle spasm wouldn't stand a chance with him holding her like that.

He waited until she'd turned and fastened her seat belt before he touched her cheek. "When do you want to make sure she knows it's not necessary? We could drive by her house tonight and honk the horn a dozen times while we hang out the windows and yell like kids."

Fia smiled at faint memories when she and nearly forgotten girlfriends had indulged in that kind of juvenile behavior. Granted, they'd been...well, juveniles.

"Or I could escort you to tomorrow's meeting of the Tuesday Night Margarita Club. I understand that's one way to hit them all at once."

"They told you about that, huh?"

He shrugged. "Lucy mentioned it. More along the lines of there will be husbands and fiancés in the bar, so if I wanted to meet someone I wouldn't be interested in dating, I should drop by and she'd provide the introductions."

"They're all really nice guys—a rancher or two, some soldiers. Guys you'd have stuff in common with." Though she suspected he could find something in common with every single person in Tallgrass. *You know cows? So do I. You like to shoot? I'm a great shot. You've driven through Kansas? So have I.* And the one everyone could answer positively: *You like food? Me, too.* No matter where he went, no matter how short a time he stayed, the man had never met a stranger.

That was not a bad thing to say about someone.

With a nod that it was settled—*health willing*—Elliot closed the door, then circled the truck to climb in. She gave him a chance to pull out of the driveway and onto the street heading out of the apartment complex before a thought occurred to her from earlier. "Where have you been staying since you got into town?"

A muscle in Elliot's jaw quirked, and he took his time slowing to a complete stop at the main street, even though there was only a *Yield* sign. After a moment, he glanced at her. "There's a great campground out at Tall Grass Lake, and the backseat is pretty comfortable once I move all the stuff out of it."

She glanced over her shoulder at the boxes and duffel bags, a laundry basket, boots on one floorboard, Stetson turned on its crown on the highest stack of boxes. He'd been living in his truck. She imagined Mouse got to sleep wherever she wanted, except on the Stetson, and everything else just got shifted around to suit Elliot's current need: home or vehicle.

When she turned forward again, she caught a glimpse of the flush on his cheeks. He should know she didn't feel sorry for him. It didn't lessen her opinion of him one bit. She'd been extraordinarily blessed that her boss had kept her on the payroll and that Scott's life insurance was invested and earning interest to help her if she ever became fully disabled. Finding jobs could be tough. Getting a new start required money, and until a person got that money coming in, he did what he had to do.

"When Scott and I got married, after we rented an apartment and paid deposits on utilities and everything, we had about two hundred bucks left over that wasn't already set aside for something. Originally we didn't plan on having a honeymoon, but we both had paydays coming up in a couple weeks, so we splurged. We loaded some clothes in backpacks and climbed on the back of his motorcycle and took off.

"I was a city girl. Did I mention that? I'd lived my whole life in Jacksonville. When he said we'd camp out at night so our money would go further, I thought it sounded great. And it was the first night. The second night I couldn't find a single spot on the ground big enough for my butt that didn't have rocks sticking up. The third night we got three inches of rain in three hours." She'd been so miserable that she'd cried that night, though Scott had never known. She'd worked hard to keep the quaver out of her voice and to pretend the tears were raindrops.

"The next day we stopped at the next town and bought a cheap little tent with walls and a floor. When it rained again, we zipped ourselves inside and..." She blew out her breath and made a show of fanning herself. After a moment, she added reverently, "Damn, I loved that tent."

Elliot was grinning when she looked at him again, all hints of his flush gone. "There's nothing wrong with close quarters when you've got someone to share them with."

"Or when you have a plan. You know, my mother used to talk about how she was going to move to New York when the time was right, when she had enough money to just make the move and not worry about getting a job right away. But the time was never right, she never stopped spending every dollar she got her hands on, and as far as I know, she's still living in Florida dreaming. Too many people are like that. They never take chances. They stay where they have a bed and a job, no matter how much they hate it, and they wish for something better, but they never try to make those wishes come true. They just can't take a chance."

Elliot's expression turned serious. "You take chances, don't you, Fia?"

"Since I was fifteen." She thought about it a moment, then admitted, "Sometimes they bite me on the ass. Most of the time, though, life is good." Gazing out the side window as buildings passed in a blur, she whispered again, this time with gratitude, "Life is good."

*   *   *

If Dillon had been given the chance to pick a worse time to have company, he didn't think he could have chosen any better than Monday evening, when Jessy told him Cadence and her aunt were on their way out. He'd been up since dawn, had a throb on his calf where a horse had kicked him, had smashed his index and middle fingers with a wrench, and still hadn't heard from BB. He was sweaty, dirty, tired, hungry, and stank to high heaven. On top of that, the chief cook—Jessy—had announced that she and Dalton were going to Walleyed Joe's for dinner and hustled his brother out the door. Now he had to entertain company *and* scrounge up his own dinner.

He breathed deeply, splashed water from the laundry room sink over his face, and dried it on paper towels as the sound of a vehicle on the drive filtered through the open windows. He wouldn't care if it was just Cadence, though no aunt in her right mind would leave her teenage niece in the care of a disreputable cowboy, and even if she were willing, he wouldn't let her. What kind of nightmare could that turn into?

Boots echoing on the wood floor, he went out the back door again—Jessy had stricter rules than his mother about wearing boots inside the house. His dog, Oliver, a big-eyed mutt, trotted over to follow him around the house while

Dalton's mutt, Oz, stayed sprawled where he was under the oak.

The SUV parked beside his pickup had been spotless before the short drive on the gravel road. It made his truck, older than he was, look even filthier in comparison. He depended on rain to rinse off the worst of the dirt. Jessy teased that if he actually washed it, he'd find that the grime and tree sap were the only things holding it together.

Cadence and Marti had wandered over to the corral, leaning on the wood fence. The girl was about to vibrate out of her skin, her weight shifting from foot to foot. The woman stood tall and still. She wore shorts but not in the way every other woman he knew wore shorts. Short, rumpled, comfortable, or meant to impress—that was what he was used to. Marti's were longer than most, made of some material that had to be expensive, and honest to God looked starched and creased. Her shirt was black, short-sleeved, clung to her breasts and her middle, and he would bet next month's paycheck that it was softer than anything he'd ever touched.

He'd bet Marti was, too.

Cadence noticed him first, a smile stretching across her face. "Mr. Smith! They're so pretty!"

He glanced from her to the horses grazing across the way. To his mind, paints and palominos were the best of a beautiful animal. He'd rodeoed on one and now raised the other, and there wasn't another animal in the world he'd rather spend his time with.

Unless he counted humans in that bunch. Then he could think of one. Six years old, round little face, dark eyes, and hair that in summer had turned the silvery golden shade of the palominos' coats. Lilah.

Rubbing restlessly at the ache in his gut, he stopped next to Cadence and whistled. Every horse's ears pricked, a few slowly continuing to munch but the rest bolting into motion. The drumming hooves of the most distant ones who reached a full gallop made the air shimmer and did something of the same inside him. Ever since he was a kid, the sound of horses' hooves pounding the ground had filled him with awe. The only thing better was when he was hearing it from the saddle instead of the fence.

"Oh my gosh, they're incredible," Cadence whispered. The horses crowded close, jostling each other for position as she stroked one velvety muzzle, then another. When one nuzzled her palm, looking for treats, she laughed delightedly. "Oh, I've missed you guys."

Dillon walked along the fence line to the corner post, where Jessy had left a bucket of apple and cinnamon flavored horse treats. He passed it to Marti, who handed it to Cadence, and she immediately popped the top off. He and Marti watched them feed for a couple of moments in silence.

A light breeze blew across the pasture, bringing with it the fragrant scents of new growth, flowering fruit trees, and horse manure. From a source much closer, he smelled sunshine and rain and ocean waves, fresh-picked strawberries and just-mown hay, favorite meals and favorite memories. Damn, Marti Levin smelled exactly like all the good things in life.

She glanced his way. "Thanks for the offer."

There'd been a time when he would have tried to charm her and probably succeeded. Now his first impulse was to grunt and leave it at that. The fact that she was Jessy's friend, though, forced him to reply. "No problem."

"I was crazy about the beach when I was her age. When

I had to stay away for more than a few days, the next time I went, I threw myself to the sand and tried to hug every single grain."

That was a difficult image to form. He'd figured she'd been every bit as proper and elegant as a child as she was now, always cool and in control of her world. A carefree, beach-loving kid just didn't compute. But life had interfered. Her husband had died far younger than he should have. Like Dillon, she'd lost dreams.

Even cool, controlled, elegant people could lose dreams.

She was tall, only a few inches shorter than him, and if the glare of the setting sun bothered her, she didn't let it show. She'd tucked sunglasses into her hair instead of covering her eyes with them. Her hands were bare of jewelry, no treasured wedding ring, no bracelet or watch. The outline in her hip pocket of a cell phone made the watch unnecessary, and if she was like the rest of the margarita club, she didn't need jewelry to remind her of the person she loved most.

As the horses kept pushing each other out of the way, Cadence kept moving down the fence in an effort to give each one attention.

"The first time I saw the ocean..." Dillon's voice sounded gritty, like he hadn't talked to anyone all day, when sometimes it seemed all he did was to talk—to Oliver and Oz, to the horses and the cows, to Jessy. Not so much to Dalton, but maybe that would change.

He cleared his throat. "I don't think I moved for twenty-four hours. I'd just left home a few months before and followed the rodeo circuit to San Diego. It was an amazing sight after riding my way across West Texas, New Mexico, Arizona, and California desert."

Marti smiled faintly. "I grew up five miles from the beach back East. My friends and I lived there, even in winter when the ocean was moody and cold." After a moment, she stated, "You were gone a long time."

Everyone in town who'd ever known the Smith family knew that. It had been Jessy who'd reconnected him with his family—or rather, Oliver, the stray dog she'd been walking who'd adopted Dillon the instant he'd seen him. He was grateful to her for that and a lot of other things. He loved her for it—though, thank God, not in a romantic sort of way. He and Dalton had enough issues between them already.

"I thought I was looking for something." The admission surprised him. He never talked to anyone about his leaving.

"Did you find it?"

He rested his forearms on the top rail of the fence, clasped his hands together, and shook his head. "Turned out, I was just running away from something else." The honesty surprised him even more.

That brought Marti's clear, sharp gaze to his face. He knew what she saw. The impassive expression he wore most of the time wasn't just an expression. It was *him*. The day he'd woken up after the accident, he'd found everything inside him frozen in place: the emotion, the regret, the anger, the self-hatred. He'd stayed that way through the trial, through the months in prison, through the months since his release. He could still hurt. He could be grateful for small things. He could laugh. He could even love again, as Jessy, Oliver, and Oz had proven.

He just couldn't get rid of that frozen knot inside him.

"Have you made peace with it?"

That wasn't a concept he had much familiarity with. For

as long as he could remember, he'd felt different—thought about different things, wanted different things. When he was riding the rodeos, drinking, and partying with all the pretty girls, he'd thought that was what he wanted. Then he'd met Tina and found some measure of satisfaction there. Lilah had deepened it before prison had ripped it right out of him.

Now he didn't know what he wanted or even what he needed. Whatever it was, he was pretty sure he didn't deserve it.

He didn't have to find out how long Marti would have let the silence drag out because Cadence came back to them, a short line of horses following her. "You've got the best job in the world, Mr. Smith, taking care of these girls."

He smiled at her enthusiasm. He had to admit, his job was one of the things right about his life now. He'd missed these pastures and woods, the house, the barn, the creek way out back. "Do me a favor. Call me Dillon."

Cadence's gaze darted to her aunt, who nodded, then back to him. "When I e-mail Mom, I'm going to tell her that instead of college, I've decided to become a rancher. That will make her freak."

"Add that you're learning barrel racing so you can win one of those great big belt buckles to wear when you get back home," Marti suggested. "That'll make her hair catch fire." They both laughed easily, their eyes crinkling the same way, their laughs full and indelicate. Not quite what he'd expected.

He suspected much about Marti Levin might not be what he'd expected. And she seriously did smell like everything good. He really needed to get himself a bottle of that.

Maybe even two.

*   *   *

Elliot liked the first day of every job he'd ever had, with the exception of the Army, when he'd been scared snotless that he wouldn't live up to his family's, the training cadre's, and his own expectations. Prairie Harts was no exception. He'd spent the morning making bread, steering clear of the professional mixers with their dough hooks and doing it the way Grandma had taught him, kneading by hand. It had been a long time since he'd made bread, but the instant he'd dug his fingers into the sticky mass, it had all come back to him: the hours he'd spent learning the right "feel" for every different bread they made, the smells, the texture, the rising, the baking, the tasting.

After work, he'd gone to one of the apartment complexes Fia had shown him last night and laid down the first month's rent plus a deposit for a good-sized studio apartment. It came unfurnished except for the Murphy bed that folded out of a closet, but hey, he and Mouse didn't need much else. The building was old, brick and stone, erected in the 1930s, recently remodeled but retaining its gracefully shabby air, and the price was within his budget. He liked gracefully shabby.

Leaving Mouse asleep on the bed, he picked up his keys, wallet, and Stetson and headed to the truck. The margarita girls liked to get an early start on their evening, and given that he had to be at work at 4 a.m., he was going to have an early end to his.

When he arrived at Fia's duplex, she was sitting on the stoop, face tilted back to catch a few rays from the setting sun. She was...

Instead of trying to narrow it to one word, he gave a heavy, happy sigh.

She would have gotten in by herself, but with a reminder that his mama didn't raise him that way, he loped around the truck, opened the door, and helped her climb up. In exchange, he got a close-up view of gorgeous legs and muscles and, beneath the shift of flowy fabric, just a hint of the nice, sweet curve of her hip.

"Good day?" she asked.

"Damn good day." When he climbed behind the steering wheel again, he repeated the question. "Good day?"

She raised her hand and made a so-so gesture. When she didn't elaborate, he kept himself from pressing for more. "So tell me who I'm going to meet tonight," he said instead.

Her expression lightened. "There's Carly. She's married to Dane, who was Airborne, and found out a few weeks ago that she's pregnant. And Therese, who's married to Keegan, who was a medic. Between them, they've got three kids and are thinking about a fourth. Ilena married a pediatrician last Christmas. Her son will be one next month, and I'm one of his many godmothers. We spoil him rotten."

"As godmothers should."

"You know Patricia and Lucy, of course. There's also Marti. Her husband and Lucy's were good friends, and they were killed in the same battle. Jessy's our Southern belle—red-haired, green-eyed, makes every man within a hundred yards look twice—and she's married to Dalton, who has a ranch outside town. His brother Dillon comes, too, sometimes. Bennie comes when her classes allow. She married Calvin just before he got out of the Army and got pregnant immediately. She's not going to wait too long the way she did with her first husband. None of them are."

After a moment's reflection, she went on, "That's all of our regular group, but there are ten to fifteen others who come when they have the chance."

Elliot turned east onto Main Street. The margarita club met at The Three Amigos, the Mexican restaurant in the strip mall where he and Fia had run into each other last Friday night. "What about you and Scott? Did you wait too long?"

"We didn't wait for anything," she replied with a laugh. "We traded phone numbers the first night we met, had sex the second night, and were married within a month. We didn't need to date a long time or have a year-long engagement to know we were meant to be together."

He was silently agreeing with her, that sometimes a person just knew, when she glanced at him. "Does it bother you? When I talk like that about Scott? I mean, when you and I are..." Again, she made that wig-wag motion with her hand.

"Dancing this dance?" he asked with a wry grin. He moved into the turn lane, then pulled into the shopping center lot. After parking, he faced her. "How old are you?"

"Twenty-four."

"That's a whole lot of living before you met me. It's a whole lot of loving." Though not as much as she should have had. Her husband shouldn't have been the first person in her life to make her feel loved. "Everything that happened in those years made you the woman you are, and I really like that woman. How could I be bothered by any of it?"

She gave him such a look—grateful, sweet, even a little bit teary. Damn, he was a sucker for looks like that.

To lighten the mood, he removed his hat, shoved his fingers through his hair in his best effort at primping, then reseated it. "Besides, it might surprise you to hear this, but I have had a girl or two who was crazy about me."

As he intended, she laughed. "Crazy in love or just plain crazy?"

"Crazy in love a couple times." Then, thinking of the girl with the tire iron, he smiled ruefully. "Just bat-shit crazy on occasion." He walked to her side of the truck and opened the door. When she took his hand, he waited until her feet were on the ground, then drew her close. The scent that drifted around her was as enticing as bread in a hot oven and as familiar as home. He had a feeling it would haunt him for a very long time to come.

Something else familiar—good old-fashioned lust—started building inside him, warming his skin, making his heart beat a little faster and his breaths a little raspier. He'd been in bed with women within an hour of meeting and had dated others without ever going that far, but Fia was different.

*You say that every time.*

Trust Emily to pop up in his head at an inopportune time.

*Everyone is different. Everyone is special. Bless you, El, you really believe it. That's why women love you.*

But Fia was even more different. Even more special.

"How do you want to play this?" His voice was ragged, and his skin tingled all over. So much reaction for so small a touch.

"Play?" she echoed as if she found an entirely different meaning in the word. Sex was serious business, true, but damn, it could be fun. Sex with Fia would be incredible fun.

He nodded toward the building behind him. "Inside. With your friends. Are we buddies? Friends? Friends with impending benefits?" He trailed one finger the length of her arm, ending at the flutter of fabric where her sleeve started. "Do I get to be your boyfriend? Are you going to introduce me to the girls, or do I just get to meet the guys?"

She snorted. "Ha. You clearly have no clue about the margarita girls. If I just left you in the bar with the guys, every single one of them would find a reason to go over and check you out—and they are *very* good at checking guys out."

Which didn't answer his question. That was okay. Meeting her best girlfriends was a big step. For a woman like Fia, who didn't love lightly, it was a public announcement of commitment. Minimizing what was between them in public was fine, as long as she was willing to acknowledge it in private.

"I'll tell you what. You just introduce us, and we'll keep them guessing. Good?"

Her fingers tightened briefly around his. "Good."

The interior of the restaurant was on the subdued side, given the bright range of colors on the outside. The hostess greeted Fia by name but didn't offer a menu or directions, unnecessary since she obviously knew where she was going. He removed his hat, then had to release her hand to wind between tables to the back, where three tables had been pushed together. A group of women sat there, each faced with chips, salsa, and contrary to their name, iced tea or water. They all greeted Fia with sincere pleasure, then all their gazes turned to him.

"Elliot!" Patricia rose from her chair and hugged him. He wasn't surprised. She reminded him of his mother, and his mom would have done the same thing. "What are you—I didn't know you knew Fia."

"She was the first person I met in town. Hey, Lucy."

His other boss looked from him to Fia, then back again, and a smile slowly curved her mouth. He knew that smile. He'd seen it on Emily plenty of times, on the wives of a few Army buddies, on every matchmaking woman he'd ever known. "Hi, Elliot. Hi, Fia."

Fia knew the significance of the smile, too, and the tone of Lucy's voice, and she flushed, but in a good way. Not an embarrassed sort of thing but more like she'd gotten caught with a naughty secret. "Guys, this is Elliot Ross. He's new in town."

She went around the table with the introductions, and he pegged each name to the few details she'd given on the way over, all the regulars plus an extra named Leah. They came in an array of hair colors, skin tones, heights, and body types, with accents that ranged from definitely Southern to back East to indistinguishable, and he knew within minutes that he would become friends with every one of them if given the chance.

He said his hellos around the table, fielded a compliment on his Stetson and another on his Texas accent, and received a tiny, intimate look from Fia, and something deep inside him sparked.

Tallgrass was looking more like home every day.

# Chapter 6

"Why don't you all just get one great big table and have dinner together?"

Fia was standing at the window in Elliot's apartment, looking toward the dimly lit horizon, while he rinsed and refilled Mouse's water dish in the small kitchen. She could see his reflection in the glass, but the real thing was much better, so she turned to face him, the broad windowsill providing a ledge for her to lean against. "I don't think it's ever come up—I think because we all like things the way they are. The guys get a night out to talk about sports or whatever, and the sisters get to catch up on everything in each other's lives."

After putting the water dish on a mat on the floor, he leaned against the cabinets, hands resting on the countertop, ankles crossed, gaze fixed on her. "Makes sense."

He was so damn handsome. She'd noticed that the first time she'd seen him—right after she'd thought how sweet it was that he was holding an umbrella for his puppy—but it still drew her up short. He had the smoldering, sexy good looks that landed guys on magazine covers and runways, along with the body to match. Put him in snug-fitting, faded, unzipped jeans that rode low on his narrow hips and nothing else but his cowboy hat, post it on the Internet, and the image would go viral in no time.

Take him out of those jeans, and... Woo.

She drew an unsteady breath and clasped her hands together around the bottle of water she held. It took some effort to push that image to the back of her mind and to concentrate on the here-and-clothed present. "Back when all the girls were single, we talked one time about what would happen if one of us met some guy and fell in love again. Would she continue to meet with us or drop out? Would he want her to be part of a group that she joined to help her mourn the loss of the first man she'd fallen madly for? It was kind of scary, especially for me. Most of the girls have family, and Carly and Lucy and Ilena are still very close to their first husbands' families. But me—these women *are* my family. I couldn't bear the idea of not having all of them in my life on a regular basis.

"Then Carly met Dane and Therese met Keegan, and there was Jessy and Dalton, and none of them *cared* why we were friends. We weren't Carly's widows' group or Therese's support group. As far as they were concerned, we were just friends. And there's Ilena and Jared and Lucy and Joe and Bennie and Calvin..." She fell silent for a moment, then murmured, "God, we are *lucky*."

Lucky to have their first husbands. Lucky to have one another. Lucky—some of them, at least—to fall in love again. How many people found one person to love them so much, much less a whole gang of them?

Sweet, but another thought to push back for a while. She didn't want to get maudlin here.

Forcing a few extra watts into her smile, she gestured around the large room. "So show me your apartment." That had been their reason for stopping by, that and to make sure Mouse was all right. Judging by the dent in the mattress, she hadn't moved much in her few hours alone.

Elliot adopted the voice of a character from a movie they both liked. "Well, this here's the sleepin' area, and this"—he held out one hand to the kitchen—"is the cookin' and cleanin' up area, and back through that door is where we do our bathin' and all."

"It's a lot bigger than I expected. I wonder why they didn't turn it into one- or two-bedroom apartments when they remodeled."

"Nah, the guy's lazy. That would have meant taking out and putting in walls, mudding and taping them, having to hire subs and getting permits and having code enforcement inspect the work. All he did was throw on some fresh paint, fix a few dings in the plaster, and change out a few sinks. Little jobs."

It amused her that, without meeting the landlord, she believed he was lazy. Had she ever trusted anyone as quickly and as completely as she did Elliot? It wasn't that he proclaimed himself as telling the truth and nothing but. There was just something about him that said he could be trusted and believed, that he was a good man, dependable, honorable, happy, satisfied. He wouldn't lie to a woman to get her into bed or to sneak around behind her back to see someone else. He wouldn't cheat or give anything less than his absolute best to anything he did.

With her upbringing, she should be skeptical of

everything everyone said or did—and for a long time, she had been. She'd thought all fathers were worthless drunks and all mothers wished their kids away on a regular basis. She'd thought grandparents were for disappointing grandkids, that aunts and uncles were just extra people in a child's life to let them down.

But she trusted Elliot. In her world, that was a huge step.

Across the room, he tried to hide a yawn, but she saw it and started toward the door. "I'd better get home before you turn into a pumpkin."

He caught the reference to their conversation last week and arched one brow. "I don't turn into a pumpkin. If I'm still up at midnight, I'll become a ravening beast with slobber dripping from my fangs while I'm trying to bake bread in the morning."

"It could go viral on the Net."

"Huh?" he responded as he opened the door for her, but she just shook her head in response. No need to tell him she'd been envisioning a naked cowboy a short while ago, not when his bed was only ten feet away.

The drive back to her house was silent, though after a few blocks, he pulled her hand onto the console and twined his fingers with her. The radio was on, old country tunes playing in the background, and she was softly singing along when Elliot joined in. Her jaw dropped, and she stared at him in the dim light. "Oh, my God, you can sing."

His grin was immodest. "I used to play some clubs in my younger days. I play the guitar, too. Guess you never noticed it under all the stuff in the backseat."

"Go on. Sing more."

He did, and she listened with her eyes half closed. The tones were sweet, the emotion fierce, the quality hands-down better than the singer on the radio. Everything she learned about Elliot was adding up to an extraordinary man.

While she remained plain, average Fia. With "issues."

"Beautiful," she responded when the song ended. At about the same time, he turned into her driveway.

He came around and held hands with her to the stoop and up the steps, where he propped open the storm door with his boot while she unlocked the door. She set her purse on the floor inside the door, then faced him. "I'm not going to invite you inside because you've got to get up early."

"Darn." He moved a step closer, fitted his hands to her waist, and leaned toward her. She met him in the kiss, her mouth parting, her hands sliding around to the back of his neck, combing through his silky hair. Dear Lord, she'd forgotten how good a kiss could be. She nibbled at his lip, pausing only when his tongue thrust between her teeth, invading, exploring, rousing a long-unsatisfied need deep inside. Moving intuitively, her hands glided over soft cotton that covered the lean muscles along his spine. When they reached the rougher texture of jeans and leather belt, the tips tingled, like the briefest touch of a live wire, singeing and searing and sparking pleasure through her body.

When she stroked a few inches lower to slide her palm over his erection, his breath caught, and so did hers. It had been so very long...would be so very easy...back up one step, don't let go, take him to the bedroom or, better, the couch, strip off their clothes...So easy. So perfect. So wrong.

Even the thought of that last word was wrong. It jangled in the midst of nerves humming with need. It pulled her out of the haze of what she could do, of the incredible satisfaction she could have, and brought back all the ugly uncertainty of her life. Elliot might be Prince Charming, but she was no princess, and her life was no simple, sweet fairy tale with a happily ever after.

Tears seeped into her eyes—disappointment, weariness—and she opened her eyes to blink them away. Apparently sensing the change in her, Elliot ended the kiss with another tiny, sweeter kiss, then clasped her hands in his. For a long time, he studied her face with an intensity that rippled along her skin, then he took a step back, putting breathing room between them.

When he spoke, he sounded as if he'd done a long hump with a heavy ruck on a hot day. "You never did tell me."

"What?"

"Is Fia short for something?"

"You never did ask." She didn't sound much better. "Sofia."

He laid his palm gently against her cheek, repeated her name, then backed away even farther. "Thank you, Sofia."

"For what?"

"Being in that parking lot Friday night. For liking me and my dog. For kissing like—" Breaking off, he grinned and shook his head. *"Damn."*

"It takes two."

His grin strengthened, then slowly faded. "Good night."

Leaning against the door jamb, she watched him go to his truck, get in, and drive away with a final wave. Sighing deeply, she stepped inside the house, closed and locked the door, and stumbled, hitting the floor with a solid thud.

\* \* \*

By the time headlights flashed across the windows fifteen minutes later, Fia had gotten herself off the floor and hobbled to the couch. Her left wrist throbbed where she'd tried to catch herself, her right knee was burning, and her left foot was in spasm, sending sharp pain from her toes all the way to her teeth. She didn't try to get up; her visitor had keys. All the margarita girls had keys for just such an occasion. She just slumped there on the couch, feeling sorry for herself.

Jessy burst into the room, all bustling energy and concern. Right behind her was Ilena, slight, slender, white-blond, mothering angel. "Are you all right?" Ilena asked as Jessy demanded, "What happened?"

"I'm sorry to call—"

They both brushed her off, Jessy sitting on the arm of the sofa and Ilena taking a spot on the cushion beside Fia. "Mamacita was with me when you called, so I sent the guys on home and she gave me a ride."

"You know you're supposed to call *any* of us at any time," Ilena chastened in her insubstantial voice. Without asking, she pulled Fia's foot onto her lap and began massaging the tight muscles. "Tell Jessy what medicine you need, and she'll get it."

Fia obeyed, then settled deeper into the couch as waves of pain radiated from her foot. "I hate for you to do that. I took a shower before dinner, but I've walked on my feet since then."

"Better than walking without them," Ilena teased. "Get real, sweetie. I have an eleven-month-old son. I've handled way nastier stuff than your feet."

When Jessy returned from the bathroom with Fia's medication, she brought a glass of water and hovered while she took the pill. It was a powerful muscle relaxant, but sometimes it couldn't overpower the spasms.

"Are you hurt anywhere else?" Jessy asked.

"My wrist is a little sore, but it's not swollen."

"She's got an owie on her knee," Ilena said with a nod. "The best cure for owies is a hug from Russell the Sheep."

"She's not a baby like John, Mamacita." Jessy checked both wrist and knee, then sat down on the coffee table. "What happened, doll?"

Fia rolled her eyes. "I'd left my purse on the floor while Elliot and I were on the porch, and at first I thought I'd tripped over it, but then I realized my foot was on fire." Pins and needles. Flames licking along her nerves. She could describe it a dozen ways, but the best was simple: hell.

"You didn't call for him?"

"He'd already left."

Jessy's green gaze studied her. "And you wouldn't have even if he'd been there."

Fia didn't say anything. She couldn't look either of them in the eye.

"Aw, Fia—"

Ilena interrupted. "Her toes are starting to loosen. Let's get her into bed before the pill kicks in and we can't move her. Not that you're big or anything, Fia."

Jessy snorted. "She's practically a foot taller than either of us."

"Good things come in small packages." Ilena wrinkled her nose. "My mom used to tell me that once it became apparent I was never going to see five and a half feet without a ladder. By the time I was sixteen, I would have sold Mom just to be average, but Juan was a little guy, too. Maybe that's what drew us together."

With their help, Fia got to her feet, and bearing only as much weight as she had to on her left heel, she hobbled into the bedroom. Ilena gave her privacy to change into her pajamas. Jessy, who'd undressed her before, helped her trade the pretty outfit chosen to impress Elliot for a comfy T-shirt advertising a 10K she'd run with Scott years ago.

"Want me to massage that foot?" Jessy offered.

"I've got it." Ilena kicked off her shoes, sat cross-legged on the bed, and went back to work on the stubborn spasm.

Jessy removed her own shoes and climbed into bed, plumping the pillow behind Fia, fixing one for herself. The first time Fia had called Jessy for help, her friend had been there in a flash, but she'd been puzzled as hell. She was no one's first call for comforting pats and *poor baby* reassurances, and Fia suspected Jessy had figured out, just as Fia had, that she was the only one available at that time.

Since then, though, she was usually Fia's first call. She had a capacity for caregiving that no one had ever guessed at, and she did it all in her usual blunt manner. She never overwhelmed Fia with too much sympathy, which tonight might have left her a hot mess.

"All right," Ilena said after a moment. "Give us the secret, inside, intimate scoop on Elliot. Where did you find him, are you going to keep him, and would you be willing to loan him out from time to time? I promise I would just look, not touch."

Fia laughed. "He's not a stray dog that wandered in looking for a place to live." But only half of that statement was true. He was looking for a place to stay, and she would very much like for that place, metaphorically, to be her.

She would also like world peace and the ability to eat all the chocolate she wanted without her butt expanding exponentially.

"Besides, what would Jared think if he knew I was loaning Elliot out to you?"

Ilena's shrug was dismissive. "When you and Elliot have kids, I'll loan Jared to you every time they get a snotty nose. Fair trade, don't you think?"

Jessy disagreed while Fia got lost somewhere in the mention of kids. It was a question she and Scott had never really decided. He just kind of assumed that one day it would happen, and truthfully, she'd just assumed if he wanted them, she'd have them. She'd never been sure she would be a good mother, though, not having had any maternal examples in her life. Now, four years older and forty years wiser, she would only have a baby if she was one hundred percent sure she wanted it. If she was married to the father, and he was one hundred percent sure *he* wanted it. If they could take care of it—him—she'd never been girly enough, she didn't think, to relate to a little girl—better than any other two people in the world. If they could love him even more than they loved each other.

*Elliot would be a great father. He would do what fathers are supposed to do and do it better than it's ever been done before,* her inside voice whispered.

But how could she be a mother when she'd fallen out of the blue? When the medication that eased her symptoms made her goofy and unable to care for herself, much less a child? When she didn't know what was wrong, whether it would get better, if it might even kill her someday?

"See that look on her face?" Ilena said in a stage whisper to Jessy. "That's the look you get when you're thinking of Dalton."

Fia shook off her thoughts to focus on her friends. "That's the look you get—well, all the time." Ilena was just so damn happy to be in the place she was in with the people she was with.

"Elliot's a friend," Fia went on.

"A very good friend," Jessy corrected her. "He kissed you good night and made you stumble over your own feet."

"How do you know he kissed me good night?"

Jessy's sigh was patient. "Because if I were Elliot and I'd brought you home and walked you to the door, I would damn well kiss you. And because I *am* a woman, and if he brought me home and walked me to the door, I'd damn well kiss him."

"We are young, but we are not naïve," Ilena said in her best South Texas drawl. She waited a moment for her comment to sink in, then the three of them burst into laughter. Ilena was naïve in the best possible way, and they all knew it. She trusted life and people, she always believed in the best, and she thought optimism wasn't a choice but the only way to live.

Must be something in that Texas soil.

Fia could use a dose of that optimism for herself, and in a sense she had it in Elliot. The thing she wanted. The thing she needed. But also the thing she couldn't have.

\* \* \*

Once the breakfast rush finished Wednesday morning, Lucy left Patricia in charge of the bakery and herded Elliot out to her car. "You need some heavy lifting done?" he asked as he slid into the passenger seat.

"Nope. I'm taking you to meet our source for sourdough starter. You met Bennie last night, right? Well, her grandmother has a starter that she got from her mother when she got married, so it's at least sixty years old. I asked on Monday if we could get some from her, and she said she was feeding it this morning so come by and we could have the discard." Lucy pulled onto the street, then abashedly grinned. "I have to admit, I know nothing about sourdough except that it tastes good, so I have no idea what she's feeding it or why or what discard is."

"Flour and water. It keeps the spores alive. And discard is exactly what it sounds like. Every time you feed it, you throw out part of it so you don't wind up with a giant mass." In his mind, he was rubbing his hands in gleeful anticipation. "My grandma's sourdough pancakes are the best pancakes that ever existed, and the bread...Damn."

"I can't wait to give it a try." Lucy slowed as she approached the middle of the block. "That house right there is mine, and Joe lives next door. Back there on the next street is Patricia's house. Remember, dinner tonight. On the way back, I'll drive by the front so you can find it easier."

"Yes, ma'am." The neighborhood was like Tallgrass itself: neat, older but lovingly cared for. The people who lived here were happy. Settled. Their contentment showed.

As they continued driving west, Lucy gave him a sly glance. "So you have some good luck, Elliot, meeting the prettiest girl in town five minutes after you crossed the city limits."

"I was born lucky." He was grateful for it every day.

"She's a sweetheart. She's had a tough time—"

Abruptly, Lucy broke off and a flush tinged her cheeks. "Aw, no gloomy talk today. Spring in Oklahoma is gorgeous but fleeting, so we keep things light and bright and sunny then. And here's where we're going."

She pulled into the driveway of a small house, where an elderly black woman sat on the porch swing. As they approached, she stood and set down her well-read Bible, and a welcoming smile spread across her face. "How are you doing, Miss Lucy?"

Lucy walked into her hug. "I'm better than ever, Mama." To Elliot, she added, "I had a heart attack last fall, and Mama prayed me through rehab. She's on very good terms with God, so if you ever need any assistance..."

While Elliot processed that information—A heart attack? She was only a few years older than him!—the old lady smiled sweetly. "I'm always happy to put a good word in with the Lord."

"Mama, this is Elliot Ross, our new baker. Elliot, Mama Maudene Pickering."

Elliot took the worn hand the old lady offered in both of his. "It's a pleasure to meet you, ma'am."

"He's a Texas boy," Lucy confided. "We're trying to break him of that *ma'am* habit, but it's awfully hard."

"Oh, shoot, a boy as handsome as this one is can call me anything, just as long as he calls me." With a great laugh, Mama picked up a pottery dish from the nearby table and held it out. "Now, do you know how to keep this going?"

He reached out, but she continued to hold on to it. "Yes, ma'am—Mama. Feed it twice a day if it's kept out and once a week if it's refrigerated. Let it rest after each feeding and come to room temperature before using it."

"All right." She let go then, entrusting the starter to him. "The stuff in that bowl is older than you by twice. You take care of it, and it'll take care of you."

"I promise I will."

She picked up a bottle and handed it to Lucy. "Bennie said you were talking about adding pulled pork sandwiches to the menu. Sweet Spirit—best barbecue sauce you'll ever have. Made right here in Oklahoma. And you see the name, you can't help but think of the song." In a clear voice, she sang, *"There's a sweet, sweet Spirit in this place…"*

Elliot harmonized with her on the next line of the old gospel tune. *"And I know that it's the Spirit of the Lord."*

"You've got a voice, son." Mama gave him a long, approving look. "You and I are going to be great friends."

"I think we are," he agreed. That was exactly what he wanted, what he missed most about home: personal connections. Friends, neighbors, buddies, co-workers. A bunch of little strings to tie him to the place; the more, the better.

After a few more minutes of chatting, he and Lucy returned to the car. She drove to the end of the street, showing him where Bennie and Calvin lived, and Calvin's parents and grandmother, then she took Patricia's street back to the bakery so he could find his way that evening.

A lot of little strings. And right in the middle of them, a big one that led to Fia. It was a little thin now, but with each shared contact, it would twine and braid and become too strong to break.

On his lunch break, he called her and left a voice mail. After work, he called again. On his way to Patricia's, he tried again. It was a good thing he wasn't insecure, or he'd be wondering if he'd done something wrong last night.

Like maybe she hadn't liked the way he kissed, except he'd *felt* her response, and it hadn't been disappointment.

After dinner with its discussions of menu items and an enthusiastic tasting of the Sweet Spirit sauce—Lucy had gone home with the intent of ordering it by the gallon—he was halfway to Fia's house before he even realized it. Her car was in the driveway, and a dim light showed through the living room windows. He sat there a moment, thinking about going to the door, knocking, interrupting her just long enough to say good night and have a chance to kiss her again, but reasons not to presented themselves in order: It was only eight thirty, but he had to get up at three thirty; Mouse had been in the apartment by herself all day and needed attention; it had been only twenty-four hours since he'd seen Fia. He didn't want to seem clingy. And she hadn't returned any of his three phone calls.

After a moment, he eased his foot off the brake and drove away.

He and Mouse were racing down the stairs to the door for a walk when his cell phone rang. For just an instant, his heart rate increased, then returned instantly to normal. "Hey, older sister."

"Hey, little brother. I just saw your text that you got a job, and at a bakery. I always figured you'd wind up in the food service industry someday."

"Yeah, but you thought I'd be bussing tables, didn't you?"

Emily's laugh made him feel good and miss her at the same time. "I thought you'd do whatever you needed to do. Isn't that the Ross family motto?"

"Just for the record, I have bussed tables a few times when we're busy. I've run the register, too, and mopped up at the end of the day." With his shoulder, he pushed open the heavy door, then followed Mouse out into the cool night. She'd discovered a park one block down the street and one over, and it was the only place she headed when she was out.

"I talked to Mom after I got your text. She said tell you congratulations, and the kids said to tell you that they're trying to finagle a road trip to Six Flags Over Texas when school is out, with a stop by to see you."

"That'd be great. I'm off Sundays and maybe another day depending on how the shop's doing. You'll see why I like Tallgrass."

"Hey, I might even want to move there myself. School will be out. The kids will be running wild."

"They always run wild. But when they get older and begin acting like human beings, you're gonna miss the hellions."

Though if he stayed here, it wouldn't make him anything but happy to have his sister move her family here. Then their parents would feel left out, so they could probably be persuaded to pack up and move, too. And then they could all have the same home again.

"If you decide to do that, let me know. I'll even clean my apartment and put out the air mattress for you."

"Don't you know your nieces and nephew would adore the opportunity to have a sleepover at Uncle Elliot's while their mom and dad sneak off to nice hotel?" Emily asked with a wistful sigh.

"It's a deal. I'll put them in the Murphy bed, and I'll even let them out the next morning."

Dusk had settled enough that the park was empty, the swings were still, and the seesaws sat empty, tilted every which way. There was no laughter, no excited squeals, no worn-out cries or impatient voices. Elliot followed Mouse across the damp grass, her nose only a half inch above the ground and her rump wiggling at the thrill of new scents.

Emily had been quiet long enough that he'd figured one of the kids had claimed her attention when her voice spoke, strong and teasing, in his ear. "If we do come, we'll also get to meet Fia. I think the last girlfriend I met of yours was the one after the crazy chick trying to crack your skull open. She was...Australian?"

He winced. "English. Chelsea." They'd met in the airport; he was coming home on leave, and she was on her first solo trip to the United States. They'd hit it off, and she'd tagged along to West Texas with him, where she'd gotten out of the car on a miserable dry 100-plus-degree day, giving everything in view—buildings, people, and animals—a disgusted look, then spouted the foulest complaint he'd ever heard from a woman.

"When she heard me say *Texas* and *ranch*, she expected something like that old TV show, *Dallas*. I warned her it was nothing like that, but..." He shrugged as Mouse circled to find the blades of grass best suited for her business, then squatted.

"I'm guessing you'd never have to apologize for Fia like that."

"No." He couldn't imagine Fia ever deliberately insulting anyone in language that would make a battle-hardened soldier blush.

Mouse kicked her feet, sending clods of grass flying, and he turned her toward home. "Hey," he said, working at sounding casual, "how many phone calls make a guy needy or, worse, creepy?"

"You could never be creepy, El. How many have you made?"

"Three today."

"Eh, just to be safe, give it a rest tonight. Try her again tomorrow." After a moment, she asked, "Trouble?"

"Nope. Just I took her home last night, kissed her, and she didn't return my calls today."

She snorted, and in the background, one of his nieces mimicked the sound in an increasingly louder voice. "People have lives. They've got jobs, people to see, things to do. But I think it's sweet you're worried."

"Not worried, just—" With a grunt, he broke off. "Thanks for calling, Em."

"I hate you."

"I hate you more."

As he slid his phone into his pocket and urged Mouse into a trot, he hoped Emily did come for a visit. He missed her and Bill and the kids. He wanted them to see that he was contented.

And it couldn't hurt to show Fia what a totally normal, affectionate family he came from, could it?

\* \* \*

It was nearly ten o'clock when Fia lowered herself onto the couch Thursday morning. She needed a shower, and even as short as it was, her hair had somehow twisted into a rat's nest. She hadn't gotten dressed since Tuesday night, still wearing the same shirt Jessy had helped her into then. She felt like crap warmed over, her muscles hurting, her head thick and cottony the way she used to get with a hangover, and emotionally she felt hungover, too.

Her stomach was unsettled, but warm tea with lemon and honey usually helped with that, and she had a cup on the coffee table. Her cell phone sat there, too, silent all morning except for a call from Ilena to check up on her. No more calls from Elliot. She should be grateful not to get calls that she shouldn't answer, but instead she just felt a little blue.

She curled on the couch, resting her head on the sofa arm, and drew a deep breath that smelled of Jessy. Her friend had spent the night on the sofa Tuesday, just a call or a groan away from the bed. Ilena had fussed over Fia in her sweet, loving mamacita way until the medication had kicked in, then Jessy had done it in her no-nonsense mushy-soft-but-not-gonna-admit-it way until the next afternoon.

*You're lucky to have them,* Scott's voice whispered.

"I know."

*And they're lucky to have you.*

She snorted and almost spilled her tea. "And what do I bring to the table, huh? I'm a mess."

*You're a mess they love. Besides, that's not who you are. It's what's going on with you right now. When you get the right doctor, the right diagnosis, you'll be the same smart, capable, independent, beautiful girl you've always been.*

Her hand shaking, she wiped her eyes on her shirtsleeve. She didn't want to cry. It turned her eyes and nose puffy and red and gave her a headache that wouldn't shake loose until tomorrow. "Scott, I can't..." *Can't talk about this. Can't talk to a spirit who's gone and never coming back. Can't even think about what seems like such slim reason to hope.*

*Can't, can't, can't,* he gently mocked. *You say that often enough, and people are going to believe it.* You're *going to believe it. Just remember, warrior girls don't give up. Ever.*

Blindly she located a tissue and dabbed at her eyes, then blew her nose. She knew people who needed a good cry now and then to stay balanced, but not her. Damn straight she was a warrior girl—maybe someday soon even a warrior woman, she thought with a wry smile—and nothing was going to change that. Not headaches, not muscle spasms, not tears, not crappy parents, not husbands who died too damn soon.

She was a survivor.

She'd finished the tea and was wondering if her stomach could handle a bit of food when a knock came at the door. Before she could do more than think about standing, the door opened a few inches and Lucy peeked in. "Hey, sweetie, can I come in?"

"Please." Fia straightened herself a little bit and tugged the afghan from the back of the couch to cover up. "Oh, my gosh, you smell good."

"Eau de fresh bread." Lucy held up a bag in one hand. "Do you think we could bottle and sell it?"

"I'd buy it for sure." Fresh bread, mixed, kneaded, and shaped by Elliot's talented hands. She would like to watch him bake a batch sometime. To see an incredibly sexy man working in a kitchen, putting his marvelous muscles into making marvelous foods...sigh...

"This other bag has a bowl of potato soup. I left out the bacon and the onions, so it might not taste as good as usual, but it's got lots of potatoes, cream, and cheese. Can I put your lunch together for you?"

Fia started to push the afghan away, to insist that she could do it herself, but Lucy gave her a chastising look.

"Don't make me call Ilena over here. I've seen her feed John. She's like a drill sergeant. That boy eats no matter what kind of mood he's in."

"Please," Fia said, gesturing to the kitchen as she settled in again. "Do whatever you need." She watched Lucy set the bags on the counter, locate dishes and napkins, fill a glass with iced tea, scoop a bit of margarine onto the bread plate. After setting up a TV tray, she brought the meal in and set it within easy reach for Fia.

She opted for a bite of bread first. It was a small brown loaf, buttery and yeasty and nutty and soft, and it dazzled her taste buds, both satisfying them and making them want more.

Lucy grinned as she broke off a larger piece. "Can you believe that gorgeous, sexy man can bake like that? You know how fast talk spreads in Tallgrass. Every single woman and foodie in town is making their way to Prairie Harts. I've seen the owners of two of the other bakeries taking home loaves of his bread."

"I'm not surprised." Fia wiped her fingers on a napkin, then took a bite of the warm soup. It wasn't as fabulous as Lucy's loaded potato soup, but it was still delicious and exactly what her stomach needed. After another bite, she hesitantly asked, "How is Elliot working out?"

"He's great. We couldn't have found a better baker if we'd put in a customized order for one." Lucy moved from the couch to sit on the coffee table, facing Fia. "Though I do think he's wondering why you're not taking his calls. He asked both Patricia and me about you last night, and again this morning."

Fia scooped up a chunk of potato, dripping cheddar, and slid it into her mouth. Finally she met Lucy's gaze. "You know why. He thinks I'm—I'm *normal* and can do all the things that all his other girlfriends have done, and I can't. I fell facedown on the damn floor Tuesday night and had to call Jessy and Ilena to get me into bed. Do you know how helpless I felt? How stupid and careless?"

"*Not* stupid or careless. People have health issues, Fia. Dane loses his balance and falls sometimes. And look at me. Can you imagine how I'm going to look in my beautiful wedding dress with bruises everywhere?" She extended her arms, showing black, blue, and purple from her knuckles all the way up to her sleeves.

"Dane had his leg amputated. You had a heart attack. Your medication causes that."

"So we've got diagnoses. You don't—yet. But you know what? When you get a diagnosis, or even if they never figure it out, no one's going to love you any less. We didn't fall in love with your zero percent body fat or your agility or your strength, and I seriously doubt that's what Elliot's thinking about when he looks at you."

Fia grudgingly admitted, "I don't look nearly as good as I did two years ago."

"Two years ago I was so jealous of you. You were solid and strong and your muscles were sleek and impressive, and there I was, overweight and so out of shape that I hyperventilated at the thought of exercise."

"But you lost that weight and you're in shape now and you're beautiful, and Joe *always* thought you were beautiful."

Lucy's familiar new smile—the soft, wondrous, living-a-dream one—brightened her face. "He did, didn't he?"

Fia nodded.

"See?" The smile turned smug. "You don't have to be

perfect for a man to fall in love with you. You think Elliot's perfect?"

*"Yes."* With a warming inside that didn't come from the food, Fia went on. "He's smart, funny, handsome, sexy, and talented. He has a gorgeous voice. He loves his family and his dog. He's sweet and kind and protective. He knows who he is, who he's always been, who he'll always be. He's satisfied with his life."

"Yeah, you've got a good point—a bunch of 'em. So don't you think he's smart enough and responsible enough and grown-up enough to know who he wants to go out with?"

Fia polished off the last of the soup, then leaned back, feet tucked beneath her, and plucked a bite from the bread. "It's not fair of me to get involved with him without telling him what's wrong with me. But if I tell him what's wrong, things will change. He'll treat me differently, look at me differently, *feel* differently. He'll feel . . . obligated."

Lucy's expression softened with sympathy that could be Fia's undoing. "And you can't bear the idea of someone feeling obligated to care for you."

Slowly Fia shook her head. "My mother told me my whole life that I was a burden. She hated me for that, Lucy, and I promised myself when I left home that I would never be a burden to anyone else again." She inhaled deeply, and even though her stomach was full, the aroma of the bread tempted her to take another bite. "I've enjoyed being with Elliot, just being a pretty woman going out with a great guy who's happy to see me. For the first time in ages, I feel like the real me."

Damn, she missed the real Fia, the bold one who'd never met a situation she couldn't face head-on, who didn't care what other people thought of her, who saw what she wanted and went after it.

She popped the last bite of bread into her mouth, and Lucy stood, carrying the dishes to the kitchen, rinsing them in the sink, putting away the folding tray. "I've got to get back to the shop. Our special today is grilled cheese sandwiches on Elliot's brioche and potato soup, and I did as much as I could to get ahead of the crowd, but he and Patricia will be needing my help soon." Bending, she hugged Fia tightly, then went to the door.

There, she turned back. "You can't just cut off contact with him, Fee. He doesn't deserve that. And a guy who makes you feel like the real you doesn't come along every day. That deserves a chance. And you know what?

"For most people, loving someone is about way more than just the issues. Carly didn't walk away from Dane when he finally told her the truth about his leg. Bennie didn't break up with Calvin because of his PTSD. Finding out Jessy was an alcoholic didn't change the way Dalton and the rest of us loved her, and Joe didn't get all freaked out by the idea of being in love with a chubby woman who'd just had a heart attack." She paused to let that sink in. "Elliot deserves a chance. This relationship deserves a chance. It's still so new that there's no telling where it's going. He may be the one, or this may run its course before you have to tell him anything. It could last forever or just be one very sweet memory. Don't go ending it before you find out."

# Chapter 7

The law office where Marti worked was unusually quiet when she stretched, then rose from her chair. Most of the staff went out to lunch, though there were a few who brought meals from home, trying to save money or watching their diet. Another few usually ordered in delivery, and a couple of women in IT used their lunchtime to power-walk around downtown.

Today, it seemed, everyone had gone out. She heard no distant music or television coming from the break room, no conversation, no tapping on a computer keyboard from any of the offices or cubicles. As she padded down the hall to refill her coffee mug with the super-premium coffee in the break room, she glanced at empty desks and quiet machines. At night, it would be kind of spooky—she'd seen too many movies where danger lurked in dark and abandoned offices.

But it was the middle of the day, and she wasn't at

all the sort to startle during the day. Sunlight was her superpower.

As she crossed the intersection with the main corridor, she glanced toward the lobby and came to an abrupt stop. A cowboy, hat in hand, was standing near the reception desk, gazing at the artwork around the office. She saw the collection of Native American art so often that she rarely paid it attention anymore. It was just always there.

Dillon Smith was paying it plenty of attention. Heels clicking on tile, she walked up to stand beside him in front of a sculpture by—

"Willard Stone," he murmured. "I can't believe this plain old building in downtown Tallgrass has a Stone sculpture."

"Three of them, actually. There's one in each of the founding partners' offices. Are you a fan of his?"

He glanced at her then. "Aren't you?"

She studied the gleaming wood figure, tall, slender, a woman, nude. It flowed in Art Deco style, sleek and free. "It's not something I would want in my house," she admitted, "but it's pretty."

He smiled, such an unexpected action that she blinked to be sure she was actually seeing it. "A Willard Stone pretty. You underwhelm with praise."

She followed him when he moved to the right. "Do you think the Blue Eagle is pretty?" he asked. "And the Crumbo?"

Her gaze shifted to the signatures: Acee Blue Eagle and Woody Crumbo. She hadn't ever known the artists' names and wasn't sure she'd ever heard them before. "They're a little, um, fanciful for my tastes. I do like the baskets and the beadwork." They crossed past the front entrance to the other side, where a half-dozen baskets filled two display cases and intricate beaded pieces were framed on the wall in glass boxes.

"Mavis Doering and Lois Smoky here in an office building."

"We do have good security," she remarked. "I thought it was because our files are filled with confidential information. Now I know it's the art that's important."

Marti walked with him as he studied every other piece on display, waiting until they reached their starting point to speak again. "It appears everyone went to lunch and left the office unmanned except for me. Can I help you with something?"

He faced her, his gaze sliding from the top of her hair, pinned into a knot on the back of her head, over her gray dress with its matching jacket all the way down to her pink-polished toes in darker gray shoes. Though the dress was flattering enough and perfectly suited for work, she couldn't help thinking that maybe Cadence was right. Maybe she did need some clothing options that weren't quite so classic... and bland... and modest.

"I don't have an appointment." His gaze came back to her face. "I came in to pick up some tractor parts and stopped by on the spur of the moment." He looked away, stepped away as if he was thinking about bolting for the door.

"As I said, everyone's out right now, but if you'd like an appointment, I can make one for you. I need an idea of what it's about so I can know which of our lawyers would be best for you."

He took another step back. "I don't know... I don't even know if there's anything... I guess I just need some advice."

She should go to the receptionist's desk and open the schedule, encourage him to meet with one of the attorneys. That was exactly what she would do if he were some stranger off the streets. But he wasn't, and she didn't. "Listen, Dillon, I'm not a lawyer. I'm a paralegal. But if you just want advice, maybe I can give it, off the record, on my lunch break, no charge, just two friends talking." Recognizing the reluctance that flashed across his face and feeling a bit of it herself at her use of the word *friends*, she quietly added, "I'm very good at keeping confidences."

He was silent a long time, long enough for her to hear voices of returning co-workers entering through the back door. As they drew nearer, she could tell one belonged to Sasha, the receptionist, who should have stayed behind to cover the desk. Marti was glad she hadn't. Sasha was beautiful, single, and there was nothing subdued or quietly elegant about her. She loved men in general, soldiers and cowboys in particular, and she could promise a good time with nothing more than a look from her big baby blue eyes.

Though why Marti should care whether Sasha showed Dillon a good time was totally unfathomable. Sure, he could take a woman's breath away, and there was zero doubt he delivered on his good-time promises, too. But he seemed...unsure. Vulnerable. And though legitimately they were much more acquaintances than friends, she thought he had enough going on inside him that he didn't need an overwhelming dose of Sasha right now.

Good thing Marti could be *under*whelming.

As the returning workers reached the broad corridor that bisected the building, Dillon shrugged. "Okay. Is there someplace private?"

Total privacy was a hard thing to find in a coffee shop or restaurant, unless they opted for someplace like Sage, with its super-spendy prices. They would never turn away a work-stained cowboy—in Oklahoma, one could never tell if he was just a cowboy or the millionaire oilman who owned the ranch—but she didn't think Dillon would be comfortable there, at least not today. Maybe not with her.

"My house is a few miles from here. We can pick up lunch and enjoy the day on the patio."

Sasha came around the corner, and a smile spread across her face. Before she could even say hello, Dillon began backing away. "I'll pick up food and meet you there. I know where it is."

After putting her purse in the bottom desk drawer, Sasha straightened and gave Marti a speculative look. "You and a cowboy. I never would have guessed that."

Marti opened her mouth to tell her they were just acquaintances, that until the past week, they'd hardly even spoken to each other, but some devil inside made her close it again and smile. "I'm taking my lunch now. I'll be back soon."

*   *   *

By the time Dillon picked up soup and sandwiches at Prairie Harts and drove to Marti's house, her SUV was already parked in the driveway. He sat there a moment, wondering what the hell he was doing. He'd known she worked for a law firm. Why hadn't he asked Jessy which one before he just walked into the biggest one in town?

Because Jessy would have wanted to know why, and he couldn't have told her.

But could he do anything stupider than telling everything to one of her friends?

Probably not. But it wasn't the first time he'd been stupid, and it wouldn't be the last. Besides, he'd believed Marti when she'd said she would keep his secrets. She worked for lawyers; she understood confidentiality and privilege. More than that, though, his gut instinct said she was the sort of person who kept her word.

She lived in a nice neighborhood, though he'd come to realize after years of traveling that *all* of Tallgrass's neighborhoods were nice compared to the places he'd seen. Some were more expensive, some older, some a little messier, but overall, the worst part of town was only moderately worse than the best part.

Her house was white with black shutters, pots of spring flowers flanking the steps, with a good-sized porch with rockers to have coffee or dessert and get to know the neighbors. Not something he could quite imagine Marti doing.

The front door was standing open a few inches. Ignoring the silent invitation, he rapped, the force pushing it open a few more inches, and Marti stepped into the hallway. "Hi. Come on back. Ooh, Prairie Harts. When you feel obligated to support your friends' new business, isn't it wonderful when the business is so fabulous that you'd go there regardless of who owned it?"

He tried not to look around too much as he walked through, catching glimpses of antiques, subtle colors, order. He wondered how big a pep talk she would have to give herself to cross the threshold of the old one-room cabin where he was currently living.

She offered coffee, water, or pop, then chose water for herself before leading the way out the back door. The yard was a nice size, fenced in, the brick patio pretty much taken over by an antique table and chairs of serious substance.

His only outdoor furniture consisted of a folding chair he'd bought at Walmart.

She sat at one end, and he took the chair at a right angle to her. He traded her soup and a sandwich for a can of pop, and they spent the first few minutes uncovering their food, opening their drinks, taking first bites. It was…odd. They could have been two strangers at a busy restaurant, sharing the only table available but having no intention of sharing anything else.

She immediately disputed that. "What's going on, Dillon?"

He took his time chewing the bite of sandwich in his mouth. After swallowing it, he drank the pop, then dried his mouth and wiped his hands. All stall tactics exhausted, he drew a deep breath. "This is confidential, right?"

She nodded.

"I—I'm looking for someone. She's six years old. Last I knew, she lived in South Dakota, but maybe now it's Wyoming or maybe Montana." He'd gotten a call from BB this morning that his questions had garnered him less than no information. What little he had learned had conflicted everything else. "Her name is Delilah, but she prefers Lilah, and…she's my daughter." He pulled the most recent photo he had from his wallet and laid it on the table between them.

Marti wiped her fingers before picking it up, her forehead wrinkling as she studied the picture. Lilah was three in it, wearing pink overalls with a white shirt and a pint-sized cowboy hat, and she smiled broadly as she pressed her cheek against his. She'd been so small and warm against his body, so full of energy and love, a lot of it directed to her mother on the other side of the camera.

After a few moments, Marti handed the picture back. "Is this a custody dispute?"

"No. I just want to know where she is. If she's okay. I'd like to see her once in a while if I could, but no, I won't ask for custody."

"Is she living with her mother?"

"Her grandparents and her aunt."

"Do they have legal custody of her? Where is her mother?"

Dillon sprawled back in the chair, his appetite gone, his stomach unsure it would keep down what he'd already eaten. He ran his fingers through his hair, then pressed the pad of his thumb hard into the inside corner of his left eye to ease the pain pounding there. "Tina and I liked to party," he said flatly, gaze fixed on the worn wood surface of the table. "We left Lilah with her grandparents one Saturday night so we could go out. It was my turn to be the designated driver, and I stuck to it. I drank pop all night. But when we left to go home...The bar was about eight miles out of town on a road that was pretty much deserted. One of the guys challenged me to a race. I know it's stupid, but we were stupid. We'd done that kind of stuff before, just for bragging rights. Tina was pushing me on—like me, she liked taking chances—so I did it. And I lost control on an S curve and wound up in a field, plowed into the only tree there. I walked away, but Tina...she had severe head injuries. The week before my trial began, she...she died. I was convicted on manslaughter charges and went to prison for eighteen months."

He exhaled deeply, ducking his head, squeezing his eyes

shut. He'd never told anyone that story. Everyone in Tina's family and those involved with the trial knew all about it, but after coming back here, he'd intended to take the details to his grave...until Lilah's birthday had come around. Until she started visiting his dreams. Until he couldn't ignore the big, empty hole ripped out of his life any longer.

He dragged in another deep breath and forced himself to meet Marti's gaze. "Lilah's mother is dead, and I'm the one responsible for it, and I haven't seen my little girl since."

\* \* \*

Elliot was feeling pretty damn weak when he got off work Thursday afternoon. He'd snagged an Italian loaf he'd made that morning, stopped by the grocery store to pick up other ingredients, and was trying to talk himself out of going to Fia's house. He'd managed not to call her all day. Patricia and Lucy had both just shrugged and said she was probably tied up with end-of-month work for the gym, but Lucy had quickly looked away when she said it. God love her, he appreciated a woman who couldn't tell a lie without cringing away from it.

Though maybe it hadn't been totally a lie. It was the beginning of May. Maybe Fia was just tying up all the loose ends of April for her boss. She didn't love paperwork, so maybe she'd just been too tired to pick up the phone when she was done.

Yeah, like the girl who ran 10Ks would be worn out by schedules and salaries and taxes.

In the end, he lost the argument with himself. He took the back streets from the grocery store to the apartment complex, turned onto her block, and pulled into the driveway. Her car sat in the same place, and the blinds were still closed. He knocked at the door a couple of times, then considered leaving a note for her. That said what?

Feeling grim, he returned to the truck and drove home, telling himself there was no reason to be down. His plans really hadn't changed. He was going to make muffaletta sandwiches for dinner, maybe watch a little TV, then go to bed early. He'd just be sharing the sandwiches with Mouse instead of the date he'd hoped to have, and that was okay.

He parked in the lot behind the building, gathered the food, and circled through the grass to the front. The building had a back door that was more convenient to the parking, but the owner had boarded it over. Probably his lazy idea of tightening security.

Walking around the corner to the broad steps, Elliot came to a sudden stop, and that grim feeling disappeared— *poof!*—like that.

"Hey." Fia was sitting at the top of the steps, wearing shorts and high-top shoes, a T-shirt from one of those races she'd run, and a hoodie, and she was shifting a little nervously, her gaze making contact with him only for seconds before moving away, then back.

"Hey." He smiled, brushed his hair back, and wished he'd had a chance to shower and change and maybe shave again.

"Are you mad?" she asked in a little voice.

"Mad? No, of course not. Maybe confused, but Emily will tell you I'm easy to confuse." What he really wanted to do was scoop her up and plant one hell of a kiss on her, but instead he set the bags to one side and crouched a few steps below her. "Are you okay?"

"Yeah. I just…" Finally she fixed on gaze on his. "I just

needed a little time." Her expression was a little sad, a little nervous, a little anxious, a little... worried.

He touched her knee the way he would a skittish animal, gentle and tentative. "You can tell me that. I mean, I got the hint after the first few calls, but seriously, you can just tell me and I'll go away for a bit. I know this is all kind of..." Sudden. Intense. Surprising. Moving way faster than either of them had expected. Getting way more serious than he had expected, and he'd fallen in love at least a dozen times.

"I know. It's just all so new." She shrugged her slender shoulders. "I don't want to make a mistake."

"You? Nah, I thought you were perfect."

A small laugh escaped. "That's what Lucy and I agreed about you. By the way, that brown bread of yours was incredible."

So that was who Lucy had taken lunch to. Checking on her? Making sure he hadn't done anything stupid or wrong? He didn't mind. Lucy had known Fia far longer than he had, and she was such a mothering sort.

He nodded toward the bags. "My Italian loaf is just as good. Add salami and cheese and olives, and you've got the best sandwich you'll find in Tallgrass. Want to share it with us?"

Finally her regular smile appeared, and his day brightened considerably. "I'd like to."

He grabbed the bags, stood, and offered her a hand. She was so slender that pulling her to her feet required practically no effort. She winced a bit when she was standing, and he scanned her legs. "What'd you do to your knee?"

She looked down at the scrape, and her face flushed. "I, uh, tripped. Bare skin doesn't slide on wood floors like clothed skin does."

"Want me to carry you up the stairs?" He expected an automatic no, but she studied him instead.

"You'd really do that, wouldn't you?"

"Sure. Well, this time it would have to be a piggyback ride. Emily's kids say mine are the best ever, but they're not always honest. They can be bought for a candy bar and a trip to the park."

"I can climb the stairs," Fia said, but even as she spoke, she slipped her hand into his free one.

It sent a rush of warmth through to his gut, but he played it cool as they climbed the stairs, then walked through the door. "This building reminds me of the school I went to down in Texas."

"Grade school, middle school, or high school?"

"Uh-huh." He laughed when the answer caught her off guard, making her blink. "The kids in our school came from all the surrounding communities, and there still weren't enough of us to need more space than this. Do you remember Garth Brooks's song, 'Nobody Gets Off in This Town'?"

*"The Greyhound stops and somebody gets on,"* she sang.

*"But nobody gets off in this town,"* he finished for her. "That's my town. Right down to the old, mean dog and the high school colors being brown."

"Really?"

His grin widened. "Nah. We had a couple mean dogs, and our high school didn't have colors." He paced his steps to hers, watching for any sign that her knee was hurting. The more they climbed, though, the more fluid her movements were. Must have just gotten stiff while waiting for him.

Waiting for *him*. He liked that.

On the second floor, he opened the door to find Mouse sitting politely, tail wagging, ears pricked. "She likes to pretend she's been waiting here for me all day, but if you go over and feel the middle of the bed, it'll be as warm as a heating pad."

"Hey, Mouse, pretty girl." Fia bent and scratched between her ears, then along her spine as the pup wriggled happily.

He set the bags on the kitchen counter, came back, and picked up the leash. "I've got to take her out for a quick run. You want to come or wait here?"

"I'll wait here."

"We'll make it quick. I don't often get to come home to a pretty female waiting."

She loosely laid her hands over Mouse's ears. "Don't say that. You'll hurt Mouse's feelings."

"A pretty woman," he corrected. "We'll be back however quick she chooses to take. Make yourself comfortable."

He and the dog ran down the stairs, burst out the doors, and turned toward the park. "Okay, Mouse, I did you a solid last week. You do me one, will you? Don't take forever with this."

\* \* \*

There were only two options for making herself comfortable: sitting in one of the two camp chairs, the kind that folded into a long tube of a bag that could be slung over one's shoulder, or on the bed. Since the bed felt just a little bit bold—something pre-Scott Fia would have done—she chose one of the chairs, the canvas shifting and adjusting beneath her. It was as comfortable as the fat armchair in her living room, at least for sitting. Curling up in it was out of the question.

Coming over here had been a big deal for her: leaving her car at home, walking the broad sidewalks, trusting her feet to stay flat and her body not to give out. She hadn't gone for a walk by herself in so long that she couldn't even remember it. Of course, whenever it was, she hadn't expected it to be the last time or she would have paid more attention.

But right now she felt great. She'd kept her pace easy but steady, pretending that she was taking in the lovely weather and newly leafed trees and lush lawns and bright-colored flowers. She hadn't pushed herself, and she'd kept her cell phone in hand in case she needed to call one of the girls. It had given her a rush, even more than driving herself to the pharmacy last Friday night. She didn't get to make many stabs at independence, so this was an accomplishment.

Though the place still looked a little bare, Elliot had unpacked. A television sat on two stacked boxes marked *Books*, and a dozen photographs hung on the walls, along with a couple of citations from his Army days. His clothes were neatly stacked in laundry baskets in the corner, and a guitar case leaned in another corner. Books lined the front windowsill: a few cookbooks but mostly biographies— George S. Patton, Omar Bradley, Norman Schwarzkopf. A fat binder, worn from heavy use, sat beside them. Grandma's cookbook?

The man traveled light. Necessary, she guessed, when he didn't stay anywhere for any great length of time. He seemed to really like Tallgrass, though—the town, his job, the people...her. But had he felt like that about other towns in the beginning? Had there been other jobs he loved, other friends, other women like her?

Women, yes, obviously. People in general were programmed to want those close relationships. Women like her? She preferred to think not for good reasons. Not just because she had this beast of an illness inside her.

His footsteps on the stairs began sounding about halfway up. Just before he reached the door, the click of Mouse's paws joined in. The door swung open, and the dog ran inside, sliding to a crouch in front of Fia, lifting her front feet to Fia's knees. "Were you a good girl?" she asked, grasping the dog around the middle and lifting her onto her lap. Mouse licked her face, turned once, and sat down.

"She's looking at me like she won the prize and I lost." Elliot hung the leash on a hook near the door, then grabbed some clothes and disappeared into the bathroom. Mouse leaped down to follow him. A couple minutes, and he was back in fresh jeans and a T-shirt that he was pulling over his head as he walked. Sometimes Fia had teased that she'd become a personal trainer because she so deeply admired the torsos of hard-bodied men. Shoulders, chest, abdomen, hips, spine, arms...Wasn't it amazing the way the skin flowed so silkenly over the ripples and hard angles of rib bones, clavicles, the humerus and collarbones? Pure art.

And if all those buff men she'd worked with over the years were works of art, then Elliot was the work of the grandest artist of all.

His head poked through the neck hole, and he grinned at her. "Did you see enough, or do I need to pull it off again?"

"I'm good for now," she assured him. Rising, she carried her chair closer to the kitchen, where she could watch him work.

He washed his hands, then emptied the shopping bags on the counter. With a flourish, he presented the paper-wrapped bread loaf to her, and she breathed deeply of its warm tantalizing taste. "Yumm. It's so pretty. I'd hate to cut into it."

"After you taste it, you won't care about the cutting. You been to New Orleans?"

"Scott and I spent a few days there on our way to Oklahoma."

"Have a muffaletta?"

She shook her head.

"It's spicy meat, cheeses, lots of olives and pimientos. Sound like too much? 'Cause I can make you something else. I saw some nice turkey breast at the deli, or I have eggs in the refrigerator."

Fia went to look at the meat—salami and ham—and the mozzarella and provolone cheeses. "They'll be fine. Sometimes I'll get a headache where just the thought of spicy food makes me queasy, but tonight I'm fine." That was the truth, as far as it went. And that was as far as she was willing to go right now.

He rewarded her with his cowboy charmer grin. "Just for that, I'll make us a small dish of bread pudding for dessert. We had some of yesterday's chocolate pastries left over, so I thought I'd see how they work in bread pudding."

"Can I help?"

"Yep. Just sit there where I can see you and look pretty."

"I'll do my best." She settled in, fluffing her hair, crossing her legs. "How was your day?"

"It was already good, but it got great about twenty minutes ago. How was yours?"

"Meh. I'm not in love with paperwork, but someone's got to do it."

He glanced up from dicing black and green olives along with pimientos. "Do you plan on going back to training at some point?"

*If I ever get well.* But that wasn't an answer she could give him—*soon*, she promised herself—so she shrugged. "I really don't know what I want to do. Becoming a trainer was really a case of me getting in shape and going all gung-ho with it, not something that I'd always thought, 'Hey, I want to be that when I grow up.'"

"Sort of like the newest Christian preaches the loudest."

New knowledge, new life, great desire to spread the word. "Yeah, I think so."

"What did you want to do when you were little?"

It was a shame she had to consider the question so long. Didn't everyone remember at least one thing they'd wanted to be when they grew up? But she could recall only one, and it wasn't a thing but a place: away from her family.

"I wanted to be a championship bull rider," he said while waiting for her. "I did some bull riding and won some prizes. Then I figured that so far I'd been damn lucky in walking away unharmed, and I didn't want to be there when the luck ran out. Beyond that, I wanted to do my stint in the Army, and then I wanted to go back to the ranch, work with my dad until he and Mom retired, then run the place with Emily and Bill. But life had other plans."

That could be her personal motto: *Life has other plans.* "What do Emily and Bill do now?"

"She works in hospital administration, and he works for the Department of Fish and Game."

"And they've got three kids?"

"Amelia, Cecilia, and Theodore." Elliot made a face, and she felt the *ouch* herself.

"Do they at least call him Teddy?"

"Nope. No Theo, either. The first full sentence he ever said was, 'It's Thee-o-door.' And believe it or not, there's another Theodore in his class this year." Switching knives, he pulled out the round loaf of bread and sliced it horizontally before laying it on a baking sheet. "Schoolteacher?"

She looked up from the pillowy softness inside the loaf. "Me? A schoolteacher? Oh, hell, no. I hated school. In my neighborhood, it was more of a prep school for prison."

"Nurse?"

"Don't like needles."

"Astronaut?"

"I get airsick."

"Lawyer? Skydiver? Circus clown?"

Laughing, she made a ding-ding sound. "You got me. My dream was to run away and join the circus. Travel, fun, good food, meeting strange and interesting people...What could be better?"

He spread the meats, cheeses, and olive salad on the bread, then slid it into the hot oven. Wiping his hands on a towel, he came toward her, pulling her from the chair, wrapping his arms around her. "I have to say, I'm glad you didn't. I was startled by a clown at a rodeo when I was little, and ever since, red noses, wigs, and big feet have freaked me out."

"I'll make a note of that for next Halloween." Then she

heard herself, felt a squeeze around her heart, and said, "If you're..."

"If I'm still here?" He grew serious, brushing his hand gently across her hair, his gaze softening in a tender way that threatened to melt her in his arms. "Darlin', I can't imagine being anywhere else."

\* \* \*

Sunday was Elliot's first day off, and he rewarded himself by sleeping in until six, then taking Mouse for a run. It wasn't by design that he found himself in a familiar maze of apartments and duplexes, but he didn't turn the other way at any of the opportunities he had. Fia's street was quiet, the only noise the occasional flapping of a flag in the breeze. He didn't need to ask to know that a lot of soldiers lived in the complex. He'd lived in similar places himself: manageable on an Army salary, close to the fort, a good place for people who shared common interests and obligations.

As they jogged past Fia's house, Mouse's nose began twitching and she tried to turn into the driveway. "You're a sucker for her, too, aren't you?" he asked, keeping her moving despite her desire to stop. "We're gonna see her later today. Lunch, remember?"

She'd offered to fix the meal this time at her place—said she would even buy a banana and some caramel sauce to put on his peanut butter—but he wanted to take her out instead. His savings had dwindled past the point where he would normally put himself on a very strict budget, but he'd decided to indulge in this one splurge. After all, he had a job, a paycheck due in a week, and if things got really tight, he could live off the recipe tasting he did and the left-overs at the bakery.

Though things wouldn't get that tight. *God willing and the creek don't rise,* Grandma would have added to that.

When he and Mouse reached Main Street, he slowed to a walk. The pup loved to run, but she wasn't as used to it as he was, and she still needed some weight on her. They were waiting to cross Main at First when Lucy called his name. He turned to find her and her fiancé, Joe Cadore, whom he'd met at The Three Amigos, approaching from the north.

"What are you doing up at this unholy hour?" Lucy's hair was pulled back, and her cheeks were pink with ex-ertion. She wore snug shorts and a snugger top, revealing muscles he wouldn't have guessed at in her regular clothes. In jeans, a T-shirt, and a Prairie Harts apron, she looked soft and motherly, not a bad impression to give when she was selling the homiest of foods.

"I got a couple hours' extra sleep, but Mouse needed some exercise." He nodded hello to Joe, then asked, "If it's an unholy hour, what are you doing up?"

She rolled her eyes at Joe, who defended himself so au-tomatically, it was clearly a conversation they'd had a few times before. "Hey, when we started this, it fit both our schedules, and a person's more likely to work out if it's part of their daily routine." Then his grin turned sly. "Be-sides, you know I'm perfectly willing to ditch the walks in favor of other activity."

Lucy slugged his shoulder, then blushed even more. Laughing, Joe hugged her close and smacked a big kiss on her forehead. They reminded Elliot of Emily and Bill—not only partners in life and love but best friends, too. According to the stories he'd been regaled with, Lucy had treated Joe like a pesky little brother while he'd waited years for her to realize there was nothing brotherly about his feelings for her.

That heart attack must have helped her along. Elliot hoped he'd never need so drastic a wake-up call.

*Ha! How many times have you been in love?* Emily taunted. *You need something to slow you down, not wake you up.*

An image of Fia popped into his head, along with one dead-certain fact: He didn't want to slow down this time. He wanted to take only the amount of time he needed and not one second more.

"Want to join us?" Lucy gestured west. "We're heading to the fire station to turn around, then back home, where I'll fix something healthy for breakfast."

"No, thanks. Too early for food." Besides, he had a bowl of buttermilk sponge on the kitchen counter, just waiting to be mixed with egg and flour and butter for Grandma's sourdough pancakes.

They traded good-byes and headed on. Double-checking traffic, Elliot and Mouse trotted across the street, then walked the half-dozen blocks to the apartment. Mouse, who'd recognized the scent of Fia's house, tried to walk on past as if the building meant nothing to her—he was sure the park just visible down the street contributed to that cluelessness—before reluctantly following him in.

He'd just gotten out of the shower when his mom made a video call. He swiped a towel over his body, pulled on a T-shirt and gym shorts, and sat on the kitchen counter to answer. "Hey, Mom."

"I told you I wouldn't wake him, Mitchell. Don't you

think I know his habits by now?" Vicky Ross turned to the computer in time to catch Elliot rolling his eyes. "Oh, no, you do not roll your eyes at me. I'll smack you until they stay that way."

"And good morning to you, too, Mom. How are you and Dad?"

"Finer than fine," his father said from the background, probably at the breakfast table with a cup of coffee and the latest edition of *American Cattlemen*. At the same time, Vicky said, "Oh, you know how it goes...Kids move out of state and take the grandkids with 'em. The only thing I hear about one comes from the other. Guess he's too busy with this new job and girlfriend of his to bother picking up the phone himself."

Dad snorted loudly, and Elliot joined in. "So far I've worked ten to twelve hours every day but today. I would have called you later." After lunch, if he didn't persuade Fia to spend the afternoon with him. After dinner, if they didn't wind up sharing that, too. Definitely before bed unless...Nope, his brain couldn't handle thoughts of Fia in bed and his mom at the same time, so he just stopped right there.

"So this is your apartment. I'm glad you're not sleeping in your truck anymore. Really, didn't you outgrow sleeping in the pickup on those camping trips we took all those years ago?"

"Nope. I like being outside under the stars, and so did you. Hey, I know you and Dad sneaked off every weekend for the first year of your marriage with a cooler of food and a bedroll," Elliot teased.

His father appeared on the screen, snuggling up to her. "That's probably where Emily was conceived."

Vicky shrieked and hid her red face behind a kitchen towel. "He doesn't need to know that, Mitchell."

Elliot leaned against the wall, then readjusted the phone. "Mom, I found out you and Dad had sex when I was, oh, about five years old. Remember? When you started locking the bedroom door?"

His dad topped off his coffee, then returned to the table, and Vicky straightened and dropped the towel, trying to regain her dignity. "I'm gonna pray for both your souls in church this morning," she informed them primly. "Now give me a tour of your new apartment, Elliot."

Slowly he panned the camera around the room, ending up in the kitchen with his feet on the counter. "Get your feet off the counter," she said. She'd spent his entire life at home telling him to get his feet off *some*thing. "You should make your bed and fold it up out of the way."

"Then Mouse wouldn't have any place to sleep."

"She's a dog, sweetheart. She can sleep on the ground like God intended her to." Without breathing in between, she changed the subject. "What's her name?"

"Mouse? Oh, no. Fia. Short for Sofia."

"Lovely name. I'm sure she's a lovely girl. All your girls are lovely."

He made a face at her. "Are you implying that I'm so shallow I only date pretty girls?"

"No, I'm saying you date girls you find lovely by your standards, not just in body and face but in character and personality—"

"With one notable exception," his father put in. "Five years later, we were still finding pieces of glass in the driveway."

"So I'm sure Fia is that kind of girl, too. How old is she?"

"Twenty-four."

"Oh, that young, huh?"

He laughed as Vicky wrinkled her nose. She looked a lot like him and Emily, olive skinned and brown haired, while they got their blue eyes—and Em's height—from their dad. "I'm only twenty-eight."

"Yes, but you're . . . you. What is she like?"

"You know, what, Mom? I'll make you a deal. Give me a week or so, and I'll call you—"

"Aw, promises, promises."

"And let you see her. Meet her for yourself."

Vicky's face lit up. "Before you let Em meet her?"

"Cross my heart."

"You know, Emily has met every single one of your girl-friends before me. Every one." She tilted her head to one side and tapped her index finger against her lips. "It's only fair that I get to meet the serious one first."

*The serious one.* That idea must have come from his sister. They were all serious in the beginning, but it hadn't taken long for some of them to become even more serious. Hadn't taken long for Fia to become *the* serious one.

"So I'll call you next week, right?"

"Right." Vicky beamed. "Any chance you'll get a hair-cut before then, too?"

Elliot winced even as Mitchell said, "Leave the boy's hair alone, Vick. He's grown up, ridden bulls, fought in two wars, and takes care of himself. If he wants long hair, he's earned the right to it."

"Thank you, Dad. Love you both."

"Love you, too," his mom said. More quietly, she mur-mured, "And I'm still gonna pray for your soul."

She said it partly as a challenge, but he didn't care.

He hadn't attended church on a regular basis since leaving home, but he was an expert at saying his own prayers. Even if he hadn't learned it as a kid, it was a skill a man picked up easily in the middle of a battle with people trying to kill him. And given that he'd come back unharmed from three combat tours, he was grateful for all the prayers anyone wanted to say.

# Chapter 8

When Elliot had asked Fia to pick a restaurant for Sunday dinner, it had taken longer than she'd expected. Zeke's was the most popular destination, a steakhouse buffet, and also where they were most likely to run into all her church-going friends. Serena's Sweets was another popular place where her non-church-going friends were liable to be. It wasn't that she wanted to avoid them; she just wanted to be selfish and keep Elliot to herself.

There were lots of other restaurants in town, but she settled at last on Sweet Baby Greens, a soul food place Bennie had introduced her to. It was family-run and served the kind of comfort food that made everything else all right. Add to that Elliot's company, and she would be in seventh heaven.

It was a few minutes before twelve when they arrived, and an elderly man seated them at a table in the farthest corner. "The most private table in the place," Elliot commented. "Did you slip him a twenty for this?"

"No, but I'll remember that for next time." She settled

into her chair, those last words echoing. It was nice knowing there would be a *next time*. It had been so very long since she'd had a good next time to look forward to. Things like doctor's appointments, muscle spasms, and double vision just weren't worth anticipating.

But she could have new first kisses and new first dates and next kisses and next dinners with Elliot. She could make new memories. For a few weeks? A few months? The rest of her life? At this point, she would settle for what she got. She wasn't greedy.

Elliot touched his hand lightly to hers. "You okay?"

Startled, she met his gaze and smiled. "Yeah. I was just thinking..."

"About Scott?"

"Actually, about you. And wondering what that incredible smell is coming from the kitchen."

He lifted his head and scented the air much the way Mouse would. "I smell ham and beans. Barbecue. Greens with vinegar and some pretty strong peppers. Corn bread. Cobbler." He sniffed again. "Cherry." After a moment of looking smug, he pointed behind her to a chalkboard on the wall that showed the day's specials.

"And here I thought your nose was so much more refined than mine."

He tried looking at his nose, making his eyes cross. "It is a pretty good nose, isn't it? But pretty much the only thing refined about me is the sugar I use when I bake."

Fia removed the silverware from the rolled napkin, then shook the linen over her lap. They studied the menu, ordered enough for three, then found themselves alone again, an expanse of distance separating them from the next nearest diners.

"Okay," Elliot said after a moment, "you don't always get to sit there and look pretty. Sometimes you have to be in charge of the conversation."

"So you can sit and look pretty?"

"I'm too tough to be pretty."

"Shows what you know." When he started to protest, she raised one hand. "You're tough enough. I'm not arguing that. You single-handedly rescued Mouse from a gang of rotten punk thugs. But you're still awfully pretty, too."

His slow smile transformed his face into sheer beauty, with a fair bit of false modesty. "Aw, there were just four of them, and they were only teenagers."

"Oh, so they were all bigger than you."

"Hey, no short jokes."

She murmured a thank-you as the waitress delivered their iced teas. Glancing around the filling room, she slid the paper from the straw, then dipped the straw into the glass, giving the tea a quick stir. It felt so good to be out. There were times she thought being confined to her apartment was cruel and unusual punishment.

But this... wonderful smells, friendly staff, happy people talking, and Elliot... This was her reward for enduring all that punishment.

"Okay," she said, mimicking Elliot from a moment ago. "The other night you said that you have had a girl or two who were crazy in love with you. Tell me about the first one. Did you love her back?"

He took a moment to resettle in his chair, leaning back, smoothing his ponytail where it had caught on the collar of his shirt. "More than I loved my horse. Her name was Cali—short for California. She had us all so intimidated about using her full name that when one of our friends moved to L.A., we could only say *out West*. She had long red hair and freckles, and she broke my heart. It was years before I could bear to look at a redhead again." With a regretful shake of his head, he went on. "So that takes care of second grade. In third grade—"

Wadding the paper from the straw, she threw it at him, laughing in a way she hadn't in ages. "You're a mess, Elliot Ross. Your mother and grandmother must have been saints to put up with you."

"Nah, I was an angel. I shoveled manure, helped herd and castrate and doctor the cattle, took my turn at baking, cooking, and cleaning, kept a B average, never got arrested, and never got anyone pregnant. The only time I got drunk in high school, I was gut-puking sick the next day so I learned to do all things in moderation."

"Wow. I never had any chores, knew nothing about baking, cooking, or cleaning, was lucky to make a C once in a while, got arrested a time or two, and got drunk more than a time or two. But—" She flashed a smile. "I never got pregnant."

"Arrested for what?"

"Vandalism. We broke out some windows in an empty building. The other time I pulled a handful of hair from a girl who was flirting hard with my boyfriend. Because she gave me a black eye, they ended up dropping the charges against both of us." She smiled slyly. "She never did that again."

They quieted while the waitress delivered plates of ribs and greens, fried okra and corn bread and corn on the cob. Elliot tasted the greens and the okra, then pointed his fork at her. "You know, I can see you pulling someone's hair out. You were a tough kid. You probably would have scared the snot out of me."

The idea of him being scared of her when they were teenagers made her feel warm inside. Being strong had gotten her through the years before Scott. It was the only thing that had helped her survive losing him. She wouldn't have the same response to an interloping woman today—She looked at Elliot and caught that thought. She wouldn't do it without being seriously provoked, but she was proud she'd been capable back then. "I was tough," she agreed. "I didn't have much, and damned if I was going to lose it."

Just like she didn't have much now. She was thankful every day, especially since having to give up her regular job, that Scott's insurance and death benefits gave her financial security and twice a day for her margarita girls, who gave her emotional security. But as far as a life, a future, she was running on fumes. It was time to slog back into the medical fray, to tell the doctor he'd had his chance at treating the symptoms; now he needed to find the cause.

Because she wanted something more than just her old life, her old future back. She had a chance at love and sharing and caring and family and all the things she'd lost, first with Scott, then with the onset of her illness.

She had a chance with Elliot.

And damned if she wanted to lose it.

\*   \*   \*

After finishing the outstanding meal by sharing a bowl of warm cherry cobbler with sweet vanilla ice cream, Elliot reached for the ticket, but Fia picked it up first. When he opened his mouth to speak, she silenced him with one warning finger. "You've paid the tab for every meal we've had. I appreciate it, but I get to contribute, too. I can afford it, and I like to do it."

He waited until she nodded emphatically, then he said, "I was about to tell you thank you."

An abashed look came across her face. "Oh. Good. You're welcome."

It was a fib on his part. He knew it was old-fashioned, but a lot about him was. He'd just been raised that on dates, guys paid. It was something he'd always done. But he liked the idea of being able to let her do it. It meant that this wasn't just a date. It wasn't a passing fling. They were sharing: time, meals, company, expenses. It was a step into a level of emotional commitment that he'd never taken before.

"We pay at the register on the way out." Fia stood, holding on to the back of her chair, stretching a moment and heaving a satisfied sigh. He followed her through the now-full dining room, weaving around tables and guests, to the register near the door, saying hello to a few familiar faces along the way.

"Who is that?" she asked curiously.

"Miz Watkins is a retired schoolteacher who meets with her friends every other day at Prairie Harts for coffee and Danishes. Miz Dauterive used to work at the bank. She was Jessy's boss, and I suspect she lit Jessy's hair on fire so many times it just turned red. She has a totally unhealthy love for Lucy's two-bite cupcakes."

"Oh, I've heard of her. The old hag."

He gave her a chastening look. "That's not nice." Then, after a beat... "But I'd have to agree." He'd rarely met a woman he couldn't charm, but Mrs. Dauterive was one.

When it was their turn at the register, Fia swiped her card, then added a generous tip. "I waited tables for a while. You get some good customers, but there are others…"

"You want to snatch their hair out?"

She smiled sweetly.

"I never had that problem when I waited tables." He held the door for a family coming in, then walked out with Fia, automatically reaching for her hand. "I usually got good tips, too."

"How many of those tips included phone numbers?"

He shrugged innocently. "A few."

"How many times did you call those numbers?"

A repeat of the shrug. "A few."

"You're a wicked man, Elliot."

"Nah, remember, I'm an angel." He breathed deeply as they crossed the parking lot. The sun had disappeared while they were inside, and the air smelled heavy and damp. The temperature had dropped a couple of degrees, and the wind was blowing in fits and starts. "Looks like we're gonna get some rain."

Fia glanced up at the sky. "The weather people predicted it for some time this weekend, but honestly, their educated predictions aren't usually any more accurate than my uneducated guesses."

"I could live without thunderstorms, but I do like rain."

"And heat."

He nodded.

"And cold. And sun. And snow. You just pretty much like everything, don't you?"

"I like to think I'm adaptable. Emily says I'm just too lazy to develop a preference."

At the pickup, Fia faced him. "You guys are really close, aren't you?"

He couldn't think of anything flip to say. "Yeah. She's two years older, and when we were kids, there was *nothing* too trivial for us to fight about, but she was always there for me. Usually pulling my hair or elbowing me in the ribs, saying, 'I told you so,' but she was there. I'd've loved her even if she wasn't my sister."

"I wish I'd had that."

The wistfulness in her tone made him swallow hard. "Yeah," he agreed hoarsely. "Everyone should have an Em in their life."

She opened the passenger door then, and he used her climbing into the truck as an excuse to touch her, to hold her lightly at the waist until she was safely inside. When he slid into the driver's seat, he started the engine and rolled down the windows before asking, "What about Scott's family?"

She brushed a strand of hair behind her ear and pondered the question for a moment as if it was a difficult one. "They weren't close," she said at last. "His mother and father divorced when he was ten, and each one seemed happy living pretty much in isolation. The only time I met his mother was at our wedding. His father came to both the wedding and the funeral, but I only know because he signed the guest book...Scott's brother was twelve years older, never married, works from home, lives in his own little world."

Her face wrinkled into a frown. "They weren't rude or hostile or anything. They seemed to be happy to hear from him, but they just didn't think about family. They were very distant people. Birthdays and holidays meant nothing to them. But Scott and me, we celebrated everything—birthdays, monthly anniversaries, the summer solstice, the spring equinox. There was so much normalcy inside him that he needed to get out."

Scott sounded like an extraordinary guy, given his upbringing. And that was exactly what Fia had needed back then, given her upbringing. But she'd learned a lot, experienced a lot, since then. Enough that maybe now all she needed was an ordinary guy like Elliot, who could share his ordinary life and ordinary family with her.

Raindrops splattered on the windshield as he backed out of the parking space. "You have any plans for this afternoon?"

"Not a one." Then she looked at him, all solemn and still. "Besides spending time with you."

*Good.*

"You want to go to a movie? Browse through the antique stores downtown? Take a drive in the country?"

She was silent a moment, waiting until he'd turned onto the highway that headed toward downtown Tallgrass, then quietly said, "I'd like to go back to your apartment, listen to you play your guitar, snuggle with Mouse a bit, and…" The way she drew out that last word offered promises of an intimate nature, and her shrug, stretching and rippling the thin fabric of her dress across her breasts, had a similar effect inside him.

Damn, it had suddenly gotten hot. Elliot tugged at the neck of his shirt and saw his hand was unsteady, like he was an inexperienced kid and the head cheerleader had just asked him to go behind the bleachers with her. His school hadn't had cheerleaders, but he'd been invited behind the bleachers at more than a few rodeos. Sometimes he'd gone. Sometimes he'd politely said no.

At this moment, the word *no* had permanently disappeared from his vocabulary.

She laid her hand on his on the console, and he turned it so they could lace fingers. The rain was falling hard enough that drops blew in the windows, splattering his arm and shoulder. He was surprised steam didn't rise.

Turning onto his street, he found one of the parking spaces out front unoccupied. He pulled in, only a few short yards from the entrance. When he jogged around to open Fia's door, a sharp bark overhead drew his attention to Mouse, sitting on the second-floor windowsill.

"She's such a doll."

"She's not supposed to be up there," he said drily. "We had a talk about it last night."

"And she said she'd stay down? She's such a smart puppy."

Pulling Fia close, he trotted across the sidewalk and up the stairs, letting go and shaking his hair under the protective cover of the roof. Fia did the same, leaving her hair rumpled and curled. With her skin damp, her eyes sparkling, and her smile dazzling, she looked young and pretty and as if she wasn't thinking for one second about the tough breaks life had given her.

He was about to open the door when she stepped in front of him, laid her palms against his face, and kissed him. Her lips found his automatically, so soft and sweet and, damn, enough to make a man weak. Luckily, there was a wall of brick behind him, solid enough to keep his feet on the ground, to support them both when he wrapped his arms around her middle and lifted her against him to deepen the kiss.

The sky darkened, the rain pounded, and rumbling came from somewhere far away, vibrating through him, jarring every nerve, every muscle, every instinct he had. He cupped his hands to the slight curve of her bottom, feeling muscle and heat. Lord, he loved a strong woman.

A gust of wind blew rain straight in beneath the roof, dousing both of them. Fia shrieked and danced away, pulling at her dress where it clung to her skin. "Ooh, that rain is cold!"

"My apartment's warm. So am I. I've even got a shirt you can borrow until your dress dries."

For an instant, no more than a few breaths, it was clear she was considering her options. Uncertainty passed through her eyes, followed by vulnerability, then determination. He would bet he was going to be the first man she'd been with since Scott, and man, that had to be tough for her. He wouldn't push her. He wanted it to be entirely her decision. She was the one recovering from a broken heart. He was just facing the possibility of one.

She took his hand, her fingers delicate in his, and they went inside the building. Their steps echoed in the stairwell, the only sound they made besides the occasional swish of her dress and drop of water splatting to the floor. As he fitted his key in the lock, she tiptoed, pressed a kiss to his cheek, then went inside as soon as the door swung open.

Mouse was waiting at the door, ignoring the books she'd knocked from the windowsill. She barked her sharp gotta-go bark, spinning in circles while Elliot got the leash. "I'll take her out real quick. You can change into something dry while we're gone." He pointed at the laundry baskets, and she nodded. She didn't move, though. When he closed the door behind him and Mouse, she was still standing in the same place.

"You're not gonna like what you find outside," he

warned the dog. "And when we come back in, I know we haven't discussed how you're supposed to behave when the grown-ups get busy, but stay off the bed. She came here to see me, not you."

He opened the door, and Mouse walked out about four steps before suddenly reversing back inside. The look she gave Elliot could too easily be read as betrayal, like he'd somehow tricked her into getting wet. Weren't they going to have fun when he had to bathe her for the first time?

"C'mon, Mouse, you gotta go."

She sat down just inside the door. When he tried to pull her a few feet, she lay down so the threshold stopped her from sliding out.

"Elliot?"

He glanced around, then realized Fia's voice came from the front window up above. "Yeah?"

"Don't forget the umbrella's in the truck. You don't want the baby to get wet."

"No, of course I don't." He looped the leash over the doorknob, ran through sheets of rain to the truck, grabbed the umbrella, and ran back. As soon as he popped it open, Mouse came out, tail wagging and happy to go.

Fortunately, the umbrella couldn't keep her feet from getting wet, and she had enough of toes squishing in grass as soon as it started. They ran back to the door, she trotted up the steps dragging her leash, and he shook out the umbrella before following her.

When he reached the landing, his door was open, and Fia was sitting on the floor, using his biggest, snuggliest bath towel to dry Mouse's feet. She'd left another smaller towel on the counter for him.

"Maybe she did come to see you," he muttered as he

wiped his face, pulled the band from his hair, and squeezed out streams of water.

"What was that?"

He startled. "Oh, uh, I'm glad you found a shirt to wear." It was a red button-down, with cuffs reaching to the tips of her fingers and tails covering everything that was modest and a bit that wasn't. It was too big, of course, and concealed all her womanly parts, but that would only make taking it off even more fun.

He took shorts and a T-shirt into the bathroom and stripped. With Fia's clothes already hanging over the shower curtain rod, there was—

He paused, fingering the fabric of her dress, looking at but not touching the hot pink bra that was covered with butterflies or the pink panties that matched. Fia was naked in his apartment. *Naked.* Damn, that knowledge was gonna make getting his wet jeans off harder than usual, but finally he was stripped, dried, and dressed again.

*Why dress again?*

"In case she changes her mind," he said quietly as he faced himself in the mirror, rubbing his hair again. "I don't want to pressure her. I want this to be her choice. And call me Captain Obvious, but I think going out there naked with a raging hard-on is pretty much the definition of pressuring her."

\* \* \*

*Bold.* That was what Scott used to call Fia, and she'd always taken it as a compliment. This was her first bold move in a long time, and it made her stomach turn somersaults. She was too skinny these days, and she didn't know what triggered her attacks. Fatigue, sometimes. Too much stress. What about a screaming-good let-me-die-now orgasm, the only kind she could imagine any woman having with Elliot? Could that make her brain go haywire, her muscles seize, her head start hurting?

She was going to find out. She hoped. If he hadn't rethought this while he was in the bathroom changing. What if she hadn't been bold enough? What if he thought that kiss downstairs had just been a kiss and now they would cuddle with Mouse and he'd play the guitar and they'd talk the way they always did? What if—

*If, if, if.* Any moment, any instance, life could change course. It could go her way this moment, turn against her the next. On that night long ago, if she hadn't walked out onto the dance floor of that particular club at that particular moment, she wouldn't have met Scott. If she hadn't had a good day and gone against advice and driven herself to the pharmacy, if the pharmacist had been a little quicker or a little slower, she wouldn't have met Elliot. If his holding an umbrella for Mouse hadn't tickled her, she wouldn't have spoken to him. Life was filled with *if*s, good and bad and in between, and the only *if* that mattered to her at that very moment was the one Elliot offered when he came out of the bathroom. She was sure she would know—by the look in his eyes, the expression on his face, the *come here* or *this is a bad idea* or *we need more time*.

And then he came back into the room, and the expression on his face was stark and hungry, and the look in his eyes was smoky and tender, and... Her gaze skimmed down his body, reaching his groin and one serious erection, and her insecurities disappeared, boom, like they'd never existed.

He walked straight to her, slow and easy, every tiny part of every gesture fluid and sensual and sending a shiver of pleasure through her. Sexual grace was a thing of beauty, so delicate and strong and purely male. It drew a primal response from her, a powerfully intense, demanding need that caught her breath and made her tremble.

He stopped a foot in front of her, helped her to her feet, and held her gaze a long time. "How'd I get so lucky?"

"I was wondering the same thing." She touched her fingertips to his arm, half expecting them to sizzle. "You didn't need to put a shirt on."

"I thought you might like to take it off."

Her mouth quivered in half a smile. "You want me to take your shirt off?"

When he nodded, she raised her trembling hands to her throat and undid the button half an inch above her breasts. He pulled her hands back, as she'd known he would, and pressed a kiss to each palm. "I want you to take this shirt off. I get to do that one."

Her feet moved her a step closer without prompting, and she curled her fingertips in the hem of the soft cotton. Taking it off filled her with anticipation, like unwrapping a gift to see what special treat was hidden inside. She already knew this special treat: an expanse of smooth, muscular, golden brown skin, soft and silky, warm enough to start a blaze. And the other special treat that was wrapped up not in the shirt but in the man himself: anticipation.

So many months without a man's touch, kiss, quick embrace. Without exploring a male body and getting the same tactile pleasure in response. So much emptiness and loneliness and yearning and longing and, for the past eighteen months, so much betrayal. Her body, her limbs, her nerves, her muscles, had turned on her, making her grateful for the tiniest acts she could still perform and leaving her to only dream of the pure, sweet, intimate acts between a woman and a man. Her dream was coming true today, and she was quivering inside and out at the prospect.

She pulled the shirt over his hard muscles, slid her hands underneath to lift it higher, up to the shadows of his throat, and took her time pressing kisses randomly across his chest. She tried to push it over his head but tangled his arms and left it there awhile so she could touch him, kiss him everywhere. "It's a shame to cover this chest all the time."

"Yeah, but working in a kitchen without clothes isn't as fun as it sounds." He sounded raspy, then his breath caught when she drew her fingers across his nipples. Ducking her head, she laved one with her tongue, then took the tiniest nip. His breath caught again, and his erection strained even harder against his shorts.

She'd lost her virginity on her fifteenth birthday, fueled by too much booze, too little food, and that angry rebellion that had driven her for as long as she could remember. She'd hardly known the guy, a classmate at the school she attended when she had nothing better to do, and her only lasting memory was of disappointment. That was it—the big deal her friends bragged about?

But she was no teenage girl, and Elliot was damn sure no teenage boy. There was magic all around him, in his eyes, his smile, his touch, his voice, in the soft warm pleasure of his body. Just touching him was enough to make her tremble, to heat her skin and her blood and to wake up her libido from its long enforced dormancy.

His fingers wrapped around her arms, drawing her so

close she had no choice but to lift her head, and his mouth claimed hers with an intensity she hadn't felt in so long. She'd forgotten how kisses and touches and love-making could make her feel *alive*, but he'd jogged her memory with a vengeance. Her skin was tingling, her nipples swelling, her intimately private places growing damp in anticipation.

After that soul-jarring kiss, he gazed down at her. "You are..."

"In desperate need." Grasping his hands, she began backing toward the bed, pulling him along. "I haven't—"

"I know."

"In so long—"

The mattress bumped her calves, and she climbed onto the bed, kneeling, pushing frenziedly at his shorts. He caught her hands, pressed kisses to her palms, then gently forced her onto her back, onto the mattress. The shirt that had seemed so adequate when she was standing now left her feeling vulnerable as it stretched the length of her body, leaving far more exposed, it seemed, than it covered. Elliot didn't mind—she could see that in the shadows of his eyes and hear it in the shallow raspy breaths.

He slid down onto the bed beside her, not face to face where she could pull him over on top, but halfway down the bed. His breath was warm against her thigh as he unfastened the bottom button of her shirt. He was leaning on his elbows, his leg pressed tight against hers, and his fingertips brushed her skin repeatedly, creating little shivers of need inside her, each stronger than the last. After an inordinate time, he moved to the second button. This time the shivers came in anticipation of his touch, tight and sharp, and her breath caught as heat moved through her, white-hot, slow, leaving her helpless to do much more than whimper, shift restlessly, reach in vain to pull him closer.

"El?" she whispered, her throat raw.

"I know, babe." He gave her a wicked grin, promising her every pleasure, every fantasy, every dream, and with a smile of complete trust, she let her eyes flutter shut while he went to work on the next button.

"I get to return the favor . . . if I survive."

"I'm counting on it."

By the time he undid the final button, she was a quaking mess of sensations, of wonder, of need. His naked body— he'd shucked his shorts at some point—was pressed against her solidly. His erection throbbed, hot and hard, nestled between her thighs, and his hands rested on the mattress on either side of her head. His stare was intense, blue fire, and his hunger was fierce. "Are you sure?"

She wrapped her arms around his neck and tugged him so close that her lips brushed his with each word. "More sure than I've ever been." Then she repeated the sentiment with a kiss, letting her lips and tongue drive the point home.

When they were both breathless from the kiss, when her body was trembling and prickling, when his muscles strained with effort, she pressed her mouth to his ear. "Let's dance this dance, cowboy."

Without leaving her, he leaned across to the night table and pulled out a packet. In seconds, the condom was in place, and so was he, sinking deep inside her, stretching, filling her, a sensation so sweet and familiar that her heart broke with the pure pleasure of it.

Oh, hell, she was in this deep, wasn't she?

\* \* \*

The rain was coming down so hard that it sheeted over the windows, obscuring the dark sky and the tall oaks and the houses across the street. Sometime in the last hour, Mouse had jumped onto the front windowsill again, scattering the books Fia had picked up back onto the floor except for one, using it for a pillow.

"I think she's thumbing her nose at the rain," Fia murmured.

Elliot glanced at the pup, then smiled lazily. "If I had the energy, I'd go dance naked in it. It seems like a hell of a way to celebrate." He shifted his weight to avoid a button on the red shirt that pressed into his shoulder blade, pulled the shirt out from beneath him, and tossed it onto the floor. It was just a simple button-front, but he was going to keep it forever. When they were old and feeble, he would show it to Fia and say, *Remember when you seduced me wearing nothing but this shirt?*

He would never be too old or feeble to return the favor.

"Celebrate?" she echoed.

"I've waited my whole life for this."

"We only met a week and a half ago," she teased.

Stuffing a pillow under his head, he pulled her closer and kissed her forehead. "The moment I saw you, I thought lightning was about to strike. Honest to God, I had to check the sky to make sure we were safe. That was why I asked you for a drink. 'Cause I knew if I let you leave without getting your name, your number, without making a connection, I'd regret it the rest of my life."

"Aw, that's sweet." She rested her hand on his chest, her fingers long and elegant and amazingly talented. "I felt…not lightning, but sparks. When we shook hands, I knew you were going to change my world."

"In a good way, I hope. But did you think it would happen this quick?"

Her smile was faint and distant. "One thing I've learned in the last few years is that everyone has a different perception of time. 'You haven't known each other long enough; you've been together too long; you've grieved too much; you need to hurry up, slow down, wait...' They don't understand that life happens in an instant. You meet somebody, and you *know* this person is going to be important. You blink, and they're gone. A baby can be created, a loved one can die, *you* can die, and if you hurry up, slow down, or wait, you'll miss everything."

Her sigh blew warm, moist air over his skin, raised goose bumps, and made his nerve endings tingle in anticipation. He vaguely remembered when she was pleading with him the first time—or was it him doing the pleading the second time?—that he had more than one time in him. He could be ready for the third go-round if she just looked at him, but not yet. Not while she was feeling bittersweet.

Tilting her head back, she gave him her regular smile, the one that had captured him the night they met. "Yes, in a very good way."

Thunder rumbled over the building, vibrating the bed, and lightning flashed, casting a faint glow over the room for an instant. Mouse's paws hit the floor with a click, and with one leap, she landed in the bed between them. After turning a circle or two, she settled between their legs, her chin resting on Fia's thigh, and snuggled in.

"You know, for a big tough pit bull, she sure is pissy about a lot of things," he grumbled.

"Aw, she's a baby. You said you don't like storms. And come on, does anyone really like peeing in the rain?"

When she began rubbing Mouse instead of him, Elliot claimed her hand and brought it back to his chest. "I'm actually surprised she's as easygoing as she is. I know her life wasn't easy before I found her. Sometimes I think she should be snarling and snapping instead of cuddling."

"I was a snarler and a snapper for a long time. I hung out with other kids like me, didn't let anyone get close. God forbid if a teacher or someone tried to be nice. But cuddling's a whole lot more fun. And having people automatically be nice to you is a hell of a lot better than them taking one look and assuming the worst."

With another strike of lightning, the overhead light flickered, then went off. The old refrigerator ticked and clanked as it settled, and another level of darkness slid over the room. "Did your forecasters call for just rain or storms?"

She was very close when she grinned, her nose only an inch from his. "Do I need to cuddle with you, too? The baby and I will keep you safe."

"I ain't scared of no storm," he said with bravado. Turning onto his side for a better look at her, he said, "Tell me about your life."

"You know all about my parents and Scott. That's pretty much it."

"That's a large part of it. In the time since Scott's death, you made a great bunch of friends for yourself."

"The margarita girls rock."

"You switched from training clients to riding a desk. What else? What keeps you going? What dreams do you have? What are you happy with, and what would you change?"

Her expression flattened, not as if he'd gotten too pushy,

but like she had to give serious thought to her answers. "What keeps me going," she said slowly, "is my girls. If I wanted to wallow in bed without showering or brushing my teeth, they'd let me do it for a couple days, but then they'd drag my butt into the shower, into clothes, and out of the house. They're the best friends I could ask for. The best people."

Elliot knew that and understood it. The bond the women shared was incredible, the sort of thing you heard about happening with guys in combat, the never-leave-a-man-behind mentality. Army wives were strong. This bunch of Army wives were damn near superheroes, and it was due, in part, to their friendship.

"As for dreams...I just want to know that one day life is going to be totally good again. It's going to take a while. No one grieves on a timetable. If I were the kind of woman who could get over losing Scott just like that"—she snapped her fingers—"then I'd have to wonder what kind of wife I was that I could set him aside so easily. I don't know if getting married again is in my future, or having kids. There's just so much I don't know." She cut her gaze to his. "Though I'm amenable to both."

The muscles deep in Elliot's gut eased their sudden tightening. He'd been born knowing he would have kids. He'd had too happy a childhood not to. Not that he got all soft and mellowy around them, but he'd never met one he didn't like. A few who needed their butts smacked, but he wouldn't raise that kind of kid.

*Mellowy? You get any more mellow, El, you're gonna be comatose.*

He concealed a snicker directed at his sister.

"But even if I don't, I dream about being surrounded by

families, sharing celebrations and sorrows, being an auntie to their babies, going to a home where I'm welcomed on Thanksgiving and Christmas, giving and asking for advice. I want to be part of a family."

*I've got a family. Damn, do I have a family, and every one of them would love you like you were theirs.* But he didn't say it out loud. He didn't want to do something crazy like ask her to marry him right now. That would really give his mom and Emily something to freak about. *You haven't been together long enough. You don't know each other well enough.*

Like Fia had said, different perceptions.

"And what would you change?"

That flatness came back to her eyes and her mouth. She shifted to stare out the side windows, at the streaky blurred view of the outside world. When thunder boomed, she didn't flinch—and missed both his and Mouse's flinches, his ego was glad to notice. He wasn't scared of storms, exactly. He just didn't think the sky should start growling and throwing random lightning bolts at them.

Moment after moment passed while she thought, while he looked at her, marveling at his luck. It was too damn amazing that they were lying here in bed together. How easily they could have missed each other in that parking lot. She might have passed with a polite nod, or she might have kept her distance from the odd guy talking to his dog and holding an umbrella for her. They both could have driven away never to see each other again, and that would have been a crying shame.

Or they could have met the next day at the grocery store. The day after that at the lake. He would have gone into Prairie Harts anyway and gotten the job, and sooner or later, Lucy and Patricia would have introduced them. If fate had intended the two of them to get together, it would have happened, one way or another.

He thought she'd decided against answering when she broke the silence. "There are a few things I'd like to change, but a very smart man once told me that everything I've been through has combined to make me who I am, and that he likes who I am a lot. If I changed one little thing, who knows what effect it would have on the big picture?"

"Very smart, huh?" He grinned smugly. "Can I quote you on that next time I talk to Emily?"

"You can. Just remember that beautiful brown Stetson that makes you look so damn sexy. What is it? Ten, twelve years old?"

"Split the difference." He leaned to the other night table, nudged aside the straw hat, and picked up the felt one, placing it on his head.

Sitting up, she let the sheet fall to her hips, her small breasts swaying as she gently shoved Mouse off the bed, then moved onto her knees and settled herself snuggly across his hips. "I would definitely have sex with the man wearing that hat, but you go bragging that I said you were smart, your head might swell too much for it to fit anymore."

He slid down, pushing the hat off his head and elbowing it to the side, wrapping his arms around her, and pulling her until their bodies were touching everywhere possible. "I got news for you, sweetheart. My head ain't the thing swelling right now," he murmured before kissing her hard and demonstrating for her.

\* \* \*

The power had come back on, and Fia's clothes had been dried for hours before she gave a thought to actually putting them on again. She was too comfortable in the shirt she'd retrieved from the floor, too taken with the scents of her and Elliot combined on it. Would he notice if she slipped out the door with it? It would certainly bring her sweet dreams.

He'd given her a perfect chance to come clean about her health problems with his question about changes, but she'd just clammed up. The way he looked at her was so incredible: like she was special, important, like he could live without her but didn't want to. All afternoon and through the evening, he'd touched her, just casual touches, but with such intense emotion. Considering how she'd been raised, the fact that not one but two men had looked at her that way, touched her that way ... the odds against it must be astronomical. She wasn't the princess who lived happily ever after; she was the plain person she'd always been.

But two Prince Charmings thought she was all that, and then some.

Who was she to argue with Prince Charming?

Wearing nothing but a pair of low-slung shorts, Elliot slid onto the bed, carefully balancing a tray holding a plate and two cups of coffee. He'd already fixed dinner for them—a pasta stew that was perfect for a night like this—and then out of nothing, he'd whipped up a pan of brownies.

"I thought only people like Lucy and Patricia could make brownies without a mix." She took a bite and made her best *yumm* sound.

"That's not the first time I've made you make that sound," he teased. "Besides, I *am* people like Lucy and Patricia. Food is my passion."

"And I thought I was."

"Want to put that brownie back on the plate and let me show you?"

"No, no, you can have two passions." She savored every bite of the small square of chewy brownie, then took a long drink of steaming coffee. He'd sweetened it, which she'd liked, but not so much that it competed with the dessert for the sugar award.

Her sigh after eating another piece was happy and lazy. "I think I've gained three or four pounds since meeting you. My doctor will be happy when he sees me next week."

Elliot's blue eyes met hers. "Everything okay?"

"Just a follow-up." And truthfully, the doctor wouldn't be too happy, weight gain or not, because she wanted him to *do* something. All the tests he'd run since last fall had been negative for this, promising for that, then turning out negative there, too. He'd exhausted his ideas, and she was left to take pills for headaches, for spasms, to help her sleep, to help her wake up, to help her live. There was an answer out there *somewhere*, and she wanted him to find it or refer her to someone who could.

She hoped she would be in shape to tell him all that. If she was having one of her attacks, Jessy would have to do the talking for her, and while she was downright scary at times, Fia wanted to speak for herself, the way she'd always done.

"I aim to feed you well."

"You've certainly done that. Tell me, is there anything you can't make?"

He pretended to think about it, though she was pretty sure he knew the answers right off the top. He wasn't the type to forget a challenge. "My cookies tend to be tough. It took a hundred pies to make a crust that earned Grandma's approval. Sometimes my meringues weep, and my macarons would shame any true Frenchman."

"Aw, poor baby. I don't even know what macarons are. But you know, if you were perfect at *every*thing, I'd be too intimidated to even talk to you." She considered another brownie, then decided she'd had enough. She'd still be working off the calories from today's lunch for a few days, while the pasta and brownies waited in the background, slowly turning to fat.

"I hate to say this," she began, and Elliot placed his fingers over her mouth.

"Then don't."

She kissed his hand before pulling it away. "You need to get to bed."

"If that's an invitation, I accept."

"Three thirty comes awfully early."

He set the tray on the floor, but when Mouse immediately pounced on it, he rethought the idea and carried it to the counter instead. Coming back, he wrapped his arms around Fia and stretched out, holding her intimately against him. "I can get by on less than four hours' sleep. For a while."

She rubbed her fingers across the beard stubble on his chin. "I need to go home. I don't have a car here, or clothes, and you really don't want to wake me up and throw me out in the predawn hours when you leave for work."

"I wouldn't do that. And you look really good in that shirt. I can come back on my break and take you home."

"Or…" She wiggled free, stood up slowly, and undid the buttons on the shirt. When she finished, she shrugged out of it and threw it at him. "You and Mouse can spend the night at my house, and you won't have to disturb either one of us when you leave."

"That's a deal." He reached for her again, but she backed away until she was in the bathroom, door closed behind her. She pulled on her bra and panties, glad that she had a fondness for wearing pretty underwear all the time and not just when she thought she might get lucky, then she tugged her dress over her head. Other than some kinks in her hair and her makeup having completely disappeared, she looked pretty good for someone who'd passed the afternoon and evening being wanton.

When she returned to the bedroom to find her shoes, Elliot was packing a small ruck with clothes, a plastic zipper bag filled with dog food, and another with brownies. He added his toothbrush, toothpaste, and razor, helped her into a slicker, and handed Mouse to her. "Is she too heavy for you to carry?"

Fia snorted. "I used to bench-press more than I weighed." She pulled the hood in place, snuggled the dog beneath the rubberized fabric, and headed for the door.

They ran through the rain, shook it off inside the truck, then made the same trip to her front door. Remembering her fall last week, she stepped inside cautiously, turning on lights, kicking off her shoes. Her little house lacked the coziness and warmth of Elliot's apartment, but that would change now that they were here. They would leave their scents in the air, all over the bathroom, in the shower, and all day tomorrow she would smell hints of him everywhere she went.

Her idea of heaven.

*    *    *

It was after ten when they finally went to bed, cuddling, playing, but going no further than that. As award-worthy as the sex had been, Fia was a tad sore where body parts that weren't used to being rubbed had been rubbed very well. In its own way, the cuddling was just as good. It was something she'd always longed for and had never gotten enough—would never get enough of.

The bedroom was dark and still, Elliot sleeping soundly with one arm flung over her hips, when Fia realized in that first groggy instant of wakefulness that she was actually awake. Rain pounded the roof and splattered against the windows, and from someplace nearer came slow, steady breathing. Opening her eyes, she saw Mouse's dim form standing beside the bed looking at her. "What's up, baby girl? Do you need to go out?"

The dog didn't turn and trot to the door but instead stood on her back legs and rested her front paws on the mattress. Her way of asking for permission to get into bed with them? Though in Fia's limited experience, Mouse didn't ask. She just did.

An instant later, pain shot through Fia's foot. Gasping, she sat up and bent her leg to massage her toes. Sometimes she could ease the spasm before it reached medication stage. *Please, God, let this be one of those times.*

Her toes were curled tight, the curve of her arch exaggerated, her foot twisting as the muscles contracted. She'd scoffed once at a story about spasms so severe that they fractured bones, but that was before they had become a regular part of her life.

As she tried to work the curve out of her big toe, Mouse trotted to Elliot's side of the bed and barked sharply.

"Hush, Mouse," she hissed, but the dog barked again.

Elliot rolled over, his face pressed into the pillow. "C'mon up. Jus' don't crowd."

Mouse barked again. If the first had been a request for attention, this one was a demand. Quickly, before Elliot could fully awaken, Fia patted his arm. "Go back to sleep. I'll see if she wants to go out."

With a grunt, he dozed off again, not moving when she eased out of bed. Her foot protested when she put weight on it, but she gritted her teeth, hobbled out of the room, closed the door as soon as Mouse was out, too, and by the dim light of the bulb over the sink, she limped into the kitchen. After giving the dog a treat to keep her quiet, Fia settled on the couch and went back to work massaging her foot. It didn't seem to be helping, she noted grimly, but at least the spasm wasn't getting worse, and hallelujah, her other foot and hands felt perfectly good.

"Really, Mouse, you have to learn to keep quiet. You could have woken your daddy up, and he has to get up soon anyway. Besides, this is *my* problem. In the future, let's keep it between you and me."

*Sitting on the couch in the dark at three in the morning, discussing your secrets with a dog. That sounds so like you, Fee.*

Fia's smile was rueful. She'd wondered when she would hear from Scott again. There were worse times, she acknowledged. Like when she and Elliot were, um, getting intimate. But Scott wouldn't have done that. Despite Elliot's claims, Scott really *was* an angel, and she knew down deep in her soul that he wanted her to make a life and be happy without him.

*I like him.*

"I do, too," she whispered.

*And he likes you.*

"Yeah." How cool was that?

*Very cool. So what are you waiting for?*

She didn't answer. She was days past the point where she should have told Elliot everything. But if she had, one of two things would have happened: He would have distanced himself from her, or he would have felt obliged to continue seeing her, even if it meant getting trapped into a situation neither of them wanted.

*Or maybe he wouldn't have cared. Maybe it wouldn't matter. So are you going to wait until one of your spells hits? Until you're having spasms and in pain and scaring the hell out of him and can't even talk to explain it to him? That's a hell of a way to break the news.* There was a brief silence, in which she could so easily see Scott shrugging that careless don't-shoot-the-messenger way of his. *I'm just telling you what you already know, warrior girl. You've got something with this guy. Give him a chance to step up and prove it.*

"I don't want that kind of proof. I want a full, free, wholehearted commitment—"

Which Elliot couldn't give if he didn't know what he was getting into. And because she'd kept her illness private, there was no way she could know how full or wholehearted his commitment would really be.

"Crap. Want to trade lives, Mouse? I think I could get used to lying around all day, getting fed when I'm hungry, and having my belly scratched when I need it."

"I don't think I'd like the lying around all day, but I'm happy to feed you when you're hungry and scratch your belly."

She jumped, twisting around to see Elliot lounging

against the wall just inside the hallway. "Oh! I didn't know—"

"I'm glad to know I'm not the only one who talks to myself." He pushed himself away from the wall and came to sit beside her on the sofa. "What are you doing up?"

Guilt and anxiety twined along her spine, one urging her to tell him, the other reminding her of the risks. In the end, the coward won, and she pushed the minuscule chances of that conversation taking place right now to the back of her mind, instead extending her leg. "Muscle spasm."

"Wow. You've got a good one going." He nudged her to put some space between them, then lifted her foot into his lap. He wore boxer briefs, navy blue, snug, and totally immodest, and she couldn't help thinking that there were so much better things he could be doing right this moment than rubbing her foot.

Then he began working his strong grip over, between, and under her toes, and the sensation was sharp-edged pain tinged with relief. "Are you getting enough magnesium and potassium in your diet? Enough water?"

"Water, yes. The others, I don't know." Not really a lie. Mineral deficiency wasn't the cause of the spasms, but since she didn't know what was . . .

"I'll pick up some food tomorrow. You like kiwis and oranges? Spinach, fish, bananas?"

"Spinach? Blech." She stuck out her tongue.

"That's only because you haven't had it the way I fix it."

She sat awkwardly for a moment, watching him, then slowly reclined back, pushing a pillow beneath her head and consciously relaxing every muscle group in her body. The exercise was part of her yoga routine, done at the end with deep breathing exercises, and usually it left her calm and peaceful. It was having no effect on her left leg, but the rest of her body was sinking deeper into the cushions, deeper into the quiet of her mind, while Elliot's hands worked their magic.

"You should mention this to your doctor next week."

The pain had subsided from needle-sharp stabs to dull throbs that she could live with. In the middle of the night, she would normally do her best to work it out, then take a muscle relaxer and let sleep take care of the rest. Elliot just might put her to sleep with nothing more than the slow, methodical deep-tissue massage he was giving her.

No doubt he was better for what ailed a woman than any grogginess-inducing pill.

"Wiggle your foot."

Her eyes fluttered open, and she saw that his hands were resting on either side of her heel. Her foot looked perfectly normal, graceful enough to slide into her most delicate sandals. Gingerly she wiggled her toes, twisted her foot left to right, scrunched up her toes, and unscrunched them again. "You're a lifesaver."

His grin appeared. "Something small, round, and sweet that you like to suck?"

"Ugh. Gross." Sitting up, she pecked a kiss on his cheek as, down the hall, the alarm on his cell rang. "I'm sorry you missed your last bit of sleep."

"I can get by. Don't worry. Think you'll be able to get back to it?"

A yawn interrupted her answer. With a laugh, he pulled her to her feet, "Come on. I'll tuck you in, run Mouse out quick, and I'll be quiet while I shower."

"Let me take Mouse out, and you go on with your shower." She put on her own slicker, hanging in the laundry room, and a pair of beat-up sneakers that couldn't be damaged by anything less than fire. Mouse was following her and wearing a cautious look. "Wondering where this is?" Fia asked, taking a long-unused golf umbrella from its hook.

The dog trotted to the back door, and Fia moved more slowly, though her caution in bearing weight on her left foot was unnecessary. The spasm, thanks to Elliot and God, was gone, leaving only a faint tingle in its place.

As she reached the back door, Elliot came out of the bedroom with an armful of clothes. "I owe you for taking her out to get wet."

"I'll collect tonight." She opened the door, popped open the umbrella, and flashed him a smile. "If you forgot anything, you can probably find it in the medicine cabinet or the linen closet, or just give me a whistle."

"Aw, damn, I never did learn to whistle. Emily can bust your eardrums. She never lets me forget it."

Laughing even as the familiar envy twisted in her stomach, she and Mouse made a dash into the rain. Cold water splashed her legs and immediately soaked through her shoes. She huddled inside the slicker while Mouse hovered beneath the umbrella, a definitely sour look on her face. "Sorry, Mouse, but it only protects you from the water up above. You still have to wade in what's already fallen."

Which was a lot. On the news they'd watched just before bed, they'd talked about flood warnings, stalled weather systems, another day or two or three of the same to look forward to. Good thing she didn't have to go to the office this week. She and Mouse could just stay warm and dry inside while Elliot made forays out to work and to bring them food.

Finally they returned to the house. Everything wet went into the laundry room, and she scrubbed them both with towels stacked on the shelf there. They were headed down the hall to the bedroom when she stopped just for a moment outside the bathroom door. The shower was running, nearly drowning out the sound of Elliot's voice as he sang. She didn't know the song, couldn't make out all the words, but it was lovely and sweet, and it made her heart hurt with joy. Leaning against the doorjamb, she listened until the last mournful notes faded, then she silently moved again.

She would remember this moment forever.

# Chapter 9

Elliot climbed out of the shower, warm and as alert as he usually was at this hour, which was not very. For a man who really liked sleeping in late, he'd sure chosen the wrong jobs: ranch hand, soldier, baker. But the shower had helped, and coffee would work wonders, too. By the time he finished his second cup, no one would guess he'd had a busy day–late evening–early morning.

He soaked up the water from his hair with a hand towel, then dried his body with a larger one. As was his habit every few weeks, he considered cutting his hair short, so he could go from drenched to ready for anything without hassle, but as was also his habit, he left the decision for another time. After all, he had someone else's opinion to consider now.

After pulling on his jeans, he rummaged through his stuff for his razor. He knew he'd stuck it in his ruck, the same time he'd dropped in the shaving cream. Damn, it must still be in the ruck. Opening the door, he saw the bedroom door was closed and the room was silent.

*If you forget anything, you can probably find it in the medicine cabinet or linen closet,* Fia had said. He checked the tub first, to make sure her razor wasn't tucked in there among all the bottles of shampoo, conditioner, and body wash, then he opened the medicine cabinet.

It was neat: toothpaste, toothbrush, and floss on the bottom shelf. Razor and extra cartridges on the second shelf. Fanciful perfume bottles filled with delicately colored liquids on the third. Pill bottles on the fourth.

The bottles stopped him short. They looked new, hadn't been handled a lot, and the labels faced forward. In the same position on every bottle was Fia's name, underneath a medication name and dosage. The first he recognized as a muscle relaxant, the next a sleeping pill. He didn't know what the third or fourth or fifth ones were.

His gut was tight, that crampy uncomfortable feeling that something bad was coming and he couldn't stop it. He didn't reach for the bottles—didn't try to see the dates they were filled, who had prescribed them, what the instructions were. He already felt guilty for seeing them, for not grabbing the razor and closing the door right away. He wasn't a snoop. He never would have looked in the medicine cabinet if she hadn't okayed it first.

He didn't think she would have okayed it if she had taken a moment to think about it.

Hand unsteady, he picked up the razor, closed the door, and caught a glimpse of himself in the mirror. He was pale, grim, and he wasn't ever going to admit it to anyone else, but even a little bit scared. Why did she need all that medication? What was wrong with her? What didn't she trust enough to tell him?

He shaved, dressed, dried his hair, brushed his teeth, and carried his boots to the living room to put them on. The towels he'd used were hanging over the curtain rod, and the razor was dry and back in its place. He put everything else back in the pack, then moved stealthily to the bedroom door, easing it open.

The instant Mouse could squeeze through, she did so, trotting to the kitchen, where he'd left a bowl of food and fresh water. He stood in the doorway, watching Fia sleep, her hands tucked beneath her cheek, her breathing shallow and steady. She was beautiful and vulnerable, and he experienced another twinge of guilt as he crept across the room and kissed her, his mouth barely brushing her skin. A faint smile appeared, but she didn't waken, so he left as silently as he'd come in.

After zipping up his slicker and tugging the hood forward, he gave Mouse a quick scratch on the sofa. "Wish you could use a phone, pup. Take care of her for me, will you?"

His mood was somber on the drive to the bakery, the sweep of wipers the only thing that broke the silence. He was so deep in thought that he drove right past Prairie Harts the first time, made a U-turn, and returned. He was the first one there, so he unlocked the door, flipped on the lights, and checked the schedule for today's specials. "If it's Monday, it must be meatballs. Italian loaves, yay." First up, though, coffee. Extra strong.

The grinder drowned out the sound of the door opening, so when Patricia appeared a few feet away, he was startled. "Morning, cowboy. You have a good day off?"

"The best." Even thinking about those hours with Fia could start warming him from inside out. "What about you?"

"It was lovely. My daughters and their family came to visit, and we all did a video chat with my son, Ben, and his wife, Avi, in Georgia. They're coming home on leave at the end of May." Patricia's smile faltered. "The first anniversary of George's death."

"Tough time," he murmured.

"Yes." She gazed off for a moment or two, lost in the past, before forcing the bittersweet expression away. "Are you going to make coffee with that or just stand there hoarding it?"

He looked down at the ground beans in the now-quiet machine. "I was thinking about just chewing it raw, but I'll share if you insist."

"Here, I'll start it. You go ahead and work on your bread."

He handed over the coffee, pulled on an apron, washed his hands, and went to his work space, a not-quite-big-enough corner of the kitchen. He warmed water, weighed yeast and flour, salt and sugar, then started.

He'd dated a girl once who'd scoffed at his interest in cooking and baking. *It's just following directions. Anyone can do it.* He pretty much agreed with her about cooking. Most recipes delivered a good product, and experience yielded the ability to make changes that took the dish from good to exceptional.

But baking...More art than science. A recipe that was perfect with eight ounces of flour today might need nine ounces next week. Yeast might not be active enough; dough could be temperamental about rising. That beautiful golden brown loaf fresh from the oven could be the most beautiful loaf ever made—mixed with precise measure-

ments, kneaded to exactly the right point, proofed until it
doubled as the recipe instructed—and be a doughy mess
inside.

As Elliot scraped the dough onto a floured board, he
couldn't help grinning. With all those uncertainties, a person would be justified in thinking he was crazy to bother
with baking at all. But iffy as it was, it provided balance
for him. Connection. It satisfied a deep need to be involved
with his food, to make it the very best he could.

Funny. He felt pretty much the same thing for Fia.

The pill bottles might not mean a thing. Just because
she had all that medication didn't mean she needed it
all the time. Even if she did, people could have health
problems that required medicine—high blood pressure, un-
deractive thyroid, allergies, depression—but it didn't mean
they were *sick*. It didn't justify that weird sense of *this is
bad* in his gut.

Yeah, Fia had lost weight. Every piece of clothing she
owned, including that pretty little bra with the butterflies,
was a little loose on her. And yeah, she'd given up a strenuous job for one that didn't even require her to leave her
house. And yeah, in the time he'd known her, she'd left the
house only twice by herself. Patricia and Lucy took her food.
Marti or Ilena picked her up for their Tuesday night dinners.

Maybe she just didn't like to drive. Maybe she'd gotten
tired of the demands of whiny clients who wanted the
benefits of a workout and a trainer without expending the
effort. And no one grieved on a timetable, she'd told him
yesterday.

"I'm no expert on bread," Patricia said, setting a coffee
mug on the counter for him, "but I think you might have
beaten that dough into submission."

He pinched off a piece of the dough, flattened it, then stretched it between his thumbs and forefingers. It thinned enough for light to shine through without tearing, a good sign that the gluten was fully developed. "Not yet," he said, "though another minute or two, and I'd be tossing this batch out and starting over."

She leaned against the counter and sipped her own coffee. "Lucy and I think we should put you to work behind glass up front. Our female customers would love to watch those muscles in action while you knead."

"Wrestling steers, humping packs, kneading dough... it's all good. But if I'm gonna put on a show, I think I need a tip jar."

With a laugh, she set her coffee down and began gathering items from the refrigerator. Breakfast treats came first: cinnamon rolls, sticky buns, Danishes, biscuits, and such. When Lucy arrived, she would work on the cakes, cupcakes, and cookies that were their best sellers, and around nine, she would start the lunch special. Today's was meatballs, served on a sandwich or in a bowl, topped with shaved parm and with a healthy serving of bread. He'd made about a hundred giant meatballs Saturday afternoon and had already warned his bosses that he was taking two or four home for dinner with Fia tonight.

Then he was going to pay back that favor he owed her. Maybe all night long.

\* \* \*

At a quarter of six on Tuesday evening, Marti was standing in front of her closet, considering her choices for dinner with the margarita girls. Nothing was calling her name—

well, except for Cadence, who'd just come home from an after-school visit with Abby. "I'm in the bedroom," she yelled back, and a moment later, her niece appeared in the doorway, hands behind her back. "Did you have fun at Abby's?"

"Actually, her mom took us to the mall. And she and Jacob and Mariah are going to Three Amigos tonight, too, and have a table of their own, and after dinner their stepdad will take them home. Can I go, too?"

"Therese already called, so of course you can go. You'd be welcome to join us without the other kids, though I'm not sure you'd want to be seen in public with the Tuesday Night Margarita Club. We might embarrass you."

Cadence snorted. "A bunch of..." She paused. "Parent-aged women? I'm sure you get really disruptive."

"Parent-aged women? Is that your way of saying 'old'?"

She shrugged, and plastic crinkled behind her back. "Not old, exactly. But you *are* just a couple years younger than my mom."

"Hmm. What are you hiding back there?"

"Not hiding. Waiting for the proper moment." With a flourish, Cadence pulled out a plastic bag stamped with the logo of a clothing store at the mall. She slid her hands inside, let the bag fall to the floor, and shook out the garment she was holding.

It was a dress: very pretty, made to fit snugly and show off its wearer's curves—and her arms, legs, and every breath she took, too. And that was the subtlest thing about it. The color was in-your-face screaming-for-attention bright-sunny-day yellow. The contrast with the school uniform Cadence wore was remarkable.

"You'll look so cute in that," Marti said.

"Not me. You. I bought it for you."

Marti lifted the tag, and her eyes widened. "That's a lot of money, Cadence."

"Nah. Mom and Dad gave me a debit card with my first three months' spending money. Consider it a thank-you for letting me stay here." The girl was beaming, looking happier in that moment than since she'd arrived. "We talked about your clothes, remember? The fact that they're pretty much boring and plain? So Abby and I were looking, and we both thought you would look great in this. You've got the body, even if you usually hide it, and Abby says it'll make your butt—I mean…" Lifting her chin, Cadence did a good imitation of her mother. "Your derriere will look fantastic. Do you like it?"

Marti resisted the urge to say of course she did just to please Cadence—the kid wouldn't be fooled—and studied the dress again. Its lines were classic, like her usual dresses. The neckline was cut a little lower than she was accustomed to—yeah, like two inches lower—and the color… Wow, the color. It would definitely be a change for her.

Hadn't she thought just last week that she needed a change?

And she wouldn't disappoint Cadence for anything.

"I do like it. Let me try it on."

"I'm sure it'll fit. We checked your sizes before we went. But go ahead, try it."

Both amused and touched by Cadence's excitement, Marti slipped out of the dress she wore—dove gray, ugh—and pulled the yellow one over her head. It required a bit of tugging here and there—adjusting it over her breasts, smoothing it over her hips, trying to get just a millimeter more coverage on her thighs—then she posed for Cadence.

"Oh, Aunt Marti, you're beautiful! It fits you perfect, and the color is even more perfect. It really pops against your hair and skin tones." Cadence went to the other closet, the one that used to be Joshua's, and scanned the shoe rack, taking out one pair of heels, putting them back in favor of another. "Here. Try these."

They were sandals Marti had bought on a whim, surely influenced by one of her bolder margarita girls, mesh and leather, with beads and bits of brightly colored satin ribbons woven through the mesh. The yellow ribbons were a close enough match to the dress, and the two items together made her look...

Well, definitely not drab. She actually looked younger, and she doubted the word *underwhelm* would come to anyone's mind. With its stretch fibers, the dress was comfortable, even when she sat down on the bed and crossed her legs.

"You look like summer," Cadence said.

"Summer who?" she asked absently.

"*Summer.* 'Shall I compare thee to a summer's day? Thou are more lovely and blah blah.'"

Marti wrapped her arms around her Shakespeare-quoting niece in an impulsive hug. Typical for their family, it didn't last long, but it was surprisingly warm. "Thank you so much, Cadence. This is wonderful. Now you'd better get changed while I finish up."

Marti was snipping the tags off when Cadence said, "Your friends will be surprised." Quickly, with a sly grin, she added, "So will Mr. Smith," before disappearing into her room.

Marti's jaw dropped as she went into the bathroom. She

hadn't mentioned Dillon having lunch there last week, at least not until Cadence saw the to-go bags in the trash.

Then, over the weekend, she'd caught Marti staring at a decade-old picture of Dillon on some rodeo website. Her grin had been big and calculating. *You like Mr. Smith?*

Did she like Dillon Smith? She actually did, considering how little she knew of him. Or maybe she should say considering how much she knew of him. She'd found some of those stories, too, about the accident and the trial. She'd never known anyone who'd gone to prison before, but now she understood that bleak, bitter look he wore so well. One bad decision, and he'd lost the two people he loved most. How did a person move on after that?

And nobody here in town knew. Not his twin brother, his sister-in-law, his other brother, his parents. Marti was the only one he'd trusted enough to tell.

Sure, it was only because she worked for a lawyer, but it still meant something to her.

Cadence didn't bring up Dillon again on the drive to the restaurant, but that didn't mean she'd forgotten him. In the parking lot, ignoring the running board and sliding to the ground from the passenger seat, she grinned. "Look, Aunt Marti. Mr. Smith's just getting here, too, and he's alone. You should go say hello."

Dillon was indeed getting out of his old truck. He smoothed his hand over his dark hair, then put on his cowboy hat. It was silver, the crown wrapped with a silver and coral hatband that appealed to her love of fine silverwork.

When she turned back to Cadence, the girl had already joined the Matheson-Logan family as they unloaded from their van. *Go talk to him,* Cadence had encouraged him, probably ninety percent sure she would do no such thing.

For that reason, when Marti finally moved, it was toward Dillon, not the restaurant.

His hands were in his back pockets, his head tilted to the ground as he walked, lost in another world. About four feet away, she stopped and waited for him to notice her. He did, starting with her feet and the silly frilly shoes Cadence had chosen for her. His gaze moved slowly to her calves and to the tops of her knees, then slid and slid and slid before reaching the hem of her new dress.

The evening was cooling off everywhere except right where Marti stood. By the time Dillon's gaze finally found her face, she was warm, her breath a little fluttery, and marveling at the difference a yard less of fabric could make.

"Marti," he said in his hoarse, hard-drinking, hard-smoking, and hard-living voice. It perfectly suited his looks: dark hair, dark eyes, strong jaw, creases etched around his mouth and eyes. He fit the iconic image of a cowboy that she'd grown up with: lanky and languid, tight jeans, hard body, brooding gaze. Pure sex in boots.

Judging by the smoky interest in his eyes, he was thinking the feminine equivalent of her: pure sex in silly frilly shoes.

And Lord help her, she liked it.

\* \* \*

Bouncing one-year-old John on her lap while his mama, Ilena, went to the bathroom, Fia felt one of those strange maternal yearnings. They were rare—the last was probably when John was born—but that didn't make them any less bittersweet. When she felt a gaze locked on her and looked up to see Elliot watching from the bar, the bitter part faded and the sweet part got even sweeter. He would make a great dad, a great husband.

But could she be a good mom, a good wife? Would her body let her?

She was torn between not wanting to consider it—disappointment was such a bitch—and wanting to believe in better days coming, one that included a diagnosis and treatment.

"What time is your appointment tomorrow?" Jessy asked, leaning close so no one else could hear.

"Ten thirty. I appreciate your taking me."

"Nah, it's good for me to see someone I can intimidate from time to time. The cows and the horses don't even give me a second glance anymore, and the dogs only associate me with food."

"Don't the brothers quake in their boots when you're going ninety miles an hour with your hair on fire?"

"They know the warning signs. There's suddenly a mare needs checking or a cow needs doctoring." Jessy tossed her head. Though she'd always worn short, sleek hair styles, now it was about the same length as Elliot's. Better for wearing her very own Resistol, she said the first night she'd shown up in the hat.

"Major change in Marti tonight. What's up with that?"

"I know, the guys can't keep their eyes off her. Well, except Dillon, who's tried real hard to look at anything but her." Jessy dipped a chip in salsa, even though she'd pushed the basket away three times already.

"Is something going on with them?" The idea surprised Fia. She would have figured Marti to choose a buttoned-down lawyer or banker or CEO—someone with more suits in his closet than she had in hers. That was the kind of man her father had been, the kind her brothers were, the kind her mother was always marrying or getting engaged to. But a cowboy...

"She waited for him in the parking lot tonight, and they walked in together. They talked by the fountain for a few minutes, then he went to the bar and she came in here and they've pretty much ignored each other since." Jessy leaned closer. "Therese says Abby says that Cadence says they had lunch together last week. At. Her. House."

"Wow. I'm surprised." Not that Dillon wasn't a fine-looking man. He was a tougher, leaner version of Dalton, and that dark air about him upped his interest level significantly. What kind of woman could resist a dark, mysterious guy?

Well, Fia could. She liked light, happy, even, on good terms with the world and everyone in it. Optimism with a dash of hope and a whole lot of faith. But angst, especially wrapped in damn good packaging, was tempting to every woman she knew, even if just for the fantasy of it.

Fia's own fantasy was across the room, drinking a beer, stealing looks from time to time. He fit in with the guys as if he'd known them forever. It was a talent, that belonging, one that she'd always wanted. Even now, though she felt with every pore in her body that she was exactly where she belonged, she couldn't imagine ever feeling the same way about other people, other places. She couldn't make temporary homes, then move on, the way Elliot could.

The way he still might.

Frowning, she gave her head a shake. She'd had a great time this evening—the Tuesday Night Margarita Club was what got her from Wednesday through Monday nights—and she didn't want to let insecurities, doubts, or mistakes put a damper on it. She wouldn't let them.

Shortly after Ilena returned to the table and reclaimed John, the other kids came to say good night: tiny blond Abby; Jacob, a heartbreaker in the making; Mariah, quite possibly the most adorable child in Tallgrass; and Marti's niece, Cadence. She was tall, coltish, and resembled her pretty aunt, and when she said good night, her gaze scanned the table, politely including everyone in her farewell, before she followed the others and Keegan.

"You didn't tell her to do her homework," Patricia remarked.

"I don't need to. She just does it. She does everything without being prompted," Marti replied. "You know, I was worried about how much she was going to change things—"

"Really," Bennie said dryly. "Your total freak-out the weeks before she came didn't give us a clue."

Marti stuck out her tongue. "But she's a good kid. Quiet, responsible, polite. She's adapted way better to the situation than I would have."

Therese nodded. "She's far more poised than I was at her age."

"Far more poised than I am at my age," Bennie said, bringing laughter from around the table.

"So...let's talk about the dress." That came from Carly, sitting one seat down from Fia, nursing a glass of water and keeping the small bowls of salsa at arm's length. If Fia ever did get pregnant, at least she would be accustomed to the bouts of nausea that were bothering Carly.

Though everyone had known the subject was coming sooner or later, Marti almost pulled off her bewildered look. "What about it?"

"In all the time we've known you—"

Lucy interrupted. "And that's like eight or nine years for me."

"You've never owned a dress like that," Carly finished. "Do we know him? Is he someone from work? A client? A lawyer?"

Jessy snickered, and so did Therese, and Fia barely kept her silence. It was good for them to grill someone else, since she'd gotten her share of it last week about Elliot. She hadn't minded a second of it, either. If there was one thing the margarita girls were good at, it was providing support. If there was anything they were better at, it was getting information. They talked, they laughed, they loved, they interrogated.

With a nonchalance that no one bought, Marti said, "It's just a pretty dress. It was a gift from Cadence, and I wanted to wear it. For her." Quickly, she took a long drink of iced tea. As if that would silence anyone.

"And the fact that it makes you look smokin' hot is just an added benefit," Jessy finished for her. "And there are a lot of guys here to see you looking smokin' hot, and we just wonder if it's meant for one guy in particular."

At that moment, Marti's gaze was drawn away from them and across the room. Everyone else looked, too, at Dillon standing beside the guys' table, his profile to them. After a moment of silence, Ilena sighed. "You know, I've always thought the Lord was having a very good day when He created our guys, but when He was working on those Smith boys, His day must have been exceptional."

Fia looked back at Marti, still gazing at Dillon. There was interest, appreciation, curiosity, and something that looked a whole lot like affection. How had Marti and

Jessy's brother-in-law developed a burgeoning friendship without anyone else being aware of it?

*The same way we all did.* Relationships weren't built in public, in groups, surrounded by friends. There could be no intimacy without privacy. Some of them chose to hide their feelings longer than others. Bennie had had to overcome anger and resentment; Lucy had needed time to move out of the best-buds groove that she and Joe were stuck in.

In fact, to date, Fia was the only one who'd brought a man into the group right up front. It had been a risk, but she'd been born a risk-taker. She'd just gotten some of it worn out of her over the past year and a half.

*But you can't keep a warrior girl down.*

Especially not as long as Elliot was in her life.

Or even if he wasn't, but he was a damn good incentive to find her spirit and be bold again.

\*   \*   \*

Elliot and Fia were the first to leave the restaurant, followed soon by the Sweets, Lucy and Joe Cadore, and Justin Stephens, the soldier kid from the Warrior Transition Unit, the only one besides Dillon who wasn't romantically involved with any of Jessy's friends. Dillon slumped on his stool, boots hooked over the rung, and considered whether he should do the same. He'd been up before dawn, had a long day, and could always use an extra hour of sleep.

But he was always up before dawn, his days were always long, and sleep never came easily just because he had the time.

Besides, Marti was still at the back table as the remaining women shuffled around, gathering stuff, drawing out their good-byes the way they usually did. They saw each other at least once a week, often more; they talked on the phone regularly, but it was always hard for them to leave.

Maybe because they knew too well that life didn't guarantee a next time.

The stool to his right scraped as Dalton pushed it back. "I'm gonna go drag Jessy out. I'm too old for these late nights."

The others snorted. It wasn't even nine o'clock yet, and they didn't keep particularly early hours. Dane Clark was finishing up his degree at OSU, and barring emergencies, Jared Conners didn't have to be in his pediatrics office until eight.

"I'll pay ten bucks to see you make Jessy go if she doesn't want to," Clark said.

"Aw, she's not much bigger than my hand. I could just throw her over my shoulder."

"That old saying *'Big things come in small packages'* became an old saying because it's so damn true," Conners pointed out. "Ilena's no bigger than Jessy, but she's got the personality and stubbornness of an eight-hundred-pound gorilla."

"Besides, Jessy fights like a girl, and she wins." Dillon admired his sister-in-law's spirit. She reminded him of his best times with Tina, the fun they'd had, the love they'd shared, the family they'd made.

He didn't need anything to remind him of the bad times. There was always that hole where she and Lilah used to be.

"Yeah, she does have a tendency to kick." Dalton picked up his hat and briefly met Dillon's gaze. "You staying awhile?"

He shouldn't. He should follow Dalton and Jessy home,

drive on past their house to the cabin, let Oliver out for a run, then crawl into bed. But he'd never been one to do what he should. "I'll head out soon."

Dalton nodded and walked through the arched doorway to the ladies' table. Contrary to his teasing, Jessy was willing to leave. Though she claimed morning always came too damn soon, she'd changed her schedule to match Dalton's earlier rising and bedtime.

Within minutes, Clark and his wife were gone, with Connors and his family right behind them. The few women left said quick good-byes and headed toward the door. At the fountain, Marti separated from them to go into the bathroom. They left without her at her urging, and when she came out a moment later, she turned to the bar instead of the exit. He watched her approach, the subconscious sway of her hips, the heels she wore making her legs look a mile long.

"Hi."

"Hey." After a moment, he nodded toward the empty stools. "Want to sit?"

"Wearing these shoes? Of course." Gracefully she slid onto the stool Dalton had vacated, crossed her legs, then tugged subtly at the hem of her dress. He would have thought a woman like her would be used to wearing revealing clothing, though now that he considered it, the dress did seem much more Jessy's style than Marti's.

Not that she didn't look incredible in it.

"If the shoes aren't comfortable, why wear them?" he asked, forcing his gaze up from those long, long legs to her face.

"Those pointed-toe boots can't possibly be comfortable."

"A custom-made pair of boots is the most comfortable thing you'll ever put on your feet."

"Are those?" She signaled the waitress and ordered cinnamon-spiced coffee. When she raised her brow in his direction, he nodded his head.

"Got 'em from a bootmaker in Edmond. Took a year to get on her list and another year to get the boots."

She studied them a moment. He hadn't opted for anything flamboyant, just good-quality leather, a little bit of suede decoration, and some damn fancy detailed stitching. "I'm guessing they were a little pricey."

He shrugged. "When you're winning regularly on the rodeo circuit, you can make some good money. I spent a chunk of mine on these boots and that O'Farrell hat." He nodded to it, hanging on a hook behind him.

"Custom-made apparel. Hmm. If I could have ordered a few extra inches on this dress..."

When she tugged at it again, a smile tugged at his mouth. "It covers what it covers. Just accept that, and all the admiring looks, and move on."

She nodded thanks to the waitress who delivered her coffee, picked up the large wide mug, and blew gently across the top. The whipped cream rippled around the edges where the heat of the coffee was warming it.

They hadn't talked much before dinner. She asked if he'd had any luck with finding Lilah, and he'd said no. She'd commented on the weather, and he'd remarked on the marvel of textiles that was her dress. At the fountain in the lobby, he'd asked about Cadence, and she'd talked of how well she was settling in, though the first call from her parents had made her homesick to the point of tears.

It was the most in-depth conversation he'd had since the

last time he'd seen her. Was that sad or satisfying? Maybe a little of both. He sometimes missed the easy way he'd had with people when he was younger, but he was okay with being a loner. Just maybe not quite so much the loner that he'd become.

Marti finally took a drink, dabbed the whipped cream from her lip with a napkin, then spoke. "I Googled you."

It was a little disconcerting, hearing that someone he didn't know well had gotten on her computer and found out who-knew-what about him. He wasn't much for computers, though of course he'd used them. Even ol' BB's Bar had already gone digital when Dillon started working there. The people he'd wanted to keep in touch with, he'd kept in touch with in person, by phone or text. But he'd never been on Facebook or Twitter or anything else that was out there. He'd never wanted any part of his life to be open to anyone who happened to have an Internet connection.

"I didn't learn anything you hadn't already told me except that you had a horse named Rebel."

"He was a good horse. He was most of the reason I ever won."

"I also Googled the Hunter family. It's too common a name to come up with anything without a lot more digging. If you want me to keep looking, I need more information. Tina's birthdate. Lilah's birthdate. Her social security number if you have it. Tina's parents' and sister's names. Any phone numbers you still have, any addresses. What kind of jobs they worked." She hesitated, then dug a small notebook from her purse, pushing it to him along with the ink pen one of the guys had used to sign his credit card receipt. "*If* you want me to keep looking."

He could do the Googling and whatever himself, though no doubt she was much more a guru of Internet searches than he'd ever be. The last thing he'd looked up had been an article on the Belted Galloway cattle Dalton raised, and that had been nearly a year ago. Besides, working for a bunch of lawyers, she probably had access to stuff he couldn't get, and it wasn't as if she would find anything worse than what he'd already told her.

She knew the worst he'd done, and yet she'd come back, spoken to him, smiled at him. There was no judgmental look in her eyes, nothing less than friendliness in her manner. He appreciated that.

Needed that.

Wondered if he would get the same response from Dalton and Noah, their mom and dad, and Jessy. Wondered if he would ever have the courage to tell them and find out.

"I'll give you what I remember. I'll have to look up the rest." Picking up the pen, he opened the notebook and began to write.

\* \* \*

Elliot's best bud in high school had been the worst pessimist he'd ever known. If he always expected the worst, Dan believed, he would be pleasantly surprised when it didn't occur and wouldn't be disappointed when it did. And man, did it. His high school girlfriend had run around on him with the nerdy science whiz the next town over. He'd freaked out so much about going away from home to college that he'd flunked out before the first semester ended. He'd joined the Navy, and God forbid, they sent him to a *ship* in the middle of the *ocean* and expected him to dress sharp, obey orders, and work damn hard. He just barely squeaked out with an honorable discharge. He totaled his new car, couldn't keep a job, two wives left him, and it turned out his kid wasn't really his... The list went on.

Elliot had been taught that a person made his own luck, and he believed it. Dan screwed up everything he ever did and then claimed the universe was against him. He never saw a correlation between his own actions and the results he got.

In the quiet of Fia's bedroom, with his two favorite girls both snoozing beside him, Elliot was feeling a bit like Dan. He never automatically looked for the bad in any situation. Hell, if it was there, it was there, and the thing for him to do was change it. His glass was never half empty. His sun was always shining.

But he couldn't get rid of the unsettling feeling every time he thought about those medications in Fia's bathroom. He kept telling himself it was normal, just maintenance meds for a woman who'd been through a hell of a hard time. Just because he never needed anything stronger than Tylenol was a blessing for him, not a comment on people who did. But something in his gut said this was different.

Just like he'd known from the moment he'd seen Fia, she was different.

He hadn't said anything to her and hadn't looked in the medicine chest again, though he'd stood there a time or two, seeing if his need to know had yet surpassed his need to behave honorably. So far it hadn't.

Communication... that was the path to smooth relationships. Leaders had to communicate with their troops; parents communicated with their kids; dog daddies communicated with their dogs; and men certainly needed to communicate with their girlfriends if they ever wanted to have wives to be happy with.

He rolled over to look at the clock. It was eleven fifty-two. Early enough to wake up Fia, ask a few questions of genuine concern, let her reassure him, and go back to sleep. How would he phrase that? *When I was looking in the medicine cabinet the other morning, I saw all the prescription bottles, and I just wonder what's wrong with you and why you take them.*

Might as well just say, *I snooped the other morning, and now I want to snoop more.*

How about, *Hey, I used your razor—you remember, you told me I could—and by the way, don't you know you shouldn't keep medications in the bathroom? Too much humidity and the temperature changes aren't good for them. So you should probably move them into the bedroom or the closet. What are they for anyway?*

"Face it," he whispered. "There's no good way to show simple curiosity about something she's chosen not to share with you." Besides, what had he thought earlier? A way for her to reassure him. This wasn't about him, except on the edges, on the serious-guy's-come-into-her-life-with-the-potential-to-be-permanent fringes.

He turned onto his side to face her, her shoulders bare, her hair sticking up in soft dark fluffs, her face completely at peace. Her breaths were slow and measured, and when he snuggled in close behind her, half a smile lit her face as she pulled his arm over her middle. *Thinking of Scott?* he wondered.

"Hey, El," she whispered, patting his hand once, twice, before sinking deeper into sleep again.

His chest was tight, his jaw clenched as if locked in

place. He wouldn't have minded if she'd spoken her dead husband's name instead. He knew the things a person could say when they were goofy with sleep. Emily used to wake him up in the middle of the night just so he could amuse her with his wild stories.

But Fia hadn't called out Scott's name. Even in her bed, sound asleep, brain off in Neverland, she had recognized Elliot's presence, his touch. The knowledge was so sweet, it cracked a thin line across his heart, too much pleasure and satisfaction, pride and humility, not to break it.

Elliot forced his jaw to relax, swallowed hard to push the lump from his throat. He thought of Dan, always unhappy, always complaining, and sent up a silent prayer that thankfully, Grandma had borne no guff from fools. *You're still breathing and thinking, so it's a good day. Make the most of it,* Grandma had greeted them every morning. She'd even smacked Dan upside the head a few times when she'd said it, but her message had never gotten through.

But Elliot had learned it and learned it well. He was a lucky guy, his buddies used to tell him. He could thank his family and God for that, and maybe even Dan for setting such a vivid example of the opposite.

Around his hand, Fia's fingers flexed lightly. "You awake, cowboy? Or is this one of those three to five erections men supposedly get while they sleep?"

"Only three to five? Slackers." With a chuckle, he scooted closer. "I hadn't even noticed, but now that you've mentioned it…"

She twined her fingers with his. "You feel so good."

"I aim to please."

When he rubbed his erection against her bottom, it

was her turn to laugh. "Not that, though it's awfully nice, too. Just you. The whole of you. You give off this air of strength and comfort and security and good humor and optimism and honesty and Zen-ness. I'm not sure I've ever known anyone who embraces life the way you do, hard knocks and all, and still loves it so thoroughly. You're a very special man."

Touched by her statement, he nuzzled her neck. "I'm here, you know? So I want to make the best of it. Which is why Fate crossed our paths. 'Cause you are definitely the best of it, Sofia."

Finally she turned to face him, sliding her knee between his, cradling her head on his arm, rubbing her soft muscular thigh against his penis. The hall light brushed her skin with its faint glow, showing her serious smile. "The world needs more people like you."

"Em used to say it needed one less—or at least, the Ross family needed one less. Her goal was always to be an only child."

"I don't believe it for a second. You people are the fantasy kind of family that some of us only see on TV. You Rosses give the rest of us hope."

He would have wanted her that instant even if she hadn't said great things about him and his family, but the fact that she had just made his desire that much stronger. Lifting himself up, he slid over her, covered her slim, lovely body, and bent to leave kisses along her jaw and down her throat. "Let me give you something besides hope," he murmured as her hands seared a path along his spine to his hips.

Her words were muddled when she abruptly kissed him, but he thought he got the gist of them.

*Please do.*

# Chapter 10

The Fort Murphy hospital wasn't huge, but it served the needs of its soldiers and their family members pretty well. Any illness too complicated to be treated there could be shipped to other military treatment facilities all over the United States or even, in critical cases, to civilian hospitals.

During her marriage to Scott and after his death, Fia had set foot inside this hospital once a year for her annual checkup. She'd admired the cleanliness of the place, the whiteness and brightness, but she'd been happy to leave.

In the last year and a half, she'd been back more times than she wanted to remember. She and Jessy took the elevator to the second-floor neurology clinic, where Fia checked in, then sat down, nervously tapping her toes.

"Cute shoes," Jessy said.

Fia stretched out her legs to show the sandals at their best advantage. "Aren't they? They're soft and spongy and comfy, I love the way they feel, and the raspberry color goes so well with the lime green and yellow and pink in my dress."

"You look like you're ready to fiesta." Jessy shimmied in her seat to the beat of a song only she could hear, catching the attention of every man, young or old, in the waiting room. She didn't even notice. "Remember when we danced the conga at Kari Okie's?"

"That was fun." It had been early in Fia's illness, when her only symptoms were a few annoying aches and spasms that came and went. They'd driven to the restaurant outside the small town of Kiefer to celebrate Lucy's birthday, eaten incredible food, danced, and even sung karaoke. It was one of many memorable moments Fia had shared with them.

"How are you feeling?"

Fia smiled faintly. "Pretty good. I never know whether to hope for a good day when I see the doctor, or if I should pray to be in the middle of a bad spell. If I walk in here on the sides of my feet with my arms curled up to my chest, my speech slurred, and my brain scrambled, don't you think they'd have to take me more seriously?"

"I think they'd slap you in a hospital bed and wire you for sound. But we can do that. Next time you have it bad, you call me, and we'll bring you to the ER and watch the doctors spaz."

When Fia's name was called, she got to her feet, wiggled her toes, and said, "Yep, but not today. All of my muscles are pretty relaxed."

"Ooh, Elliot's good for something more than gazing upon with great appreciation and awe, isn't he? I knew he would be. I mean, look at him. How could he not be? Just that Texas accent alone is orgasm-inspiring."

Fia smiled all the way to the exam room, which looked like every other exam room she'd ever seen. Jessy took the comfy chair and Fia had to step up onto the paper-covered table. She settled in with a crinkle, exhaled deeply, and wondered what to say to the doctor.

*I appreciate all you've done, but it's not enough.*

*I don't care about your other patients. Make me your first priority.*

*You're a healer, so heal me, damn it.*

*For the love of God, heeelllp me!*

The medic checked her vitals, told her the doctor would be in soon, and left them alone again. Flipping through a golf magazine disinterestedly, Jessy asked, "How serious are you about Elliot?"

Fia studied her feet in the raspberry-hued flip-flops and grimly admitted, "Enough that it's gonna break my heart when he leaves."

That brought Jessy's piercing gaze to her, one she could feel as surely as if she were looking. "Where do you think he's going? Because from what I've seen, he's getting really comfortable here. He's got a job, he's got friends, he's got you."

Fia tried to make her shrug casual, but her muscles were suddenly too tense to pull it off. "I don't know if he'll leave Tallgrass, but me..."

Jessy let the last pages of the magazine flutter and tossed it on the counter. "Little sister's keeping secrets, hm?" One finger tipped with glossy red polish wagged in Fia's direction. "Don't deny it. I was the master secret keeper for a long time. I recognize the signs in others. You haven't told him about this." Her wave took in the room.

"No." Fia wagged her own finger. "And you *were* the master secret keeper, so don't tell me I shouldn't be doing it."

"That's exactly why I get to tell you now you shouldn't.

Because I know how hard it is on you. It killed me to even think about you guys figuring out the truth about me. I was terrified, trying to figure out how the hell I would get by without you. I had this incredible part of my life where I could be happy and laugh and feel grateful I was here, and this other big part where I was scared all the time. About Aaron. About my drinking. About you guys disowning me and Dalton wanting nothing to do with me. About being totally alone." Jessy shook her head ruefully. "It was no fun, and it just made everything harder. Coming clean...aw, Fee, it was like breathing again after spending way too long underwater."

Fia gazed out the window, though all she could see were treetops interspersed with the roofs from the nearby housing area, remembering that evening when Jessy had confessed all to the sisters: that she'd fallen out of love with her husband; that she'd intended to ask for a divorce after he'd returned from his deployment; that she'd coped with her guilt and her grief by numbing herself with way too much booze. She'd fought her way back, though, through their help, through Dalton's, but mostly through her own stubborn strength. She'd refused to throw away her life and had begun living it instead.

That was what Fia wanted.

"But you could handle your problem," Fia said quietly. "You could fix it. I can't. I have to depend on other people to take care of mine. You guys keep me going. You cook for me—"

Jessy looked scandalized. "I do not cook."

A laugh broke free. "Okay, the others cook for me. You drive me places. You take me shopping if I can go and you do it for me if I can't. I'm guessing it's not too bad because there's a bunch of you, so I don't take up too much of any one person's time. But Elliot's just one guy, and he has a life. He spends long hours at work. He takes care of his dog. I'm sure there are times when all he wants to do is go out and have a beer—"

"Tuesday night with the guys."

"Or strip down to his underwear and play the guitar—"

"Who cares if he plays stark naked? As long as one, um, instrument doesn't get in the way of the other." Jessy grinned, and even if Fia hadn't wanted to, she couldn't have stopped herself from joining in. Granted, she'd seen both instruments and was seriously impressed by both.

"My point is, I'm kind of a full-time commitment. A lot of the time, I don't need help, but a lot of the time, I do, and it doesn't come on schedule. I don't get a text saying, 'Today at two thirty-eight p.m., you're going to get a migraine,' or 'Pull the car to the side of the road because in the next sixty seconds, your legs are going to spasm and go numb.'"

"Driving's overrated."

Fia shook her head. "Driving is freedom." Didn't statistics show that giving up their cars was one of the hardest things for senior citizens? It was such a huge gift, the key to independence. More than anything, the realization that she was too big a danger to get behind the wheel had brought home to her how serious her condition really was.

"Okay, yeah, driving is freedom. I get that. But Fia, who's given you rides and fixed your meals and brought you whatever you need since you met Elliot?" Jessy waited a moment, one brow arched. "Elliot has. He's a guy. He *wants* to take care of you."

"That's the problem." Fia shifted, paper crumpling beneath her. "Right now he wants to because he doesn't know the extent of what's going on. But if he sticks around, it won't be his choice anymore. He'll have to. He's too good a guy to walk away."

A lump formed in her throat, and a sorrowful tear seeped down her cheek. "And that's a situation I just can't bear."

\*   \*   \*

The lunch rush was slowing Wednesday, and Elliot was making a start on the next day's special—individual chicken pot pies—when Fia and Jessy stopped by the shop. Elliot liked the redhead and could easily imagine meeting her at any of the bars he'd frequented before Fia. They would have danced a few dances, shared a few beers, then gone back to her place or to a motel or even the back-seat of her car. And when it was over, he still would have liked her, and she still would have liked him. Then, the way those things usually ran, he would have gone to some sort of party a few weeks or months later, and there she would be with one of his buddies.

Good times.

But not as good as these times with Fia.

The two women bypassed the counter and came into the kitchen. "Morning, ladies," Jessy said, giving quick hugs to Patricia and Lucy, then patting Elliot's arm. He grunted hello and watched Fia do the same before coming around the table to him. She looked incredible in a thin, flowy dress and sandals in bright, summery colors, no sleeves in the way to hide her impressive biceps and triceps. He'd known some female soldiers who'd clearly counted fitness as one more tool in their arsenal to help keep them alive. They'd been buff and hard, but not like Fia.

"Hi," she greeted him softly, brushing her mouth to his cheek.

"Hey, you. Did the doc give you a clean bill of health?" He kept his voice as light as he could, but the question made his breath catch in his lungs. If there was something wrong...

The other women stopped their conversation to look at her, too, and Fia wrinkled her nose and shook her head. "This was more a checkout than a checkup. He got orders to his next assignment, and the doctor who's taking his place hasn't arrived yet. So I got all dressed up and even put on my prettiest underwear just to talk for a few minutes."

"You always wear your prettiest underwear," Lucy pointed out. In an aside to Elliot, she said, "You ever want to get her a gift, try underwear—pretty—no black, white, or beige—or flip-flops in cool colors." Lucy lifted her own foot to display a shoe identical to Fia's except in color. "The brand is Oofos. The comfort is supreme, and the periwinkle, lilac, and melon shades are adorable."

"I'll keep that in mind," he said with a laugh, while his brain was wondering why the hospital clinic had scheduled an appointment for Fia with a doctor who was already halfway out the door in the transfer process.

"So what did you talk to him about?" He narrowed his gaze and feigned a frown. "Was it you he was checking out? Saying, 'Hey, pretty girl, I'm a doctor. Want to go to—'"

"Fort Wainwright," she filled in with a shudder. "Alaska? It would take way more than a doctor to get me up to the land of eternal cold. So, no, he wasn't checking me out...though I did see him give Jessy a few admiring looks."

"Men have been giving Jessy admiring looks since she was in the cradle," Patricia said. "It's her birthright. You kids want some lunch? We've got chicken with Elliot's most delicious dumplins'." At their looks, she made shooing motions toward the front. "Go look on the specials board out there."

Jessy tiptoed to see out the pass-through, then laughed. "It says that, Fee. 'Chicken with Elliot's most delicious dumplins.' Where's the *g*?"

"There's no *g* in that word," Patricia admonished as she began rolling out another batch of piecrusts. "A good Georgia girl like you should know that."

Jessy tossed her red hair. "I have been many kinds of girl, Patricia, but good has never been one of them."

When the laughter quieted, Elliot asked, "You want to eat?"

Fia hesitated before nodding. "I do."

Had he ever known a woman who needed to think when asked that question? On the Ross ranch, food was sustenance that provided the strength to work twelve-hour days. A person ate whether they wanted to, and they ate well. Of course, Fia didn't work on a ranch in hotter-than-hell Texas, but she still needed regular high-calorie meals until she put back on the weight she'd lost.

"Go ahead and take your break, Elliot, and have lunch with the girls," Patricia suggested. "If we get busy, we can give a shout out."

"Nah, I can help," Jessy volunteered. "Dalton's parents are stopping by this evening on their way home to Texas, and his mom insists on feeding me enough for two or three. I fast a day before she comes and another after she leaves. Tell me what to do."

So Elliot wound up sitting alone at a corner table with Fia, two bowls of steaming dumplings between them, along with two glasses of pop. "It's kind of nice to be on this side of the counter once in a while," he commented as he watched her scoop a dumpling, blow on it, then bite into it.

"Yumm. Oh, Elliot, that's good. Your grandma's in Heaven smiling at you."

"She always smiles on me. That's what grandmas do." Belatedly, he remembered that Fia's grandmothers hadn't smiled on her when they were around and probably weren't in a place now where smiles came easily.

They ate a few minutes in silence before he casually returned to the earlier conversation. "It's a shame you had to interrupt your day, go to the hospital, and wait, just to find out that the doctor's not going to actually do anything."

She cut a large dumpling with the side of her fork, ate half, then speared the other piece without lifting it from the bowl. When she looked up, she gave him a sunny smile. "It's not like my day really had anything going on to interrupt. Besides, it was a nice chance to visit with Jessy."

Elliot's fingers tightened around his own fork. "Why did she go with you? Did your car not start?"

An uncomfortable shade of pink crept into Fia's cheeks, and she broke gazes with him under the guise of reaching for her drink. "When Lucy had her heart attack, it was so sudden and unexpected that the poor woman couldn't get any time to herself for weeks afterward. Her mom came out when it happened, and she came again with her dad at Christmas. Between them, Joe, and all of us, we went everywhere with her. You know, family's there when you need them, when you want them, and sometimes when you don't."

"Yeah, I know. But..." Should he drop it? Just let go for now? He didn't want to be pushy or intrusive. He should wait until she was ready to tell him, but what if she never was? How much farther would things have to go between them before she trusted him with a little medical information?

"But?" she repeated, prodding him.

He shrugged, managed half a grin, and said, "I was just going to say that you didn't have a heart attack...did you?"

"Oh, hell, no. My heart is incredibly strong considering that it's been broken more than once." She ate a few more bites. "I grew up poor, and Jessy grew up in luxury, but other than that, we come from kind of the same place. Her parents didn't approve of her. They didn't love or support her. If she wasn't going to be the same snooty, phony, fake people they were, they wanted nothing to do with her. They turned their back on her, and she sailed out of their life after high school without ever looking back. She's kind of like the big sister I never had, and I'm the little sister she does have who pretends not to know her."

"So you're all friends, but she's special."

Fia nodded, then grinned slyly. "Besides, Dalton and Dillon are likely to ask for her help with one of the animals, and she really prefers to be gone when that happens."

It sounded reasonable. Women did things together, like shopping, going to the bathroom, accompanying each other on appointments. And Elliot could hear in Fia's voice, could see in her eyes, the affection and respect she had for Jessy.

Wryly he polished off the last of his lunch. He'd met Fia so easily, hit it off with her so easily, fit into her life and fallen into her bed and gotten emotionally involved so easily. He'd expected it to continue that way. Perfect match, perfect romance, perfect life. He hadn't expected road bumps.

*Your life has been filled with blessings,* Em used to say. *Don't get greedy.*

He wasn't greedy. He was grateful for everything he had. He just wanted a little more.

But that was pretty much the definition of *greedy*, wasn't it?

\* \* \*

Fia hadn't been truthful with Elliot yesterday about the doctor's visit. They had just talked a bit, true enough, and the doctor really was getting assigned elsewhere, but the details of the conversation she'd kept to herself. Jessy would have told Patricia and Lucy, of course, and that was fine, but no one would rat out Fia to Elliot.

*I appreciate the fact that you've listened to me,* she'd told him, *but I need results. I can't go through life never knowing when I'm going to fall apart. You've ruled out a lot of stuff, but I need someone to rule something in. I need a diagnosis. I need treatment. I need my life back.*

She'd been proud of herself for getting the speech out without tears, theatrics, or swearing. And he'd nodded somberly—the way he did everything—and told her a new doctor would be taking over her care. Basically, she would be starting over again. Same old stories to repeat to him. Old x-rays and EEGs and MRIs for him to review. New ones to order. And all on a snail's timetable.

And this morning she'd woken up with a migraine and a tender left arm that she couldn't straighten. It made getting dressed awkward, so she tossed aside the polka dot bra she adored and the button-front shirt and chose gym shorts and a T-shirt instead. Even getting those on one-handed with every movement threatening to split her skull was tough. Thank goodness she'd cut all her hair off, or she would go around all day looking as if she'd caught her head in a blender.

Mouse followed her from the bedroom to the bathroom, where she pocketed a pill for her headache, then trotted to the back door. Fia held on to the wall with her good hand, made her way to the laundry room, and found a length of clothesline she used to stretch above the bathtub to hang her lingerie. Judging from Mouse's ever-more anxious barks, it was taking her forever, but soon she had one end of the line knotted to the ring on Mouse's collar and the other to the stair railing.

"I hate to send you out like this, pretty girl, but stairs and migraines are a dangerous combination for me." After making sure the knot at the post was secure, she stepped out of the way, and Mouse raced past her. She didn't go to the grass, of course, but squatted on the patio and peed, cringing every time it splashed back on her legs. Then she chose a clean square of concrete to poop on.

"That'll teach me to skip taking you for a walk." Leaving the door open, Fia went to the kitchen and pulled a bottle of water from the refrigerator before surveying the food there, wondering if anything would stay down. Leftover dumplings, hamburger patties, a variety of cheeses, kiwis, spinach, oranges. Elliot was determined to keep her potassium and magnesium levels up to stave off any more muscle spasms.

If only it were that simple.

She closed the door, took a loaf of his bread from its wrapper, and tore off a small piece. She was on her way to check on Mouse when she almost tripped over her.

"Sweetie, I'm your best friend when your daddy is working. Please don't break me."

Fia unhooked the puppy, and totally unapologetic, Mouse went to her dish and chowed down on the nuggets Elliot had poured for her. Nibbling a tiny bite of bread, Fia closed the back door and gauged the distance between where she stood and the bed versus the couch. The bed was more comfortable, but the couch was closer, so she was shuffling that way when the phone rang.

Though she didn't recognize the ringtone, Fia's hand went automatically to her pocket before she realized it was Elliot's phone on the kitchen counter. Tucking the water into the crook formed by her stiff arm, she picked it up. Caller ID showed it was Emily of the funny stories, devoted sister and all-around good person. It would be polite to let it go to voice mail, but Fia couldn't resist.

"Elliot's phone."

There was a moment of silence, then a female version of Elliot's voice chuckled. "Elliot's sister here. And you must be Elliot's girl."

*Elliot's girl.* Oh, she loved the sound of that. But her brain insisted on adding *for the moment,* and the pleasure faded.

"I'm Fia." She reached the couch and sank onto the cushions. Snagging the throw from the back, she spread it over her and snuggled deep into the cushions. "Elliot must have been in a hurry this morning since he left his phone here. He has to be at work at oh-dark-thirty."

"Oh." Was there a wealth of meaning in that small syllable, or was Fia imagining it? Probably imagining, because when Emily went on, there was no change in her tone. "I bet he's loving that job. He's always had way more interest in food than most people. I thought any woman he settled down with would be doubly lucky, not only in getting a great guy but an outstanding personal chef, too. His red onion and olive focaccia bread...Oh, my."

"I haven't had that yet. Everything else has been fabulous, though."

"Just wait. He'll fix you every dish in his repertoire before long. I think it's part of his way of taking care of people. It was important to our grandmother that everyone was happy and comfortable and provided for, and El's the same way. It's a lot of responsibility, but it's what makes him happy. And as long as he's being such a giver, I don't have to." Her laugh denied the truth of her last comment. "So you're an Oklahoma girl—or as the men in my family like to say, Far North Texas."

The crunching in the kitchen stopped, and Mouse appeared around the counter, nails clicking on the floor before she lightly jumped onto the couch and settled in next to Fia's legs. "I'm actually from Florida, but God rescued me and brought me here."

Letting her eyes drift shut, Fia mentally sighed. A quiet dark room, Mouse curled up against her, warm and snuggly, and a friendly voice on the phone. For a bad time, it was pretty good.

"He talks about you a lot," she said. "Sounds like you two had a great childhood."

Emily laughed. "We did, despite driving each other crazy, along with our parents and the rest of the family. We picked on each other, played practical jokes, wished each other out of our lives from time to time, but if anybody else said or did anything against one of us, all hell broke loose. I didn't fully appreciate him at the time, but he's the best brother a woman could ask for."

*And the best man a woman could ask for.* Ignoring the twinge around her heart, Fia asked, "So you have three kids?"

"Two girls and a boy. They drive each other and the rest of us crazy. When school's out, we're taking them to Six Flags, and we're planning to spend a few days in Tallgrass. We're looking forward to sharing the insanity and meeting you."

Their trip would probably be the end of May, the beginning of June. Would she and Elliot still be together? *He's such a giver,* Emily had said. Would he give too much to Fia and stick around? Or would he understand why she couldn't commit to him and let things end?

A tear slid down her cheek to land on the pillow, but her voice still sounded pretty even. "That would be nice." In a normal world, she would love to meet his family, to be welcomed and embraced as one of their own, to have parents, a sister, nieces, and a nephew, even if they were all in-laws. It would be a totally new experience for her, and she could hardly even imagine how wonderful it would be.

But her world wasn't normal, and her heart could break only so many times.

"Listen, Fia, I didn't mean to interrupt your day. I was just going to let Elliot know that the trip is definite. If Bill and I tried to back out now, there would be rioting in the streets. Tell him that, will you?" Emily's voice turned sly. "I'll tell him myself that I like his girl. I think we'll be great friends, Fia."

In a normal world, Fia thought they could be, too. But...

"Thanks. It's nice meeting you, Emily."

After hanging up, Fia dug the migraine pill from her pocket, lifted her head high enough to swallow it with some water, then lay back down with a sigh. Whatever happened, she could deal with it, right?

Though, God help her, she would be more than happy to stop dealing with problems for a while.

\*   \*   \*

"Tell me again why you rented an apartment?"

Elliot looked up from the kitchen, where he was applying a piece of duct tape to the bag of dog food. It was kind of pointless keeping it there when Mouse was spending way more time at Fia's place than their own. He was spending way more time there, too. In the week since they'd first made love, the only night he'd come home to sleep was Thursday, when her migraine had left her too worn out to do anything but sleep.

And he'd lain in that bed across the room, missing her, and worried himself to sleep.

"Because you didn't fall into bed with me the night we met."

Fia gave him a sweet smile. "You didn't ask me to."

"It just seemed kind of tawdry."

"Tawdry?" She laughed. "What twenty-eight-year-old man uses the word *tawdry*?"

"This one. I learned it from my grandma. Anything she didn't approve of was tawdry. And it's kind of a fun word to say. Tawww-dry." He set the food bag near the door, then checked the refrigerator, tossing out a mostly empty carton of milk. "Besides, I'd never made love to a woman in a Murphy bed."

She lifted one brow. "It wasn't any different from a regular bed, though if it had folded up with us inside... They would have found our naked bodies with smiles on our faces."

"Hey, I'm a tough guy. I can fight my way out of a creaky old fold-up bed." He picked up the basket holding what was left of his clean clothes, then grabbed the one overflowing with dirty clothes, too. It was time to do some laundry.

It had been a very good Saturday, and not just because weekends were sort of obliged to be good or risk losing their *thank-God-it's-here* status. He'd also had the day off, so he'd gotten to sleep in late, and he'd awakened with Fia snuggled behind him. They'd done pretty much nothing: had a breakfast with far too many calories, cleaned the mostly clean house, gone to the grocery store and debated menus, and driven out to the lake, parking in the spot where he and Mouse had camped, sitting on the tailgate, watching the dog run wild, and even casting a fishing line into the water. They'd thrown back their catches, though, little guys that had probably scurried to the lake bottom and hidden for the rest of the day.

Now the sun was setting, Mouse was at Fia's house, probably sleeping on the bed, and as soon as he got the stuff he'd come for into the truck, he and Fia were heading to Tallgrass's most popular cowboy bar. They'd done plenty of dancing in private without music. Now he was looking forward to doing it with music.

A person might think he'd dressed for the occasion—

button-down shirt, jeans, boots, Stetson—but they were his regular clothes. Fia, though...Man, was she dressed for it.

Her dress was tan with a western-diamond-ribbon pattern in subdued browns, greens, and rusts. It left her arms bare and was almost short enough to pass for a shirt. The leather belt buckled around her waist was decked with silver conchos and fringe the color of rich caramel that dangled beyond the hem, brushing her thigh when she moved. She'd traded her usual sandals and running shoes for a pair of well-worn brown cowgirl boots studded with silver and dangling fringe down the outside seam. Their six-inch shaft, like the dress, left an awful lot of leg to admire.

"For a Florida girl, you sure make a good cowgirl."

"I'm a fake cowgirl. Never been on a horse in my life, and the only ranch I've ever set foot on was Dalton's, for a barbecue last month." Slowly she walked toward him, a mesmerizing sight, the fabric of the dress shifting with each step, the fringe swaying, the muscles in her long legs flexing. When she stopped a few feet in front of him, he hooked his finger inside her belt and drew her close, slid his arm around her waist, and snugged her hips up to his.

"Being a cowgirl is all about the spirit, darlin', and you've got that in spades." He brushed his mouth back and forward across her cheek, slowly kissed his way to her ear, then down her neck. He was getting hard—nothing new about that—and she was making a tiny, soft sound that fed the need inside him. They could forget about Bubba's, the only functioning part of his brain suggested. Tell her how gorgeous she was in that dress and those boots, then take them off her and tell her how much more gorgeous she was without them. Make love until they were too weak to do it again, feed her to restore her strength, and start all over again.

With a long sensual sigh, she lifted her head, opened her eyes, and gave him the sexiest smile he'd ever been lucky enough to receive. "Hold that thought for later, cowboy. You promised me music and dancing, and I'm holding you to it." She touched her fingers lightly to his mouth, then pulled out of his arms and sashayed to the door.

It was proof of just how far he'd fallen that putting sex on hold for a few hours sounded promising.

She gave him directions to the bar, located on the west side of town, and he found a space in the crowded gravel lot. As soon as they got out of the truck, they heard the music and laughter, voices, good times. There was a party going on inside, and when it was over, he and Fia would have their own intimate party for two at home.

There was nothing quite like walking into an honest-to-God cowboy bar. Though there were plenty of people inside who just liked the lifestyle, he would guess probably half of them lived it. The place was loud, the dance floor was crowded, and people stood three deep at the bar. He felt at home.

Leaving Fia leaning against a wooden post near the door, Elliot joined the crowd at the bar, finally getting a cold beer for himself and pop for her. While he waited, he counted three guys who approached her. He watched her smile, talk, and after a moment, send each one on his way. He didn't blame the guys for trying, but he was damned glad she'd said yes to him.

He rejoined her about the same time a woman in tight jeans and tighter shirt tapped her on the arm. "Hey, Fia, how are you?"

The two women hugged and talked for a minute before the friend pointed toward the wall. "My friends and I are leaving if you want our table. My date left me here. Can you believe that? Said he didn't like country music and wouldn't have come if he'd known that's what it was. Sheesh, *Bubba's*? He thought that was going to be high class?" Abruptly the woman looked at him. "Oh. You're together. My, oh my."

"Sorry. Laurel, this is Elliot. Elliot, Laurel. She's a trainer at the gym."

He didn't need a second look at the woman to confirm that. Given the looks she got as they followed her to the table, he doubted she would go home alone unless she wanted to.

There were more friends to meet, a couple who didn't look like they were going home alone, either. They cleared the table, and Elliot and Fia claimed it before anyone else could think twice about it.

"Before Scott, I spent entire nights in places like this. I'd crash for a while, go to work, then go back and party. It seemed so important back then." She graced him with a smile. "Then I grew up."

"Bars are great places to have fun, as long as you don't overdo it." He tilted his beer bottle at her. "Everything in moderation. That's my motto. Except you."

Her smile remained, though something about it changed a bit. It was still sweet, still enough to make a man look twice, but a tinge of sadness had appeared. Thinking about Scott and all the good times they'd had here? Missing him more than usual? Maybe feeling a little guilty about bringing Elliot here?

He understood that as much as he could, not ever having

lost the woman he loved dearly. He wasn't possessive or jealous. He didn't want her ever to forget one ounce of the love she'd felt for Scott, to suppress a single memory or put him in some dark corner of her mind as if he'd never existed.

He just wanted some of that love for himself. To add new happy memories to the old ones. To make a future to complete Scott's past.

When the waitress swung by, Fia ordered a burger and fries. Not bothering with a menu, Elliot doubled the order, then settled back, beer in hand, and just gazed at her.

She shifted a bit, glanced at him, crossed her legs, then awkwardly laughed. "What are you looking at?"

"The prettiest girl in the place."

With another choked laugh, she made a show of looking over her shoulder. "Really? Which one?"

Teasingly he pointed across the room with the beer bottle. "That blonde over there."

Fia's head spun around so fast that he was surprised she didn't get whiplash, then she turned back and slugged his shoulder. "Don't tease the girl you're going home with tonight."

*Home.* Oh, hell, yeah.

Drawing his index finger lightly along the curve of her knee, he was rewarded with the tensing of her muscles, the slight swing of the boot fringe. Touch was a wondrous thing, that he could make her shiver with no more than the slightest contact. He could relax her, calm her, excite her, please her. He could make her feel safe. And she could do all that and more for him.

He'd been dancing around it for a while now, but there was no use denying it anymore.

He'd fallen in love with Fia.

*You fall in love with every woman you date,* Emily reminded him.

That was true. Emily called him things like *sentimental* and *flighty.* He liked to consider it keeping himself open to all possibilities.

*You've only known her two weeks,* she added.

*And one day. It's not the quantity, Em, it's the quality. It feels like I've known her forever. Like no matter how much time we have together, it'll never be enough.*

The sister in his head just gave a big, heavy sigh in response to that. Em liked Fia—she'd told him so when he'd called her back Thursday. She had really good feelings about her. *But...*

Was the *but* really Emily's? Or was it his? The medications, the muscle spasms, the migraines... Doing a desk job, fussed over and mothered by the margarita girls, somebody taking her everywhere... If something was wrong, he wanted to know. Needed to. He needed her to trust him enough to tell him.

And if something *was* wrong, what difference would it make? Any, some, none?

His gut said none, but could he commit to that when she kept him in the dark?

"Woohoo." Fia's long slender fingers waved in front of his face. When he focused on her, she smiled. "Welcome back. You looked like you were a thousand miles away."

"More like seven." That was about the distance to her house, and the flush pinking her cheeks showed she knew it.

"You are determined to cut this evening short, aren't you?" She shook her head admonishingly. "I need my burger and fries. I need to hear some music. I need to dance. Besides, you know what they say about anticipation." She leaned closer and trailed her fingertip along his forearm and lowered her voice to a sexy murmur. "It makes the pleasure so damn much better."

He moved, too, until the distance between them was minimal, until his mouth brushed the delicate shape of her ear, and he whispered, "Darlin', if it gets any better, it might damn well kill me."

* * *

Dear Lord in heaven, Fia had forgotten how much she absolutely *loved* to dance. Being in the middle of the crowd, the music loud enough to vibrate through her body, swaying and spinning, losing her breath on a fast song and losing it in a different way on a slow one...Her body tingled, felt alive, and the only thoughts in her mind were good ones.

Sexy ones, she amended as Elliot pulled her close for another slow song. She'd always liked tall guys before, but she and Elliot fit together as if they'd been designed for one another. His arms held her close, her arms were around his neck, and his gorgeous blue gaze was locked on her. She had no clue how long they'd been on the dance floor—maybe an hour, maybe a lifetime—but with each passing moment, she felt *more*. Happier, freer, looser, calmer, easier.

And more aroused than she could remember. Every place her body touched his tingled with sensation, hot and electric, and God help her, when it was her skin against his with no fabric for protection, it was searing. Her nerves itched to cast off the clothing, to be naked and feverish, to feel him deep, deep inside her, to connect with him as intimately as two people could.

"Elliot?"

"Hm?"

"What do you say we blow this popsicle stand?"

His smile was sweet and lazy. "What twenty-four-year-old woman says that?"

"This one. I don't even know where I learned it, but it's fun to say." She kissed his jaw, touching the tip of her tongue to his warm skin for just an instant. "Wanna go?"

Taut lines formed in his jaw, muscles tightening down his neck, and he pulled her hands from his neck, clasped one tightly in his, and guided her in a weaving line around the other dancers to their table. She took her jacket from a hook on the wall, and he collected his hat from the next one.

They'd made it only a few steps outside the door when Fia was forced to an abrupt stop. A broad porch fronted the building, a place where customers went to light up, talk without shouting, or just to cool off for a moment. The only people out there at the moment were three men in dark denims and felt cowboy hats that were probably too warm for the evening and a woman, standing beside the rail, clutching her cell phone tightly in her hand. She was faced off against the biggest of the men, her muscles tensed as if they were deciding whether the situation called for fight or flight, and the air practically crackled with emotion. Anger, fear, frustration.

Fia looked from the woman to the man, a good six inches taller and at least seventy-five pounds heavier. She couldn't just walk away—she wasn't built that way—but her quick assessment said the guy could pick up both her and the other woman, one in each hand, and not even feel the effort.

But she wasn't on her own here. Elliot's hand rested lightly in her back as he nudged her to the side and asked, "Everything all right here?" His voice was calm, even—so much so that hearing it directed at her would have raised goose bumps on Fia's arms.

The man didn't take his gaze from the woman. "Taryn and I are just talking, aren't we, babe?"

"I'm not your babe, Brian," Taryn spat back.

Brian moved closer to her, but Elliot stepped between them. The look Brian gave him made clear that he didn't consider him a threat. Stupid man. Fia had worked with clients like him, big and strong and arrogant enough to think that was all that mattered. She doubted he'd had many fair fights—his type always picked on weaker people—which would just make seeing him get his ass kicked that much sweeter.

Elliot's muscles were taut, his stance alert but loose. He handed his hat to Fia, held one hand in the air, inches from Brian's chest, and turned his head slightly toward the woman. "Taryn, you want to talk to this guy?"

"No. Not ever again. I told you, Brian, no more!"

"You want him to leave you alone?" Fia asked, shifting closer to her.

"Yes! Then I want him to drop dead. You pissy little bastard!"

*Don't be stupid,* Fia hoped, but this guy was too mad to be anything else. He had a little booze in him, his girl had rejected him in front of buddies and strangers, and now some little dude and a woman were getting in his way. She'd bet next month's pay that Brian really didn't like women.

He telegraphed his punch, clumsy and slow. Elliot easily ducked it and responded with a quick jab to his jaw, sending him staggering a few feet back. The expression on his face would be something to laugh about later: shock that someone was actually going to fight back, the realization that this might not end well for him. With a roar, he charged, and Elliot sidestepped, catching him with a sharp blow to his ribs.

"Should I call 911?" Taryn whispered.

"You should go get in your car and leave." Fia shifted her gaze from the men to her. "Has he done anything like this before?"

Taryn grimaced. "I broke up with him last week because of his temper."

"Go ahead. Get out of here. And make a complaint with the sheriff's office. Don't let him get away with this."

With a nod, Taryn backed away a few steps, then spun around and ran remarkably fast for a woman in heels.

Brian staggered against the railing, breathing hard, before taking another wild swing. Fia split her attention between him and his friends, wondering if she should call 911 or leave Elliot alone with the three to try to locate the bouncer inside. But Elliot moved lightning fast, driving his fist into Brian's nose, using his own momentum against him. For long seconds, Brian teetered on the top step, then in sweet slow motion, he tumbled backward to the gravel below. He tried feebly to get up, then sank down again, mumbling curses.

Still loose and light on his feet, Elliot turned to Brian's friends. "Either of you got a problem with me?"

They both grimly shook their heads.

"Okay then." He took his hat from Fia, seated it, and slid

his arm around her waist. As they started toward the steps at the far end of the porch, she looked over her shoulder to make sure the men weren't following. Elliot grinned, giving her a squeeze. "Are we safe?"

"We're safe. They're just standing there. Not even helping their friend up."

"Good." He flexed his right hand and winced. "I hate people who can't take no for an answer."

"Me, too. But they give good guys like you a chance to impress girls like me."

"Were you impressed?"

"Oh, hell, yeah."

He nuzzled her neck, throwing them both off balance. He caught her, swung her into his embrace, and kissed her. "You should have gone to the truck when Taryn left. What if he'd left me on the ground bleeding?"

"I'd've kicked his ass myself. I am not a fragile flower. I learned how to fight dirty a long time ago."

His laugh was husky and made her feel warm and happy all the way through her soul. "Aw, Fia, you're my perfect woman. You know that? Everything I ever wanted... everything I will ever need..."

This kiss was longer, slower, hungrier, and robbed the breath right from her lungs. Her legs were so weak, she wasn't sure she could stand, much less walk, and the heat inside her burned so bright that tearing off her clothes right now, right there, was a terribly tempting idea. Hell, forget her clothes. Tearing off *his* was what she really needed.

Before she'd managed to undo even one shirt button, Elliot lifted his head, grasped her hands in his, and gave her that incredibly charming cowboy smile. "Let's go home, Fia."

# Chapter 11

Walking really wasn't Marti's thing. It wasn't that she held anything against the great outdoors or exercise in general. It was just that she didn't like to sweat. That was an activity she thought should be reserved for sex and catastrophic disasters, such as running through the jungle with a T. rex on her heels.

But Cadence had asked to go for a walk this evening, and since Marti wasn't going to send her out alone after dark, no matter how safe Tallgrass was, here she was in shorts, a tee, and sandals, strolling toward Main Street. They'd talked about school, the weather, Cadence's parents, and Cadence had even brought up a boy she liked at school.

Giving advice to a fourteen-year-old with her first serious crush...not something Marti had ever imagined herself doing. Though Lucy would say she was quick to give advice to grown-up women with their serious crushes. It was only because she never planned to have another crush herself, so someone might as well make use of her experience.

And the fact that she was just a little bossy.

"Grandmommy sent me a text this afternoon and said she may come to Tallgrass for Christmas," Cadence announced without warning.

Marti nearly tripped over a crack in the sidewalk. "She did, huh?" Thank God, her house had only two bedrooms. Though Eugenie wouldn't hesitate to kick Cadence out of her room and onto the couch. The thought of sharing her own personal private space with her mom was daunting. She'd done it once before for a few weeks, and by the time she left, Eugenie had not only been on Marti's last nerve but was stomping it with four-inch heels. The evening of her departure, the margarita girls had added an extra night out to their schedules and dragged Marti from bar to bar until she was so happy and relaxed that they then took her home and poured her into bed.

"I always like when Grandmommy visits. But last time Mom told Dad that the house wasn't big enough for both of them." After a moment's reflection, Cadence added, "I think Grandmommy does some of it on purpose. She wants to see if she can make steam come from Mom's ears."

"Eugenie's always making steam come from someone's ears." Marti stopped at the intersection with Main Street and gestured. "Which way?"

Cadence looked to the left, her gaze skimming over the businesses, then turned right. "Bronco's is right up there. This girl Gillian in my class, her older sister is a waitress at Bronco's, and she wears this teeny little outfit and makes really good tips. Gillian says she's gonna work there when she's old enough."

Marti stopped herself from rolling her eyes only by biting her tongue. The prep school Cadence attended before coming to Oklahoma prided itself on the fact that ninety-some percent of its graduates went on to college, that seventy-some percent earned advanced degrees, that they turned out top doctors, lawyers, military leaders, scientists, and civic leaders. And here, Cadence's classmate's goal was to work in a soldier bar. If Belinda knew, she would probably deem Marti a failure and whisk her daughter off to that boarding school after all.

And Marti would miss seeing Cadence's sweet face every evening when she got home from work.

Maybe she would get a cat.

"So her goal is to be a waitress in a bar in skimpy clothes?"

"And make really good tips. That's the important part of it. And if that's what she wants, Aunt Marti, then that's what she should do. You know, the teachers back home always tell us we can be whatever we want to be, but then they treat you like a failure if you want to be something traditional, like a waitress or a nurse or a stay-at-home mom. They say, 'Why would you settle for being a nurse when you could be a doctor? Why would you waste your talents staying at home taking care of babies when you can hire someone to do it for you while you take care of your career?'" She shrugged her thin shoulders. "They don't have much respect for the people who make their world work, like waitresses and nannies and chauffeurs."

And paralegals. Bakers. Kindergarten teachers. Cowboys.

"Ah, Cadence, you're a wise girl."

"I know." Her gaze was directed ahead, probably on the neon lights at Bronco's, but a tiny smile curved her mouth.

They strolled another block or so before she spoke again. "Look, Aunt Marti. There's Mr. Smith."

Oh, Marti was *not* proud of how quickly her head snapped up, or of the pleasure that rushed through her the instant her gaze found him standing outside a café on the next block. One of the down sides of a cowboy who lived and worked on a ranch outside town, the opportunities to just casually run into him were somewhere between slim and none, unless she started hanging out at the farm and ranch supply places in town.

"He's really cute. I like him."

"I do, too."

Cadence's grin lit her face. "I know." In a totally uncharacteristic manner, she waved one hand high above her head and yelled, "Hey, Mr. Smith!"

He looked up, looked their way, and Marti hushed her niece even as anticipation spiked inside her. "Child, weren't you taught better manners than that?"

"Abby says sometimes being subtle doesn't work. Besides, if I hadn't gotten his attention, he would've gotten in his truck and driven away. Come on, hurry up." Cadence didn't sprint, but she lengthened her steps until Marti had to work to catch up to her.

Dillon met them at the street corner, his hand going automatically to the brim of his hat in salute. "For such a slender kid, when you bellow, you sound remarkably like an angry cow that's been separated from her baby."

Cadence smiled. "You heard me, didn't you?"

"I think the whole block heard you," he said mildly, then bumped her shoulder in an easy, friendly manner. His gaze shifted to Marti, and he almost smiled. Not completely, but it was enough to know that he was happy to see her.

God, how long had it been since a man was happy to see her?

He tipped his head. "Marti."

She mimicked his motion and his tone. "Dillon."

"We're going to the ice cream shop," Cadence announced. "Want to go with us?"

While one side of Marti's brain pointed out that there'd been zero mention of ice cream, the other side was holding its breath for his response. Going for ice cream was a sweet, old-fashioned thing to do, even with a teenage girl along, and last Tuesday seemed a long time ago while next Tuesday was still a long time away.

"I'm always ready for ice cream."

Something warm and gooey burst open inside Marti. Crap, she wasn't a warm and gooey person. She was practical and logical and analytical and never, ever overly emotional. But she couldn't deny that his small gesture turned a lovely evening into something much more spectacular, that anticipation was edging out complacency, that things in general had just gotten better.

If that wasn't being overly emotional, she didn't know what was.

*   *   *

The tension in the truck was heavy, electric, the air damn near too thick to breathe, but it was good tension. Claw-inside-and-make-him-ache tension. Expectancy. If they had to drive one half mile farther, Elliot didn't think he could make it. He would have to turn into the first empty parking lot, find the spot farthest from the street, and do with Fia what cowboys had been doing in pickups for decades.

Releasing her hand, he parked in the driveway, hustled around the truck, and opened the passenger door. She slid into his embrace, her arms going around his neck, her legs wrapping around his waist. Aw, she felt so damned good, so damned hot. They would be lucky if they made it into the house in time to avoid arrest for being lewd and lascivious in public. Her mouth was sending incredible sensations along his cheek, his jaw, his ear, as he blindly made his way to the steps, then the stoop, then inside the house. Getting keys from his pocket had never been so damn near impossible.

Happy to see them, Mouse was barking and circling around Elliot's ankles as he stumbled toward the couch. When the back of it banged against his legs, he bent, lowering Fia to the cushions, sliding after her, his hands tangling with hers as they tried to undo each other's clothing.

His blood was boiling, his skin supersensitized to every touch from her, his erection about to burst, when Mouse barked, then pawed at him. "Not now, Mouse."

She did it again, adding a pathetic whine that made Fia chuckle. "Aw, poor baby needs to go out." She kissed him, greedy, demanding, then pushed him back a few inches. "You take her out. I'll wait in the bedroom."

He tried to kiss Fia again, but she pursed her lips and shook her head. "Take care of the baby first." As he rose, she gave him a look. "Then I'll take care of you."

"Promises, promises." He headed toward the back door. "Come on, Mouse, and make it quick."

The pup ran down the steps and across the patio, then started sniffing. Depending on how urgent her need, the sniffing part could be over in seconds or take as long as he was willing to give her. Apparently, she'd exaggerated her need tonight, because she was on a trail and showing no signs of losing it.

"Come on, Mouse, you're killing me here."

The dog glanced up at her name, then bent her head again, pulling him across the yard. Finally, hallelujah, she circled, then squatted, and they got to return to the house.

The couch was empty, but a light shone from the bedroom. Elliot left Mouse snacking in the kitchen and headed that way, but when he walked through the door, the room was empty. He turned back, saw a wedge of light coming from the bathroom, and knocked on the door. "Fia?"

The door wasn't closed completely, so it swung open under the weight of his hand, showing Fia sitting on the floor, her back to the tub, hugging her arms to her chest. No, not hugging. They were drawn up that way in what looked like a spasm to match the one he'd massaged from her foot the other night. Her knees were bent, her left foot bare and turned inward, and her head was bowed, her forehead resting on her knees, her face hidden.

"Fia?" Elliot crouched in front of her, his heart booming like artillery, a shiver of fear rushing over him, icy enough to extinguish the heat that had been building inside. Gently he lifted her chin, forcing her to look up. "What's wrong? What's happening?"

She tried to turn her head away but seemed to lack the energy. "Ah can't…"

Her voice was weak, her words slurred. If he didn't know better, the words and the paleness of her face would make him think she'd gotten gut-puking drunk. His hands trembled as he cupped her cheeks to tenderly turn her face to him. "Do you need to go to the emergency room? Should I call 911?"

"No, no, no. Please. Jus'...jus' bed." A tear slipped from her eye and rolled until it hit his finger. "I didden want...S-s-sorry."

Hearing the sadness in her voice made his heart hurt. Why not, since his gut was knotted and his lungs were so tight he could grab only the shallowest of breaths? "Shh, shh, shh. It's okay." He scooped her into his arms, then stood, barely feeling her weight. Mouse was waiting curiously in the hall, and she followed them into the bedroom, where he carefully laid Fia on the bed. Straightening, he switched on the bedside lamp, but she flinched and squeezed her eyes shut, so he turned it off again. "What do you need, Fia? Tell me what to do."

"Pills," she whispered.

"Okay, pills." Yeah, he was familiar with the pills. They'd been raising too many questions without answers in his head. He took two steps that way, then pivoted back. "Which ones? Darlin', which ones do you need?"

With a moan, she rolled onto her side away from him, curling up in the fetal position. When he realized she was trying to toe off her other boot, he pulled it off for her and saw with despair that those toes were curling under, too, muscles pulling them painfully taut. She was in a lot of pain—any fool could see that—and he felt as damn helpless as a newborn baby.

And scared. Panic tumbled in his gut, threatening to spill over and leave him a quivering mess.

"Fia? Baby, can you hear me? Tell me what pills to give you."

Slowly she shook her head, mumbling words he couldn't make out even when he bent close enough to feel her breath. Straightening, he ran his fingers through his hair, then his gaze skimmed across her cell phone on the nightstand. She must have left it there before going into the bathroom, where this—this whatever the hell it was started. He grabbed the phone, scrolled through to the listing for Patricia, and hit Send.

Patricia's hello was cheery and motherly and eased his panic enough to just barely keep him from hysteria. "It's Elliot, Patricia. Something's wrong with Fia. She, just, uh, she has these spasms, and she can hardly talk, and—and her feet and her arms...She's whimpering." The sound was like a razor-sharp blade scraping his skin raw. "I'm gonna call 911—"

A weak *No!* came from the bed, muffled by Fia's position.

Patricia's cheeriness disappeared, replaced with concern. "No, sweetie, it upsets her. Besides, they've seen her like this before. They'll just give her the same medication she takes at home, run her through tests she's already had a dozen times, make her really uncomfortable and tired, and then send her home. What you need to do first is give her the pills."

"She can't tell me which ones she needs or how many."

"Go to the bathroom, on the top shelf of the medicine cabinet."

He covered the short distance in a few strides, jerked open the cabinet door, and asked, "Which ones?"

"Two from the bottle on the left, one from the second bottle, one from the third."

He popped open the bottle, hands shaking so badly he poured a half dozen in the sink. Clenching two in his fist, he got the next two. "Okay, so four pills. Is that all?"

"Yes. Get those down her and make sure she keeps them down."

He left the bathroom, turned to the bedroom, then spun around to sprint into the kitchen for a bottle of water as Patricia continued.

"If the lights aren't already off, turn them off. These spells make her really sensitive to light. If you can, get her undressed and into something comfortable, or I can help. I'm on my way over. Massages help with the spasms. Just be careful. You're a lot stronger than any of us. That's all you can do until the pills kick in. I'm already in my car. I'll see you in a few minutes." Patricia hesitated, then asked, "You didn't know about any of this, Elliot?"

"No." Though he'd known *something* was wrong. Though he'd wanted to know what. At this moment, he wasn't sure if he wanted to know more—everything—or wanted his ignorance back.

"Okay, start with those pills. I'll see you."

After hanging up, he pressed his forehead against the cool stainless of the refrigerator, trying to calm his breathing. He was worried. And scared. And just a little bit pissed that Fia had known this could happen when she was alone with him and still hadn't confided in him. Forget the trust and the falling in love. This was a serious health issue, and she hadn't told him how to deal with it.

Then his jaw tightened. He could think about that later. All that was important right now was getting the pills down her.

Back in the bedroom, he uncapped the bottle of water, set it on the night table, and lifted her up until she was leaning against his arms and chest for support. Her eyelashes fluttered as if seeing was too painful, and her skin was cool. "El?" she whispered.

"I'm here, darlin'. I've got your pills. Open your mouth so I can put the first one in."

"Doan wanna puke on you."

He'd never felt worse, but a chuckle came out on its own. "I'm a tough guy. I've been puked on before. Don't worry about it." He slid the first tablet into her mouth, then lifted the water to her lips. She drank, swallowed, and shuddered. Though he wanted to cram the last three down her throat with a big suck of water, he took his time, limiting the water she got, waiting a moment or two between pills.

When she swallowed the last one and let her head sag against his shoulder, he silently sighed. *Get her into something comfortable,* Patricia had said. Damn, he had so looked forward to taking off this dress tonight. He'd just expected it would be a whole lot more fun.

The buckle at her waist came open easily, and he tossed the belt on the bed. The zipper at her back slid open all the way past her waist, and he pulled her arms free, then shifted to lay her back. "This was supposed to be a whole different thing," he said in an even voice. "Me undressing you and you thinking, 'Wow, Elliot's the sexiest guy in the entire world. He's handsome, he's sweet, he knows all the tricks and has all the talent, and he's hung like a—'"

He was pretty sure her choked sound was meant to convey amusement, since it was accompanied by a pitiful attempt at an elbow gouge. "You are . . . sexiest . . . world."

"Thank you, darlin'." He pulled the dress past her waist, under her butt, and down her legs. He tossed it aside, too, and wasted a moment wishing for the next chance to see her in it and take her out of it.

By the time Patricia knocked at the door, Elliot had

removed Fia's bra, gotten her into a cozy T-shirt, and begun massaging her hand. He didn't try to talk to her. She was clearly fatigued and still in pain, groaning occasionally when he pressed too firmly or tried to work out a particularly strong spasm. He had a thousand questions, and that quiet anger still simmering, but all that could wait.

Patricia set down her purse and a tote bag that a pair of house slippers stuck out of. Clearly she'd come prepared to spend the night if necessary. Leaning forward, she hugged Elliot tight, the kind of hug his mom had given him for every upset and disappointment. He had an urge to bury his face, hold on forever, and let tears fall. It was amazingly comforting.

"How are you?" she asked, letting go, then cupping his face in her palms.

"She scared me out of my wits." He half wished Emily were there for one of her wisecracking responses: *Aw, El, you were always a dimwit.* "What's wrong with her? Is she gonna be okay?"

"We don't know. Let's see if we can make her comfortable, then when the medicines put her to sleep, you and I will talk, all right?"

"All right."

Grimly he led the way to the bedroom. He'd been wondering all week, and tonight, for better or worse, he would find out. He prided himself on being a good guy, honorable and decent, but he couldn't remember anything involving a woman that had scared him as badly as finding Fia on the bathroom floor. He hoped this situation proved him to be honorable and decent, but his gut was worrying the uncertainty like Mouse with a bone.

*God, don't let this be more than I can handle.*

* * *

The ice cream shop Cadence had so quaintly referred to was Braum's, sitting at the back of a crowded parking lot with cars lined up eight deep for the drive-through and families and friends crammed into booths or sharing tables. If Dillon were home, he would be getting ready to take his last walk around the barns and the pastures with Oliver, then going to bed. Town people didn't have the same concept of bedtime and late nights as he did. They didn't get up the same time he did, either.

They joined the line to order ice cream, Cadence stretching on her toes to see the various flavors in the freezer case. "Ooh, Aunt Marti, why haven't we been here before?"

"Because if I come here very often, I'll have to take up real exercise, and you know I just can't do that."

Dillon's gaze slid over Marti, from her sleek hair to her sleek outfit, all creased and pressed and showing a whole lot less skin than that yellow dress had. "You don't need real exercise."

"You haven't seen my butt after a few quarts of cherries, pecans, and cream or birthday cake ice cream," she retorted.

"The blue stuff?" He snickered. "That's such a kid flavor."

Her left brow arched as she looked at him. "I see you know it, too."

"Yeah," he admitted. On the rare occasions he and Tina had made it to Braum's, it had been Lilah's favorite. Tina had taken a picture once, snapped on her cell phone, of his baby with a blue-smeared grin, her expression pure delight. He supposed her family had it now. Why not? They had everything else.

They got their ice cream cones and were on their way to a table when a chorus of voices called Cadence's name. Looking pleased, she waved to the kids grouped around a table, then her gaze turned pleading. "Aunt Marti, can I sit with my friends? I'll be right in the same room with you. I'll never be out of your sight."

"Go on." They watched her walk to the table as casually as if she'd done it a hundred times, then Marti pointed to a table for two against the wall. He nodded, and she made a beeline for it, getting there ten feet ahead of another couple. There was a tinge of triumph to her smile as she took a seat. She moved with an easy grace, every movement flowing naturally, as if she didn't even think about it, as if it was pure muscle memory, inborn, smooth. Impressive.

"Cadence's parents don't give her a lot of freedom, do they?" Dillon sat opposite her, laying a handful of napkins on the table between them, swiping a lick of his chocolate chip ice cream.

"I don't think so. Her life is pretty tightly scheduled at home: prep school, dressage for a long time, dance, gymnastics, violin lessons, language immersion, cultural outings." She rolled her eyes. "Her mother is rigid about taking Cadence to museums, the theater, the opera, twice a month. It may not show, but my mother put me through the same stuff, only she didn't go, too. She sent me with other people. I had more culture growing up than a yogurt factory."

He smiled—at least, his best attempt in a while. "The first time I set foot in a museum was on a field trip our sophomore class took to the National Cowboy Museum in Oklahoma City, and the only way you'd get me to an opera or symphony is to hog-tie and drag me."

"Did you get kicked out of the museum?" At his look, she shrugged. "I hear you were a little, um, unruly when you were a kid."

"Just because I got thrown out of Bubba's a few times? Had a few suspensions from school? Spent a night or two in jail?"

"Oh, no, my sources were wrong," she said agreeably. "You weren't unruly at all."

"I prefer the word *spirited*." After a moment, he relented. "No, I didn't get kicked out of the museum, but my friend and I had to stay at the teacher's side for the last hour of the tour. She wouldn't even let us go to the bathroom by ourselves."

"You probably would've set it on fire." Marti sighed. "I never got in trouble in school my whole life. I was such a good girl. Really, the worst thing I did was negotiate with my mother: time at the beach for every time she sent me off for culture's sake."

She took a bite of her ice cream, swiping a cherry from the cone, her tongue licking the last bit of cream from her lip. Dillon watched a moment longer than he should have, realizing with a start that this was the best Saturday evening he'd had in years: ice cream, conversation, and a beautiful woman to look at. Ten years ago he would have been partying hard, lots of booze, maybe some fighting, plenty of women before settling on the one he would go home with. Was this an improvement or a sorry commentary on his life?

Marti glanced up and smiled, and the question answered itself: definitely an improvement.

"So how did a rich girl from back East with tons of culture wind up in Tallgrass?"

"I married a soldier. Some younger wives go back home when their husbands deploy, but I wasn't that young, and I had a house, a job, some good friends. Then Joshua died, and..." She shifted her gaze out the window.

He didn't regret asking the question. Joshua was a major part of her life, just as Tina had been a major part of Dillon's. Blocking them out, pretending they didn't exist, wasn't normal or healthy. He'd been doing it long enough to know that for a fact.

"I didn't really have anywhere to go," she finally continued. "I wasn't the same girl who'd grown up in Connecticut, so it didn't feel like home anymore. By then, my mother had moved to Florida, but I'd been too independent to move back under her thumb again. None of the places I'd lived were home, but Tallgrass came closest. And since I did have a job, a house, and friends, I decided to stay for a while. 'A while' became eight years and counting, and now it really is where I want to be. Where I belong."

Funny. When she'd faced trauma, she couldn't go home. When he'd faced it, he'd had nowhere to go but there. If he hadn't come back to Tallgrass when he did, if he hadn't met Jessy and Oliver, then seen Dalton and their mom, he didn't know what would have happened to him.

"What are you doing in town alone on a Saturday night?" Marti asked before taking a crunchy bite of her cone.

"I could ask the same of you."

"I'm not alone. I'm with Cadence. Besides, I am determinedly single. All my margarita sisters might be falling in love and getting married again, but I'm content exactly the way I am."

Contentedness wasn't happiness, he wanted to point

out. Being content sounded an awful lot like settling for what life had chosen to give her. He knew because, other than his desire to find Lilah, he'd done the same thing.

And settling could be awfully lonely.

\*  \*  \*

If Elliot hadn't spent so much time kneading bread over the past days, he was pretty sure kneading Fia's muscles would have worn out his hands and biceps long before he saw results. He didn't know how long it had been—since he'd found her on the floor, given her the medicine, called Patricia. He just knew at least some of the meds had kicked in a while ago, putting her into a deep sleep even though her limbs were still crampy and drawn taut.

Now, finally, Patricia stood and stretched out the kinks in her back. "I think that's the best we're gonna get tonight. Want a cup of coffee?"

Not particularly. In fact, the nerve-numbing provided by a bottle or two of whiskey sounded much more appealing. But the liquor stores were closed, and he wasn't going to go looking for a bar to drown his sorrows. "Okay."

She left the bedroom. He gazed at Fia, her breathing deep and steady, her T-shirt twisted a little around her shoulder, a strand of hair fluttering against her cheek. She looked peaceful, but he knew that was an illusion. Her sleep came from drugs and exhaustion.

He shared the exhaustion.

Quietly he went out, leaving the door halfway open. He found Patricia in the kitchen, coffeepot in hand, cups on the counter. "This isn't the first time you've done this," he said as he slid onto a barstool.

"Made coffee?" Her laugh was throaty and deep, but she sobered quickly. "Fia calls Jessy or me usually. Ilena's got the baby, Therese has her kids, Carly and Bennie are pregnant, everyone has a job. Well, me, too, since I joined Lucy at the bakery. We've all spent our share of time here. We all have a list of Fia's medications, which one's for what, how many."

He opened his mouth for a simple question, four words. He'd been wondering for nearly a week, had wanted to ask her and everyone who knew her, but now that he could, he had to force the words out. "What's wrong with her?"

Patricia started the coffeemaker, and within seconds, a rich aroma drifted onto the air. She took cream from the refrigerator, sugar from the cabinet, and set them with spoons on the counter in front of him. "We don't actually know."

"Don't know? She's on five medications—some powerful stuff. How can she be taking all that if they don't know what's wrong with her?"

"They treat the symptoms. As far as her diagnosis..." She shrugged, palms up. She went to her bag on the sofa, pulled out a plastic container, and came back. As she opened it to reveal fresh apple turnovers, she explained. "I didn't know Fia when all this happened. I just met the margarita girls, except for Lucy, at George's funeral about a year ago. When I met Fia, she was already having problems. They'd started over the winter. Little injuries, clumsiness, pulled muscles, that sort of thing. She was a personal trainer; she could run circles around most of the soldiers in town; the doctors said it was a hazard of her job. Take it easy, be more careful, rest more.

"Then it began getting worse. She started having migraines, trouble seeing, walking, and talking, and those awful muscle spasms. She went to the ER, and they did tests and ruled out pretty much everything they'd expected it to be. She did follow-ups with Neurology, same thing. She saw different doctors; each one just echoed the same response. 'I don't know.' After a while, she got so tired of it all that she stopped going. You're so darn healthy, Elliot, I doubt you've experienced the frustration of trying to get a diagnosis when everyone's stumped."

She put two of the turnovers in the microwave for half a minute, plated them, then filled two cups with coffee. Ordinarily, he would have offered to do all that—after all, this was as much his home as anyplace else, and he always did the work in his own kitchen—but he was too numb to get up from the stool. After setting the pastries and coffee on the counter, she came around and slid onto the stool next to him.

"After a while, Jessy and I began going to her appointments with her. We thought she needed an advocate who wasn't shy about demanding results. Jessy, as you know, has never been shy a day in her life, and I learned to be pretty commanding as a colonel's wife. We asked for a new doctor, and she got it. He started from scratch—new tests, more advanced ones. He was more proactive, but she still didn't get answers. Now, he's been transferred, and she'll be starting over again."

Elliot automatically picked up his fork and took a bite of the turnover. The baker inside him acknowledged that it was every bit as good as his own—maybe even better—but the rest of him was focused on the conversation. "So…" He didn't know what to say. He knew more now, probably as much as any of the others did, but he still didn't know a damn thing.

"Sounded like a better sentence starter when you said it, didn't it?" Patricia patted his arm before picking up her coffee and blowing lightly on it. "So she's been sick a year and a half, and no one knows why. She has a lot of good days. She has a lot of bad days. She gave up driving for the most part because she was terrified of what would happen if she had an attack in the car. She had to give up the training stuff, too. Luckily, her boss is a good man who kept her on staff. She doesn't love paperwork, but she hasn't hurt herself doing it yet."

Elliot ate more turnover, drank coffee, and let more questions tumble around in his head. How could they not find a diagnosis? They were doctors; they had all the tools of modern medicine to help them. Was it something that would get worse? Would the bad days start to outnumber the good days until the good days were completely gone?

Would there be more symptoms yet to come? Would she wind up bedridden? Would they ever be able to help her, or was she doomed to go on the way she had been? Would she ever have a normal life again?

Or God help him, would she die young and in pain?

Again, Patricia patted his arm. "I know it's a lot to take in. She should have told you when she realized that things were getting serious—at least enough so you'd know what to do on a night like this one—but..."

"Things started getting serious about five minutes after we met."

"Ah, the magic of love. My granddaughter says that when God chooses two people who are meant for each other, He puts a tiny piece of her heart into his, and a tiny piece of his into hers. And when they meet, they may be totally clueless, but their hearts recognize that their missing pieces have come back. Mind you, she's checked her own heart, and it's one hundred percent hers, so there won't be any icky boys coming around her house soon."

He smiled despite his mood. He loved kids and their logic and their faith.

Loved them. Wanted some. Fia was amenable to both marriage and kids, she'd said. But *could* she have a baby? Could she be a mother?

"I can see where it would have been hard for Fia to bring up the topic when we met. In the first five minutes, she caught me standing in the rain holding an umbrella for a dog taking a leak, talking to myself, found out I'd once chased my sister with an umbrella but didn't have a chance of catching her because she's got all the height in the family." He shrugged. "She was probably too busy trying to figure out if she should get in a truck with someone who was just crazy or was bat-shit crazy."

After a moment, he added quietly, "But there were plenty of other chances."

"You know about her background?"

"Yeah. Her parents should be—" Too late he remembered a few details about Patricia's life—how she'd fallen in love with her second husband while still married to her first; how she'd disappeared from her children's lives without warning and stayed away for the better part of twenty years.

"It's okay, Elliot. They should be whipped. And I should have been, too. I thank God and my family every day that my kids were able to forgive me. Forgiving someone doesn't sound so hard, but I think it's the hardest thing some people ever do."

He took the last bite of his turnover, got up to top off

his coffee, and refilled Patricia's, too. When she slid off the stool to stand, he followed her into the living room, taking seats at opposite ends of the couch, where she took up the conversation again.

"Probably the single biggest lesson Fia took away from her parents, other than the fact they didn't love her, was that they didn't want her. She was a stupid mistake they would be burdened with for eighteen years. They'd done nothing wrong, nothing to deserve her. Why should they suffer when it was all her fault for being born in the first place?"

Forget whipping; it was too good for them. The state should have taken Fia before the damage was done, put her in a good home, and shot the parents. They would never have caused any more harm, would never have brought any other children into the world to abuse and neglect, and Fia wouldn't remember a damn thing about them. She would only know the love and support of her second family.

*Nice fantasy, El. It's shameful that even today it proba-bly wouldn't come true. Twenty-plus years ago...Poor kid didn't have a chance.*

He shoved Emily back, then dragged his fingers through his hair, tugging hard enough to pull a few strands free. Mouse jumped onto the sofa, putting her front feet on his legs so she could lean close and sniff. For a long moment she stared at him—a silent accusation for not sharing his apple turnover?—before she stepped back and curled so her head rested on his knee. He moved his free hand auto-matically to the pup's head, finding the favorite scratching spot right between her ears.

"You're a good man, Elliot," Patricia said quietly. "Fia recognized that from the beginning. She couldn't bring herself to tell you right up front that she had problems. She's been alone a long time. She needed to feel like a woman again and not just a patient. She needed someone who was smitten with her, who could bring the sunshine back into her life. I don't think she intended to let it go this far, but she liked you too much to end it."

"She didn't have to end it. All she had to do was tell me." Even to himself, he sounded like a petulant kid.

"What would you have done? Would you have thought you hadn't signed on for that kind of burden? Would you have stayed around of your own free will? Or would you have stayed because that was what a good guy would do?"

He opened his mouth automatically, because the answer was obvious. He'd never walked away from someone he really cared for, and he'd never turned his back on someone who needed him.

But the words didn't come out. If he'd known the truth from the start, in those first few days when they were getting to know each other, when he liked her, was attracted to her, but could have gone on without her... Would he have done so? Would he have thought, *She's a great woman, and we could probably have something awesome together, but I'm not interested in taking on that kind of problem*?

All the confidence he'd claimed his whole life had deserted him. He couldn't say whether he still would have been gung-ho for the relationship or if he would have refused to give it a chance, if he would have moved on— another town, another woman—and thought of her from time to time with fondness and/or regret as the one he couldn't have.

Restlessly he dislodged Mouse and got to his feet. "I, uh, I need to go out for a while. Will you stay? Watch her?"

"Of course. I brought my jammies just in case."

At the door, he looked back. "I'm sorry. I just, uh..."

Patricia's smile was tinged with sadness. "It's all right. Go. Think. Be careful."

He nodded, walked outside, and climbed into his truck. As he started the engine, he felt like a jerk for leaving but couldn't find it in him at the moment to stay.

"Not much of a white knight now, huh, Em?"

# *Chapter 12*

Every muscle in her body hurt.

Fia lay in her bed, too aware of the emptiness on the other side. Even though Elliot had been spending the night for only the last week, she allowed herself a moment for self-pity. She ached, her headache hadn't completely given up its grip on her brain, and something miserable and tight had lodged in her chest, making each breath difficult.

The evening had been going so damn well. Nothing could have made it more perfect: the food, the music, the dancing. Even Elliot's run-in with Brian the bastard had reinforced her appreciation for his character, his honor, his plain and simple basic goodness.

And then her body had ruined it. Ruined everything.

A tear seeped from her eye, and she raised one hand to dash it away. The muscles protested, as if she'd overdone it on the weight bench. Spasms always left a bit of pain behind even when they were nothing but a memory.

The bedroom door was open, dim light shining from down the hall. Mouse was stretched out on Elliot's side of the bed, head resting on his pillow. *Just like a person*, he'd said once, and she had scoffed. *Of course she's a person.* The clock showed it was nearly 5 a.m., and the house was still. She was pretty sure someone was there—she had a vague memory of Patricia crooning to her—but she was just as sure it wasn't Elliot.

Hey, the man came over expecting incredible sex, not nursemaiding her through a crisis. No wonder he'd taken off, right? Wasn't that what she'd been afraid of?

One more tear sneaked out, the pain around her heart in liquid form. She let it slide, leaving cool damp in its wake, then mentally squared her shoulders and stiffened her spine. Elliot might be gone, but she was here, and she had things to do. Hurt feelings wouldn't stop her.

Cautiously she sat up and assessed her body again. A little nausea, nothing threatening. A lessening throb behind her eyes. Her head felt like a pumpkin stuffed with cotton, heavy and too dense for easy thought. Her bladder was functioning just fine, though, reminding her it was past time for a trip to the bathroom.

She eased to her feet, but before she turned down the hall, she looked out the window and confirmed what she already knew: Elliot's truck was gone. Patricia's car and her own were the only ones in the driveway.

Disappointment turned her walk into a shuffle, her feet too clumsy to work normally. After peeing, she slipped down the hall to the living room, hoping against hope that she would find both Elliot and Patricia there.

She didn't.

She went back to bed, curled under the covers, and let

one more lonely tear slide down her face before dozing off again.

*   *   *

The sun was shining bright when Fia awoke again, thin slivers of light showing at the edges of the windows. She still felt like a pumpkin head, but an experience like last night's could, and usually did, do that to her.

She thrust out one arm, feeling cold sheets where Mouse had lain. She wasn't surprised the dog had abandoned her. A person could only lie in bed sleeping for so long. By now, surely Mouse had moved on to lying on the couch sleeping.

But Fia wasn't alone. Without opening her eyes, she felt Elliot's presence. Smelled his cologne. Heard his slow, steady breathing. Waking with him nearby stirred such sweetness inside her, warmed her in that spot around her heart that had been cold for so long.

Then memory returned. Her body declaring war on itself. The fear in his eyes and his voice when he'd found her on the floor. The worry, the trembling hands. The waking up without him. Where had he gone? How long had he stayed away? Was he back now only to pick up Mouse and say good-bye? Worse, would he look at her with pity and say, *I'll stand by you*, when all he really wanted was to run far, far away?

It took all her courage to open her eyes and see.

He sat in a chair he'd brought in from the dining table, his hair pulled back into a ponytail, his clothes from last night rumpled, his jaw stubbled with beard. Wherever he'd gone, it hadn't been to shower or, judging by the weary lines etched into his face, to sleep.

The desire to close her eyes again, to feign sleep, was intense. The longer they could put off this conversation, the longer she could believe the fantasy: that she'd found a wonderful guy, who thought she was pretty wonderful, too. That she could have another happily ever after, one that would last more than a few short years. That her heart wasn't going to break.

"Hey, you." His voice sounded rusty, hoarse.

"Hey." So did hers. She rolled onto her back, sat up, scooted until the headboard was behind her. Her calf muscles protested when she bent her knees, and her biceps did the same when she tucked the sheet under her arms.

"It's after eleven. You ready for some lunch?"

Throwing up was one of her least favorite things in the world, and her gut was already tied in knots, so good sense said skip the food for a while. She shook her head, clasped her hands together, and swallowed. "You have questions?"

"Patricia answered a lot of them. She spent the night here."

"I know." *Where were you? Were you afraid to stay? Did you not want to? Are you angry?*

She would be pissed if she were him. She'd known chances were good she'd have a serious episode when he was around. She had prepped the margarita girls so they would know what to do, but she hadn't had the courtesy to do the same for Elliot. But prepping him would have meant telling him everything, and she'd wanted so very much for him not to know. For the way he looked at her and touched her and felt about her not to change.

"You should have told me." His tone was flat, but there was a hint of disappointment, maybe hurt, wavering in there.

"I know. But I didn't think it was much of an introduction to say, 'Hi, I'm Fia Thomas, I'm twenty-four and widowed, and I have an ailment that doctors can't diagnose that turns me from totally normal to totally disabled in seconds.'"

He conceded that with a nod. "You didn't owe me your life history when we met."

But she'd pretty much given it to him, except for her medical issues.

"But at some point…"

*What point?* By the time she'd realized her mistake in hiding it, there'd been no easy way to bring it up. No good lead-in, no guarantee of an outcome that wouldn't break her heart and probably his, too.

And honestly, there'd been that part of her that didn't want to deal with it. That just wanted to *be* with Elliot.

"Were you ever going to tell me?"

She pressed her lips together, and her palms, and her knees. Her toes curled beneath the sheet, but this time it was voluntary because she didn't think he was going to like her answer.

"I accepted a long time ago that a relationship was out of the question for me. I can't hold my regular job. I can't drive without risking my own safety and everyone else's. I have to depend on people in ways I haven't since I was eight years old. I'm no prize in this shape."

He didn't argue with her—didn't say anything at all. Though she hadn't said it in hopes of him denying it, pain twinged anyway.

She shook her head, trying to focus on getting out what she had to say in the best way possible. "Before I could possibly get involved with someone, I needed answers and successful treatment and, aw, what the hell, maybe even a cure. I wouldn't be a burden. I couldn't. But that night we met, I realized I could have a few good times, make a few good memories, without a chance of anything permanent. Without requiring a huge lifelong commitment. I could quit worrying, quit being the center of everyone else's worry, and pretend I was okay, that I was an everyday average woman doing everyday average things like flirting with a gorgeous man. Having dinner with him. Hanging out with him for a few hours. For just a little while, I wanted to be the woman I used to be, before the illness crippled my life."

Elliot sat still, stoic, his gaze locked intensely on her. She loved his intensity, but she loved it more when it was soft and aroused and full of warm, gooey emotion. "So I went to Sonic with you, and I had such a good time that I couldn't say no to the next time or the next. Then I didn't know how to tell you everything because I knew one or both of us was going to get hurt, and I couldn't bear that." She said the last part on a rush of breath, then inhaled deeply. Even with the six or eight feet separating them, his scents teased and tempted her.

Finally, he moved, shifting position, crossing one booted ankle over his knee. "You never gave me a chance."

"No, I didn't, and I apologize for it." The sentiment was way too inadequate, but it was the best she could offer. "But I learned a lot about you that first night, Elliot. I knew you had a sense of honor and responsibility and integrity that's rare today. I knew you lived by your own code: loving your family and your friends and your country; protecting anyone more vulnerable than you; being responsible; living up to your commitments; saving the world for everyone in your part of it. I knew..."

Her spine was aching from the slumped position, and a lump was forming in her throat. If she wasn't such a warrior girl, she'd think she was about to cry, but she never cried. At least, not in front of men.

Moving slowly, she pushed back the covers and scooted to the foot of the bed, closing most of the distance between them. His chair was at an angle in the corner, and she faced the wall, but she still had a very good view of him. His scents were stronger, and heat radiated from his body as the fine muscles in his jaw twitched.

"The unshaven look works for you."

"The rumpled look works for you."

His voice faded, and so did the lightness of the moment. What settled in its place was regret, resignation, despair. She knew all three well.

"I figured there were two possible outcomes. You wouldn't want to tie yourself down to a woman with as many needs as I have, or you would feel like you had a duty to finish what you started and stay with me." Her smile was brief. "Duty holds one hell of a meaning to a guy like you."

"Yeah. And now it's my duty to get some food into you and get a couple of pills down you." He rose from the chair, walked past, then stopped, resting his hand lightly on her shoulder. "You forgot the third outcome, Fia. That I would fall in love with you because you're the sweetest, funniest, strongest, and most open woman I know, and that I wouldn't care about your illness because it's not your health I'm in love with."

Her throat swelled again, a lump forming so hard and so big that it might never sink down. If it did, it would probably crush her heart. She tried to smile but couldn't, tried to sound casual but couldn't manage that, either. "What are the odds of that?"

He went to the door, pausing for one quiet question before walking out of the room.

"We'll never know, will we?"

\*    \*    \*

Elliot stalked down the hall to the kitchen, stumbling when Mouse circled around his ankles. He caught himself with one hand on the bar and snarled at her. Sitting politely on her butt, she snarled back, then gave him a look as if to ask what they would do next. Damn dog didn't even blink when he scowled at her.

*You're her rescuer, her protector. Why would she take a scowl seriously?*

Maybe it was time to hang up his white hat. This morning it seemed it caused him nothing but trouble.

He nudged Mouse with his boot until she moved aside. She'd already emptied her breakfast dish and drunk half the fresh water Patricia had put out, but she was never so full that she would turn down a snack. Maybe not yet totally confident that her luck had really changed and that he would continue to feed her?

He preheated the oven, buttered a half-dozen slices of bread, and slid them in. After tossing a slice of bread to Mouse—because the idea of anyone scared of being hungry sucked—he got two bottles of water and the pills Patricia had told him to give Fia when she woke up.

Once the toast came out of the oven, he plated it, tucked the water bottles under his arm, and carried it all back to the bedroom. Fia had put on gym shorts that barely showed under the baggy T-shirt, straightened the covers, pulled back the drapes, and tilted the blinds to let light into the room. It was the first time he'd seen the blinds open.

Damn, listening to her talk had been tough. *Be careful what you wish for,* Grandma had often warned, and she'd been right. He'd wanted answers, and he'd got them. Now he had to deal with them.

He set the toast on the bed, gave her a water bottle, and grabbed a couple of tissues from the nightstand before sitting down. She swallowed the pills without comment, chose the least buttery toast, and took a small bite. She swallowed, waited, then bit off another piece.

He waited, eating his own toast, until she'd eaten half the slice like that before he spoke. "Let me see if I have this straight. Your plan was to pursue the mutual attraction we felt for each other, have some fun, and then dump me before things got too serious?"

She looked affronted. "Wasn't that your plan, too?"

"No. I knew there was a chance it wouldn't go anywhere, that we'd have some good times and then it would run its course, but I always stay open to the possibilities. I didn't go into it with the intention of dumping you." *Of using you,* he almost said, but that wasn't fair. There had been women in his life that he'd known he wouldn't be with after a month or two weeks or, hell, even for a second date, but that hadn't stopped him from enjoying the time they did have to its fullest extent.

Besides, her intentions weren't the problem. He wasn't even sure exactly what the damn problem was. He'd driven out to the lake last night and spent hours hiking and staring at the stars and trying really hard to figure out what he was feeling. *Betrayed* was too strong a word, *disappointed* not strong enough. He'd thought she trusted him—had thought she was falling in love with him.

Damn it, he knew she trusted him. Knew a woman who'd been raised the way she was didn't let just anyone into her life. Knew she'd been as attracted to him from the start, knew she'd been hurt, knew she was wary.

He knew she loved him. Knew her heart had recognized its tiny missing piece in his heart, just the way his heart had recognized its missing piece in hers.

Hell, he wasn't even really disappointed. He just couldn't put his finger on what he *was*.

But he had time to figure it out. *They* had time.

Fia finished the toast and delicately wiped her fingers on the tissue. "I know you're angry—"

"I'm not angry," he interrupted a little too angrily to be effective.

"And I don't blame you. I never wanted to hurt you. I never thought…things happened so quickly…you're just so freaking special…" Her smile was unsteady, and as she looked away, the light glistened in her eyes.

Or were those tears? *Aw, man, don't cry. I can't handle crying.*

Her gaze came back to him. Definitely tears. "So now you know everything, and I can quit worrying, and you can start over. Move on. Find someone else."

His eyes widened, and his jaw damn near hit the floor. "Move on? Find someone else? You're dumping me *now?* Are you *serious?*"

She flinched at either the tone or the volume of his voice, but she managed to maintain some level of calm. "Elliot, I'm sick. I don't know whether I'm going to get better or get worse or if I'll even be alive a year from now. I don't have a future to share with you!"

Forgetting his hair was in a ponytail, he raked his fingers through it, snagging the band and yanking loose a half-dozen hairs in the process. He'd never met a woman who literally drove him to pull out his hair in frustration, but this one was doing a pretty good job of it. "That's bullshit, and you know it, Fia. Remember what you told me? Life happens in an instant. No one's guaranteed anything beyond this moment. The future can mean fifty years or twenty years from now, but it can also mean next month or next week or tomorrow. *Everyone* has a future. Maybe not as long as they'd like, but we all have one."

Yep, definitely tears. First one, then another, slid down her cheeks, catching at the corners of her mouth. That weakness he'd always had for a crying woman surfaced with a need to wrap his arms around her, stroke her hair, and swear to her on all that was holy that everything would be all right.

But he didn't know that for a fact. That big uncertainty was still gnawing in his gut, growing slowly but steadily, and he still didn't know what it was.

"You want kids, Elliot?"

The abrupt change of subject gave the uncertainty a big growth spike. His impulse was to blurt out, *Hell, yeah*, but good sense clamped his jaw shut first, giving him time to choose his words carefully. "I would love to have kids. But you know, there are a lot of people that just doesn't happen for. It wouldn't be the end of my life." Just the end of a few dreams.

"I can't have kids."

His gut clenched, and the tightness spread upward

through his chest and into his throat before he realized what she was really saying. She would be open to both marriage and kids, she'd told him, so in this case, *can't* didn't actually mean *can't.* "You mean you won't."

"You saw me last night. Imagine if I were thirty-six weeks' pregnant and that happened. What if I had a baby and fell while holding her? What if she choked and I was too dopey with my medications to help her?" A plea for understanding rang in her voice. "How could I take care of a baby when I can't even take care of myself?"

"They're called babysitters. Nannies."

"You work at a bakery. I do office work for the gym. You think we could afford babysitters or nannies?"

"They're also called grandmothers."

"Really? Well, I've been out of those for twenty years." Her forehead wrinkled, her look disbelieving. "Your parents live in Arizona. They've got lives there. You think they'd just pack up and move to Oklahoma to be full-time caregivers because their son's girlfriend is a crappy mess who can't be trusted with an infant?"

"It's called considering your options." Elliot shrugged. Honestly, he had no idea what his parents would think. Vicky and Mitchell wanted more grandbabies, no denying that, but enough to uproot themselves again and start over in another new state?

Probably. His dad's immediate family had all lived on the ranch for the convenience of the work, but he had other relatives who'd moved from here to there to help out an ailing grandmother, a mama with a new baby and three kids under five, a cousin who'd relocated permanently to keep her uncle from having to go into a nursing home. The Rosses cared about family; Fia had picked up on that right away.

She paced the room, then stopped at the window, one hip leaning against the sill. "If you were any kind of ordinary guy, last night would have scared you off."

"If I were any kind of ordinary guy, you wouldn't have brought me home with you last night." He mimicked her position at the other side of the window, but while she kept her gaze fixed outside, he kept his on hers.

"You didn't sign up for this."

"I don't remember signing anything. I asked you for a drink. You asked me for a burger. I invited myself to your house to cook. You dragged me into bed—"

"Not that quickly, and you weren't exactly resisting." The memories softened the sadness on her face, sent a good deal of it fleeing. Those memories could brighten his day, too, from drab and dreary to blinding sunshine, flowers, and rainbows. Damn near every memory of her had that effect on him.

"You can't make a commitment, Elliot. Because I blindsided you with my monster, you never had a chance to back off. You lacked valuable information that most likely would have led you to avoid intimacy with me. Now I can't let you commit to me until we find out what's wrong and what the prognosis is."

His snort told her what he thought of that. "You can't *let* me? Aw, darlin', do you even *know* me?"

He stepped toward her, and she stepped back. "I know you'd never force yourself into a situation where you're not wanted."

"True." He moved again, and so did she. "So you're saying you don't want me."

Heat flushed her face, and her gaze shifted away. She couldn't look him in the eye and lie. "That's what I'm saying."

The last step put her back to the wall, the bed table wedging her in. He didn't crowd her, but he didn't leave her room to escape, either. "Then you have to say it."

"S-say it?"

" 'I don't want you, Elliot. I don't want to spend time with you. I don't want to make love with you. I don't like your hair or your body or your dog or your cooking or even your bread. I don't like or want anything about you.' "

He fully believed she was capable of lying for someone else's good, but not today. Her mouth opened, and a few breathy sounds even made it out, but she couldn't say the words. Maybe it was pride; maybe her dignity didn't want to put herself in the position of telling blatant untruths. Whatever the reason, when her jaw closed, it stayed closed.

Leaning forward, he kissed her, then teasingly rubbed his jaw against hers. She gasped at the stubble and pushed him back. Sometime in those last moments, she'd surrendered, at least for the time being. He could see it in the faint hope in her eyes. "You do that again, I'll have new rashes to show the doctor tomorrow."

"The new neurologist?"

She nodded.

"Can I go with you?"

She hesitated before giving half a nod. "My appointment's at three thirty. You should already be off."

"I'll definitely be off." An easy promise to make when his bosses were her best friends. "Do you feel up to some real lunch now? Maybe egg salad sandwiches?"

He was walking away when she caught his arm. The hope was gone, sadness back in its place. "This isn't over. When I find out what's wrong, you'll be free to go. I won't let you stay if it's bad."

Another spike of uncertainty ripped through his gut. But he gently patted her hand where it rested. "Yeah, you'd better be looking for some middle ground there, Sofia. I'm not so easy to get rid of."

Leaving her to think about that, he left the bedroom, hooked on Mouse's leash, and took her outside for a go around the yard. "Fia's not the only one who needs to do some thinking, pup," he murmured. "I need to figure out what that big mess of something in my stomach is and get rid of it."

*   *   *

Fia had never been so nervous going to a doctor's appointment. She'd worn a flowery, flowy dress and her favorite flip-flops and put on makeup—when she spent so much time at home, she grabbed whatever excuse she could find to pretty up—and knowing she looked good helped her confidence a little.

But confidence wasn't the problem this afternoon. It was fear, a word she hated with a passion, that gnawed at her. Fear that the little hope flaring inside would soon die. Fear of expecting too much from the new doctor. Of being disappointed yet again or, worse, of hearing news so bad that she had no choice but to send Elliot away.

*You didn't have much luck with that yesterday.*

Covering her grimace at Scott's droll comment, she shifted awkwardly on the exam table. She'd never told a guy it was over and gotten a response like Elliot's before. He was crazy for not taking the chance to run like hell.

*He is crazy. About you.*

It was a lovely thought that sent all sorts of sweet, warm

feelings through her, quivering her nerves and shivering everything else. But...

Aw, hell, she hated that word with a passion, too.

It was nearing five o'clock when the doctor came in. All doctors ran late, she'd learned, though sometimes it seemed military doctors ran later. He was a slight, nice-looking guy, his black hair cut high and tight, his glasses reminding her of Harry Potter. He looked about as old as Harry in the first movie, way too young to be a board-certified neurologist. Had he graduated medical school at the same time he finished Hogwarts?

He extended his right hand. "I'm Dr. Haruno. You're Sofia?"

"Fia, please. And this is Elliot."

After they exchanged handshakes, he sat on the wheeled stool and adjusted his glasses. "I apologize for being late. I just got here last week, and I've been trying to go over all my patient records on the run. It's a good thing we've gone digital because a print copy might weigh more than you."

She smiled faintly. Her health record before all this began had been minimal: patient healthy, blood work and Pap smears normal. Hardly even enough to qualify for a file.

"They've tested you every which way, haven't they?"

She nodded grimly, hoping he wouldn't want to redo the tests looking for different results. She'd been taken enough electroencephalograms, slid into enough MRI chambers, and had enough blood tests and lumbar punctures to last a lifetime.

"I won't repeat all the tests, but I noticed that it's been a while since your last MRI and lumbar puncture, and I'd like to see how things look now. I also didn't find any record of an electromyogram, which you should have had back in the beginning. It's a test that records the electrical activity of muscles. It's not too bad. They'll ask you to wear loose shorts and a T-shirt, or they'll put you in a gown, then poke a few needles in you and zap them with current. Does that sound like something you could put up with?"

Fia glanced at Elliot, swiftly looking away before she made eye contact. "I can give it my best shot."

"Okay then." The doctor's owlish gaze met Elliot's before fixing on hers. "According to his notes, your previous doctor discussed the possibility of MS with you."

"Yeah, but he ruled it out." She'd been grateful for that, since she knew just two details about multiple sclerosis, and they both scared the crap out of her: It was a disease that attacked the central nervous system, which she needed for, well, *everything*, and it had no cure. When the last doc had taken MS off the table, she'd thanked God.

Was Dr. Haruno putting it back up for consideration?

Still avoiding looking into Elliot's face, she swiped her damp palms on her dress. That big tight feeling in the pit of her stomach was familiar, anxiety and fear and nausea and hope and dread, a combination she'd tolerated every time she'd thought the staff was going to tell her something important.

Wheels squeaking, Dr. Haruno rolled the stool to the cabinet, where he could have back support. "Generally speaking, multiple sclerosis isn't really something you rule out. There's no definitive test that says yes, you have it or no, you don't, though researchers are working on that. Usually, the way you diagnose MS is by ruling out everything else with the same or similar symptoms."

Elliot leaned forward in his chair. "Are you saying that pretty much everything else has been ruled out?"

"Like I said, I want to dig deeper into her records and make sure I haven't overlooked anything. But given what I've seen so far, I'm thinking that's what we're looking at here."

"Why didn't any of the other doctors think that?" It was Elliot speaking again because Fia was fixated on the turmoil in her stomach that was rising into her chest, tightening her throat, and swirling up into her brain. This appointment day had been just like every other appointment day. Was it really possible it was going to turn out to be totally different? Was she actually going to get a diagnosis after so many months of praying and hoping? And did it have to be a diagnosis that was so damn scary?

Dr. Haruno's expression remained solemn. "MS can be difficult to diagnose because the symptoms vary widely from patient to patient. There's a term in medicine, the Great Imitator, that refers to a number of systemic diseases that have nonspecific symptoms, symptoms that can be found in numerous other conditions. MS is one of the Great Imitators."

Then his manner changed from confident and serious to awkward, as if he wasn't comfortable with what he was about to say. More bad news? Did he suspect she had the most aggressive form of the disease?

"I don't mean to criticize your other doctors. I don't know them. I wasn't here. But...doctors are like any other professionals. Some are passionate about what they do. Some can't stand a problem they can't solve, so they don't quit until they do. Some see it as a job. They show up on time, put in some effort, but they don't really invest themselves in their patients' problems. And some are just calling it in." His face flushed, he shrugged. "I'm just saying that in my opinion, MS should have been fully explored as a likely diagnosis a long time ago."

Fia's shoulders slumped before she stiffened them. A diagnosis was good, even when it was bad. A diagnosis meant treatment, medication, knowledge, support, understanding. And if it couldn't be cured, maybe it could be managed decently. And with all the billions of dollars going into research, maybe a cure was around the corner. Maybe five years, ten, fifteen, they'd have a magic pill that would make her all better.

A lump swelled in her throat, and tears filled her eyes. She would not cry, not in front of the high school doctor boy and for damn sure not in front of Elliot. She'd wanted a diagnosis; now warrior girl had to deal with it.

Dr. Haruno laid his hand over hers. "It's not an easy thing to hear. But it's treatable, Fia. You'll have a normal lifespan. You can have children if you want them. The disease is important, and it always will be, but the treatments provide work-arounds. You can live a fairly normal life when you're in remission, and hopefully we can lessen the occurrence and severity of your relapses."

So her good days were remissions, and the bad ones were relapses. See? She'd already learned something new about MS.

"Do you have any questions?"

Her smile was unsteady. "I need to go home and learn something so I can figure out what questions to even ask."

He opened a cabinet door and pulled out a handful of pamphlets. "These will get you started, and of course there's tons of information on the Internet. Just remember, a lot of what's on there isn't true, so don't let any of it scare you before we talk again. So here's the plan: I'll get you scheduled for an MRI, a lumbar puncture, and an EMG as soon as they can work you in, then see you back here. We'll talk about medication, physical therapy, alternative therapies like yoga and acupuncture, and we'll figure out a plan for you. Sound good?"

"Yeah." She had to force in a breath. "About as good as being told I probably have an incurable disease can sound."

He stood, and so did she, stepping down from the table while he held her hand. "Remember what they say: Knowledge is power. Knowing what you're up against takes away most of the fear."

She clenched the pamphlets in one hand. "Then I'd better go home and absorb a whole lot more knowledge. Thank you, Dr. Haruno."

When he left, Elliot claimed the hand he'd held. There was such comfort in his fingers around hers. This was a hand she could hold forever...depending on what she learned.

"You ready to go home?" he asked in that husky voice she adored so much.

She squeezed her eyes shut to force back the tears, breathed deeply to clear her throat and lungs, then gave him a dismal smile. "Yup." As they walked through the clinic, then out to the elevator, she asked, "What did you think of him?"

"I think he's one of those passionate people who don't rest until they solve every problem they come across."

"Me, too." Though the last doctor had fooled her. He'd jumped to attention and seemed all passionate and concerned once Jessy and Patricia had told him what they expected, but apparently he'd just gone through the motions. With her *life*.

She remained quiet until they'd left the building and crossed the lot to Elliot's truck. With a heavy sigh, she stood next to it, head tilted back, the sun warm on her face. The hardest thing about adjusting to Oklahoma had been the winters. Though her home state didn't hold many good memories for her outside of Scott, when it came to weather, she was definitely a bright-sunshine-and-sandy-beach girl. It healed what ailed her.

But not this time.

Elliot had opened the door and was waiting, a grim look replacing his usual Zen-ness. She glanced at the booklets, the words *multiple sclerosis* jumping out at her, then gazed into the distance. "All along, I've been nursing this secret hope that everything was going to be okay. That it was just some funky fluke, some mysterious ailment that would run its course and miraculously disappear." Her voice quavered, but for the first time, she didn't try to hide it. "Even when I tried to prepare myself for the worst, there was always this optimistic little voice inside, whispering, *But maybe...just maybe...*"

The sun's warmth drained away, leaving her chilled and empty. "Now there's no more maybe."

Elliot wrapped his arms around her, pulled her close, enfolding her in the security of his embrace. She wanted to stay there forever. Wanted to break down and sob and be weak and let the fear consume her, knowing he would keep her safe, that when she was done, he would put her back together again.

She didn't break. She couldn't. But she leaned against him, drew strength from him, absorbed heat and life and hope from him. She stayed there until everything inside her began to settle, until the need to fall apart passed, and then she lifted her head and smiled weakly at him. "I guess we should go home."

"And learn things," he said, then a hint of his usual demeanor cracked his solemn façade. "Knowledge is power."

With his help—she didn't need it, just wanted it—she climbed into the truck, fastened her seat belt, and watched him walk around to the driver's door. If the two most important men in her life said it, then it must be true.

But she could barely resist the urge to point out to them that, sometimes, ignorance could be bliss.

\* \* \*

The last time Marti had invited someone to her house for dinner had been more than eight years ago, before Joshua's last deployment, when he'd been there to man the grill and her only responsibility had been tossing a salad and taking bread from the oven. The guests had been Lucy and Mike Hart and another couple from the guys' squad, and they'd sat on the patio late into the night, filled with steaks and grilled potatoes, and laughed and drunk cheap wine and beer.

Idly she wondered what had happened to that other couple. The husband had deployed with Joshua and Mike; he'd survived the battle that killed them; and his wife had basically removed herself from Marti's and Lucy's lives. Sometimes people just didn't know what to say. Sometimes they found the widow too frightening a reminder of the danger their spouses were in. Some widows resented it, were hurt, but it had just made Marti appreciate the ones who stuck around, like the margarita girls, that much more.

"Is the table set?"

She glanced up from laying the last piece of silverware on the dining table and smirked. "Yes, Mom, it's done."

Cadence, wearing an apron over her tee and shorts, placed her hands on her hips and tilted her head the way Eugenie always did when she was inspecting someone's work. "Did you use real napkins, not paper?"

"Yes."

"Real plates, not foam?"

"Of course."

"The good silver?"

"It's all good." Passing her, Marti pinched her cheek on her way into the kitchen. "I can't believe you brought an apron from home with you."

"I didn't. It's yours."

"I have an apron?"

"I found it in the pantry."

Marti widened her eyes. "I have a pantry?"

Cadence swatted her before returning to stir the sauce on the stove. When Marti had mentioned that she needed to talk to Dillon—the paper bearing the information she had for him crinkled in her hip pocket—it had been Cadence's idea to invite him for dinner. *But I can't cook,* Marti had reminded her, and Cadence had rolled her eyes. *I'll cook.* She knew only one dish—spaghetti and meat sauce—but it was very good. Add a loaf of garlic bread from the bakery, and *poof!* Dinner.

So Marti had called Dillon and invited him over. Cadence had been cooking, and Marti had been fluttering for the past hour.

*I don't flutter,* her dignity insisted.

*You do around Dillon,* her brain pointed out.

*A typical female reaction to a hot guy.*

Her brain and everything else snickered.

"Aunt Marti?" Cadence stirred the sauce, placed a lid over the stock pot of boiling water, then finished spreading garlic butter on thick slices of bread. "It's so sad about Mr. Smith's—Dillon's little girl. Where is she?"

Three glasses in hand, Marti froze in mid-turn from the cabinet. When two of the glasses clinked together, she realized her hands were less than steady and set them on the counter. "How do you know about her?"

Cadence compressed her lips for a moment before saying, "You're not the only one who knows how to Google."

"Of course not," she murmured, slowly placing one glass under the ice dispenser, pressing to start the flow of cubes. At any time, Jessy, Dalton, Noah, or their parents could type Dillon's name into any search engine and, on an idle whim, find out his greatest sorrow.

Life just wasn't fair.

The doorbell rang before she'd formulated an answer, and Cadence spun around, taking the glass from her. "You go answer and sit down and talk graciously until I call you for dinner. Go on, and don't disturb the chef."

There were some people Marti just didn't argue with—when every part inside her laughed, she amended that: at least this one—so she went to the door. For an instant, she studied herself in the mirror near the door: new jeans snug and fitted, top equally so, hair sleekly pulled back. A sniff of her wrist showed her perfume was still detectable, and her smile... Yes, definitely in place.

When she opened the door, Dillon removed his hat, his fingers flexing carefully. Cowboy hats, Marti decided, were no different than any other clothes. The more expensive they were, the better care a person took with them.

Then she noticed the vase in his other hand. "They're beautiful, but you didn't have to bring flowers."

"Good, because they're not for you. They're for the cook."

Stepping back so he could pass, Marti deliberately took a long, slow breath so she could breathe in leather and cologne and fresh clothes and cowboy. "She prefers to be called chef. She already likes you, Dillon. Now she'll be so impressed, she'll think you can do no wrong." Though she knew he could. She knew about Tina and Lilah.

But it was good to learn that people weren't infallible, that good people could make bad mistakes. And Cadence was a smart, compassionate, empathetic kid. She wouldn't rush to judgment. She probably wouldn't judge at all.

"What about you?" Dillon set the vase on the coffee table, laid his hat upside down on the hassock, then faced Marti. "Do you like me?"

The question caught her off guard. She could tease or make light of it, but a simple question deserved a simple answer, a truthful answer, and she tried pretty much always to tell the truth. "Yes, I do."

Would he now say that he liked her, too? It would only be fair, after all, and she always liked hearing good things.

He didn't say anything, but a smile slowly spread across his face, starting with his mouth, easing upward into his eyes, and there was warmth and appreciation and pure simple pleasure that sent a shiver all the way to her toes.

And that was better by far than any words.

# Chapter 13

I think it's a rule in most places that the chef doesn't have to do dishes." Cadence looked at her aunt, brows raised, and Dillon suppressed a smile. He didn't blame her. When he was her age, he would have chosen shoveling manure over washing dishes.

Marti nodded. "I may not cook, but I am a whiz at doing dishes."

"Good." The girl's smile was big and just a little sly. "Then I'm going to go to my room, *close the door*, and look over my homework." She stood, laid her napkin next to her plate, then pushed her chair back in place. She got a few feet away before pivoting back to pick up the vase. "Dillon, you're the first person who's ever given me flowers. Thank you." She brushed a kiss to his cheek, then hustled from the room as if an angry bronc were on her heels.

His cheeks grew hot. He hadn't been kissed by a fourteen-year-old girl since he was a fourteen-year-old boy, and it hadn't been quite so sweet back then. He liked Cadence. Wished he had a niece like her. Wondered if his daughter might be like her.

"Her parents never told me she had an interest in match-making." Marti showed no inclination to rise from the table and start clearing. Instead, she settled in, a cup of coffee in front of her, her pink polished nails tapping lightly on the china.

Dillon picked up his own coffee. "You ever wonder how they could leave her for a year?" Granted, it had been a hell of a lot longer than that since he'd seen Lilah, but that hadn't been his choice. Voluntarily picking up and moving halfway around the world...he just couldn't imagine it.

"It didn't surprise me. Nothing my family does surprises me anymore. I think..." She glanced toward the hall as if making sure Cadence's door was closed, then shrugged, "I understand Frank doing it, but Belinda...He doesn't need her in Dubai as much as Cadence needs her at home." Then she smirked. "But I get to be the good relative for taking her in instead of making her go to boarding school."

"That's what family does, isn't it? If Tina's family hadn't wanted Lilah, I have no doubt my parents or Dalton or even Noah would have taken her, even though they'd never known she existed."

"When are you going to tell them she does exist?"

He stared past her at the wedding portrait on the wall. Like all wedding portraits, it was full of happiness and joy and hope and possibilities. She and Joshua had had it all...until he'd died.

There were some pictures of Dillon and Tina where they'd looked like they had it all, too. They'd loved each other, hated each other, fought like wild animals, made up like soul mates. She'd been his best friend and, on occasion, his worst enemy, because she'd known which buttons to push, which tender points to jab when she was pissed.

If she'd lived, though, he didn't know that they would still be together. Sometimes he'd imagined a quieter, more peaceful life, just him and Lilah, without all of Tina's passion and drama.

Marti was quiet and peaceful, happy with herself and contented with her life. There was passion inside, but it smoldered rather than flaring regularly into fireworks. She was too serene and self-possessed to have caught his attention when he was young and stupid, but now that he'd grown, learned, lost...

"Well?"

His gaze shifted back to her while he tried to recall her question. Oh, yeah. Telling. About Lilah. "I don't know. It doesn't seem fair to tell them about a granddaughter that they'll probably never get the chance to know because of me."

"What if they find out about her some other way?"

"How?"

An air of discomfort came over Marti, unusual enough that it damn near shimmered in the air around her. After a moment, she stood, still holding her coffee. "Let's go outside."

Walking behind a pretty woman was always a good place to be. He could admire her dancer's posture, her slender waist, the curvy sway of her hips, and keep it to himself, though he doubted she was entirely unaware. Some things a man just couldn't hide, and attraction to a woman like Marti was high on the list.

They sat at the old wooden table, her tucking her feet

onto the oversized seat, him sliding a chair around to face her. It was a nice evening, warm enough to remember it was May, cool enough to remember that Oklahoma had gotten snow in May. Thanks to the lights of the city, there weren't many stars visible, though that didn't stop her from gazing at the sky for a moment before she met his gaze.

"They could find out the same way Cadence did. On the Internet." Her shrug was delicate. "It's what people do, Dillon, out of interest, curiosity, boredom. They Google your name and find out everything ever made public about you."

An ache stabbed through him, cold and sharp, that Cadence knew he'd killed his baby girl's mother. *She already likes you,* Marti had said earlier, so how disappointed in him had she been? Disappointing people was an old habit of his, but he didn't want to let down Cadence. She was a sweet kid.

Marti rested her hand on his. "She knew before you came over. Knew before she offered to cook dinner. She thinks it's sad, but she doesn't blame you."

He held Marti's gaze a long time, reading no subterfuge in her face. Was it possible? Cadence's attitude toward him through dinner had been the same as usual. She'd exclaimed over the flowers, waited expectantly for his compliments on the food, then kissed his cheek. He never would have guessed she knew, based on her behavior.

"Your family will probably feel the same way," Marti said, giving his hand a squeeze. "But it's got to be better coming from you than finding out online. And who knows? Maybe they will get a chance to meet Lilah."

Releasing him—damn, he missed the contact before the sensation had time to fade—she pulled a piece of paper from her pocket and offered it. "I located your daughter.

She's living in Colorado with her aunt Kayla. Here's the address, the phone number, and..."

His hand shaking, he took the paper and unfolded it. The information was written in a graceful hand across the top, and underneath it was a picture of a neat little house with a pink bicycle in the yard, pink flowers in the beds, and a puppy wearing a pink collar.

"I'm guessing Lilah's favorite color is pink," Marti said quietly. "It's a mapping photo taken last summer. At the time they drove down the street and snapped the pictures, Lilah happened to be playing in the yard with her dog." Her voice quavered to match the unsteadiness of his hands. "There's your daughter, Dillon."

And there she was, sitting on the sidewalk, her legs spread wide. A half-dozen old metal jacks were spread across the concrete—he didn't know little kids even knew what jacks were—and a small rubber ball was captured bouncing in midair. Her dark blond hair was pulled back in a ponytail with loose strands framing the smile that split her face from ear to ear, and just looking at her broke his heart in two.

His daughter.

Lilah.

He tried to swipe at his eyes subtly, tried to disguise his sniff as a normal breath. His baby wasn't a baby anymore, five years old in the picture, taller and heavier and looking all grown up, but she was still her mama's daughter. Still her daddy's girl.

"Oh, my God...I can't believe...Durango, Colorado. I've rodeoed in Durango before. Tina liked it there."

"Maybe that's why Kayla settled there with Tina's daughter."

He swiped his eyes again. "What about the grand-parents?"

"They live in Nebraska. Kayla has custody of Lilah. She works part-time and goes to school part-time at Fort Lewis College."

Dillon studied the picture again, wishing it were bigger, brighter, billboard-sized with brilliant colors. His little girl, caught at random playing outside her house, looking so damn happy.

"All you have to do is call Kayla, Dillon. You've pre-pared yourself for the worst, thinking you'll never see Lilah again. Now you need to take a chance at the best. Call Kayla. Talk to her."

His muscles twitched as if they craved immediate action—climbing in the truck, stopping at the ATM, and heading straight for Durango. He could just show up to-morrow, maybe have the same good fortune the mapping people had, and find Lilah outside playing. Ten, twelve hours' driving, no sleep, all this emotion rolling inside, he would probably look like a madman and scare both Lilah and her aunt half out of their minds.

He settled for standing up from the chair, walking stiffly to the edge of the patio, then back again. He didn't want to call. It was so easy to hang up on someone, to block their number, and put them out of your mind. But if he could show up, if Kayla could see that he was no threat, if Lilah remembered him and hadn't been too badly poisoned by her grandparents...

"I've got to think about this," he said. "I've got to figure out what to say, how to say it, how to not scare her, to—to not screw up." He looked at the picture again, then at Marti, who'd also stood in the last moment. Her smile was sweet, her gaze warm. He briefly considered asking if she would call Kayla for him, but no, that was something he had to do himself. Besides, there was something else he wanted to say to Marti.

He took a few steps until they were close enough to feel each other's breath, inhale each other's scents, absorb each other's heat. He raised one hand to her face, traced his fingers along her soft cheek. Leaning even closer, his mouth brushing her ear, he whispered, "I already liked you, Marti, but now I'm so impressed that I'm pretty damn sure you can do no wrong. Thank you."

He might have left it there, but something about her being so close tempted him, drew his arms around her. Maybe it was the huge emptiness he'd lived with so long. Maybe it was the basic needs of a man for a woman. Maybe it was her arms twining around his neck, her body pressing against his, her mouth seeking out his.

Whatever reason, it was the best kiss, the best moment, of his life.

\*   \*   \*

Elliot's eyes hurt, the muscles in his neck and shoulders were taut, and the hunger in his belly had surpassed his ability to concentrate on the computer screen anymore. Between them, their smart phones and Fia's laptop shared a history of searches that would do any brain doctor proud. And the doctor had been right: Knowledge was power. With each new article he read, with each new input of information, the knot that had lived in his gut since Saturday night had started shrinking. It wasn't completely gone, but it was easier to face an enemy he knew than one he didn't.

He rubbed his eyes before sprawling more comfortably and asking, "You hungry?"

Fia closed the lid of her laptop and stretched her arms over her head. "How'd you guess?"

"Your stomach's rumbling like a fully loaded eighteen-wheeler laboring up a mountainside."

"You can hear—" Grabbing the pillow beside her, she threw it at his head. He ducked and let it sail on past to the floor, where Mouse pounced on it. "What are you hungry for?"

"Hm. Let's see. As I remember, you made a deal with me a couple nights ago that if I took care of Mouse, then you would take care of me. I kept my end of the bargain. I've just been waiting for you to feel good enough to keep yours."

A flush tinged her cheeks pink before she stood and did another stretch, spreading her feet apart, bending from the waist until her palms touched the floor. The position muffled her voice since she wound up talking to the couch cushions instead of him. "That would have been an incredible night. It's too bad it got interrupted, because now, you know, all the anticipation is gone. We had that whole sexy-dancing-touching-music-holding-hero-cowboy thing going on."

She began easing into an upright position, her movements slow, one inch at a time. He loved watching her move. He knew from experience it was easier to speed through an exercise than to glide at a snail's pace from position to position while keeping perfect form. Her form was very, very perfect.

It was hard to reconcile this grace with the *spasticity*— a new word he'd learned—that he'd seen Saturday night.

"To get that back, we'd have to start all over again, and given that you have to be at work at four a.m., I don't see that happening until at least Saturday. However..."

She crossed to his chair in a few steps and slid onto his lap, her head resting on his shoulder, her feet dangling in the air, as her hands snaked around his neck. "I might be able to do something on a lesser scale." She kissed his jaw, his cheek, the rim of his ear, drawing a shudder and a groan from him before sweetly smiling. "After you feed me."

"Where?" If she would reply, *In bed*, he would be more than happy to feed her, and to do his share in making a grander scale for her offering.

"There's an IHOP near the main gate. I like their coffee, and they're open all night. And..." She shifted her gaze away and ended her embrace. "We can talk. Unless you're too tired."

He wished he could truthfully claim to be too tired, but he couldn't. Would he like a full eight hours' sleep tonight? Sure. Would he get it even if they didn't talk? Of course not. There was still dinner to eat, Mouse to feed and walk, Fia to make love to. Sleep was overrated anyway.

Talking was overrated sometimes, too. Especially the talk he was pretty sure she wanted to have. While reading tonight, she'd mumbled a comment or two about prospects *she* faced with MS, not them. She read articles about the progression of the disease, and the look on her face just about broke his heart. She'd started to read a few points aloud, scanned ahead, and said, *Never mind*, as if they were just too depressing to know.

He couldn't deny, a lot of it was damn depressing. But things could *always* be worse, so he was grateful for what they had.

"Get your shoes on, pretty girl." Elliot boosted her to her feet, making sure she was steady before he rose, too. "I'll give Mouse a quick once-around the backyard."

Hearing her name, Mouse left the pillow and trotted to the back door. He slipped her leash on, stepped outside, and followed her to the grass.

A lot of the information he'd learned danced around in his brain. Some had been too technical to understand, and some had been overwhelming, and some had actually been hopeful. Words like *not fatal*, *treatable*, *manageable*, *normal activity* were singing in his head like the "Hallelujah Chorus."

He was pretty sure the accompaniment in Fia's head was more along the lines of a funeral dirge. Her old life was gone, and it wasn't coming back. She needed time to grieve, accept it, and move on.

And she probably expected him to move on, too.

Damn, he hated to disappoint her. Not.

By the time Mouse headed back up the steps, Fia was waiting. She'd filled the pup's food dish and put fresh water in her bowl, and she'd gotten a jacket from the closet, a faded orange jean jacket that matched the flowers on her dress.

He remembered passing the IHOP his first night in town. It was just a few minutes' drive, only a block or so from the gym Fia pointed out where she worked. Despite the time—half past eight—the parking lot was full, the gym was well lit, and people scurried from machine to treadmill to weight room.

"I haven't been in a gym in too long. Should I try yours?"

"Oh, sure. The fittest, buffest, toughest women in town

either work or work out there. They'll treat you like a king."

"Huh. I've never been treated like a king before." He laughed at the sharp jab she gave him. He liked it when the right woman displayed a bit of jealousy.

He found a parking space near the restaurant door, and they walked in together, hands clasped. Her palm seemed damp, or was that his? Were those his fingers shaking or hers?

With the dinner rush over, they got a small table in a far corner with no other diners to disturb them. The waiter brought a pot of coffee and a bowl of flavored creamers, took their orders, and left them alone facing each other.

She rested her palms on the table, probably because they'd tremble if she put them in her lap, like his were. "Did you read enough to form an opinion?"

He chuckled. "I read enough to diagnose the next patient Dr. Haruno sees."

"It's awful."

"It's manageable."

She scoffed. "Fifteen years after diagnosis, twenty percent of patients are bedridden, and twenty percent more require a wheelchair, a cane, or crutches to walk."

The scorn in her voice couldn't hide the fear. If she found losing the ability to drive tough, losing the ability to walk would kill her, so he kept his voice level when he responded, "What happens to the other sixty percent?"

She opened her mouth, stopped, and closed it again. She was by nature, he knew, an optimist; it had gotten her through the crappy years with her family, had kept her safe and whole until she met Scott, had kept her here when Scott died because she was needed here. Now thin lines formed between her eyes as she scowled at him. "They're waiting for the ax to fall on them."

He poured two cups of coffee, dumped a tub of creamer into his, and stirred it with a spoon. "The other sixty percent are taking their medicine, doing their yoga, watching their diet, and soldiering along. There are even some who have very little deficit at all in their whole lives."

She reached for her own coffee and breathed deeply of the steam. "I have deficits, Elliot."

"Because you're not on the treatment plan yet. The medications are very good and getting better."

She shuddered. "I take enough medicines now, and just how much do they help? I don't want to be a walking pharmacy."

"The pills you take now are just treating symptoms. We're talking medications that alter or slow the course of the disease. And stop whining about how many pills you take now. I can shove a hundred down your throat every day and smile while doing it if it keeps you healthy."

She stopped in the middle of sweetening her coffee, everything about her going still. "Did you just tell me to stop whining?"

Her eyes were narrowed to laser-like beams, and he wasn't sure if the steam was coming up from her coffee or blowing down from her nose. He'd been in situations like this before, occasionally with a girlfriend but usually with Em. He used what had worked best for him in the past: the sweetest, most charming smile he could pull off and equally sweet words. "I love you."

The impact of the words didn't escape him. Sure, he'd said them hundreds of times before, but never to this woman. Never to the one who'd been nurturing a piece of his heart forever. And he didn't care if she said them back because he knew. He *knew*.

Her expression was comical, torn between outrage and laughter. This time the laughter won out. "I don't whine. If I do, you've got my permission to smack me upside the head."

"Aw, I'd never smack you. But I might tickle you until you lose control."

With that poorly chosen image, the cheer fled her face. "Bladder dysfunction occurs in eighty percent of all patients. So does bowel dysfunction. And sexual dysfunction. Elliot, you can't possibly..."

He got all solemn, too. "What, Fia? Be with a woman like that? Be with you no matter what happens?"

She leaned forward, the color drained from her face, and whispered, "I could lose sensation in important places. Sex could be off the table. Damn it, you could end up changing my diapers!"

He leaned forward, too, their noses nearly touching over the coffee cups. "Yeah, my dick could shrivel up and fall off tonight from too damn much anticipation. A meteor could crash through that window—or a ninety-year-old woman who can't tell the gas pedal from the brake. *Any*thing *can* happen, but that doesn't mean it's going to, and if it does, well, we deal with it."

Heat radiated from her, fading as she slowly sat back. "*I* deal with it. You...you're free to walk away anytime."

His jaw clenched on all the words he wanted to say, letters clawing with their fancy curled tips to get out of his mouth and into the air, but his muscles clamped tighter. The waiter provided a respite, bringing their meals, offering condiments not on the table. If he noticed the frost between them, he didn't let it show other than with his quick retreat.

After a couple moments, followed by maybe ten or twenty more, Elliot forced his mouth open, forced a smile and a pleasant tone. "You tried dumping me yesterday, and yet here I am. Why do you think I'll be any more amenable tonight?"

Fia folded her arms across her middle and ignored the ham, egg, and white cheddar crepes in front of her. "You can't refuse to be dumped. Guys don't do that. They yell at you, call you names, then go get drunk and screw around with other women."

"I don't do that." He arranged his eggs over easy on the toast, then speared the yolks and let them run. With sausage, hash browns, a biscuit, and gravy, it was a totally heart-unhealthy feast that he rarely indulged in. Tonight just seemed that kind of night.

"Then they follow you places, get in your face, make threats, and get their asses kicked by a white knight passing by."

"I don't do that, either. How are your crepes?"

She looked down at them, and he swore he saw her nose twitch as the flavor drifted up to meet it. "I've lost my appetite."

"Really? The way your stomach growled all the way over here? Huh. Imagine that." He cut a slice of sausage, dipped it in gravy, and made a show of *yum*ming it.

Grudgingly Fia picked up her fork and poked the crepes as if she wasn't sure they wouldn't poke back. She cut a tiny slice, slid it into her mouth, put the fork down, and crossed her arms again. A silent declaration: *I'm done.*

"Elliot," she began after a while. "I know I never should have gotten involved with you without telling you about my mystery condition. And I know you have this huge sense of duty to other people, and you want to make them happy, and you want to fix them, and it's hard for you to not do that. Like the girl at Bubba's the other night...you'd never seen her before in your life, but you felt obligated to help her out, even though her boyfriend was twice your size."

"I'm the one who walked away while he sprawled in the dirt," he reminded her, then relented. "As far as feeling obligated, hell, yeah. I wasn't raised to just walk past someone who was being mistreated by someone else. Emily's the same way, though she wouldn't have bothered throwing any punches. She would have kicked his family jewels so far up inside him they'd need a spotlight to find them." He raised one brow and pointed his fork at Fia. "That's what you would have done, too."

She wanted to deny it just to be contrary—he could read her so well. Instead, she whacked off another bite of food as if it had offended her and stuffed it in her mouth.

Elliot ate a few more bites, enough to satisfy his hunger for the moment, and set his fork and knife down. "Okay. I know what you want, Fia, what you need, and what you fear. Now I'm going to tell you what I want and need and fear."

\* \* \*

When Fia's fingertips went numb around her fork, her first distressed thought was the spasms were starting again. After an instant, she realized she was gripping her fork so tightly that she'd cut off circulation. Gingerly, she peeled them loose and waited for Elliot to speak.

He was going to make an argument that staying with her knowing what he now knew should be entirely his decision. That it had nothing to do with duty or feeling somehow responsible. That he knew what he was giving up—a normal life with a normal woman and a normal household. That he loved her too much to make any other choice.

He would tell her all those things, and like any other woman in the world, she would want desperately to believe them. She wanted it so bad that she ached with it. Accepting a commitment like that would make life so much easier. She'd learned that from Scott. But what right did she have to accept a commitment like that in her condition? How could that possibly be fair to Elliot?

"This huge sense of duty...that's just who I am, Fia, whether I'm with my family or you or my Army buddies or anyone else. It's the way I was taught: to care about others, to protect them when they need it, to help them when they want it. I couldn't change that if I wanted to, and I don't want to. I think being a good person is a better goal in life than being one who just doesn't care. And I know you understand that because you taught yourself to be a good person. To get involved. To make a difference in people's lives."

Slowly she took another forkful of dinner, actually tasting it for the first time. The crepe was delicate, the flavors of the eggs and ham and cheddar melding together beautifully. She let the surface of her mind focus on each taste, each bite, while deeper in her brain she concentrated on Elliot.

"As far as acting responsibly, wanting people to be happy, and making commitments, yeah, I plead guilty to that, too. I prefer to live in a better world than a worse one. It would be disrespectful to my parents and uncles and grandparents to act any other way. Now, you have damn good reasons to not respect your parents after the way they treated you, but me..." He shook his head. "They made me who I am, and they did it with love and responsibility and commitment, and that stuff is so deeply ingrained in me I can't ignore it."

She swallowed hard—ugh, another problem she might face as the disease progressed—and for a flash, envied him. Her parents had contributed to who she was, too, though not in a good way. The good stuff had come from her own stubborn determination, from Scott and the friends she'd been blessed with.

Elliot was a blessing, too, wasn't he? She'd known that from the instant she'd realized she was falling for him—no, even before that. The night they met, the tender care he'd taken with a scrawny, vulnerable puppy, umbrella and all...That was when she'd realized he was a very special man. A man who brought happiness to everyone in his path. A man her friends adored and respected from the start.

A man who could spend hours studying the effects of a disease, then look at the woman who had it and say, *I love you.*

He sipped his coffee, his strong fingers gripping the mug with just the right pressure, the way he touched her. She had vague memories of Saturday night, but there were flashes of recall, of him unfolding her fingers so gently, rubbing away the pain, never pushing harder than she could take.

*When he could have taken off instead,* came Scott's

drawl. *He's a stand-up guy, Fia, and I know you have trouble believing this, but you're damn well worth standing up for.*

"I know the word you hate most in the world," Elliot went on. "Your worthless parents made you feel like a burden. Even though you've overcome pretty much everything else, you've never overcome that fear of being someone else's burden. Do you think Carly feels burdened by Dane, or Bennie by Calvin, because they've got health issues?"

She thought of her friends, both pregnant and happy and deeply in love with their husbands, and envy turned her voice into a breathy squeak. "No."

"Did Carly know from the beginning that Dane had lost his leg? Did Calvin tell Bennie right from the start that he had PTSD?"

"No."

"You guys take privacy to extremes around here, don't you?" Elliot shook his head, his expression bemused. "For what it's worth, I had the measles when I was a kid, but the vaccinations took care of everything else. I've been stepped on by a few horses, had a few black eyes, mostly from Em, and had stitches a few times, along with a couple bruised ribs after encounters in drinking establishments that didn't turn out as well as the one at Bubba's. I also discovered once that I could be too drunk to get an erection, much to the disappointment of myself and a pretty little Carolina girl, and I have never been that drunk since."

Fia didn't want to soften or be amused, but she couldn't stop herself from adding to his record. "And you've still got scars on your ankle from a miniature poodle with pink bows on her ears."

"That was one ferocious dog," he defended himself. "Of

course, if I had to go around with bows on my ears, I'd be pretty pissed off at the world, too."

After his grin faded, he took her hand. "Fia, the point is, loving somebody and making a commitment to them doesn't have anything to do with health or wealth or social status or career or any of that stuff. It has to do with who you are and who I am and the fact that we're better people together than we are apart. You having some disease... yeah, it's awful, and I wouldn't wish it on anyone, but it doesn't change who you are, and it doesn't change who I am. Who you are is a strong, intelligent, hardheaded woman who's been on her own so long that you're afraid to let someone else in for the long haul."

At least he got the *hardheaded* part right. Strong? She used to be. Intelligent? Her head had been so muddled with frustration and helplessness that she wasn't sure how much intelligence remained. After all, she was trying her best to break up with the best guy she'd ever met since Scott. Nothing smart about that, was there?

"And who are you?" Her voice was tight, broken between words by the lump rising in her throat.

He gazed at her with the intensity that had made her shivery from the start. "I'm the guy who's in it for the long haul, no matter how hard you push me away. You may not have learned this yet, darlin', but I'm a little on the hard-headed side, too. I know, I know, I come off as all soft and easygoing and biddable—"

She snickered. "What twenty-eight-year-old man says *biddable*? Wait, I bet your grandma used to say it."

"Nope. I picked that one up totally on my own." He flashed a grin, but the fierce look in his eyes didn't lessen. "Now, where was I? Oh, yeah, biddable. But deep down,

I'm like a dog with a bone. When I want something, I don't give up."

She waited for him to go on, but he didn't. "Until you get it," she prompted. "You don't give up until you get it."

"No. I don't give up. I never give up."

He would never give up on her. So how in the world could she give up on them so easily?

*We're better people together than we are apart.* He really believed that. Did she?

All it took to answer that was a scan of the past few weeks. All the tenderness, all the feelings that she was once again part of a whole, all her smiles and happiness and hopefulness—all of it had come from or been in response to Elliot. He had that missing part of her heart. She could live without it, but why in the world would she want to?

Slowly she lifted her gaze to Elliot. A smile was tugging at her mouth, pulling wider until it spread across her face, sending warmth and pleasure through her. She hadn't really smiled since Saturday night, and damn, how she'd missed it.

She slid to her feet, picked up the ticket, grabbed his hand, and pulled him up. "You've been taking care of Mouse the past few days. Now it's time for me to live up to my end of the bargain and take care of you. After all..." She gave him a wicked look over her shoulder. "We don't want any body parts falling off, do we?"

# *Epilogue*

It was Saturday night, the evening was still, the heat was hanging around, and sheet lightning was putting on a show off in the northwest sky. Exhausted in a totally comfortable happy way, Elliot lay on a chaise longue on the patio, Mouse curled by his feet, with a beer resting on an upside-down bucket serving as a table. Beside him, Fia lay on a matching chaise. She wore shorts that left her long legs bare, a thin top that left glimpses of her belly bare, and his straw Stetson, tipped forward to cover most of her face. Her water bottle sat on the bucket, too.

It had become their habit to come out on warm still nights and laze—or as Elliot liked to think of it, be one with the universe. They watched the sun set, looked for comets and shooting stars, and mostly found airplanes. It was a peaceful, restful end to their days—peaceful and restful being something Dr. Haruno highly recommended.

This second Saturday in June, while a hell of a lot of fun, had been far from either one.

"Are you awake under there?"

"Yup." She removed his hat and looked at him. "The margarita girls throw one hell of a party, don't they?"

"Yes, ma'am, they do." It had started as a simple little barbecue to celebrate that school was out, for the students—the kids, Dane, Bennie, and Noah—and the teachers, Carly and Therese. Then since it was June, they'd added Carly and Dane's anniversary, and they couldn't overlook little John's big oh-one birthday. Patricia's son and daughter-in-law, Ben and Avi, were heading back to Georgia from leave, the Smith family was meeting Dillon's daughter, Lilah, for the first time, and Elliot's own family was coming to town to meet Fia for the first time. The simple little school's-out party had become a huge celebration of everything.

It had been the best first meeting in the history of family first meetings. "You know my family adored you," he mentioned, just in case she'd let uncertainty blind her to the obvious.

Her smile was broad and teasing. "I know. Your mom said after tire-iron girl and foul-mouthed English girl, she'd begun to worry about your taste in women, but I was even better than she dared hope for."

His expression wrinkled into a grimace. "She told you about them, huh?"

"Oh, babe, while you were off with the guys, your mom and Emily told me *every* embarrassing moment and bad choice in your life."

"Nah, couldn't have. That would take way more than one day."

She reached across to tuck her hand in his. "I like the Emily-saves-Elliot stories."

He chuckled. "To be honest, some of the Emily-saves-Elliot stories happened because Emily got Elliot into the bad situation to start."

"But she never left him there. You said everyone should have an Em in their lives." Fia gazed into the sky, satisfaction radiating in lazy waves around her. "And now I do."

"Damn right you do." While Elliot had been "off with the guys," he, his father, and Bill had talked at length about the future with regards to Fia's health. Mitchell's and Bill's offer had been simple: If and when her MS began progressing more rapidly, they were more than open to a move to Tallgrass to help out. Family was family. They celebrated together when things were good and pulled together when they were bad.

It had been enough to bring a lump to Elliot's throat, but he hadn't been surprised. That was the way the Rosses were. They took care of their own.

And Fia was theirs now, too.

Damn, he'd been blessed.

After a moment's silence, Fia spoke. "I counted four pregnant women today: Carly, Bennie, Avi, and Ilena. Jessy and Marti and I are betting Lucy's next."

"Maybe you'll be." He said it casually, but everything inside him tightened, awaiting her answer. He tried not to pressure her about it, but he couldn't help wanting. He hoped that as time went on and her medications returned her to relative normalcy, she'd get more comfortable with the idea.

And the meds were working. She'd had only a few minor episodes since that awful Saturday night. Her energy was coming back; she wasn't afraid to walk Mouse by herself; she'd regained the weight she'd lost, thanks to his cooking, she teased; and she'd even talked about taking on a couple of her favorite training clients this summer.

She gave him a long look, then set his hat aside and slid across the small space between them to share his chaise. He turned on his side to make room for her, though it meant lying very, very close and touching, well, everywhere. Anticipation started in his belly, spreading with each beat of his heart.

"Who knows?" Fia said at last, her tone thoughtful. "Maybe it *will* be me." In a voice so soft he barely heard it, she said, "And then everything will be perfect."

Wrapping his arms around her, sliding onto his back again and lifting her onto him, he said, "It's all a matter of attitude, darlin'. From my perspective, everything *is* perfect. Right now. Right here. You know, life happens in an instant. You blink, and you miss it. We're not gonna blink, either one of us. We're not gonna miss a thing." Not in the six weeks since they'd met, not in the six weeks, six months, or sixty years they had ahead of them. Whatever future they faced, they faced it together.

With a sweet sigh, she rested her head on his shoulder. "I love you, Elliot."

"I love you, too."

"I'm so glad you came to Tallgrass."

"I couldn't have stayed away. Remember, I told you I was looking for a place that felt like home."

"And you even made a list of what it needed to be home." She lifted her head to look at him "What's on that list?"

He gazed into her solemn eyes a long time, raising one hand to gently brush through her hair. He'd been born knowing he was damn lucky but never so much as he was right that moment. "You are, darlin'," he said in a husky voice.

"Just you."

After losing her husband in Afghanistan, Carly Lowry rebuilds her life in Tallgrass, Oklahoma. She has a job she loves and the best friends in the world. She's comfortable and content...until she meets ruggedly handsome Staff Sergeant Dane Clark who rekindles desires Carly isn't quite sure she's ready to feel.

Please see the next page for an excerpt from

## *A Hero to Come Home To*

and see how the Tallgrass series began...

# Chapter One

*One year later*

It had taken only three months of living in Oklahoma for Carly to learn that March could be the most wonderful place on earth or the worst. This particular weekend was definitely in the wonderful category. The temperature was in the midseventies, warm enough for short sleeves and shorts, though occasionally a breeze off the water brought just enough coolness to chill her skin. The sun was bright, shining hard on the stone and concrete surfaces that surrounded them, sharply delineating the new green buds on the trees and the shoots peeking out from the rocky ground.

It was a beautiful clear day, the kind that Jeff had loved, the kind they would have spent on a long walk or maybe just lounging in the backyard with ribs smoking on the grill. There was definitely a game on TV—wasn't it about time for March Madness?—but he'd preferred to spend his time off with her. He could always read about the games in the paper.

Voices competed with the splash of the waterfall as she

touched her hand to her hip pocket, feeling the crackle of paper there. The photograph went everywhere with her, especially on each new adventure she took with her friends. And this trip to Turner Falls, just outside Davis, Oklahoma, while tame enough, was an adventure for her. Every time she left their house in Tallgrass, two hours away, was an adventure of sorts. Every night she went to sleep without crying, every morning she found the strength to get up.

"There's the cave." Jessy, petite and red haired, gestured to the opening above and to the right of the waterfall. "Who wants to be first?"

The women looked around at each other, but before anyone else could speak up, Carly did. "I'll go." These adventures were about a lot of things: companionship, support, grieving, crying, laughing, and facing fears.

There was only one fear Carly needed to face today: her fear of heights. She estimated the cave at about eighty feet above the ground, based on the fact that it was above the falls, which were seventy-two feet high, according to the T-shirts they'd all picked up at the gift shop. Not a huge height, so not a huge fear, right? And it wasn't as if they'd be actually climbing. The trail was steep in places, but anyone could do it. She could do it.

"I'll wait here," Ilena said. Being twenty-eight weeks pregnant with a child who would never know his father limited her participation in cave climbing. "Anything you don't want to carry, leave with me. And be sure you secure your cameras. I don't want anything crashing down on me from above."

"Yeah, everyone try not to crash down on Ilena," Jessy said drily as the women began unloading jackets and water bottles on their friend.

"Though if you do fall, aim for me," Ilena added. "I'm pretty cushiony these days." Smiling, she patted the roundness of her belly with jacket-draped arms. With pale skin and white-blond hair, she resembled a rather anemic snowman whose builders had emptied an entire coat closet on it.

Carly faced the beginning of the trail, her gaze rising to the shadow of the cave mouth. Every journey started with one step—the mantra Jeff had used during his try-jogging-you'll-love-it phase. She hadn't loved it at all, but she'd loved him so she'd given it a shot and spent a week recovering from shocks such as her joints had never known.

One step, then another. The voices faded into the rush of the falls again as she pulled herself up a steep incline. She focused on not noticing that the land around her was more vertical than not. She paid close attention to spindly trees and an occasional bit of fresh green working its way up through piles of last fall's leaves. She listened to the water and thought a fountain would be a nice addition to her backyard this summer, one in the corner where she could hear it from her bedroom with the window open.

And before she realized it, she was squeezing past a boulder and the cave entrance was only a few feet away. A triumphant shout rose inside her and she turned to give it voice, only to catch sight of the water thundering over the cliff, the pool below that collected it and Ilena, divested of her burden now and calling encouragement.

"Oh, holy crap," she whispered, instinctively backing against the rough rock that formed the floor of the cave entrance.

Heart pounding, she turned away from the view below, grabbed a handful of rock and hauled herself into the cave. She collapsed on the floor, unmindful of the dirt or any crawly things she might find inside, scooted on her butt until the nearest wall was at her back, then let out the breath squeezing her chest.

Her relieved sigh ended in a squeak as her gaze connected with another no more than six feet away. "Oh, my God!" Jeff's encouragement the first time she'd come eye to eye with a mouse echoed in her head: *"He's probably as scared of you as you are of him."*

The thought almost loosed a giggle, but she was afraid it would have turned hysterical. The man sitting across the cave didn't look as if he were scared of anything, though that might well change when her friends arrived. His eyes were dark, his gaze narrowed, as if he didn't like his solitude interrupted. It was impossible to see what color his hair was, thanks to a very short cut and the baseball cap he wore with the insignia of the 173rd Airborne Brigade Combat Team. He hadn't shaved in a day or two, and he was lean, long, solid, dressed in a T-shirt and faded jeans with brand-new running shoes.

He shifted awkwardly, sliding a few feet farther into the cave, onto the next level of rock, then ran his hands down his legs, smoothing his jeans.

Carly forced a smile. "I apologize for my graceless entrance. Logically, I knew how high I was, but as long as I didn't look, I didn't have to *really* know. I have this thing about heights, but nobody knows"—she tilted her head toward the entrance where the others' voices were coming closer—"so I'd appreciate it if you didn't say anything."

Stopping for breath, she grimaced. Apparently, she'd learned to babble again, as if she hadn't spoken to a stranger—a male stranger, at least—in far too long. She'd babbled with every man she'd met until Jeff. Though he'd been exactly the type to intimidate her into idiocy, he never had. Talking to him had been easy from the first moment.

"I'm Carly, and I hope you don't mind company because I think the trail is pretty crowded with my friends right now." She gestured toward the ball cap. "Are you with the Hundred Seventy-Third?"

There was a flicker of surprise in his eyes that she recognized the embroidered insignia. "I was. It's been a while." His voice was exactly what she expected: dark, raspy, as if he hadn't talked much in a long time.

"Are you at Fort Sill now?" The artillery post at Lawton was about an hour and a half from the falls. It was Oklahoma's only other Army post besides Fort Murphy, two hours northeast at Tallgrass.

"No." His gaze shifted to the entrance when Jessy appeared, and he moved up another level of the ragged stone that led to the back of the shallow cave.

"Whoo!" Jessy's shout echoed off the walls, then her attention locked on the man. The tilt of her green eyes gave her smile a decided feline look. "Hey, guys, we turn our back on her for one minute, and Carly's off making new friends." She heaved herself into the cave and, though there was plenty of room, nudged Carly toward the man before dropping to the stone beside her. She leaned past, offering her hand. "Hi, I'm Jessy. Who are you?"

Carly hadn't thought of offering her hand or even asking his name, but direct was Jessy's style, and it usually brought results. This time was no different, though he hesitated before extending his hand. "I'm Dane."

"Dane," Therese echoed as she climbed up. "Nice name. I'm Therese. And what are you doing up here in Wagon Wheel Cave?"

"Wishing he'd escaped before we got here," Carly murmured, and she wasn't sure but thought she heard an agreeing grunt from him.

The others crowded in, offering their names—Fia, Lucy, and Marti—and he acknowledged each of them with a nod. Somewhere along the way, he'd slipped off the ball cap and pushed it out of sight, as though he didn't want to advertise the fact that he'd been Airborne. As if they wouldn't recognize a high-and-tight haircut, but then, he didn't know he'd been cornered by a squad of Army wives.

*Widows*, Carly corrected herself. They might consider the loose-knit group of fifteen to twenty women back in Tallgrass just friends. They might jokingly refer to themselves as the Tuesday Night Margarita Club, but everyone around Tallgrass knew who they really were, even if people rarely said the words to them.

The Fort Murphy Widows' Club.

Marti, closest to the entrance, leaned over the edge far enough to make Carly's heart catch in her chest. "Hey, Ilena, say hi to Dane!"

"Hello, Dane!" came a distant shout.

"We left her down below. She's preggers." At Dane's somewhat puzzled gesture, Marti yelled out again, "Dane says hi!"

"Bet you've never been alone in a small cave with six women," someone commented.

"Hope you're not claustrophobic," someone else added.

He did look a bit green, Carly thought, but not from claustrophobia. He'd found the isolation he was seeking, only to have a horde of chatty females descend on him. But who went looking for isolation in a public park on a beautiful warm Saturday?

Probably lots of people, she admitted, given how many millions of acres of public wilderness there were. But Turner Falls wasn't isolated wilderness. Anyone could drive in. And the cave certainly wasn't isolated. Even she could reach it.

Deep inside, elation surged, a quiet celebration. Who knew? Maybe this fall she would strap into the bungee ride at the Tulsa State Fair and let it launch her into the stratosphere. But first she had to get down from here.

Her stomach shuddered at the thought.

After a few minutes' conversation and picture taking, her friends began leaving again in the order in which they'd come. With each departure, Carly put a few inches' space between her and Dane until finally it was her turn. She took a deep breath...and stayed exactly where she was. She could see the ground from here if she leaned forward except no way was she leaning forward with her eyes open. With her luck, she'd get dizzy and pitch out headfirst.

"It's not so bad if you back out." Despite his brief conversation with the others, Dane's voice still sounded rusty. "Keep your attention on your hands and feet, and don't forget to breathe."

"Easy for you to say." Her own voice sounded reedy, unsteady. "You used to jump out of airplanes for a living."

"Yeah, well, it's not the jumping that's hard. It's the landing that can get you in a world of trouble."

On hands and knees, she flashed him a smile as she scooted in reverse until there was nothing but air beneath her feet. Ready to lunge back inside any instant, she felt for the ledge with her toes and found it, solid and wide and really not very different from a sidewalk, if she discounted the fact that it was eighty feet above the ground. "You never did say where you're stationed," she commented.

"Fort Murphy. It's a couple hours away—"

"At Tallgrass." Her smile broadened. "That's where we're all from. Maybe we'll see you around." She eased away from the entrance, silently chanting to keep her gaze from straying. *Hands, feet, breathe. Hands, feet, breathe.*

\* \* \*

Dane Clark stiffly moved to the front of the cave. A nicer guy would've offered to make the descent with Carly, but these days he found that being civil was sometimes the best he could offer. Besides, he wasn't always steady on his feet himself. If she'd slipped and he'd tried to catch her, she likely would have had to catch him instead. Not an experience his ego wanted.

His therapists wouldn't like it if they knew he was sitting in this cave. He'd only been in Tallgrass a few days. The first day, he'd bought a truck. The second, he'd come here. The drive had been too long, the climb too much. But he'd wanted this to be the first thing he'd done here because it was the last thing he'd done with his dad before he died. It was a tribute to him.

The women's voices were still audible, though all he could really make out was laughter. What were the odds he would drive two hours for a little privacy and wind up sharing the cave with six women—seven if he counted the pregnant one, now handing out jackets—from the town where he was stationed?

It really was a small world. He'd traveled a hell of a lot of it. He should know.

Sliding forward a few inches, he let his feet dangle over the edge. God, how many times had doctors and nurses and therapists told him to do that? Too many to think about, so instead he watched Carly's progress, her orange shirt easy to pick out against the drab shades of rock and dirt. Why had she volunteered to lead the climb if she was afraid of heights? To prove she could?

Finally, she jumped the last few feet to the ground and spun in a little circle that he doubted any of her friends noticed. She joined them, and what appeared to be a spontaneous group hug broke out, congratulating each other on their success.

He'd had buddies like that—well, maybe not so touchy-feely. Still did, even if they were scattered all over the world. But after years filled with one tour after another in Iraq or Afghanistan, a lot of them were gone. Sometimes he thought he couldn't possibly remember all their faces and names. Other times, he knew he would never forget.

After posing for more pictures, the women headed away from the falls. With the trail empty as far as he could see, he stood up, both hands touching the rock just in case. Time to see if his right leg and the miracle of modern medicine that served as his left could get him to the bottom without falling on his ass.

He succeeded. Uneven ground made for uncomfortable walking, the prosthetic rubbing the stump of his leg despite its protective sleeve. It was odd, standing, moving, climbing, without more than half of his leg. He could feel it, and yet he couldn't, sensed it was there but knew it wasn't. It was the damnedest thing—sometimes the hardest of all to accept.

He stood for a moment watching the water churn where the falls hit, giving the ache in his leg a chance to subside. Another month or two, and the pool would be filled with swimmers on weekends. He'd always liked to swim, and his various medical people had insisted he would again. He wasn't so sure about that. He'd never considered himself vain, but putting on trunks and removing his prosthesis in public...He wasn't ready for that. He was beginning to think he never would be.

Determinedly he turned away from the water and started for the parking lot. It wasn't far, maybe a quarter mile, sidewalk all the way, but by the time he reached his pickup, his leg and hip were throbbing, and the pain was spreading to his lower back. The two-hour drive home, plus a stop for lunch, would leave him in need of both a hot bath and a pain pill, but he didn't regret the trip.

Dane drove slowly through the park and onto the highway. Once he reached the interstate, he turned north, then took the first exit into Davis. A quick pass through town showed the fast-food options, and he settled on a burger and fries from Sonic. He was headed back to the interstate when traffic stopped him in front of a Mexican restaurant. Inside were the seven women from the cave, toasting each other, margarita glasses held high.

He'd noticed without realizing that most of them wore wedding rings. Were they just friends from Tallgrass, Army wives whose husbands were stationed there or maybe soldiers themselves? Carly, at least, had some military experience, with the way she'd pulled the name of his old unit out of thin air. And neither she nor Jessy nor any of the others had sounded as if they were native to Oklahoma, though he knew how easily accents could be

picked up and lost. Best bet, they'd been brought to Tallgrass by the Army, and when their husbands deployed, so
did they.

But he knew from firsthand experience there were worse
ways for a wife to entertain herself when her husband was
gone than hiking with her girlfriends.

He reached Fort Murphy in good time, turning at the
end of Main Street into the post's main entrance. A sand-
stone arch on either side of the four-lane held engraved
concrete: WELCOME TO FORT MURPHY on the left, a list of
the tenant commands on the right, including the Warrior
Transition Unit. That was the unit that currently laid claim
to him. In the future...

Once he'd had his life all laid out: Twenty years or
more in the Army, retirement, a family, a second career
that left him time to travel. He'd thought he might teach
history and coach, open a dive shop or get into some type
of wilderness-adventure trek business. Now he didn't have
the vaguest idea what the future held. For a man who'd
always known where he was going, it was kind of scary,
not knowing where he was going or how—or even if—he
could get there.

After clearing the guard shack, he drove onto the
post, past a bronze statue of the base's namesake, cowboy, actor, and war hero Audie Murphy. The four-lane
passed a manicured golf course, a community center
with an Olympic-size pool and the first of many housing
areas before he turned onto a secondary street. His quarters were in a barracks, opened only months ago, small
apartments to help their occupants adjust to life outside
the hospitals where most of them had spent too many
months. Dane's own stay had lasted eleven months. Long

enough to bring a new life into the world. *Not* long enough to adjust to a totally new life.

He was limping painfully by the time he let himself into his apartment. Tossing the keys on a table near the door, he grabbed a beer from the refrigerator and washed down a couple pills, fumbled his way out of his jeans, then dropped onto the couch before removing the prosthesis. He had two—one that looked pretty real from a distance and this one that seemed more of a superhero bionic thing. He was grateful to have them—he'd seen nonmilitary people forced by the cost to get by on much less efficient models—but neither was close to the real thing.

Absently rubbing his leg, he used the remote to turn on the television, then surfed the channels. There were lots of sports on today that he didn't want to watch. They reminded him too much of his own years playing football and baseball and running for the pure pleasure of it. No chick flicks, no talking animals, no gung-ho kick-ass action movies. He settled on a documentary on narrow-gauge railroads that let his mind wander.

How had he filled his Saturday afternoons before the amputation? Running for his life sometimes. Taking other people's lives sometimes. Jumping out of helicopters, patrolling barren desert, interfacing with locals. Before Iraq and Afghanistan, it had been riding his motorcycle through the Italian Alps, taking the train to Venice with his buddies, sightseeing and drinking too much. Hanging out, using too many women badly trying to get over his failed marriage.

He replayed weekends all the way back to his teens. Chores, running errands, homework, extra practices if the coach deemed them necessary, dates on Saturday night with Sheryl. Before she'd married him. Before she'd fallen out of love with him. Before she'd run around on him—adding insult to injury, with guys from his own unit.

He was over her. By the time she'd actually filed for divorce, he'd been so disillusioned by her affairs that he hadn't cared. But there was still this knot of resentment. They'd been together since they were fourteen, for God's sake, and she hadn't even had the grace to say "It's over." She'd lied to him. Betrayed him. She'd let him down, then blamed him for it.

And her life was great. She'd gone back home to Texas, married a rich guy who only got richer and lived in a beautiful mansion with three beautiful kids.

Dane's mother gave him regular updates, despite the fact that he'd never once asked. *"You let her get away,"* Anna Mae always ended with a regretful sigh.

Yeah, sure. *He'd* screwed up. It was all his fault. To Sheryl and Anna Mae, everything that had gone wrong was his fault, even the IED that had cost him his leg. *If you'd listened to Sheryl and me and gotten out of the Army...*

A dim image of the women he'd met that day—Carly, Jessy, and the others—formed in his mind. Did they lie to their husbands, betray them, let them down? It would be easy to think yes. The unfaithful-always-ready-to-party military wife was a stereotype, but stereotypes became that for a reason.

But today, after driving to the park, hiking to the falls, and climbing up to the cave, he'd rather give them the benefit of the doubt. That was something normal people did, and today, he was feeling pretty normal.

\* \* \*

"Do you ever feel guilty for looking at a guy and thinking, 'Wow, he's hot; I'd like to get to know him'?"

The quiet question came from Therese, sitting on the far side of the third-row seat of Marti's Suburban. Carly looked at her over Jessy's head, slumped on her shoulder. The redhead's snores were soft, barely noticeable, and due more to the third margarita she'd had with lunch than anything else, Carly suspected. Jessy was full of life until she got a few drinks in her, then she crashed hard.

"You mean, do I feel like I'm being unfaithful to Jeff, his memory, our marriage, his family, myself? Yeah. We had such plans." Regret robbed her voice of its strength. "Life wasn't supposed to turn out this way."

"But are we meant to spend the rest of our lives honoring our husbands' memories and...alone?"

*Alone.* That was a scary word even for women as independent as the Army had forced them to become. Even before their husbands had deployed to Iraq and Afghanistan, they'd been gone a lot, training at various bases around the country. They'd worked long hours to get themselves and their troops combat-ready, and most home-life responsibilities had fallen on their wives.

But then, *alone* had been okay. There had been an end to every training mission, to every deployment. The men had come home, and they'd made up for all the time missed.

For the seven of them, though, and the rest of the margarita club, the last return home had been final. There would be no more kisses, no more hugs, no more great sex, no more making up for missed time. There were only flags, medals, grave sites, and memories.

Yes, and some guilt.

"Paul wouldn't want you to spend the rest of your life alone."

The words sounded lame even to Carly. Lord knows, she'd heard them often enough—from friends, from her in-laws, from therapists. The first time, from a grief counselor, she'd wanted to shriek, *How could you possibly know that? You never met him!*

But it was true. Jeff had loved her. He'd always encouraged her to live life. He would be appalled if she grieved it away over him instead. Her head knew that.

Her heart was just having trouble with it.

Therese's laugh broke halfway. "I don't know. Paul was the jealous type. He didn't want me even looking at another guy."

"But that was because *he* was there. Now..." It took a little extra breath to finish the sentence. "He's not."

A few miles passed in silence before Therese spoke again. "What about you guys? What if one of us..."

After her voice trailed off, Fia finished the question from her middle-row seat. "Falls in love and gets another chance at happily ever after?"

Therese swallowed, then nodded. "Would it affect *us*? We became friends because we'd all lost our husbands. Would a new man in one of our lives change that? Would we want to share you with him?"

"Would he want to share you with us?" Ilena asked. "What guy would want his new girlfriend spending time with a group that's tied at its very heart to her husband's death?"

Shifting uncomfortably, Carly stared out the window. She had other friends—a few from college, teachers she worked with, a neighbor or two—but the margarita club, especially these six, were her best friends.

She wanted to say a relationship could never negatively affect their friendship, but truth was, she wasn't sure. She'd had other best friends before Jeff died—they all had— other Army wives, and they'd grown apart after. They'd shown her love and sorrow and sympathy, but they'd also felt a tiny bit of relief that it was *her* door the dress-uniformed officers had knocked at to make the casualty notification, that it was *her* husband who'd died and not theirs. And they'd felt guilty for feeling relieved.

She knew, because she'd been through it herself.

She forced a smile as her gaze slid from woman to woman. "I'll love you guys no matter what. If one of you falls in love, gets married and lives the perfect life with Prince Charming, I'll envy you. I'll probably hate you at least once a week. But I'll always be there for you."

The others smiled, too, sadly, then silence fell again. The conversation hadn't really answered any questions. It was easy to say it was okay to fall in love, even easier to promise their friendship would never end. But in the end, it was actions that counted.

The closer they got to Tallgrass, the more regret built in Carly. Though their times together were frequent—dinner every Tuesday, excursions every couple months, impromptu gatherings for shopping or a movie or no reason at all—she couldn't ignore the fact that she was going home to an empty house. All of them were except Therese, who would pick up her resentful stepchildren from the neighbor who was watching them. They would eat their dinners alone, watch TV or read or clean house alone, and they would go to bed alone.

*Were* they meant to spend the rest of their lives that way? Dear God, she hoped not.

By the time the Suburban pulled into her driveway, Carly was pretty much in a funk. She squeezed out from the third seat, exchanged good-byes with the others, promising to share any good pictures she'd gotten, and headed toward the house as if she didn't dread going inside.

It was a great starter house, the real estate agent had told them when they'd come to Tallgrass. *"That means 'fixer-upper,'"* Carly had whispered to Jeff, and he'd grinned. *"You know me. I love my tools."*

*"But you never actually use them."*

But the house was close to the fort, and the mortgage payments allowed plenty of money left over for all those repairs. Jeff had actually done some of them himself. Not many, but enough to crow over.

She climbed the steps he'd leveled and inserted the key in the dead bolt he'd installed. A lamp burned in the living room, a habit she'd gained their first night apart, shining on comfortable furniture, good tables, a collection of souvenirs and knickknacks and, of course, photographs. The outrageously sized television had been his choice, to balance the burnished wicker chair she'd chosen for her reading corner. Likewise, he'd picked the leather recliner to hide at least part of the froufrou rug she'd put down.

Their life had been full of little trade-offs like that. He would load the dishwasher if she would unload it. He would take his uniforms to the dry cleaner for knife-sharp creases, and she wouldn't complain if he wore sweats at home. She mowed the lawn, and he cleaned the gutters.

She'd stayed home, and he'd gone to war and died.

And she missed him, God, more than she'd thought possible.

To stave off the melancholy, she went to the kitchen for a bottle of water and a hundred-calorie pack of cookies. Before she reached the living room again, her cell phone rang.

It was Lucy. "I sent you some pictures. Check 'em out." She sounded way too cheerful before her voice cracked. "Norton, don't you dare! Aw, man! I swear to you, that mutt holds his pee all day just so he can see my face when he soaks the kitchen floor. Gotta go."

"Hello and good-bye to you, too." Carly slid the phone back into her pocket and made a turn into the dining room, where her computer occupied a very messy table. She opened her e-mail, and pictures began popping onto the screen—group shots, individuals, posed, candid, all of them happy and smiling.

No, not all. She hovered the cursor over one photo, clicking to enlarge it. Their cave-mate Dane. He was looking directly at the camera, a hint of surprise in his eyes as he realized he was being photographed, as if he wanted to jerk his gaze or his head away and didn't quite manage.

It was a stark photo of a good face: not overly handsome, with a strong jaw and straight nose, intense eyes and a mouth that was almost too sensitive for the rest of his features. He looked capable, a command-and-control kind of guy, except for his eyes. They were tough to read, even when she magnified the photo until the upper half of his face filled the screen, but there was definitely something haunted—or haunting?—about them.

He had a story to tell, and probably a sad one. It wasn't likely she would see him again to hear it. Tallgrass wasn't a large town, but it was easy enough for people to live their lives without ever running into a specific individual. Unless Dane had a child at the elementary school or happened to crave Mexican food on a Tuesday night, they would probably never see each other again.

Whatever his story, she wished him well with it.

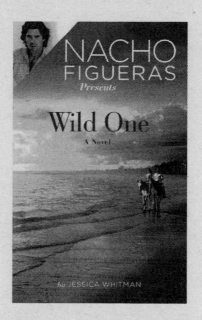

**NACHO FIGUERAS PRESENTS: WILD ONE**

Ralph Lauren model and world-renowned polo player Ignacio "Nacho" Figueras dives into scandal and seduction in the glamorous, treacherous, jet-setting world of high-stakes polo competition. Sebastian Del Campo is a tabloid regular as polo's biggest bad boy, but with an injury sidelining him, he's forced to figure out what really matters...including how to win the heart of the first woman who's ever truly understood him.

*Fall in Love with Forever Romance*

"Will get you in the spirit for love all year long."
—Jill Shalvis, *New York Times* bestselling author

# HAPPY EVER AFTER
## in
### Christmas

GREAT
LOW
PRICE!

## Debbie Mason
*USA TODAY* BESTSELLING AUTHOR

## HAPPY EVER AFTER IN CHRISTMAS
### By Debbie Mason

*USA Today* bestselling author Debbie Mason brings us back to Christmas, Colorado, where no one in town suspects that playboy Sawyer Anderson has been yearning to settle down and have a family. But when his best friend finds out the bride Sawyer has in mind is his off-limits baby sister, it might be a hot summer in Christmas in more ways than one...

# *Fall in Love with Forever Romance*

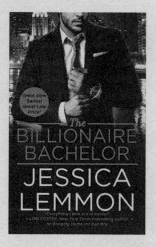

### THE BILLIONAIRE BACHELOR
### By Jessica Lemmon

Bad boy billionaire Reese Crane needs a wife to convince the board of Crane Hotel that he's settled enough to handle being CEO. And beautiful Merina Van Heusen needs money to save the boutique hotel she runs. But what will they do when love intrudes into their sham marriage? Fans of Jessica Clare and Samantha Young will love this new series from Jessica Lemmon.

### A SUMMER TO REMEMBER
### By Marilyn Pappano

In the tradition of RaeAnne Thayne and Emily March comes the sixth book in Marilyn Pappano's Tallgrass series. Can Elliot Ross teach the widow Fia Thomas to love again? Or will the secret she's hiding destroy her second chance at forever?

*Fall in Love with Forever Romance*

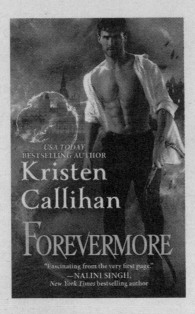

**FOREVERMORE**
**By Kristen Callihan**

Sin Evernight is one of the most powerful supernatural creatures in heaven and on earth, and when his long-lost friend Layla Starling needs him, he vows to become her protector. Desperate to avoid losing her a second time, Sin will face a test of all his powers to defeat an unstoppable foe—and to win an eternity with the woman he loves. Don't miss the stunning conclusion to *USA Today* bestselling author Kristen Callihan's Darkest London series!